COME THE SPRING

"What began so beautifully in *For the Roses* and continued with the Clayborne Brides series comes to a truly lovely conclusion in *COME THE SPRING*. . . . You'll find it as hard as I did to say farewell to a family you have come to love like your own. Thank you, Ms. Garwood, for Mama Rose and her children."

—Kathe Robin, *Romantic Times*

"Garwood does her usual superb job. . . . [A] fascinating tale of western romance and adventure."

—*Abilene Reporter-News* (TX)

"The Rose series [is a] tremendous collection. . . . *COME THE SPRING* is as good if not better than the previous novels. . . . With its tremendous prose and building suspense, this book [is] a long-term literary classic."

—Harriet Klausner, America Online

"Julie Garwood has become a trusted brand name in romantic fiction . . . [featuring] characters of the Old West, especially the ruggedly handsome gunslingers and the sassy, beautiful women who love them."

`—*People*

Also available from Simon & Schuster Audio

Praise for Julie Garwood's Clayborne Brides novels

ONE PINK ROSE

"[An] utterly charming little book. . . ."
—*The Philadelphia Inquirer*

"Great dialogue. . . . Wonderful characters."
—*Denver Rocky Mountain News*

ONE WHITE ROSE

"As charming as *For the Roses*, as sweet and funny and sensual as anything Ms. Garwood has written. . . . A must-have book if you love the Claybornes."
—*Romantic Times*

"Vintage Garwood, funny and tender, familiar yet new."
—*BookPage*

ONE RED ROSE

"Charming and heartwarming. . . . Garwood has a gift for sending our hearts soaring."
—*Romantic Times*

"Absolute dynamite story. . . . A scrumptious romance, nonstop action, and delightful dialogue."
—*Rendezvous*

These collected novels are also available from Simon & Schuster Audio

Julie Garwood wins raves for her smash *New York Times* bestseller—a tour de force of passion and suspense

HEARTBREAKER

"*Heartbreaker* moves along at a racehorse pace, its plot swerving and darting with sudden turns and jolts. . . . Garwood's characters are well-drawn."

—*New York Post*

"*Heartbreaker* dances between suspense and romance."

—*USA Today*

"Just when it looks like the ride is over, the action ratchets up again and doesn't let up until the final shot has been fired."

—*The Kansas City Star*

"Garwood has quite a flair for intrigue and suspense!"

—*Romantic Times*

"A heart-thumper."

—*The Ottawa Citizen*

"Engrossing. . . . Addictive. . . . By turns explosive and unpredictable. . . . You cheer for the good guys and are glad when the bad guys get caught. . . . [Garwood] has found a niche for herself in contemporary romantic fiction."

—*The Anniston Star* (AL)

A Main Selection of the Doubleday Book Club

Books by Julie Garwood

Gentle Warrior
Rebellious Desire
Honor's Splendour
The Lion's Lady
The Bride
Guardian Angel
The Gift
The Prize
The Secret
Castles
Saving Grace
Prince Charming
For the Roses
The Wedding
Come the Spring
Ransom
Heartbreaker
Mercy

The Clayborne Brides
One Pink Rose
One White Rose
One Red Rose

Published by POCKET BOOKS

JULIE GARWOOD

COME THE SPRING

POCKET BOOKS

New York   London   Toronto   Sydney

This book is a work of fiction. Names, characters, places and incidents are products of the author's imagination or are used fictitiously. Any resemblance to actual events or locales or persons, living or dead, is entirely coincidental.

POCKET BOOKS, a division of Simon & Schuster, Inc.
1230 Avenue of the Americas, New York, NY 10020

ISBN 978-0-7434-6712-4

First Pocket Books paperback printing October 1998

10 9 8 7 6 5 4 3 2

POCKET and colophon are registered trademarks of Simon & Schuster, Inc.

For information regarding special discounts for bulk purchases, please contact Simon & Schuster Special Sales at 1-800-456-6798 or business@simonandschuster.com

Front cover illustration by Lisa Litwack
Photo credit: Darrell Gulin/Stone

Printed in the U.S.A.

For my daughter, Elizabeth,
who has the mind of a scientist, the heart of a saint,
the determination of a champion,
and the twinkle of a true Irishman.
Oh, how you inspire me.

Acknowledgments

A special thanks to the following:

To Jo Ann for keeping me accurate, focused, and on track . . . and for putting up with me.

To my agent, Andrea Cirillo, and my editor, Linda Marrow, for believing in my dreams . . . and for never saying the word "impossible."

And, to all the readers who fell in love with the Claybornes and encouraged me to continue their story. Thank you, thank you, thank you.

For winter's rains and ruins are over,
And all the seasons of snows and sins;
The days dividing lover and lover,
The light that loses, the night that wins;
And time remembered is grief forgotten,
And frosts are slain and flowers begotten,
And in green underwood and cover
Blossom by blossom the spring begins.

—From *Atalanta in Calydon*
Algernon Charles Swinburne

Part One

For winter's rains and ruins are over,
And all the seasons of snows and sins;

One

*B*ut for the grace of God and an untied shoelace, she would have died with the others that day. She walked into the bank at precisely two forty-five in the afternoon to close her account, deliberately leaving the task until the last possible minute because it made everything so final in her mind. There would be no going back. All of her possessions had been packed, and very soon now she would be leaving Rockford Falls, Montana, forever.

Sherman MacCorkle, the bank president, would lock the doors in fifteen minutes. The lobby was filled with other procrastinators like herself, yet for all the customers, there were only two tellers working the windows instead of the usual three. Emmeline MacCorkle, Sherman's daughter, was apparently still at home recovering from the influenza that had swept through the peaceful little town two weeks before.

Malcolm Watterson's line was shorter by three heads. He was a notorious gossip, though, and would surely ask her questions she wasn't prepared to answer.

Fortunately Franklin Carroll was working today, and she immediately took her place in the back of his line. He was quick, methodical, and never intruded into anyone's personal affairs. He was also a friend. She had already told him good-bye after services last Sunday, but she had the sudden inclination to do so again.

She hated waiting. Tapping her foot softly against the warped floorboards, she took her gloves off, then put them back on again. Each time she fidgeted, her purse, secured by a satin ribbon around her wrist, swung back and forth, back and forth, like a pendulum keeping perfect time to the ticktock of the clock hanging on the wall behind the tellers' windows.

The man in front of her took a step forward, but she stayed where she was, hoping to put some distance between them so that she wouldn't have to smell the sour sweat mixed with the pungent odor of fried sausage emanating from his filthy clothes.

The man to her left in Malcolm's line smiled at her, letting her see the two missing teeth in the center of his grin. To discourage conversation, she gave him a quick nod and turned her gaze upward to the water stains on the ceiling.

It was dank, musty, and horribly hot. She could feel the perspiration gathering at the nape of her neck and tugged on the collar of her starched blouse. Giving Franklin a sympathetic glance, she wondered how any of the employees could work all day in such a dark, gloomy, stifling tomb. She turned to the right and stared longingly at the three closed windows. Sunlight streaked through the finger-smudged glass, casting jagged splotches on the worn floorboards, and fragments of dust particles hung suspended in the stagnant air. If she had to wait much longer, she would incite Sherman MacCorkle's anger by marching over to the windows and throwing all of them open. She gave up the idea as soon as it entered her mind because the president would only close them again and give her a stern lecture about bank security. Besides, she would lose her place in line.

It was finally her turn. Hurrying forward, she stumbled and bumped her head against the glass of the teller's window. Her shoe had come off. She shoved her foot back inside and felt the tongue coil under her toes. Behind the tellers, dour-faced Sherman MacCorkle's door was open. He heard the commotion and looked up at her from his desk behind a glass partition. She gave him a weak smile before turning her attention to Franklin.

"My shoelace came untied," she said in an attempt to explain her clumsiness.

He nodded sympathetically. "Are you all ready to leave?"

"Just about," she whispered so that Malcolm, the busybody, wouldn't poke his nose into the conversation. He was already leaning toward Frank, and she knew he was itching to hear the particulars.

"I'll miss you," Franklin blurted out.

The confession brought a blush that stained his neck and cheeks. Franklin's shyness was an endearing quality, and when the tall, deathly thin man swallowed, his oversized Adam's apple bobbed noticeably. He was at least twenty years her senior, yet he acted like a young boy whenever he was near her.

"I'm going to miss you too, Franklin."

"Are you going to close your account now?"

She nodded as she pushed the folded papers through the arched, fist-sized opening. "I hope everything's in order."

He busied himself with the paperwork, checking signatures and numbers, and then opened his cash drawer and began to count out the money.

"Four hundred and two dollars is an awful lot of money to be carrying around."

"Yes, I know it is," she agreed. "I'll keep a close eye on it. Don't worry."

She removed her gloves while he stacked the bills, and when he pushed the money through the opening, she stuffed it into her cloth purse and pulled the strings tight.

Franklin cast his employer a furtive glance before leaning forward and pressing his forehead against the glass. "Church won't be the same without you sitting in the pew in front of Mother and me. I wish you weren't leaving. Mother would eventually warm up to you. I'm sure of it."

She reached through the opening and impulsively squeezed his hand. "In the short while that I have lived here, you have become such a good friend. I won't ever forget your kindness to me."

"Will you write?"

"Yes, of course I will."

"Send your letters to the bank so Mother won't see them."

She smiled. "Yes, I'll do that."

A discreet cough told her she'd lingered too long. She picked up her gloves and purse and turned around, searching for a spot out of the traffic where she could retie her shoelace. There was an empty desk in the alcove beyond the swinging gate that separated the customers from the employees. Lemont Morganstaff usually sat there, but like Emmeline MacCorkle, he too was still recovering from the epidemic.

She dragged her foot so she wouldn't step out of her shoe again as she made her way across the lobby to the decrepit, scarred desk in front of the windows. Franklin had confided that MacCorkle had purchased all the furniture thirdhand from a printer's shop. His thrifty nature had obviously compelled him to overlook the ink stains blotting the wood and the protruding splinters lying in wait for an uncautious finger.

It was sinful the way MacCorkle treated his employees. She knew for a fact that he didn't pay any of his loyal staff a fair wage, because poor Franklin lived a very modest life and could barely afford to keep his mother in the medicinal tonic she seemed to thrive on.

She had a notion to go into MacCorkle's brand-spanking-new office, with its shiny mahogany desk and matching file cabinets, and tell him what a cheapskate he was in hopes of shaming him into doing something about the deplorable conditions he forced his staff to endure, and she surely would have done just that if it hadn't been for the possibility that MacCorkle would think Franklin had put her up to it. The president knew they were friends. No, she didn't dare say a word, and so she settled on giving MacCorkle a look of pure disgust instead.

It was a wasted effort; he was looking the other way. She promptly turned her back to him and pulled out the desk chair. Dropping her things down on the seat, she genuflected in as ladylike a fashion as she could and pushed her petticoats out of her way. She adjusted the tongue of her shoe, slipped her foot back inside, and quickly retied the stiff shoelace.

The chore completed, she tried to stand up but stepped on her skirt instead and was jerked back to the floor, landing with a thud. Her purse and gloves spilled into her lap as the chair she'd bumped went flying backward on its rollers. It slammed into the wall, rolled back, and struck her shoulder. Embarrassed by her awkwardness, she peered over the top of the desk to see if anyone had noticed.

There were three customers left at the tellers' windows, all of them gaping in her direction. Franklin had only just finished filing her documents in the file cabinet behind him when she fell. He slammed the file drawer closed and started toward her with a worried frown on his face, but she smiled and waved him back. She was just about to tell him she was quite all right when the front door burst open with a bang.

The clock chimed three o'clock. Seven men stormed inside and fanned out across the lobby. No one could mistake their intentions. Dark bandannas concealed the lower part of their faces, and their hats, worn low on their brows, shaded their eyes. As each man moved forward, he drew his gun. The last one to enter spun around to pull the shades and bolt the door.

Everyone in the bank froze except for Sherman MacCorkle, who rose up in his chair, a startled cry of alarm issuing through his pinched lips. Then Franklin screamed in a high-pitched soprano shriek that reverberated through the eerie silence.

Like the others, she was too stunned to move. A wave of panic washed through her, constricting every muscle. She desperately tried to grasp control of her thoughts. *Don't panic . . . don't panic . . . They can't shoot us . . . They wouldn't dare shoot us . . . The noise of gunfire . . . They want money, that's all . . . If everyone cooperates, they won't hurt us. . . .*

Her logic didn't help calm her racing heartbeat. They would take her four hundred dollars. And that was unacceptable. She couldn't let them have the money . . . wouldn't. But how could she stop them? She took the wad of bills out of her purse and frantically searched for a place to hide it. *Think . . . think. . . .* She leaned to the side and looked up at Franklin. He was staring at the robbers, but he must have felt her watching him for he tilted his head downward ever so slightly. It dawned on her then that the gunmen didn't know she was there. She hesitated for the barest of seconds, her gaze intent on Franklin's pale face, and then silently squeezed herself into the kneehole of the ancient desk. Quickly unbuttoning her blouse, she shoved the money under her chemise and flattened her hands against her chest.

Oh, God, oh, God . . . One of them was walking toward the desk. She could hear his footsteps getting closer and closer. Her petticoats! They were spread out like a white flag of surrender. She frantically grabbed them and shoved them under her knees. Her heart pounded like a drum now, and she was terrified that all of them could hear the noise. If they didn't spot her, they would leave her money alone.

A blur of snakeskin boots, spurs rattling, passed within inches. The smell of peppermint trailed behind. The scent shocked her—children smelled like peppermint, not criminals. *Don't let him see me,* she prayed. *Please, God, don't let him see me.* She wanted to squeeze her eyes shut and disappear. She heard the shades being pulled down, sucking out the sunlight, and she was suddenly assaulted with the claustrophobic feeling that she was in a casket and the man was pushing the lid down on top of her.

Bare seconds had passed since they'd entered the bank. It would be over soon, she told herself. Soon. They wanted only the money, nothing more, and they would surely hurry to get out as quickly as possible. Yes, of course they would. With every second that they lingered, they increased the odds of being captured.

Could they see her through the cracks in the desk? The possibility was too frightening. There was a half-inch split in the seam of the wood all the way down the center panel, and she slowly shifted her position until her knees were rubbing against the drawer above her head. The air was thick, heavy. It made her want to gag. She took a shallow breath through her mouth and tilted her head to the side so she could see through the slit.

Across the room the three gray-faced customers

stood motionless, their backs pressed against the counter. One of the robbers stepped forward. He was dressed in a black suit and white shirt, similar to the clothing the bank president wore. Had he not been wearing a mask and holding a gun, he would have looked like any other businessman.

He was terribly polite and soft-spoken.

"Gentlemen, there isn't any need to be frightened," he began in a voice that reeked with southern hospitality. "As long as you do as I say, no one will get hurt. We happened to hear from a friend of ours about a large government deposit for the army boys, and we thought we might like to help ourselves to their pay. I'll grant you we aren't being very gentlemanly, and I'm sure you're feeling mighty inconvenienced. I'm real sorry about that. Mr. Bell, please put the Closed sign in the window behind the shades."

The leader gave the order to the man on his right, who quickly did as he was told.

"That's fine, just fine," the leader said. "Now, gentlemen, I would like all of you to stack your hands on top of your heads and come on out here into the lobby so I won't have to worry that one of you is going to do anything foolish. Don't be shy, Mr. President. Come on out of your office and join your friends and neighbors."

She heard the shuffle of feet as the men moved forward. The gate squeaked as it opened.

"That was nice and orderly." The leader oozed the praise when his command was promptly followed. "You did just fine, but I have one more request to make. Will all of you please kneel down? Now, now, keep your hands on your heads. You don't want me to worry, do you? Mr. Bell would like to lay you out on the floor and tie you up, but I don't think that will be necessary. No need to get your nice clothes dirty. Just squeeze yourselves together in a tight little circle. That's fine, just fine," he praised once again.

"The safe's open, sir," one of the others called out.

"Go to it, son," he called back.

The man in charge turned to the desk, and she saw his eyes clearly. They were brown with golden streaks through them, like marbles, cold, unfeeling. The man named Bell was coughing, and the leader turned away from her to look at his accomplice.

"Why don't you lean against the railing and let the others take care of filling up the bags. My friend's feeling poorly today," he told the captives.

"Maybe he's got the influenza," Malcolm suggested in an eager-to-please voice.

"I'm afraid you might be right," the leader agreed. "It's a pity because he so enjoys his work, but today he isn't up to entertaining himself. Isn't that right, Mr. Bell?"

"Yes, sir," his cohort said.

"Are you about finished, Mr. Robertson?"

"We got it all, sir."

"Don't forget the cash in the drawers," he reminded him.

"We've got that too, sir."

"Looks like our business is almost finished here. Mr. Johnson, will you please make sure the back door isn't going to give us any trouble?"

"I've already seen to it, sir."

"It's time to finish up, then."

She heard the others moving back into the lobby, their heels clicking against the floorboards with the precision of telegraph equipment. One of them was snickering.

The man in charge had turned away from her, but she could see the others clearly now. All of them stood behind the circle of captives. While she watched, they removed their bandannas and tucked them into their pockets. The leader took a step forward, then put his gun away so he could carefully fold his bandanna and put it in his vest pocket. He stood close enough for her to see his long fingers and his carefully manicured nails.

Why had they removed their masks? Didn't they realize that Franklin and the others would give the authorities their descriptions . . . *Oh, God, no . . . no . . . no . . .*

"Is the back door open, Mr. Johnson?"

"Yes, sir, it is."

"Well, then I expect it's time to leave. Whose turn is it?" he asked.

"Mr. Bell hasn't taken a turn since that little girl. Remember, sir?"

"I remember. Are you up to it today, Mr. Bell?"

"Yes, sir, I believe I am."

"Then get on with it," he ordered as he drew his gun and cocked it.

"What are you going to do?" the president asked in a near shout.

"Hush now. I told you no one would get hurt, didn't I?"

His voice was horrifically soothing. MacCorkle was nodding when the man named Bell fired his shot. The front of the president's head exploded.

The leader killed the man in front of him, jumping back when the blood from the wound he'd inflicted spewed out.

Franklin cried, "But you promised . . ."

The leader whirled toward him and shot him in the back of the head. Franklin's neck snapped.

"I lied."

Two

The ceremony was unique. The guest of honor, Cole Clayborne, slept through it and the celebration that followed. An hour after most of the guests had departed, the effect of the unnatural sleep was wearing off. In a stupor, he floated somewhere between fantasy and reality. He felt someone tugging on him, but he couldn't summon enough strength to open his eyes and find out who was tormenting him. The noise was making his head ache fiercely, and when he finally began to wake up, the first sounds he heard were the clinking of glasses and loud, rambunctious laughter.

Someone was speaking to him, or about him. He heard his name, yet he found it impossible to concentrate long enough to understand what was being said. His head felt as though there were little men inside, standing between his eyes, pounding his skull with sharp hammers.

Was he hung over? The question intruded into his hazy thoughts. No, he never got drunk when he was away from Rosehill, and even when he was home, he rarely had more than an occasional beer in the heat of the afternoon. He didn't like the aftereffects. Liquor, he'd learned the hard way, dulled the senses and the reflexes, and with half the gunslingers in the territory wanting to build their reputations by killing him in a shoot-out, he wasn't about to drink anything more dulling than water.

Someone was having a mighty fine time. He heard laughter again and tried to turn his head toward the sound. Pain shot up from the base of his neck, causing bile to rush to his throat. Ah, Lord, he felt like hell.

"Looks like he's coming around, Josey. You'd best get on back home before he starts growling and spewing. You're liable to get your feelings hurt." Sheriff Tom Norton stared through the bars of the cell while he addressed his wife of thirty years.

Josey Norton scurried away before Cole could get his eyes focused. It took him a minute to realize where he was. He gritted his teeth as he sat up on the narrow cot and swung his legs to the floor. His hands gripped the mattress and his head dropped to his chest.

He studied the sheriff through bloodshot eyes. Norton was an older man with weather-beaten skin, a potbelly, and melancholy eyes. He looked like a harmless hound dog.

"Why am I in jail?" The question was issued in a sharp whisper.

The sheriff leaned against the bars, crossed one ankle over the other, and smiled. "You broke the law, son."

"How?"

"Disturbing the peace."

"What?"

"No need to shout. I can see it pained you. You've got a nice bump on the back of your head, and I don't suppose yelling is gonna make you feel better. Don't you remember what happened?"

Cole shook his head and immediately regretted it. Pain exploded behind his eyes.

"I remember being sick."

"Yes, you had the influenza. You were sick with fever for four days, and my Josey nursed you back to health. Today was your second day out of bed."

"When did I disturb the peace?"

"When you crossed the street," he said cheerfully. "It was real disturbing to me, the way you walked away while I was trying so hard to convince you to stay in Middleton until the appointment came through. I gave my word to someone real important that I would keep you here, son, but you wouldn't cooperate."

"So you hit me over the head."

"Yes, I did," he admitted. "I didn't see any other way. It wasn't much of a hit though, just a little thump with the butt of my pistol on the back of your head. No permanent damage was done, or you wouldn't be sitting there growling at me. Besides, I did you a favor."

The sheriff's chipper voice was grating on Cole's nerves. He glared at him and asked, "How do you figure that?"

"There were two gunslingers waiting for you to get into the street. Both of them were determined to make you draw—one at a time, of course. You were just getting over your sick spell, and even though you won't admit it, I'd wager a week's pay you weren't well enough to take either one of them on. The influenza hit you hard, son, and you're only just now getting your color back. Yes sirree, I did you a favor."

"It's all coming back to me."

"Put it behind you," he suggested. "'Cause it's water under the sink now. The appointment came through, and we had us a nice ceremony right here in the jail. It seemed kind of odd to file into your cell for a big do, but the judge didn't mind and it worked out all right. Yes, it did. Too bad you had to sleep through the celebration, since you were the honoree and all. My wife, Josey, made her special yellow cake with sugar icing. She cut you a nice big piece and left it on the table over there," he added with a nod toward the opposite side of the cell. "You'd best eat it before the mice get to it."

Cole was becoming more frustrated by the second. Most of what the sheriff was telling him didn't make any sense. "Answer my questions," he demanded. "You said that someone important wanted to keep me here. Who was it?"

"Marshal Daniel Ryan, that's who. He should be along any minute now to let you out."

"Ryan's here? That no-good, low-down, thieving—"

"Hold on now. There ain't no need to carry on. The marshal told me you've been bearing a grudge against him. He said it had something to do with a compass and gold case he's been keeping safe for you."

Cole's head was rapidly clearing. "My mother was bringing me the compass, and Ryan stole it from her. He doesn't have any intention of giving it back. I'm going to have to take it from him."

"I think you might be wrong about that," Norton said with a chuckle.

It was futile to argue with him. Cole decided to save his wrath for the man who was responsible for locking him up . . . Daniel Ryan. He couldn't wait to get his hands on him.

"Are you going to let me out of here and give me my guns back?"

"I'd surely like to."

"But?"

"But I can't," the sheriff said. "Ryan's got the keys. I've got to take some papers across town to the judge, so why don't you sit tight and eat some cake? I shouldn't be gone long."

The sheriff turned to leave. "One more thing," he drawled out. "Congratulations, son. I'm sure you'll do your family proud."

"Wait!" Cole called out. "Why are you congratulating me?"

Norton didn't answer him. He sauntered into the outer office, and a minute later Cole heard the front door open and close. He shook his head in confusion. He didn't know what the old man had been rambling on about. Why would he congratulate him?

He glanced around the stark cell—gray walls, gray bars, and gray floor. On a three-legged stand in the corner was a gray-speckled basin and a water jug next to the piece of cake the sheriff's wife had left for him. The only other adornment was the black spider crawling up the painted stones of the wall. There was another one hanging from its web in the barred windowsill high up by the ceiling. Cole was over six feet tall, but in order to look out, he would have to stand on a chair. There weren't any inside the cell. He could see a fragment of the sky, though, and like his temporary home, it too was gray.

The color fit his mood. He was in a no-win situation. He couldn't very well shoot Norton, since his wife had nursed him back to health. The sheriff had probably saved his life, as well, by knocking him out before the gunslingers had challenged him. Cole remembered the influenza had left him weak and shaky. He would have died in a gunfight all right, but damn it all, did Norton have to hit him so hard? His head still felt as if it had been split in two.

He reached up to rub the knot in the back of his neck, and his right arm bumped against cold metal. He looked down, then froze when he realized what he was staring at. A gold case dangled from a chain someone—Ryan, most likely—had clipped to the pocket of his leather vest.

The son of a bitch had finally given him his treasure back. He gently lifted the precious disk into the palm of his hand and stared at it a long minute before opening it. The compass was made of brass, not gold, but it was still finely crafted. The face was white, the letters red, the dial black. He removed it from its case, smiling as he watched the dial wobble back and forth before pointing north.

His Mama Rose was going to be pleased to know that he had finally gotten the gift she'd purchased for him over a year ago. It was a handsome treasure. He couldn't find a nick or a scratch anywhere. Ryan had obviously taken good care of it, he grudgingly admitted. He still wanted to shoot the bastard for keeping it so long, but he knew he couldn't if he wanted to stay alive a little longer—killing marshals was frowned on in the territory, no matter what the reason—and so Cole decided to settle on punching him in the nose instead.

Carefully tucking the compass into his vest pocket, he glanced over at the pitcher and decided to splash some water on his face. His gaze settled on the piece of cake, and he focused on it while he tried to sort fact from dream.

Why were they eating cake in his cell? The question seemed too complicated to think about now. He stood up so he could stretch his knotted muscles and was about to take off his vest when his sleeve caught on something sharp. Pulling his arm free, he glanced down to see what was jabbing him.

His hands dropped to his knees as he fell back on the cot and stared down at his left shoulder in disbelief. He was stupefied. It had to be a joke—but someone had a real warped sense of humor. Then Sheriff Norton's words came back to him. The appointment had come through . . . Yeah, that's what he'd said . . . And they celebrated . . . Cole remembered Norton had said that too.

And Cole was the honoree . . .

"Son of a bitch!" He roared the blasphemy at the silver star pinned to his vest.

He was a U.S. marshal.

Three

By the time Sheriff Norton returned to the jail, Cole was seething with anger. Fortunately, Norton had gotten the keys from Ryan. His wife, Josey, was with him, and for that reason Cole kept his temper under control. She carried a tray covered with a blue-and-white-striped napkin, and as soon as the sheriff swung the door open, she brought the food inside the cell.

Norton made the introductions. "You two haven't officially met, since you were burning up with fever every time my Josey got near you. Josey, this here is Marshal Cole Clayborne. He doesn't know about it yet, but he's gonna be helping Marshal Ryan chase down that slippery Blackwater gang of murderers terrorizing the territory. Cole . . . You don't mind if I get familiar and call you by your first name, do you?"

"No, sir, I don't mind."

The sheriff beamed with pleasure. "That's mighty nice of you, considering the inconvenience you must be feeling over getting yourself thumped on the head.

Anyway, as I was saying, this pretty lady blushing next to me is my wife, Josey. She fretted over you something fierce while you were ill. Do you remember?"

Cole had stood up as soon as Josey entered the cell. He moved forward, nodded to her in greeting, and said, "Of course I remember. Ma'am, I appreciate you coming by the hotel and looking after me while I was so sick. I hope I wasn't too much trouble."

Josey was a rather plain-looking woman, with round shoulders and crooked teeth, but when she smiled, she lit up the room. Folks tended to want to smile back, and Cole was no exception. His smile was genuine, as was his appreciation.

"A lot of people wouldn't have taken the trouble to nurse a stranger," he added.

"You weren't any trouble at all," she replied. "You lost a little weight, but my chicken ought to put the fat back on you. I brought some from home."

"My Josey makes mighty fine fried chicken," Norton interjected with a nod toward the basket his wife carried.

"I felt I ought to do something to make up for my husband's orneriness. Thomas shouldn't have knocked you out the way he did, especially since you were feeling so puny and all. Does your head pain you?"

"No, ma'am," he lied.

She turned to her husband. "Those two no-good gunslingers are still hanging around. I spotted both of them on my way here. One's squatting north of our avenue and the other's due south. Are you going to do something about it before this boy gets himself killed?"

Norton rubbed his jaw. "I expect Marshal Ryan will have a talk with them."

"He doesn't seem the talking type," Josey replied.

"Ma'am, those gunslingers want me," Cole said. "I'll talk to them."

"Son, they don't want to talk. They're itching to build their reputations, and the only way they can do that is if one of them shoots you in a draw. Just don't let them aggravate you into doing anything foolish," Norton said.

Josey nodded her agreement, then turned to her husband again. "Where do you want me to lay out the plates?"

"It's too stuffy to eat in here," Norton said. "Why don't you put it all out on my desk?"

Cole waited until Josey had gone into the outer room before speaking to the sheriff again. "Where's Ryan?"

"He'll be along soon. He was headed here, but then he got called over to the telegraph office to pick up a wire. I expect you're anxious to have a word with him."

Cole nodded. He kept his temper under control by reminding himself that the sheriff had only done Ryan's bidding. It was the marshal who'd ordered Norton to keep Cole in town, and it was also the marshal who'd pinned the star on his vest. Cole had in mind another place for the badge. He thought he might like to pin it to the center of Ryan's forehead. The thought so amused him, he smiled.

Josey had removed the papers from the desk and covered it with a red-and-white tablecloth. There were two chipped china dinner plates, white with blue butterflies painted on the rims, and two matching coffee cups. In the center of the desk was a platter of fried chicken sitting in a thick puddle of grease, along with bowls of boiled turnips with their hairy roots, like gauze, still wrapped around them, congealed gravy that resembled day-old biscuit dough, pickled beets, and black-bottomed rolls.

It was the most unappealing meal Cole had ever seen. His stomach, still tender from the influenza, lurched in reaction to the smell. Since Josey had already left, Cole didn't have to be concerned that his lack of appetite would offend her.

The sheriff took his seat behind the desk and motioned for Cole to pull up another chair. After pouring coffee for both of them, he leaned back and pointed to the spread. "I might as well warn you before you get started. My wife means well, but she never quite got the knack for cooking. She seems to think she's got to fry everything up in a kettle of lard. I wouldn't touch that gravy if I were you. It's a killer."

"I'm really not hungry," Cole said.

The sheriff laughed. "You're gonna be a mighty fine marshal 'cause you're so diplomatic." Patting his distended belly, he added, "I've gotten used to my Josey's cooking, but it's taken me close to thirty years to do it. There was a time or two I thought she was trying to do me in."

Cole drank his coffee while Norton ate two large helpings of food. When the older man was finished, he restacked the dishes inside the basket, covered it with his soiled napkin, and stood up.

"I believe I'll mosey on down to Frieda's restaurant and get me a piece of her pecan pie. You want to come along?"

"No, thank you. I'll wait here for Ryan." One thought led to another. "What did you do with my guns?"

"They're in the bottom drawer of my desk. That's a right nice gunbelt you've got. It makes it easy to get to your guns, doesn't it? I expect that's why Marshal Ryan wears one."

As soon as the sheriff was out the door, Cole got his gunbelt out and put it on. All of the bullets for the two six-shooters had been removed. He scooped them up, filled the chambers of one gun, and was working on the second when Norton came rushing back inside.

"I expect Marshal Ryan could use your help. Those two gunslingers are waiting at both ends of my street, and he's strolling right smack across the middle. He's gonna get himself killed."

Cole shook his head. "They want me, not Ryan," he said as he slammed the loading chamber into place and shoved the gun in his holster.

"But that's the problem, son. Ryan ain't gonna let them have you. If one of them kills you, then you won't be able to help him get the Blackwater gang, and he's said more than once he needs your special kind of help."

Cole didn't have the faintest idea what the sheriff was talking about. What special kind of help could he give? He guessed he was about to find out, though. His suggestion that the sheriff remain inside was met with resistance.

"Son, I can lend a hand. Granted, it's been a while since I've been in a shoot-out, but I figure it's like drinking out of a cup. Once you've learned how, you never forget. I used to be considered quick with a pistol too."

Cole shook his head. "Like I said, they want me, but thanks for the offer."

Norton rushed forward to open the door for him, and before Cole stepped outside, he heard the older man whisper, "Good luck to you."

Four

Luck didn't have anything to do with it. Years of hard living had prepared Cole for these annoying nuisances.

Cole took everything in at once. The gunslingers were waiting at opposite ends of the dirt street, but he didn't recognize either one of them. Gunslingers all looked the same to him—God, how many had there been, chasing after the empty dream of being the fastest gun in the West? Dressed alike in leather chaps, the two men shifted from foot to foot, letting Cole see their eagerness. They weren't boys, which was going to make killing them easier, Cole supposed. He had already figured out exactly how he would do it. The plan called for him to hit the dirt—but damn, he really hated diving and rolling around in the mud, especially today, since his stomach was acting so persnickety. Still, he would do what he had to do in order to survive.

Marshal Ryan was the fly in his ointment, however. The lawman was standing stock-still in the center of the street, and that would put him right in the middle of the gunfire.

Cole was about to call out to him when Ryan motioned for him to come forward. Keeping his hands down and loose at his sides so he wouldn't spook the eager-to-die gunslingers, he stepped off the boardwalk and headed for the marshal. His fingers itched to reach for his gun. He didn't particularly want to shoot the lawman, just hit him on the back of his head with the butt of a gun so Ryan would have an inkling of the pain Cole had endured because of his order to keep him in town.

As he sauntered closer, the gunslingers, like rodents afraid of the light of day but craving the prize between them, edged forward.

Cole decided to ignore them for the moment. He and Ryan were both safe . . . until one of the gunslingers went for his gun. The challengers were there to build their reputations, and the only way they could do that would be to shoot it out in a draw with witnesses watching. Fair and square. Otherwise, the kill didn't count.

Sheriff Norton peered through the crack of the doorway, watching. He smiled at the sight before him, for it was something to behold, and remember. The two marshals, both as big and mean-looking as Goliath, were sizing each other up like contenders in a boxing ring. They made a striking pair, just like Josey said. She'd been afraid of Daniel Ryan when she'd first met him, and later on she'd had the very same reaction when she met Cole Clayborne, though she did a decent job of masking it. The two marshals spooked her, she'd confessed, and Norton remembered vividly her exact words when she'd tried to explain why she felt the way she did. "It's in their eyes. They've both got that cold, piercing stare, like icicles going right through a body. I get the feeling they're looking into my head and know what I'm thinking before I do."

She also admitted that, in spite of her timidity, she couldn't help but notice what handsome men they were . . . as long as they didn't stare directly at her.

Cole shouted to Ryan, drawing the sheriff's full attention.

"Get the hell out of the street, Ryan. You're going to get killed."

The marshal didn't budge. His eyes narrowed as Cole moved closer. Cole stopped when he was a couple of feet away. He stared into Ryan's eyes. Ryan stared back. He was the first to break the silence. "Are you thinking about shooting me?"

There was a hint of laughter in his voice Cole didn't particularly like. "The idea crossed my mind, but I've got other things to worry about now. Unless you want to catch a stray bullet, I suggest you move."

"Someone's going to die, but it isn't going to be me," Ryan announced in a lazy drawl.

"You think you can take both of them?" Cole asked with a nod toward the gunslinger on his left, who was slowly creeping closer.

"I'll find out soon enough."

"They want me, not you."

"I'm just as fast, Cole."

"No, you're not."

Ryan's smile took Cole by surprise, and he would have asked Ryan why he was so amused if the gunslinger on his right hadn't shouted at him.

"My name's Eagle, Clayborne, and I'm here to take you out. Turn and face me, you lily-livered bastard. I'm gonna draw on you, damn your hide."

The competing gunslinger wasn't about to be left out. "My name's Riley, Clayborne, and I'm the man who's going to kill you."

The gunslingers Cole had encountered so far had all

been stupid. This pair, he decided, wasn't the exception.

"I should probably do something about those two," Ryan said.

"Like what? Are you thinking about arresting them?"

"Maybe."

His casual attitude was irritating. "What kind of a marshal are you?"

"A damned good one."

Cole clenched his jaw. "You're sure full of yourself."

"I know my strengths. I know yours too."

Cole's patience was gone. "Why don't you go on inside with the sheriff, and you can tell me all about your strengths after I'm finished here."

"Are you telling me to get out of your way?"

"Yeah, I am."

"I'm not going anywhere. Besides, I've got a plan," he said with a gesture toward one of the gunslingers.

"I've got a plan too," Cole replied.

"Mine's better."

"Is that right?"

"Yes. On the count of three, we both drop to the ground and let them kill each other."

In spite of his dark mood, the picture Ryan painted made Cole grin. "That would be real nice if it worked, but neither one of them is close enough to hit the other. Besides, I'd get my new shirt all dirty dropping to the ground."

"What's your plan?" Ryan asked.

"Kill one, then dive, roll, and kill the other."

"Seems to me you're going to get that brand-new shirt dirty with your plan too."

"Are you going to get out of my way or not?"

"Lawmen stand together, Cole. That's a real important rule to remember."

"I'm not a lawman."

"Yes, you are. You should be sworn in, but that's only a formality."

"You've got a twisted sense of humor, Ryan. You know that? I'm not going to be a marshal."

"You already are," Ryan explained patiently.

"Why?"

"I need your help."

"I think maybe you don't understand how I feel. I'm fighting the urge to shoot you, you son of a bitch. You kept my compass for over a year."

Ryan wasn't at all intimidated by Cole's threat. "It took that long for the appointment to come through."

"What appointment?"

"I couldn't just pin a badge on you," Ryan said. "The appointment came from Washington."

Cole shook his head.

"They're moving in on us," Ryan said. He rolled his eyes in Eagle's direction. "Do you know either of them?"

"No."

"I'll take the one at five o'clock."

Cole started to turn, then stopped. "Your five or mine?"

"Mine," Ryan answered.

They each turned to face an approaching gunfighter, then slowly stepped backward, stopping when they were shoulder to shoulder.

"Don't shoot to kill."

"You gotta be joking."

Ryan ignored the comment. He shouted to the gunslingers to put their hands in the air and walk, slow and easy, toward him, but Eagle and Riley stayed where they were with their right hands hovering above their guns.

"If you miss Riley, his bullet is going to go through you and hit me," Cole said.

"I never miss."

"Arrogant bastard," Cole whispered just as Eagle

went for his gun. Cole reacted with lightning speed. The gunfighter didn't even get his weapon out of his holster before a bullet stabbed through the palm of his hand.

Ryan fired at the same time. He shot the gun out of Riley's hand just as he was bringing his weapon up. The bullet cut through his wrist.

Keeping their guns trained on their targets, the two marshals strode forward. Ryan reached Riley first. He removed his weapons, ignoring the man's squeals of agony, and prodded him toward Sheriff Norton's jail.

Eagle was bellowing like a wounded boar. Much to Cole's frustration, he wouldn't stand still, but danced around in a gyrating jig.

"You ruined my shooting hand, Clayborne. You ruined my shooting hand," he screeched.

"I heard you the first time," Cole grumbled. "Stand still, damn it. I'm taking your guns."

Eagle wouldn't comply, and Cole quickly tired of chasing him. He let out a sigh, grabbed hold of the gunslinger by his collar, and slammed his fist into his jaw, knocking him unconscious. He continued to hold him up until he'd removed his gun, then let him drop to the ground. Gripping the scruff of his neck, he dragged him to Norton.

The sheriff was beaming at the two marshals from the boardwalk. "Guess I'll have to go get the doc to patch them two up," he remarked.

"Guess so," Cole replied.

The sheriff rushed back inside, snatched his keys off the desktop, and hurried on to unlock two cells. A moment later, the gunfighters were pushed inside.

There wasn't time for the sheriff's congratulations, for no sooner had the cell door slammed shut than Ryan was called outside by the telegraph clerk. When Cole joined him on the boardwalk, one look at the marshal told Cole something bad had happened. He was surprised when Ryan handed the wire to him.

Cole read the contents while Ryan gave the news to Sheriff Norton. "There's been another robbery." His voice was flat.

Norton shook his head. "How many dead this time?"

"Seven."

"Where did it happen?" Norton asked.

"Rockford Falls."

"That ain't far from here. I can tell you how to get there."

"How far is it?"

"About forty miles over some rough terrain."

"You might want to keep your eyes open in case any of them pass through here again. I doubt they will," Ryan added. "They've already hit this bank. Cole, are you riding with me?"

He shook his head and handed the wire back to Ryan. "It's not my problem."

Ryan said nothing. Squinting against the sunlight, his eyes narrowed and his brow wrinkled into a frown. Suddenly he grabbed hold of Cole's vest and shoved him backward off his feet. Before Cole could recover and retaliate—his fingers were flexing into a fist—Ryan stole his thunder by apologizing.

"I'm sorry. I shouldn't have done that. I let my temper get the upper hand. Look, you're right. You didn't ask for any of this, and the robberies aren't your problem. They're mine. I just thought . . . hoped, anyway . . . that you would want to help. I won't accept your resignation, though. You're going to have to ride to the regional office and surrender your badge to the marshal there. Sheriff Norton will give you the directions. I've got to get going to Rockford Falls before the trail grows cold. No hard feelings?" he asked as he put his hand out.

Cole shrugged and shook Ryan's hand. "No hard feelings."

Ryan headed for the stable at a run. Cole watched

him leave and then followed the sheriff inside the jail to find out where in tarnation the regional office was located.

"If it isn't close by, I'm sending the badge back," he told the sheriff.

Norton sat down heavily behind his desk and stacked his hands on top of his papers. "I don't think Marshal Ryan will cotton to that idea. Those badges are considered sacred, son. I wouldn't get him riled up if I was you. He went to considerable trouble getting you appointed, and it sure seems peculiar to me that he didn't want to argue with you a little more. He gave up easy, didn't he?"

"I don't know Ryan well enough to judge," he replied.

"You sure you want to give the badge up?"

"I'm sure. I'm not cut out to be a lawman."

"You thinking you ought to be a gunslinger? Some folks think there ain't no difference at all between a marshal and a gunman."

"I'm just a rancher, nothing more."

"Then why are so many gunslingers coming after you? Like it or not, you got yourself a reputation for being fast. Those boys ain't gonna quit chasing after glory. It seems to me the only way you can change your future is to hold on to that badge. Some gunslingers will think twice before taking on a U.S. marshal."

"Some won't," Cole argued. "Are you going to tell me where the regional office is or not?"

Norton ignored the question. "I'm gonna tell the facts to you plain and simple is what I'm gonna do. Marshal Ryan didn't nag you into doing the right thing, so I guess I ought to, and you're gonna have to be polite and listen to me because I'm old enough to be your father and age gives me the advantage. We got us a terrible problem with this Blackwater gang running over our territory, and since you happen to live inside the boundaries, I'd say it was your problem too. Not too long ago our little bank got robbed and we lost us some good friends. They were decent, law-abiding folks who just had the bad luck of being inside the bank at the time. Every one of them was killed like a dog. We had us a witness too. His name was Luke MacFarland, but he didn't last long."

"Sheriff, I'm sorry about what happened, but I don't—"

Norton cut him off. "Luke got shot up when the robbery was going on, and he wasn't even inside the bank at the time. He was just passing by on the boardwalk, which was another piece of bad luck all right. Still, the doc had him mending. He would have recovered—the doc said so—and he did see a couple of faces through the crack in the shades of the bank. He would have made a good witness when those no-good bastards got caught."

"What happened to him?"

"Luke got his neck sliced like a bow tie, that's what happened to him. His wife got cut too. They were both sleeping in their bed, but I think maybe one of them woke up. You should have seen that room, son. There was more blood than paint on those walls. I ain't never gonna forget it. Their little boys saw it too. The oldest, just ten last month, found them. He ain't never gonna be the same."

The story struck a nerve deep inside Cole. He leaned against the side of the desk, his gaze directed outside, as he thought about the children. What a hell of a nightmare for a child to see. What would happen to that little boy now? Or the other ones? Who would take care of them? How would they survive? Would they be split up and shipped to various relatives, or would they take to the streets, the way he had when he was a youngster? Out of the corner of his eye he noticed Ryan on a black horse riding at a gallop down the main street. He hoped the marshal would catch the monsters who had made those children orphans. In one night, their lives had been changed forever.

He turned back when the sheriff spoke again. "There was no call to kill those two, no call at all. You know what Ryan said?"

"No, what's that?" Cole asked.

"That it was a miracle they didn't kill those little boys. If one of them had come into the room while they were butchering, they would have killed him for sure . . . the others too."

"What's going to happen to them?"

"The boys?" The sheriff looked bleak, disheartened. "My Josey and me offered to take them all, but the relatives back east said they'd give them a home. I think they're gonna farm them out between them. That doesn't seem right to me. Brothers ought to stay together."

Cole agreed with a pensive nod.

"I got my own opinion why they killed Luke's wife. Want to hear it?"

"Sure."

"I think they were sending folks a message." His voice dropped to a whisper of confidentiality as he continued. "Word gets around fast, and anyone who might see something or hear something in the future is gonna think long and hard before stepping forward. Witnesses don't survive. That's the message."

"They're bound to make a mistake one of these days."

"Son, that's what everyone is hoping will happen. I'm praying it happens soon, 'cause a lot of good people have died, and not just men, but women and children too. Those men are gonna burn in hell for what they've done."

"They've killed children?"

"I heard about one little girl that got killed. She was in the bank with her mama. Of course it could just be speculation. I asked Ryan about it, but he got a real strange look in his eyes and went out the door without answering me, so I don't know if it's true or not. The marshal sure has his hands full," he concluded with a shake of his head. "Are you thinking about heading back to your ranch?"

"Right now I'm headed for Texas to bring some steers back. The regional office better be on the way or—"

Norton wouldn't let him finish. "I got a little favor to ask you." He put his hand up to ward off any interruption and hastily added, "I know I don't have the right, since I went and knocked you over the head. Still, I'm compelled to ask."

"What is it you want?"

"Hold on to your badge until tomorrow before you make up your mind. It's already going on dusk, so you don't have to wait long. In the morning, if you're still determined to give the badge back, then I'll be happy to tell you the fastest way to get to the regional office. With that fancy compass, you won't have any trouble finding it. Now, don't shake your head at me. At least consider it, and while you're at it, answer another question for me."

"What?" Cole asked with a bit more surliness than he intended.

"Why do you suppose Ryan went and shoved you the way he did before he took off?"

"Frustration," Cole answered.

The sheriff grinned like a big cat sitting in a tub of cream. "You wanted to hit him, didn't you? I saw you make a fist, and—yes, son, I did—and I saw something else happening too, but never you mind about that. You showed considerable restraint," he added. "And Marshal Ryan did apologize—I heard it with my own ears—but now I'm wondering to myself if he was apologizing for shoving you or maybe something else he'd done."

Before Cole could ask him to explain what he was

chattering on about, the sheriff pushed the topic around to the badge again.

"Will you stay on tonight? I'll treat you and Josey to supper at Frieda's fancy restaurant, and if you ride out now, you won't get far before dark hits. If I were you, I'd want to spend one more night sleeping between clean sheets before I headed out on such a long trip. Come morning, I'll give you the directions you're wanting and you can be on your way lickety-split. Course you'll probably want to go on over to Rockford Falls first. It ain't too far away from here."

Cole raised an eyebrow. "Why would I want to go to Rockford Falls?"

Norton chuckled. "To get your compass back."

Five

The town of Rockford Falls was reeling with shock. In the past two days, they had lost eight of their finest citizens and one who wasn't quite so fine but who mattered to all of them just the same.

Influenza was responsible for two deaths. The epidemic had been gathering strength during the past week, striking down half the population. The old and the young were hit hardest: Adelaide Westcott, a spry seventy-eight-year-old spinster who still had all of her own teeth and who never had a cranky word to say about anyone, and sweet little eight-month-old Tobias Dollen, who had inherited his father's big ears and his mother's smile, both died within an hour of one another of what Doc Lawrence called complications.

The town mourned the loss, and those who could get out of bed attended the funerals, while those who couldn't leave their chamber pots for more than five-minute intervals prayed for their souls at home.

Adelaide and Tobias were buried on Wednesday

morning in the cemetery above Sleepy Creek Meadow. That afternoon, six men were brutally murdered during a robbery at the bank. The seventh man to die and the last to be noticed was Bowlegged Billie Buckshot, the town drunk, who, it was speculated, was on his way from his dilapidated shack on the outskirts of town to the Rockford Saloon to fetch his breakfast. Billie was a creature of habit. He always started his day around three or four in the afternoon, and he always cut through the alley between the bank and the general store, thereby shortening his travel by two full streets. Because he was found cradling his rusty gun in his arms, it was assumed by Sheriff Sloan that he had had the misfortune to run into the gang as they were pouring out of the bank's rear exit. It was also assumed that the poor man never stood a chance. Everyone knew that until he had his first wake-up drink of the day, his hands shook like an empty porch swing in a windstorm. Six hours was a long time to go without whiskey when your body craved it the way Billie's did. He wasn't shot like the others, though. A knife had been used on him, and judging from the number of stab wounds on his face and neck, whoever had done it had thoroughly enjoyed his work.

As luck would have it, no one heard the gunshots or saw the robbers leaving the bank, perhaps because more than half the town was home in bed. Folks who wanted to get out for some fresh air waited until the sun was easing down to do so. Those few strolling down the boardwalk certainly noticed Billie curled up like a mangy old dog in the alley, but none of them gave him a second glance. It was a sight everyone was used to seeing. They figured the town drunk had simply passed out again.

Yet another precious hour passed that could have been used tracking the killers. Heavy clouds moved in above the town and rumbles of thunder were heard gathering in the distance. Emmeline MacCorkle, still weak and gray-faced from influenza, was nagged by her mother to accompany her to the bank to find out why Sherman MacCorkle thought he could be late for supper. Sherman's wife was in a snit. She caused quite a commotion banging on the front door of the bank, drawing curious glances, and when it wasn't promptly answered, she dragged her daughter around to the back door. Neither Emmeline nor her mother looked down at the curled-up drunk. Their disdain evident, they kept their noses in the air and stared straight ahead. Emmeline had to lift her skirt to step over Billie's feet, which were sticking out from the filthy tarp she thought he was using as a cover. She did so without giving him so much as a fleeting glance. Once they had rounded the corner, her mother unlatched her grip on her daughter's arm, flung the door open, and marched inside shouting her husband's name. Emmeline meekly followed.

Their blood-curdling screams were heard as far away as the cemetery, and folks came running to find out what was happening. Those who saw the grizzly tableau inside the lobby, before Sheriff Sloan could get there and seal the doors, would never be the same. John Cletchem, the photographer the sheriff summoned to take pictures for posterity, became so sick at the eerie sight, that he had to keep running outside to throw up in the street. Two of the victims, Franklin Carroll and Malcolm Watterson, had been shot simultaneously and had fallen into each other. They were both still on their knees and appeared to be embracing, with their heads drooping over each other's shoulder.

Daniel Ryan had a near riot on his hands when he rode into town at five minutes past one the following afternoon. Because of a torrential downpour, the journey had taken longer than expected. Sheriff Sloan met him in front of the bank, gave him the details, and then unlocked the door and followed him inside.

The bodies hadn't been removed from the lobby. If Ryan was sickened by the sight before him, he didn't show it. He slowly walked around the scene and stared down at the dead from every possible angle. There was only one telltale sign that he was affected. His hands were in fists at his sides.

In a strangled whisper, Sloan said, "I didn't know if I should let the bodies be taken out or leave them alone for you to see. Did I do the right thing?"

Before Ryan could answer him, the sheriff continued. "There was another body found in the alley next to the bank. His name was Billie, and he was the town drunk. They used a knife on him, and before I could tell the funeral men to leave him be, they carted him off and put him in the ground. I had pictures taken of these poor men, but Billie was already gone, so I didn't get any pictures of him."

The stench was getting to him. Sloan held a handkerchief over his mouth and nose to block the smell. He couldn't make himself look at his friends, but stared at the ceiling instead. "I don't want the families of these men to see . . ." Sloan couldn't go on. He gagged, spun around, and clawed at the doorknob. Ryan had to turn it for him. The sheriff ran outside, doubled over in front of the crowd that had gathered, and threw up in the street.

Returning to his inspection, Ryan squatted down next to one of the bodies to get a closer look at a bullet he'd spotted half buried in the floorboard. He could still hear Sloan's retching outside when the door opened again, letting in another blessed whiff of fresh air. Cole came striding inside. Ryan turned to him and waited for a reaction.

Cole wasn't prepared for what he saw. As though he'd just run headlong into a stone wall, he staggered back and whispered, "Ah . . . Lord."

"Are you going to run, or are you going to stay?" Ryan demanded.

Cole didn't answer. Ryan's eyes were blazing with fury now. "Take a good look, Cole. Any of these men could have been one of your brothers. Tell me, how often do they go into a bank? Or your mother? Or your sister?" he taunted in a voice that lashed out like a whip.

Cole shook his head and continued to stare at the two corpses on their knees leaning into one another. He couldn't look away.

"Don't you dare tell me this isn't your problem," Ryan said. "I've made it your problem by getting you appointed marshal. Like it or not, you aren't walking away from this. You're going to help me catch the bastards."

Cole didn't say a word. He was fighting the urge to join the sheriff outside, yet at the same time he could feel his anger fueling to a rage. No one should have to die like this. No one.

He wouldn't allow himself to be sick. If he turned his back on these men and ran outside, he would be committing a blasphemy. He couldn't reason his reaction. He just knew it would be wrong for him to be repulsed by them.

He shook his head as if to clear his thoughts, then slowly moved away from the door and walked around the circle of dead. Ryan watched him closely.

Another minute passed in silence, and then Cole said, "I don't know how many of them were in here, but I'm pretty sure several men did the shooting."

"How do you figure that?" Ryan asked.

"Powder burns and the angle of the bullets." He pointed to two of the bodies and whispered, "The bullet came through the back of this man's head, went out through his forehead and into the neck of the man facing him. The same thing happened with those two.

41

They were playing a game," he added. "Trying to kill two with one bullet. You already figured that out, didn't you?"

Ryan nodded. "Yes."

"The robbery was yesterday. Why weren't these bodies buried?"

"The sheriff thought he should leave them here for us to see. I have a feeling he hasn't been a lawman long."

Cole shook his head again. "There's a funeral cart outside. These people need to be buried."

"Then order it done," Ryan challenged.

Cole turned to go outside, but stopped with his hand on the doorknob. "Whenever I'm away from the ranch, I work alone."

"You don't work alone any longer."

"I should warn you. I do things different . . . Some of it won't be legal."

"I figured as much," Ryan replied.

He followed Cole outside and stood by him on the boardwalk while Cole ordered the crowd to back away so the funeral cart could be pulled closer. The body collector, a moonfaced man with hunched shoulders, stepped forward. Cole told him that he wanted the bodies covered with sheets before they were carried out.

The reporter for the Rockford Falls newspaper objected to the order. "We want to see them," he shouted. "Why do they have to be covered with sheets?"

Cole wanted to punch the ghoulish curiosity seeker. With effort, he resisted the impulse and said, "They wouldn't want to be remembered this way."

The reporter wouldn't let up. "They're dead," he shouted. "How do you know what they want?"

A woman in the crowd started crying. Cole looked at Ryan, waiting for him to answer, but the marshal ignored him and kept his gaze directed on the men and women in the street.

"Yes, they're dead," Cole shouted back. "And now the law becomes their voice. Get the damned sheets."

Ryan nodded his agreement. He pulled the compass out of his pocket and handed it to Cole. "You just became a lawman."

Six

It took over an hour to remove the six bodies. Because of the heat, rigor mortis had set in rapidly, and the owner of the funeral parlor had a hell of a time getting the two men who had died on their knees wrapped up and carried out.

The men who were assisting him whispered while they worked. Cole wasn't certain if they kept their voices low out of respect for the dead or if they were just plain spooked, but one of them started gagging and had to run outside when the funeral director worried out loud that if the families wanted to bury the men that day, he would have to either build two special coffins to accommodate the bent knees, or cut off their legs. One day's delay would ensure that the troublesome rigor mortis would have worn off. And if he sealed the coffins tight, no one would notice the smell.

The floor near the center of the lobby where the bodies had knelt was black. Blood had seeped into the dry wood, and it was there to stay. Not even lye would remove the stains.

Ryan questioned Sloan for a while before he searched through the president's office and behind the tellers' counter. He collected the papers, put them in a box he'd found, and carried them over to an old, ink-stained desk in front of the windows. While Cole roamed around the bank, trying to figure out exactly how, why, and when it all happened, Ryan sat on the edge of the desk and began to read.

Sloan stood by the door, fidgeting.

Ryan finally noticed him. "Is something bothering you, Sheriff?" he asked, without looking up from the document he was scanning.

"I was thinking I ought to get another posse together and go looking for the gang again. We had to disband last night when it got so dark. The trail's going to get cold if I wait much longer."

"That's a good idea," Ryan said. "Why don't you take charge and see to it."

"I figure I should pick the men I want to ride with me, like I did yesterday before you got here."

Ryan shrugged. "You know these people better than I do. I don't want to hear you did anything stupid though, like stringing someone up because you think he might have been involved. If you catch anyone, you bring him back here."

"I can't control an entire posse. Folks know what happened here. Someone might—"

Ryan cut him off. "You *will* control them, Sheriff."

Sloan nodded. "I'll try."

"That isn't good enough. No one takes the law into his own hands. You got that? If any of your friends thinks otherwise, you shoot the son of a bitch."

Ryan expected Sloan to leave, but he stayed where he was. His face turned bright red, and he shuffled from foot to foot as he stared down at the floor.

"Was there something else?" Ryan asked.

"It seems to me . . . and a lot of folks in town . . . that I ought to be in charge of this investigation."

Ryan cast Cole a quick glance to see how he was reacting to the sheriff's claim.

"How do you figure that?" Ryan asked.

"I'm the sheriff in Rockford Falls, so this is my jurisdiction, not yours. Like I said before, I ought to be in charge and you two should be taking orders from me."

"You think you could do a better job?"

"I maybe could."

"You can't even look at the stains on the floor," Ryan said. "What makes you think you can—"

"It's my jurisdiction," Sloan stubbornly insisted.

Ryan's patience was all used up. "Marshal Clayborne and I are here by special appointment, and I don't particularly care if you've got a problem with that or not. Stay out of our way," he ordered harshly. "Now, go get your posse together."

Cole listened to the exchange without saying a word. He waited until the sheriff left, then crossed the lobby to the windows and opened one. A clean, sweet breeze, tinged with the scent of pines, brushed over his arms and neck. He took several deep breaths to rid himself of the metallic smell of blood inside the bank, and then turned around and leaned against the ledge.

He stared at Ryan's back. "It rained hard last night and most of this morning," he remarked.

"Yeah, I know. I got soaked."

"There isn't going to be a trail this afternoon. It's been washed away."

Ryan glanced over his shoulder. "I know that too. I just wanted to get rid of Sloan."

Cole folded his arms across his chest and leaned back. "The men who did this are long gone."

Ryan nodded. "Wires were sent to every lawman in the territory yesterday. By now all the main roads are being watched. There are also men at the train stations and the river. The bastards will still get through the net, though. They're slick, real slick." He let the paper he'd been reading drop down to the desk and turned around to face Cole. "You know what I used to be worried about?"

"What's that?"

Ryan's voice lowered. "That they'd stop and I wouldn't be able to catch them."

Cole shook his head. "They aren't going to stop." Nodding toward the bloodstains, he added in a whisper, "They're having too much fun."

"Yeah, I think you're right. They've developed a real taste for killing."

"How many banks have they robbed?"

"This makes almost a dozen."

"They've gotten away twelve times?"

"They're either very lucky or very smart."

"Where and when was the first robbery?"

"It happened late spring two years ago. They robbed a bank in Texas—Blackwater, Texas, to be exact. That's how they got their name."

"The Blackwater gang," Cole said.

"Yes," Ryan said. "Anyway, they went in during the night with kerosene and burned the building to the ground when they left. No one saw anything."

"Was anyone killed?"

"No," Ryan answered. "Then, two weeks later, they hit another bank in Hollister, Oklahoma. Once again, they went in during the night, but they didn't use kerosene."

"Did they tear up the place?"

Ryan shook his head. "They were nice and tidy. They didn't touch anything but the money, and they didn't leave any evidence behind."

"How do you know the two robberies were related?"

"Gut feeling mostly," Ryan said. "There were a

couple of similarities. As I said before, they went in during the night, and in both cases, government money had just been deposited for the army salaries at the nearby forts."

"Where was the third bank?"

"Pelton, Kansas," Ryan answered. "They changed the way they did things with that robbery. They went in at closing time, just like they did here. There were seven people inside. Two were killed. The shooting started when one of the employees went for his gun. He died gripping it in his hand, but he didn't get a shot off."

"So you did have witnesses?"

"Yes, but they weren't helpful. They said the men wore masks and that only one did all the talking. They said he had a southern drawl."

"How many men did they say came into the bank?"

"Seven."

"And they were after army payroll again?"

"Yes."

Cole filed the information away. Then he asked, "Where did they strike next?"

"They went back to Texas," Ryan answered, "and robbed a bank in Dillon."

"That's your hometown, isn't it?"

Ryan looked startled. Cole quickly explained. "I did a halfhearted search for you when you took the compass from my mother."

"What else did you find out?"

Cole shrugged. "Nothing much. Was anyone killed in the robbery in Dillon?" he asked, switching the topic back to the more pressing matter.

"Yes." His voice turned harsh, angry. "Too damned many."

Cole waited, but Ryan didn't give him any particulars. When Cole prodded him for details, he became agitated.

"Look, it's all in the files. I've gone through them at

least a hundred times, but maybe when you read the reports, you'll find something I missed. The bank in Dillon was the last one they hit that year. They lay low in the fall and winter months, then start in again in the spring and summer months. It's sporadic, yet consistent," he added. "Last year they moved north and became even more violent, and this year, all three banks they've robbed have been in Montana Territory."

"Probably because there are so many places to hide."

"Yes. I think so too. They've stayed away from the big cities."

"Sheriff Norton told me about the witness you had in Middleton."

Ryan nodded. "Luke MacFarland was his name. He happened to be walking past the bank during the robbery. He told me he heard gunshots, but that he was already looking in through the space between the window and the shades because of something else he heard."

"What was that?"

"Laughter."

Cole wasn't shocked. "I told you they enjoy their work. It's going to get much worse unless you stop them."

"Unless *we* stop them," Ryan corrected. "You're in this now."

"Yeah, I guess I am. Did Luke tell you how the people inside died? Did they make them kneel down?"

"No, they were taken into the back room and killed there. The kneeling . . . that's new. So is the knife."

Ryan reached up and began to rub the knot in the back of his neck. "Damn, I'm tired."

Cole could see how exhausted Ryan was. "You shouldn't have slept outside in the rain. You're too old for it."

Ryan smiled. "I'm only a year older than you are."

"How do you know my age?"

"I know everything there is to know about you."

If Cole was surprised by the comment, he didn't let it show. "Why didn't you protect your witness in Middleton?"

"I sure as hell tried to protect him. Honest to God I did, but another robbery was reported over in Hartfield, and I left to check it out. Marshal Davidson was put in charge of Luke MacFarland and his family."

"Besides telling you that he heard laughter, what else did Luke say?"

"He could only see two men through the seam. One of them took his mask off, and Luke got a glimpse at his profile. He didn't think he could point him out in a crowd, though. He did say he was tall, lean."

"Anything else?"

"No."

"What was Marshal Davidson doing while his witness was being killed?"

"He'd already gotten hit. He's going to recover, but it will take a long time. The doctor dug three bullets out of him."

"They wouldn't have left him unless they thought they'd killed him."

"Yes, that's what I think."

"Sheriff Norton told me how MacFarland and his wife were killed. A knife was used on both of them. He thinks they murdered his wife to send folks a message. He says you're going to have a hell of a time getting anyone to admit he saw anything. Word travels fast in the territory."

"Did Norton happen to tell you anything about his background?"

"No, he didn't. Why do you ask?"

"Just curious. Have you ever heard of a gunslinger named the Laredo Kid?"

"Sure," Cole answered. "He was a legend when I

was growing up. Everyone knew what a daredevil he was . . . crazy, but fast with a gun. Real fast. He's probably dead by now. Did Norton kill him?"

Ryan smiled. "The Laredo Kid isn't dead. Fact is, he became a sheriff."

"Norton is . . . ?" Cole was incredulous.

"I swear it's true."

"He should have been killed years ago. There's always someone faster with a gun waiting to prove himself. He's lucky he's still alive."

"I agree, especially with that wife of his cooking for him. Did she make you eat her fried chicken? It damn near killed me."

Cole burst out laughing. He was surprised how good it felt. The tension in his gut eased up a little. "She tried," he admitted. "But I didn't touch it."

Ryan also relaxed, until he looked at the blood-stained floors again. It was a sobering sight.

"You've had time to look around. Tell me what you think happened."

The laughter was gone from Cole's eyes when he answered. "I'll tell you what I know didn't happen. None of them fought. There aren't any signs of a struggle. Hell, they were as meek as sheep. There are guns in all three cash drawers behind the windows," he said with a tilt of his head toward the tellers' stations. "They're loaded, but they haven't been touched. Now, you tell me something, Ryan. Why did you come after me? There are better men out there to wear this badge."

"I wanted you."

"Why?"

"It's complicated."

"That's an excuse, not an answer."

Ryan sent the chair flying backward when he stood up and leaned against the desk. Both men ignored the crash that followed as the chair struck the wall; their gazes were fixed on each other.

A long minute passed in silence before Ryan made up his mind. "All right, I'll tell you why I chose you for the job. A long time ago I started getting curious about you when I heard about the trouble you ran into down near Abilene and how you handled it."

"I'm sure the story was exaggerated."

"No, it wasn't. I checked it out. You knew what they were going to do to that woman, and you—"

"Like I said," Cole interrupted, "the story was exaggerated."

"You shot through her to get him."

"I shot through her arm, that's all. The bullet didn't touch bone. She only got a nick."

"But that same bullet killed him."

"He needed to die."

"I can give you at least twenty other examples."

"I'm good with a gun. So what?"

"You want the best reason of all?"

"Yes."

"You think like they do."

"Like who?"

"The bastards who came in here and killed all those people."

"Son of a bitch!" Cole roared. "Do you think I could do something like this?"

Ryan diffused his anger. "No, I don't think you could do something like this. I said you think like they do. You can get into their minds, Cole. I've tried, but I can't do it."

"You're nuts, Ryan."

"Maybe, but I need a man who won't hesitate and who doesn't mind bending the law in certain situations. I also have to trust him, and I trust you."

"How do you know you can trust me?"

"All the stories you say didn't happen. I rode with your mother on the train to Salt Lake, and she told me all sorts of saintly things about you only a mother could believe. Does she know how ruthless you can be?"

Cole refused to answer the question.

Ryan plunged ahead. "She thinks you're headed in the wrong direction. That's why she gave you the compass."

"The compass you kept for over a year."

Ryan shrugged. "She also told me the compass was to remind you to stay on the right path. The way I see it, I'm helping you do just that."

"I'm not ruthless."

"When the situation calls for it, you are. I also heard about Springfield."

"Ah, hell."

"Are you going to help me or not?"

Cole had already made his decision. The sight of those bodies would stay in his mind for a long, long time, and he knew he wouldn't be able to sleep at night unless he helped find the men who had committed this atrocity. He simply couldn't walk away.

"I want to get all of them," he whispered. "I'll keep the badge, but as soon as this is over, I'm giving it back."

"You might decide to stay on."

"Maybe," was all he would allow. "Are there any special rules for marshals? I never was one for rules," he warned.

"Marshals are assigned to territories, but you and I are the exception because we're on special duty. As for the rules, you don't need to worry about them. It's all common-sense stuff anyway. Marshals can't be tried for murder, you know." He told the lie with a straight face.

Cole laughed. "That rule will come in handy."

Ryan stood up and rolled his shoulders to work the stiffness out. "Why don't you go through this box while I go in the back and look through the drawers again."

Ryan had already headed toward the president's office when Cole called out to him. "What am I looking for?"

"The names of the people who did their banking yesterday. Sloan told me that the president insisted his tellers keep accurate records. They were ordered to write down the name of every customer they helped."

"Once we make the list of the names, then what?" Cole asked.

"We talk to all of them because one might have noticed something out of the ordinary."

"Has that ever happened before?"

"No, but we still have to ask. Those bastards are going to slip up one of these days. Maybe one of them came into the bank earlier to look it over."

"That's wishful thinking, Ryan."

"Yeah, I know, but we still have to go through the routine. We have to cover all the possibilities. From the looks of all these stacks of paper, there were quite a few customers yesterday. It's going to take us the rest of the day to go through them."

They divided the stacks between them. Ryan went back into the president's office to work there. Cole stayed out in the lobby. He searched through the top drawer of the ink-stained desk for a notepad and pencil so that he could make his list, found what he needed, and put them on the desktop. He was on his way to get the chair Ryan had kicked over when a glimpse of blue on the floor under the desk's kneehole caught his attention.

"We're going to have to go through everything in here at least three times," Ryan warned. "Just in case we miss something the first and second time around."

"We'll be here a week," Cole shouted back as he bent down on one knee and reached inside the kneehole. He pulled out a pale blue bag with a blue-and-white satin string.

He opened it and looked inside. There wasn't anything there, just blue satin lining. Cole stared at the thing for several seconds, then called out, "Hey, Ryan, do you know who works at this desk?"

"Yes," Ryan shouted back. He was seated at the president's desk, methodically going through the contents in the top drawer. "I've got the name written down in my notes."

"Do you remember if it is a man or a woman?"

Something in Cole's voice caught Ryan's attention. He glanced up, saw him down on one knee, and called out, "A man sits there."

"Was he one of the men killed?"

"No. He was home sick yesterday."

Cole stuck his head into the opening. "Well . . . well," he whispered.

"Did you find something?" Ryan shouted.

"Maybe," Cole answered. "Then again, maybe not." He stood up and turned to Ryan. "Do you happen to know how often this place gets cleaned?"

"That's the first question I asked Sloan, since we also have to go through the trash. According to him, MacCorkle was obsessed about keeping the place spotless. He had it cleaned every night and inspected every nook and cranny in the morning. All the trash in the bins is from yesterday's business."

"You're positive it was cleaned Tuesday night?"

Ryan stopped what he was doing and walked back to the lobby. He spotted the wad of blue fabric in Cole's hand.

"Yeah, I'm sure. Why? What have you got?"

"A possibility."

"A possibility of what?"

Cole smiled. "A witness."

Seven

Three women had been inside the bank between the hours of one and three o'clock in the afternoon on the day of the robbery. Cole and Ryan knew that was fact, not speculation, because of Sherman MacCorkle's taskmaster rules. Just as the sheriff had told Ryan, the president of the bank had demanded that every transaction—even change for a dollar bill—be recorded by name on a piece of paper and filed in the cash drawer. If the figures on the papers didn't balance with the money in the drawer, the teller had to make up the difference. MacCorkle had also insisted that each day's tallies be separated into the morning and afternoon hours. The receipts for Wednesday morning's transactions were still on MacCorkle's desk in three neat piles. There was also an open filing cabinet behind MacCorkle's desk filled with documents, loan applications, mortgages, and records of foreclosures. Every piece had a date on top.

God love Sherman MacCorkle for being such a stickler for details.

With all the interruptions, it took until evening to sort out all the names. In all, twenty-nine men and women had come into the bank that day. Eighteen had taken care of their business during the morning hours, and none of them were women. The bank had been closed for lunch from noon until one o'clock, and that afternoon, eleven people had come inside, and of those eleven, three were women.

One of them had left her bag behind.

Ryan and Cole were cautious about the discovery and decided in hushed, urgent voices to keep the possibility of a witness to themselves for the time being.

"We could be jumping the gun on this," Cole warned. "In fact, we probably are."

"Yeah, but I got a feeling . . ."

"Me too," Cole whispered. "The thing is . . . it could have been under the desk for weeks."

"We should talk to the couple who cleans the place right away. I've got their names and address somewhere in my notes," Ryan said as he flipped through the pages of his notepad. "Here it is. Mildred and Edward Stewart. They live over on Currant Street. Let's go talk to them now. I want to get out of here for a few minutes and get some fresh air."

"It's past nine," Cole said. "They might be in bed."

He was already moving toward the front door as he reminded Ryan of the time. They locked the door on their way out and walked over to the Stewarts' cottage on the outskirts of town. The couple's daughter opened the door for them and explained that her parents were working. They cleaned the bank, the church, and the general store every night.

The marshals backtracked. They could see the lights inside the general store. The shades were drawn, but Edward Stewart opened the door as soon as Ryan knocked and told him who he was.

Mildred was down on her knees scrubbing the floor. The heavyset woman got to her feet and wiped her hands on her apron when the marshals came inside. Both she and her husband were older—around fifty or so, Cole speculated—and from their haggard expressions and their stooped shoulders, he knew they had had to work hard all of their lives.

Ryan made the introductions, and then said, "We know you're busy, but we sure would appreciate it if you would answer a couple of questions."

"We'll be glad to help any way we can," Edward said. "There's some chairs behind the counter if you want to sit down. The floor should be dry by now."

"It won't take that long," Ryan said. "Did you and Mildred clean the bank Tuesday night?"

Edward nodded. "Yes, sir, we did. We clean it every night but Sunday, and MacCorkle paid us every Monday morning."

"Do you think the new people running the place will keep us on?" Mildred asked. "We do a good job and we don't charge much."

They could tell she was worried. She was wringing her apron in her hands and frowning with concern.

"I'm sure they'll keep you on," Ryan predicted. "When you clean the bank, do you wash the floors or sweep them?"

"I do both," Mildred answered. "First I give them a good sweeping, and then I get down on my hands and knees and wash every inch of my floors. I use vinegar and water, and when I'm done, the hardwood shines, doesn't it, Edward?"

"Yes, it does," he agreed.

"You don't move the furniture, do you?" Cole asked.

"I don't move the heavy pieces, but I move the chairs and the trash tins. I get under the tellers' windows, under the desks, and behind the file cabinets that aren't against the walls. We do a real thorough job," she insisted.

"MacCorkle always inspected our work. Sometimes he'd get down on his knees and look into the corners just to make sure we didn't miss a speck of dust or a cobweb, and if he found any, he deducted from our pay. He was real finicky about his bank."

"He bought old, used-up furniture for the lobby and his loan officers, but he told us, with enough elbow grease, we could make the wood shine again. Some of those desks should have been thrown away years ago, but MacCorkle wasn't one to waste anything," Edward said.

"He had fancy new furniture put in his office," Mildred interjected.

Cole spotted a basket of green apples on the counter. He took a coin out of his pocket, tossed it on the counter, and then selected two. He threw one to Ryan and took a bite out of the other.

"Ma'am, did the folks who came into the bank ever leave anything behind?"

"Sure they did," Mildred answered. "I found a pretty brooch once, and Edward found a wallet with six whole dollars inside. Anything that's left behind is put in the lost-and-found box in MacCorkle's office. It's in the corner by the safe."

"Did you happen to find anything Tuesday night?"

Both Mildred and Edward shook their heads.

"Do you remember cleaning under the desks Tuesday?" Cole asked.

"Sure I remember," Mildred said. "I clean under the desks every night, but Sunday. Why are you asking?"

"I was just curious," Cole lied.

"Even if we were tired, we cleaned every inch of the bank because MacCorkle wouldn't pay us our full wage if we didn't."

"He was a hard man to work for," Mildred whispered.

"You shouldn't be speaking ill of the dead," Edward told his wife.

"I'm speaking the truth," she argued.

"We'll let you get back to your job," Ryan said. "Thanks for your help."

Edward moved forward to let them out the front door. "Do you think you could get MacCorkle's wife to pay us for the two nights we cleaned?"

"I'll be happy to talk to her, but if she doesn't pay you, I'll make sure the new manager does."

Edward shook his head. "If we can be of any help catching those men who killed our friends, you let us know, Marshal."

"I'll do that," Ryan promised.

The marshals started down the boardwalk. "Now what do we do?" Cole asked.

"Go back to the bank and box up all the papers from yesterday's business. It won't take long."

"Do you think the restaurant's still open?"

"No, it's too late. Your apple's going to have to do for the moment. I wish we could go talk to those three women now, but I don't know where they live."

"We can get the addresses from the sheriff as soon as he gets back with his posse."

"Yes," Ryan agreed.

They walked along in silence for several minutes, and then Cole said, "At least we know the bag was left during the day of the robbery. MacCorkle was a real sweetheart, wasn't he?"

"You mean holding back their wages if they didn't do a thorough job?"

"Exactly," Cole said. "Why would a woman leave her purse behind?"

"She must have been in a panic."

"If she was hiding in the kneehole, she saw the whole thing."

"*Maybe* she saw the whole thing," Ryan said. "We should talk to the man who sits at the desk."

He handed Cole the key to the front door of the bank while he dug his notepad out again. After Cole had gone inside and turned up the gas lamp, Ryan found what he was looking for.

"His name's Lemont Morganstaff. We'll talk to him in the morning," he said. "He might know something about the bag."

"What's he gonna know?" Cole asked.

Ryan shrugged. "Probably nothing, but we have to ask him anyway."

"And then what?"

"If he doesn't know where the bag came from, we still can't assume a woman was hiding in the kneehole. It could have ended up there a hundred different ways. One of the three women could have sat down at the desk to go through some papers. She might have dropped it when she got up. Damn, I wish it wasn't so late."

"You're right. There could be a hundred different explanations. A woman could have left it during the morning. She could have come inside with a friend and been sitting at the desk while he did his banking."

"Why would a woman carry around an empty purse?"

"I don't know why they carry them in the first place. Pockets are more efficient."

"We shouldn't get our hopes up. A woman might have dropped it, then kicked it into the corner of the kneehole when she stood up. Does that make sense to you?"

Cole shook his head. "The women I know keep track of their things."

"God, I hope she saw it."

"Now who's being ruthless? If she did see the murders, she has to be scared out of her mind. The last thing she's going to want to do is come forward."

"We'll protect her."

"She won't believe that, not if she heard what happened to Luke MacFarland."

Ryan began to pace around the lobby. In the shadows of the gas lamps, the bloodstains resembled ghoulish outlines.

"We're going to try to follow procedure on this one. I don't want to leave any stone unturned."

Exasperated, Cole said, "I've been a marshal one day. I don't know what the procedures are."

"We interview the three women first, but we also question every man who came in here yesterday."

"It seems like a waste of time to me," Cole said.

"It's procedure."

Cole leaned back against a desk and took another bite of his apple. "Fine, we'll do it your way. There were twenty-nine people inside the bank. You talk to fifteen and I'll take the other fourteen."

"No, that isn't how it works. We interview them together, then compare notes afterwards. I might miss something that you will pick up," he explained. "We'll talk to the women first," he repeated. "Then the others. And that's only the beginning. We need to talk to everyone who happened to be on the street, near the street, or in one of the buildings close to the bank. We also—"

Cole interrupted him. "In other words, we talk to everyone."

"Just about," Ryan replied. "As much as I hate to, we're going to have to involve Sloan on this. I don't know these people. He does, and people here might tell him things they won't tell us. I'll give him the list of names as soon as he gets back."

Ryan stopped pacing and looked around the lobby. "I think we're finished here. I'll put yesterday's papers in the safe just in case one of us wants to go through them again. The bookkeepers from the bank in Gramby will be here Sunday to examine MacCorkle's records, and when they're finished, we'll know the exact amount stolen. Let's meet back here at seven in the morning and have Sloan round up the people we want to talk to."

"I don't think it's a good idea to question them here. We should use the office at the jail."

Ryan shook his head. "Jails make people nervous."

"Seeing the bloodstains is going to make them more nervous."

"Yeah, you're right. We'll use the jail."

After collecting the papers and locking the safe, they left the bank.

"Have you checked into the hotel yet?" Ryan asked.

"No, I went directly to the bank. What about you?"

"I didn't take the time either. Are you still hungry?"

"Yeah, I am," Cole answered. "Maybe the hotel will open the kitchen for us."

"They will," Ryan assured him. "We're marshals. We'll make them."

Cole laughed. "I knew there had to be a couple of benefits to this job."

They walked in companionable silence down the middle of the street, the only light supplied by a full moon.

"How much money do you think they got away with?" Cole asked.

"Like I said before, we won't know the exact amount until the examiners go through the records. I do know from the receipt I found on MacCorkle's desk that an army paymaster made a deposit that morning. The amount was seventeen thousand eight hundred and some change."

Cole whistled. "That's a lot of money. I'll bet the bastards knew before MacCorkle did that the money was coming."

"I'm sure they did. All they had to do was follow him."

"Why bother robbing the banks?" Cole asked. "Why not rob the paymaster on his way to the fort with the cash?"

"It's too dangerous and unpredictable, that's why. The paymaster doesn't ride alone, and the guards assigned to him are all crack shots. Banks are easier if you know what you're doing, and the men we're up against obviously do."

The discussion ended when they reached the hotel. The only rooms available were in the attic and were about the size of clothes closets. Cole's room faced the street. Ryan's room was directly across the hall. The beds were soft though, and with a little persuasion, the night manager agreed to send up supper.

Neither Ryan nor Cole got much sleep that night. Cole kept thinking about the grisly scene he'd walked into, and Ryan spent his time thinking about the possible witness.

Eight

❦

Morning came all too quickly. As agreed, the marshals met at the bank, where Sheriff Sloan was waiting to report that the posse hadn't had any luck finding a trail. Ryan handed him the list of people he wanted to report to the jail to be interviewed. The three women's names were at the top.

The sheriff looked over the names and shook his head. "Some of these folks are sick as dogs with influenza. It hits hard and fast," he warned. "And some of the others are getting ready to head out of town. I ran into Doc Lawrence at the restaurant, and he was up all night tending to the Walsh family, and you've got John Walsh's name on the list. Doc told me Frederick O'Malley is heading out of town with his brood as soon as the general store opens and he can get some more supplies."

"No one leaves Rockford Falls until Marshal Clayborne and I have talked to them. That includes Frederick O'Malley."

"I can't make him stay."

"I can," Ryan replied.

Sloan wanted to argue. "This seems like a waste of time to me. If anyone saw anything, he would have spoken up by now."

"Marshal Ryan wants to follow procedure," Cole explained.

Sloan was staring at the blue bag on the desk. "Where did that come from?"

Ryan answered. "It was on the floor under the desk."

"You think someone left it?"

"That much is pretty obvious," Cole said. "We're curious to know who it belongs to."

A gleam came into Sloan's eyes. "It had to have been left here on the day of the robbery because the Stewarts, who clean the place every night, would have found it if someone had left it the day before. They would have put it in the lost-and-found box. They're honest people," he thought to add. "You don't think one of the robbers left it behind, do you?"

"No, we don't think that," Cole said dryly.

"Which desk was it found under?"

"Lemont Morganstaff's," Ryan answered. "We're going to talk to him right away. Do you know where he lives?"

"Sure I do. I know just about everybody in town. I'll take you over to Lemont's as soon as you're ready. Are you going to ask him about the bag?"

"Yes," Ryan answered.

Sloan's mind was whirling with possibilities. "Where exactly was the bag found? Was it right by the chair or was it way under the desk?"

"It was in the kneehole," Ryan answered. "In the corner."

Sloan's eyes widened. "You don't think that maybe someone was hiding under the desk, do you?"

"We haven't drawn any conclusions yet," Cole told him.

"But it's possible, isn't it?"

"Yes," Ryan agreed. "It's possible. The matter of the bag is confidential, Sheriff. I don't want you telling anyone about it."

Sloan dropped down to his knees. "You can see through here . . ."

"I want to get started," Cole said impatiently. "Show us where Lemont lives, and then start rounding up the people on the list. We'll use the jail to talk to them."

"I'll wait out front to take you to Lemont's," Sloan said, bolting for the door.

As soon as Sloan had stepped outside, Cole said, "It was a bad idea to tell him where the bag was found."

Ryan shrugged. "He's a lawman, and he'll only get in our way if we don't feed him a little information now and then. What harm can he do?"

Nine

As it turned out, Sloan could do a great deal of harm. Before the day was over, Ryan actually considered locking the sheriff in his own jail. Unfortunately, the law frowned on incarcerating a man just because he was stupid.

In a town the size of Rockford Falls, everyone knew everyone else's business, and carefully guarded secrets had a way of leaking out like water through a sieve. The employee who worked at the desk where the purse was found, Lemont Morganstaff, a prissy old-maid of a man, was shown the cloth bag and duly questioned. The interview took place in the claustrophobic parlor of Lemont's home. Dressed in a bright lime green velvet robe and slippers, Lemont resembled a parrot. He sat in a faded yellow velvet chair, rested his arms on the lace-covered arms, and puckered his lips in thought for several minutes before declaring that the purse couldn't have been found by his desk. He made it a rule, he explained, never to let any of the customers, man or woman, past the gate.

However, since he hadn't been working on the day of the robbery, he couldn't be certain the other employees had enforced his rule.

Sheriff Sloan, who had insisted on being part of the interview, blurted out the fact that the purse had been found in the kneehole of Lemont's desk. "It couldn't have been kicked there," he said, "because your desk faces the lobby and that front panel goes all the way to the floor. Someone had to go around, past the gate, and get behind your desk. I've had a little time to ponder on it, and I think that maybe there was a woman hiding there during the robbery. I'd wager the marshals think the same thing. Now, there were three women in the bank—their names are on the list Marshal Ryan gave me—and I'm going to go round them up as soon as I'm finished here. I'm hoping the woman who saw the murders is just too timid to come forward, but if she's deliberately keeping the information to herself because she's scared, I'm going to have to arrest her."

Lemont covered his mouth with his lace handkerchief and looked horrified. "You think a woman saw the murders? Oh, that poor dear," he whispered.

Ryan quickly tried to repair the damage Sloan had done, while Cole shoved the sheriff toward the front door.

"We don't believe any such thing," he said. "The purse could have gotten under the desk a hundred different ways. There could have been a lot of women inside the bank, and any one of them could have sat at your desk and accidentally dropped it."

Lemont wasn't paying very much attention to the marshal's explanation. "It had to have been left on the day of the robbery," he said excitedly. "The bank's cleaned every night by the Stewarts, and they always do a thorough job. Still, you're right. A woman could have left the bag sometime during the morning hours.

If you look in the tellers' drawers, you'll find a record of every customer who did any business that day."

Sloan elbowed his way back over to Lemont. "I got a feeling the three women on my list were there in the afternoon. I got their names right here. There was Jessica Summers, Grace Winthrop, and Rebecca James. Do you know any of these, Lemont?"

"As a matter of fact I do. I know Rebecca James. I saw her just last night, but she was feeling very poorly, and I fear she's caught the influenza. I sent her home, of course.

"I met the dear woman last week," he continued. "She stopped by to tell me how glorious she thought my garden was. She appreciates beauty," he added. "I don't know the other two women, but then I keep to myself. By the time I get home from the bank, there are only two hours left before dark, and I spend every minute of it tending my flowers."

"None of the women on the list have lived in Rockford Falls long," Sloan said. "Are you sure you've never met Jessica Summers or Grace Winthrop?"

"I might have, but if I did, neither one of them made much of an impression."

Cole grabbed hold of Sloan's arm and pushed him out the doorway. Ryan kept his attention on Lemont.

"The sheriff spoke out of turn," he began. "His conclusions aren't based on fact."

"Perhaps a stranger left the pocketbook behind," Lemont said. "There are so many of them in town this time of year. They come to see the falls and trample all over the glorious flowers growing wild on the hills outside of town. Some of the men and women are quite audacious, Marshal. Why, just two weeks ago one of them vandalized my garden and picked all of my tulips. I've asked and asked Sheriff Sloan to do something about it, but now that you're here, perhaps you can apprehend the culprits. I'll press charges," he added. "I don't care if it was the work of a child or not. The hooligans belong in jail."

Cole returned to the parlor in time to hear Lemont's remarks. "It seems you're more concerned about your garden than—"

Lemont interrupted him. "Than the people who died in the bank? You're right, Marshal, I am. Flowers, you see, are more precious to me. They serve only one purpose. To be pretty, and I like pretty things."

"Let's go," Cole told Ryan. "We've taken enough of Lemont's time."

The two men headed for the door. "I don't want to hear that you've told anyone about our talk," Ryan ordered, "or you'll end up in jail."

Lemont immediately gave his word to keep quiet. He found it impossible to keep his promise, however. He received a visitor an hour later and simply had to relate every word of the conversation he'd had with the marshals. He also told his housekeeper, Ernestine Hopper, who just happened to have a mouth the size of the stuffed bass mounted on the sheriff's office wall. A rather dull-witted woman, she also led a rather dull life, and news such as this couldn't be kept to herself. She told everyone she knew that there was a possibility of a witness to the murders, and after retelling the story four or five times, she stopped using the word "possibility" and made it fact. By the time the rumor circled around to Ryan and Cole, the story had blossomed into front-page news in the *Rockford Falls Gazette*. Convinced the story was the hottest news to hit town, the reporter had talked the owner into printing an evening edition. It was the first time in the history of Rockford Falls that folks were treated to two newspapers in one day, and needless to say, the special edition caused quite a stir.

Ten

$\mathcal{R}$yan wanted to kill someone. Cole suggested he start with the sheriff and then head on over to Morganstaff's house and shoot him and his damned flowers too. The men, furious and frustrated, discussed the problem of dealing with Sloan on their way to Melton's restaurant that evening. They still hadn't talked to the three women. Jessica Summers and Grace Winthrop had gone to do an errand and weren't expected back at the boardinghouse until suppertime. Rebecca James was staying at the hotel, but was too ill to receive visitors. Hopefully she would be well enough to talk to the marshals tomorrow.

Ryan and Cole had already talked to eighteen of those who had been in the bank, and thus far, the investigation had proven to be a waste of time, for they hadn't gleaned one morsel from any of them. No one had seen or heard anything unusual.

Although darkness was fast approaching, their day wasn't over yet. After they had their supper, the two of them were going back to the boardinghouse to talk to Jessica and Grace.

The few men and women strolling down the street gave the marshals a wide berth, and as soon as the two men sat down inside the restaurant, most of the other diners got up and left.

"Does this bother you?" Ryan asked Cole, nodding toward the doorway where three men were comically tripping over one another in their hurry to leave.

"No," Cole answered. "I'm used to it. Every time I'd ride into a new town, for some reason folks automatically jumped to the conclusion that I was a gunslinger."

"You were a gunslinger," Ryan reminded him.

Cole wasn't in the mood to argue with him. He moved back so that the owner could place the bowls of rabbit stew and a basket of hot bread on the table.

"If you two don't mind hurrying, I'd like to get you fed and out of here so my business will pick up."

Cole tried to hold on to his patience. The woman was old, tired-looking, and thin as a stick of straw. He politely asked for coffee. She impolitely demanded to know if he planned to linger while he drank it.

"Ma'am, neither Marshal Ryan nor I killed the seven men who were just buried, and we'd both appreciate it if you'd stop treating us like we did."

"Why haven't you caught any of the men who killed them? That's what folks are wondering."

"We're trying," Ryan said, his voice weary.

"I know you've been talking to the folks who were in the bank the day of the murders."

Cole nodded. "Word gets around fast, doesn't it?" he remarked to Ryan. He turned back to the woman. "None of your friends and neighbors saw anything. They didn't see them ride into town or out. They didn't hear any gunshots either," he added.

She gave the marshals a sympathetic look. "Oh,

some of them probably heard the shots. They were maybe too scared to do anything about it. You boys are tired, aren't you? My name's Loreen," she added. "And I'll go fetch your coffee now."

She returned a minute later, poured two cups, and put the coffeepot down on the table between the men.

"The way I see it, some folks would tell you if they'd seen or heard anything, but most probably wouldn't. We all know what happens to people who talk. The Blackwater gang comes back to get them. Everyone knows that's how they do things. In all my days I've never heard of men who are so pure evil. I read a while back that they robbed a bank in Texas and killed a woman and her little girl. The baby wasn't even three years old."

"She was four," Ryan said.

Loreen's head snapped up. "Then it's true."

His voice was soft, chilling. "Yes, it's true."

"Dear God, why would they want to hurt such an innocent little lamb? She couldn't have told anything. She was too little."

Cole's appetite vanished. They were dealing with monsters, and all he wanted to think about was catching them.

Loreen put her bony hand on her hip and shook her head. "I know you're trying to do your best. You boys take all the time you need. Business is suffering anyway because of the influenza spreading through town. Even the strangers who come to gawk at the falls are getting sick—at least most of them are, according to the doc. He says the sickness isn't contagious, but I say it is. Have you talked to that poor woman who saw the murders?"

Lost in their own thoughts, the marshals were jarred by her question. Cole asked her to repeat it.

"I asked you if you talked to the poor woman who saw the murders," she said. "I heard you suspect that one of the three women who were in the bank during the afternoon saw everything while it was happening. If she isn't too scared, she might tell you what she saw, and if she is too scared, well then, maybe you could persuade her to talk. I'm not trying to tell you how to run your investigation," she hastily added. "But since you suspect . . ."

"We don't suspect anyone," Cole interjected.

Lorene didn't pay any attention to his comment. "It has to be true because I read about it in the paper. We had us a special edition this afternoon. Sheriff Sloan was interviewed by the reporter, and he told him that he got under the desk himself and looked, and sure enough, he could see the lobby through the cracks in the wood. He said a woman was hiding there, all right."

"Ma'am, the sheriff didn't get under the desk," Cole argued.

"It says in the paper that he did," she countered. "You know, I could have been in that bank while the robbery was going on. I usually make my deposits about that time of day, but lately, enough cash hasn't come in for me to go every day. No one feels like eating when they're sick," she explained. "Still, I can't understand why you would put all three of those poor ladies in jail. Why, I heard the sheriff dragged one of them out of her sickbed, and the other two had just sat down for their supper. I think you should have asked them your questions at the boardinghouse. That's what I think. Jail isn't a proper place for ladies. No sir, it doesn't seem right to me the way you're treating them as though they're common-trash criminals. Aren't you boys going to eat your supper? Where are you going?"

As soon as the word "jail" had been mentioned, Cole and Ryan had jumped to the same conclusion. Sloan was responsible for another fiasco.

Eleven

Their guess proved to be right. They ran back to the jail, cursing under their breath most of the way, and found that the sheriff had indeed locked all three women in one of his cells.

The idiot was actually proud of what he had done. His chest was puffed up like a rooster's as he strutted around the office giving his explanation.

"I had to do it," he began. "I asked all of them which one was in the bank during the holdup, and none of them would own up to it, so I put them in a cell to think it over. I'm predicting there's going to be a lynching mob out front in no time at all, because people have heard by now that we have a witness who won't step forward, and folks saw me bring them in."

Ryan was so furious with the sheriff his hand instinctively went to the butt of his gun. He forced himself to stop before he did anything he would regret. Cole's hand went to Sloan's throat. He didn't stop. He was trying to choke some sense into the lawman when he heard what sounded like a baby laughing.

Incredulous, he roared, "Are you out of your mind? You locked a baby in jail?"

Ryan was rigid with anger. He sat behind the desk glaring at the sheriff.

"Cole, quit choking him so he can explain. I want to hear what he has to say for himself. He's going to tell me why he would lock three women and a baby in jail."

The second Cole let go, the sheriff started stammering. "I didn't know what else to do with the little boy. He wanted to stay with his mama, and he wouldn't listen to reason. He threw himself down on the floor and had himself a real tantrum. He isn't a baby, Marshal. He's got to be a year and a half, maybe even two. He's still wearing nappies, but he can talk, so he can't be a baby. Babies don't talk," he added authoritatively.

The muscle in Ryan's jaw twitched from clenching his teeth together. "Where are the keys to the cells?" he demanded.

"You aren't going to let them out, are you?"

"Hell yes, I am," Ryan snapped. "Now, tell me where the keys are."

"They're hanging on the peg behind you," Sloan answered, his attitude insolent. "I did what had to be done."

Ryan ignored the comment. "Is there a back door in here?"

"Yes. It's at the end of the hallway. Why?"

Ryan tossed Cole the ring of keys. "Here's what you're going to do, Sheriff. Marshal Clayborne will let the ladies out of the cell. You're going to wait for them outside the back door, and when they come out, you will escort them home."

"You're also going to apologize to them," Cole

77

interjected. "And you damned well better sound like you mean it."

Sloan took another step back from Cole. "But I locked them up," he protested. "If I apologize, they'll think I don't know what I'm doing."

Cole let out a weary sigh. "No, they'll think you're just plain stupid. Now, get going."

Tight-lipped and red-faced, the sheriff stomped his way to the back exit. Cole opened the door that connected the cells to the main office, ducked under the overhead frame, and started down the long, narrow corridor. The walls were damp from rain that had seeped in through the roof, and the air smelled like wet leaves. He suddenly came to a quick stop. For a second he imagined he was looking at a priceless painting framed by cold gray stone walls inside an old museum. Three of the prettiest women he'd ever seen were sitting side by side on the narrow cot. Shoulders back, heads held high, they were perfectly still, as though an artist had ordered them to pose that way for their portrait.

Cole was completely unprepared for this vision. They were young . . . they were incredibly beautiful . . . and they were seething with anger.

The woman closest to him sat demurely with her hands folded in her lap. Her long black hair fell in soft ringlets to her shoulders, framing a porcelain complexion and clear green eyes that peered up at him through thick dark lashes. There was definitely a regal bearing about the woman, an aristocratic refinement that suggested a wealthy upbringing. She wore a pink walking dress with pearl buttons, but the lace collar adorning her delicate neck was frayed around the edges. On the seat next to her lay a wide-brimmed straw hat with pink ribbons, and resting on the brim was a pair of bright white gloves.

She had put on a hat to come to jail, Cole surmised

with an inward smile. Only a woman of gentle breeding would do such a thing. Her gaze was direct, curious, and not at all uppity, and he sensed a gentleness in her that could withstand any circumstance.

Seated next to her was the most exquisite beauty Cole had ever seen. She was a bold contrast in her richly textured sapphire blue dress. Her features were flawless—alabaster skin, full red lips, patrician nose, and blue eyes. Her chin tilted up in a haughty gesture of contempt. Her golden hair was pulled back in a severe bun, which would have detracted from any other woman's appearance, but only enhanced hers. Such perfection would take most men's breath away. She knew the effect she was having on him too. She gave him an impatient look that suggested he stop gaping at her and get on with it. Obviously used to turning heads, she had developed a bored, unapproachable demeanor.

The last of the three was seductive. Her cinnamon-colored hair was also pulled back, but several wayward tendrils had worked loose and fell gently to the sides of her oval face. Her frown blended the spray of freckles across her nose, and her piercing, dark almond-shaped eyes bored through him. She wore a faded lavender dress with the sleeves rolled to her elbows, indicating that she had been interrupted from a chore to be brought to jail. Her stare was unsettling, and he detected beneath the smoldering glare a burning passion that wouldn't be squelched . . . and that was even more unnerving.

On her lap sat a curly-headed cherub, curious but unaffected by the unexpected upheaval in his life. He seemed content to sit wrapped in his mother's arms and was oblivious to the animosity surrounding him.

They were fit to be tied all right. The hostility radiating from the three of them would have knocked a lesser man off his feet. If glares could kill, Cole thought the three beauties would have been throwing dirt on his grave now. Their pale complexions indicated they weren't feeling well, and he figured they were also scared. He felt bad about that. He pulled himself out of his thoughts and moved forward to unlock the door. As soon as he took a step, the baby turned and buried his face in his mother's bosom.

Swinging the door open, he said, "I'm real sorry about this inconvenience, ladies. I know you would rather be home."

The golden-haired woman stood up first. The other two promptly followed.

"Who are you?" she demanded.

"Cole Clayborne," he answered. "Marshal Clayborne."

"Are you the man in charge?"

Cole shook his head. "No, ma'am. Marshal Ryan's in charge."

"Is he aware that the sheriff in this town is a complete imbecile?"

The question made Cole smile. "He's beginning to get that idea, ma'am."

His honesty deflected some of their hostility. "Then neither you nor Marshal Ryan gave the order that we be locked up like common criminals?"

"No, neither one of us gave that order."

"Sheriff Sloan is power hungry and ignorant. It's a dangerous combination," she muttered. She glanced at the other two women, and then nodded. "Very well. We shall save our wrath for the sheriff. Allow me to introduce myself, Marshal Clayborne. My name's Rebecca James, and I was rudely ordered out of my sickbed by the sheriff. He made quite a scene in the lobby, and I was horribly embarrassed and feeling quite ill at the time. The dear lady on my left is Grace Winthrop. She came here all the way from England because she heard all about our wonderful country. And how does this town show their hospitality? They lock her in jail."

She was getting all worked up again. "Miss James, if you would calm—"

She cut him off with a wave of her hand. "And last but certainly not least, I would like to introduce you to Jessica Summers and her son, Caleb. She was just about to feed her baby supper when she was ripped out of her home and dragged here."

"I'm sure she was neither ripped nor dragged," he argued, though a part of him wouldn't have put it past Sloan to do such a stupid thing. "As I said before, I'm real sorry about the inconvenience."

"Inconvenience? It's an atrocity," Rebecca cried out.

Both Grace Winthrop and Jessica Summers nodded their agreement.

It was apparent to Cole that while they had been locked up together, Rebecca had taken on the role of speaker for all of them. Grace and Jessica both seemed content to let her do their talking. It was also evident that the three of them were united in their outrage.

"Are you certain Marshal Ryan didn't give the order to lock us up?" she asked once again.

"No, I didn't give that order."

Ryan answered the question from the doorway. Cole noticed he was staring at the three women with a look of surprise on his face. He was obviously reacting to the sight the very same way Cole had.

"Ladies, if you wouldn't mind, I'd appreciate it if you would stay inside the cell for a few more minutes."

Rebecca took a step forward and answered for all of them. "We most certainly do mind. Come along, ladies. We're leaving this vile place."

Cole had only just noticed the rifle in Ryan's hands when Rebecca tried to get past him. His arm shot out to block her.

"I think you'd better wait here a little longer," Cole said.

"I cannot believe such rudeness," she declared before she backed away. Jessica tried to get past him then. He shifted so that he blocked her with his body.

They stood toe-to-toe. She didn't back away, and so he gave her a look that suggested she shouldn't tangle with him.

She gave him the identical look. Hell, she was better at it than he was. She didn't even blink. She could stare a rattlesnake down, he thought to himself, and, Lord, she smelled good. Like fresh air and flowers. He quit scowling at her. It wasn't working anyway, and it was his own fault because he wasn't concentrating. He couldn't seem to get past the fact that she had such pretty eyes.

"Cole, we've got a little situation developing out front. I could use your help," Ryan said.

The baby was peeking up at him. Cole winked at him, then swung the door closed in his mother's face. He locked the door and went back to the front office, her outrage ringing in his ears.

Twelve

✦

*T*he little situation turned out to be a mob. Ryan had left the front door open and stood on the boardwalk with the rifle at his side. He was in the process of trying to convince forty to fifty angry men to go back home.

"I'm ordering you to disperse," Ryan shouted. "Go home and let us do our jobs."

A man near the middle of the group shouted, "Give us the women. We'll get them to talk."

Curious, Cole shouted, "How are you going to do that?"

"We'll hang them, that's how," he answered in a bellow.

"That makes a lot of sense," he muttered to Ryan.

Ryan glanced over at him. "You can't reason with angry people."

"They aren't angry. They're just a little riled up. That's all. You want angry, go back inside and let those women out. They're going to flay you alive."

83

Ryan hid his smile. "All right. You take care of this crowd, and I'll take care of the women."

"Deal," Cole agreed. He stepped forward to address the men. "No one's going to hang anyone. You've all been listening to idle gossip. We don't have a witness."

"We read it in the paper that you do," a man in front shouted.

"The paper's wrong."

"Then why did the sheriff lock those women up?" someone yelled.

"You'll have to ask him," Cole replied. "Now go back home."

"Why don't you and the other marshal go home and let our sheriff take care of the women? He'll get them to talk."

Before Cole could answer, a man in front stepped forward and turned around to face his friends and neighbors. He put his hands in the air to hush them. "I know for a fact that the lady with the funny accent was in the bank before it got robbed. I stood in line with her, and I heard her talking to the teller."

"Then it's got to be one of them other two," yet another man called out. "Did anyone see either one of them in the bank?"

"I did," a man in the back shouted. "I seen the yellow-haired woman when I was getting change for my bills from Malcolm. I remember her real good 'cause she was about the prettiest thing I ever laid my eyes on."

A snicker rolled through the crowd. "What about the woman with the baby?"

"I seen her," a man called out. "The boy made MacCorkle angry because he was swinging on his gate, and his mama had to get out of line to fetch him. She blistered old man MacCorkle good for raising his voice to her young'n."

"If all of them women were seen in the bank, then it

don't appear we got a witness after all," the placater, waving his hands in front of the crowd, concluded.

"Maybe one of them sneaked back inside to hide under the desk," someone else suggested.

"These people aren't real bright, are they?" Cole whispered to Ryan.

"Sloan has gotten them all worked up," Ryan said.

"All right," Cole shouted to the group. "Here's what's gonna happen. All of you are going to go home. I want you to think about what you were doing on the day of the robbery. If any of you saw or heard anything unusual, then come back to the jail tomorrow morning and tell us about it."

"You don't have the right to tell us what to do," a man near the edge of the crowd shouted. Cole recognized him. He was the reporter from the *Rockford Falls Gazette* who didn't want the bodies covered with sheets. Cole had taken an instant dislike to the man.

The reporter took a step forward. His eyes darted back and forth from the crowd to the marshals. "This is a local matter, Marshal. Sheriff Sloan ought to handle it."

"Federal money was stolen," Ryan shouted. "And that makes it our business. Do as Marshal Clayborne ordered. Go home and let us do our job."

"I'm not going anywhere until I talk to those women," the reporter shouted.

Cole wasn't in the mood to argue any longer. Quicker than the man could blink, he drew his gun and shot the hat off the reporter's head.

"You had no right to do that," the reporter screamed.

"Sure I did," he answered. "Marshal Ryan explained I can't be tried for murder now that I'm a U.S. marshal, so the way I figure it, I can shoot every one of you and get away with it. This is the last time I'm going to tell you. Go home."

"Cole?" Ryan whispered his name.

He kept his attention centered on the crowd as he answered. "Yeah?"

"I made that up."

Cole smiled. "They don't know that."

The marshals continued to stand their ground until the crowd ran out of steam. Grumbling to themselves, the mob dispersed. Then Ryan let the ladies out.

Ten minutes later Sloan came slinking around the corner. He had escorted the ladies home and was returning with a proclamation from them—if they were to suffer an inquisition, it was best to get it over with tonight so that they wouldn't have to worry about it any longer.

Ryan and Cole decided to accommodate the women. They started with Rebecca James.

She was staying at the Rockford Falls Hotel, where Cole and Ryan had also taken rooms. The old, four-story building was located one block north of the jail on Elm Street. A veranda circled the hotel on three sides. One of the housemaids was sent up to tell Rebecca the marshals were waiting for her on the porch.

The sunlight was fading, and a cool breeze was a welcome respite after the blistering heat of the day.

"We won't learn anything important," Cole predicted. "We already know all three of the women were spotted in the bank earlier in the afternoon. Talking to them is a wasted effort. What could they have seen?"

"We won't know the answer to that question until we talk to them. It shouldn't take long."

Thirty minutes later, he had to revise his estimate. Rebecca kept them waiting until well after eight o'clock. Cole paced around the veranda. Ryan was sprawled out in one of the wicker chairs when Rebecca finally arrived. She didn't apologize for being late, and from the expression on her face as she walked across the porch to join them, they could tell she was still fuming.

Ryan stood up as soon as he spotted her coming toward him. He waited for her to take her seat, then pulled up another chair to face her. Cole leaned back against the railing and folded his arms across his chest.

She sat on the edge of the chair, her back straight and her hands in her lap. She was furious all right, and if she became any more upset, Cole thought smoke would start pouring out of her ears.

He leaned back, content to let Ryan question the woman while he watched her. He knew he was being rude; he didn't care. The woman was magnificent. He searched for a flaw, hoping that if he found one, he would be able to get past his fascination with her.

Ryan was also staring intently, and Cole wondered if he was playing the same game.

"We appreciate your cooperation," Ryan began. "And we're both sorry about the trouble earlier."

"I don't believe I'll be much help with your investigation," she said. "But I'll be happy to answer your questions. Then I'm going to leave this horrible town and never look back. The town is charming, I'll admit, and the waterfalls are spectacular, but the people are a bit . . . backward, and since the rumor was put in the paper, it's been very difficult. I'm happy I'll be getting back home."

"Where is home?" Ryan asked.

"St. Louis. I had planned to leave a couple of days ago to meet some friends in Salt Lake City, but then I became ill and had to delay my trip."

"Are you feeling better now?"

"A little, thank you. The doctor told me I was fortunate because I have only a mild case."

"Are you originally from St. Louis?" Cole asked.

"I grew up in the east," she explained. "I moved to St. Louis to be near close friends."

She turned back to Ryan. "I thought you wanted to talk about the robbery."

"We do," Ryan answered. "Do you remember what time you were in the bank?"

She took several seconds to answer. "As a matter of fact, I do remember. I was inside the bank at two o'clock, give or take ten minutes. I stood in line, but I don't remember any of the other people who were there. I wasn't paying any attention to them. I'm sure someone will remember seeing me there. Are you writing down every word I say on paper?"

Ryan glanced up and smiled. "I'm trying to," he said.

"Why?"

He leaned back in the chair, finished jotting down his notes, and then said, "There have been so many robberies, it's the only way I can keep the information straight. Does it bother you?"

She shook her head. "No, I simply found it curious, that's all."

Sheriff Sloan interrupted the questioning when he came lumbering up the steps. He looked sheepish, and as soon as he saw the marshals' hostile expressions, he turned around and tried to leave.

Ryan's voice lashed out at him. "Sit."

As quick as a trained dog, Sloan obeyed the command. He grabbed the nearest chair and fell into it.

"You have caused considerable trouble, Sheriff," Rebecca said. "Because of you, people in this town believe there was a witness to the robbery and murders at the bank. I read the article in the paper. So did everyone else. You were quoted numerous times. Do you have any idea what you've done? If the men who murdered all those people read the *Rockford Falls Gazette* or hear the rumors *you* started, they'll come back here and kill Jessica and Grace and me. My God, don't you realize what those fiends are capable of? They've already killed other women. They certainly wouldn't think twice about killing three more."

"Ma'am, I wouldn't fret about the Blackwater gang coming back here. They've probably left the territory by now."

His cavalier attitude infuriated her. "Witnesses don't last long," she cried out. "Everyone knows what happened to that poor man in Middleton. I believe those murderers killed his wife too, didn't they? If either Grace or Jessica had been in the bank during the holdup, do you honestly think she'd admit it? She'd be signing her death warrant."

"I'm real sorry about your situation," Sloan said. He blushed with embarrassment. "I wouldn't worry about the gang reading our little paper, though. No one outside Rockford reads the *Gazette*," he added in a halfhearted attempt to placate her. "And I didn't have a choice about the interview. That reporter was hounding me for details, and I am the authority in this town. I had a duty to tell him what I knew, but all I remember saying was that the marshals happened to find a purse under one of the desks. He jumped to his own conclusions."

After giving his explanation, Sloan stood up and excused himself. "I promised a lady friend that we'd go out walking, and she's waiting for me inside. Did you need me to hang around, Marshal Ryan?"

"No," Ryan answered.

Rebecca waited until Sloan left the porch with the silly little woman giggling on his arm before continuing. "The sheriff showed all of us the purse. It doesn't belong to me. I never carry one," she added. "May I leave now? I really would like to go to bed. It's been an exhausting day."

"I don't have any other questions at the moment," Ryan said. He closed his notepad and looked at Cole. "Do you?"

"Just one," Cole answered. "How long will you be staying in town?"

"Until the day after tomorrow when the coach comes through again."

Ryan offered Rebecca his hand to help her stand. She looked startled by the gentlemanly gesture and hesitantly took hold of him.

"You aren't going to bother Jessica and Grace tonight, are you? It's already well after eight," she said. "They were both so weary this afternoon. Neither one of them is feeling well," she added. "You should let them get a good night's sleep before you hound them with questions. Good night, gentlemen."

They watched her walk away. Each was lost in his own thoughts until she paused in the doorway and looked at them again. Tears streamed down her cheeks. Because she had been as cool as ice during the questioning, the emotional display surprised them.

"Are you ever going to catch those horrible men? Do you have any leads at all? The sheriff told me you didn't, but I was hoping he was wrong."

Ryan's shoulders slumped. "No, we don't have any leads now, but that could change."

"One thing's certain," Cole interjected. "We will catch them. It's only a matter of time. You can count on it."

"Yes, of course you'll catch them," she said. "If you think of any other questions, I'll be here."

Once she was inside, Cole muttered an imprecation. "I don't like being a marshal. It's depressing."

"You know what's really bothering you? You feel sorry for all three of the women, don't you?"

"Yeah, I do. Thanks to Sloan's incompetence, those ladies have been thrown into the middle of a boiling pot. They shouldn't have to be afraid. Besides, it's pretty certain none of them was in the bank during the robbery, but now everyone in town thinks one of them was. Folks around here don't think things through, do they? I guess I hated seeing Rebecca so scared."

"I can't blame her for being afraid," Ryan said. "She knows what the Blackwater gang can do."

"Do you think any of them will come back to Rockford Falls? Would they go to such an extreme because of a rumor?"

"People believe what they read in the paper. It would be a lucky break for us if they did come back. Stop glaring at me, Cole. I'm only being honest. It *would* be a break, and God knows we're due for one. We can protect the women. Come on, let's go talk to Jessica Summers and Grace Winthrop."

"It seems kind of pointless," Cole said. "They didn't see anything."

"We have to go through the motions," Ryan stubbornly insisted. "And by the way, you're supposed to take notes during the interviews."

"You take them. I hate paperwork. Besides, I can remember what everyone said."

"Maybe now you can, but later, after one or two more robberies, all the names and dates start blending together."

"Then I guess we better catch the bastards before they rob again." Hungry and weary, he grudgingly followed Ryan down the steps. "Rebecca told us that Jessica and Grace were exhausted. Remember? Maybe we ought to wait until tomorrow to talk to them."

"No, I want to talk to them now."

Cole gave up trying to argue with him. He found the job of marshal incredibly frustrating thus far. He wanted to act. Sorting through the mire of paperwork and talking to potential witnesses was like putting an intricate puzzle together. One had to be patient, and Cole hadn't quite learned how to accomplish that feat.

Part Two

The days dividing lover and lover,
The light that loses, the night that wins;

Thirteen

Tilly MacGuire's boardinghouse was at the end of Elm Street, a winding road lined with hundred-year-old trees. The front door of the hotel where Rebecca was staying actually faced the front door of the house, but because of the meandering road and the trees, it wasn't possible to see one building from the other.

The old homestead had just been treated to a fresh coat of white paint. The trim of the window shutters and the doors was a dark burgundy red. The color matched the lounging chairs scattered about the porch. The pristine house sat back from the white picket fence that surrounded the property, and while that too had recently been painted, tenacious spurs of ivy were already working their way back up the slats.

Both the house and the rambling lawn in front were shaded by a cluster of ancient walnut trees on either side of the porch. The leafy giant sentinels stood guard over the occupants inside. A faint breeze moved unnoticed through the massive limbs that arched out to one another over the gabled roof.

Tilly MacGuire's home was a charming, idyllic place to raise a brood of children, and she had done just that. The spry sixty-five-year-old woman had married at age fourteen, produced eight offspring— all girls—but after her youngest had married and moved away and her third husband had passed on, she converted her six-bedroom home to a boarding facility.

She didn't need the money; she needed the companionship. She was a discriminating landlord and chose as boarders only those ladies for whom she felt a kinship. She boasted of being a stickler for rules. Men weren't allowed above the first floor, no matter what the reason; her ladies had to be home by ten o'clock every night, including Saturday; they must attend church with her on Sunday morning, and none of them could miss supper. Her houseguests put up with the regulations for the simple reason that as long as they followed the rules, they were gloriously pampered. The food was always delicious and plentiful; the bedrooms were spacious and beautifully adorned, and the linens were changed every other day. More important than the luxuries, though, was Tilly herself. She was a sweet-hearted woman who treated her selected guests like long-lost family members.

If the truth were known, Tilly was also a real softy under her tough, no-nonsense exterior. She had already broken one of her ironclad rules by allowing Jessica and her son to stay with her. Since her own children were grown, Tilly didn't allow babies or children because of the mess they made, but little Caleb turned out to be her one exception. The toddler, a pistol if ever there was one, stole her heart when he batted his big brown eyes and stuck his tongue out at her.

She was laughing at the baby's antics when the marshals knocked on her screen door. Tilly was a little acorn of a woman with sparkling eyes and deep-set wrinkles. She was smiling until she spotted their badges. Latching on to Caleb's hand, she slowly walked to the door.

"You're here to question my girls, aren't you?"

"Yes, ma'am, we are," Ryan answered.

Her frown intensified. "They're both worried and scared, and only just getting over a hard bout of influenza. Poor Jessica was almost well and then suffered a setback. She was throwing up most of Wednesday evening. It's a shame those girls have got to be scared too. You might as well come on inside. They're both in the kitchen doing my dishes. I don't regularly allow houseguests to set foot in the back of my house, but my hired girls are both home sick, and I'm feeling a little puny myself tonight, so I'm breaking my own rule. I can do that," she hastily added, "because this is my home. Do you want to talk to both of them together? I'll let you sit at my kitchen table if you do."

The freshly scrubbed baby was clutching a rag doll by its hair and looking up at Cole. He pulled his hand free from Tilly's grasp and put his thumb in his mouth.

"We'd prefer to talk to each one separately," Ryan said. "If you wouldn't mind asking Jessica Summers to come out on the porch, we'll wait here."

"Go find your mama, boy," she ordered the child.

The baby pulled his thumb out of his mouth long enough to shout, "No," then turned around and went running toward the back of the house.

Tilly grinned. " 'No' is that baby's favorite word. He must say it a good hundred times a day. He isn't sassy or slow-witted, though, just stubborn."

She glanced behind her to make certain the baby was out of earshot before she spoke again. "Like I was saying, Jessica and Grace are scared as rabbits, and it's all because of that rumor someone started, saying one of them was a witness to the murders. It was even written down in the paper. Now, my girls didn't see anything because they would have told me if they had. I don't want to be hearing you marshals browbeat them with your questions either. You hear me?"

"Yes, ma'am, we hear you," Cole replied.

"I'll go get Jessica," she said. "Then I'm going upstairs with a pot of tea Grace is kindly brewing for me, but I'll be back down to lock my doors at ten o'clock on the dot. You expect to be finished by then, don't you?"

"Yes, ma'am, we do," Ryan answered.

Tilly wasn't quite ready to leave. She had something more to say to the marshals, and whenever she wanted to speak her mind, she did exactly that, believing that time was too precious to waste dancing around a sensitive topic.

"It's a crying shame the way this town is acting. Just because my girls haven't been here long, they're fair targets for every rumor. I feel sorry for poor Rebecca James too. She was feeling just as poorly as my girls. Have you hounded her with questions yet?"

Ryan didn't answer. "When did you happen to meet Rebecca?"

"At church Sunday last," she answered. "We had us a nice talk after services, and she told me she was considering moving into my house because her hotel room was so cramped. She would have been welcome," she added. "And I'm persnickety in my old age, but I took to her right away. She's got a good heart. Why, she was even nice to nasty old Lemont Morganstaff. She made him blush with her compliments about his garden."

"How many boarders do you take in?" Cole asked.

"There's room for five, but I only have two now. Just Grace and Jessica, and the baby of course."

Caleb came running past Tilly, pushed the door open, and scurried outside before she could grab hold of him. The little boy was dressed in a white cotton gown that came down to his ankles. He was barefoot and full of mischief.

"I'll let you boys keep an eye on that critter while I hunt Jessica down. Then I'll take Caleb upstairs because I promised him a story."

She was turning away when Cole stopped her with a question. "Ma'am? Where's the boy's father?"

"That's a good question, and if I were at liberty to talk about it, I'd tell you where I think he is, but I gave my word to Jessica to keep my mouth shut. I can tell you that sweet boy's mama died giving birth," she added. "Her husband wasn't at her side, though. No, sir, he wasn't."

"Jessica isn't the boy's mother?" Daniel asked.

"Caleb thinks she's his mama because she's been taking care of him for so long, but she isn't his blood mother."

"Is Caleb's father dead or alive?" Cole asked.

"I don't honestly know," she answered with a scowl. "But I'm hoping he's drunk himself to death by now. I'm not going to say another word about him," she vowed. "You'll have to ask Jessica for the details."

She disappeared into the dining room. Cole and Ryan both turned to look down at the baby. Caleb was standing near the front steps, grinning up at them. All of a sudden he dropped to his knees and crawled backward. He wasn't housebroken yet, and when he tried to shimmy down the front steps on his belly, the ties on his diaper came loose.

"Where do you think you're going?" Cole asked as he bent down and picked the baby up in his arms. Ryan grabbed hold of the diaper before it slipped past Caleb's thighs and quickly retied the straps. Caleb dropped the rag doll and reached for Ryan's badge.

"You act like you know what you're doing," Cole remarked, ignoring the baby's squirming and grunting to get down.

"I've had a little experience."

"Nieces and nephews?"

"No. A daughter." He patted the baby before walking away. "He smells like apples and soap. It brings back memories."

He crossed the porch and leaned against a post, staring out into the darkness. "I'm tired tonight," he remarked.

"I didn't know you were married."

"You never asked."

His voice had taken on a hard edge, an unspoken suggestion to let the topic go. Cole was too curious to take the hint. "How long have you been married?"

"It would have been seven years last month."

"Would have been?"

Ryan nodded. "They're both dead."

Cole's mind began to race with questions.

"When did you say you started working on this investigation?"

"I didn't say."

"Okay, you didn't tell me. So when did you?"

"I was appointed to head the special force after one of the robberies."

"Quit being so evasive. Tell me which one of the robberies it was."

"Dillon," Ryan answered. "After the robbery at Dillon."

"Your hometown."

"Yes, my hometown."

Silence settled between them as Cole recalled the accounts he had heard of Dillon.

"Did your wife and daughter get sick?" he finally asked.

"Stop asking so many questions, Cole."

"Did they?" he persisted.

Ryan shook his head. "No, they didn't get sick. They were simply in the wrong place at the wrong time."

Cole let out a long breath. "Ah . . . hell, Daniel. They're the ones, aren't they?"

Fourteen

✤

 $\mathcal{J}$ essica Summers stood at the kitchen counter and stared out the window, daydreaming. She was trying to recall what it had felt like to be carefree.

She couldn't remember.

She was tired tonight, and surely that was why her burdens and worries seemed so overwhelming to her now. There had been so many changes in her life over the past two years, and lately there were moments when she felt like an old woman.

This was one of those moments. She wasn't feeling sorry for herself—there simply wasn't time in her busy day for such a silly self-indulgence—and as weary as she was, she was still able to thank God for the blessing he had bestowed on her by giving her little Caleb. She couldn't imagine life without him, as chaotic as it sometimes seemed.

Forcing herself to get back to the task at hand, she picked up a wet cloth and began to wash one of Tilly's prize Redbird china plates. Water splashed her skirt. She looked down and noticed for the first time how old and faded the dress was. It didn't quite fit anymore; the bodice was uncomfortably tight across her chest, but all she had to do was move the buttons, if and when she found the time, and then the dress would be almost as good as new. She certainly wasn't about to throw it away as Tilly had suggested, because that would be a waste, and she couldn't afford to waste anything these days. Besides, the dress was serviceable and she was quite fond of the color. Age, wear, and countless washings had turned the bright lavender material a much paler shade. Tilly had told her it looked like an old, used hand-me-down, and Jessica had shrugged indifference. The dress was decent, and that was all that mattered.

Lord, how her priorities had changed. She remembered another dress she had coveted a lifetime ago when such frivolous things actually mattered to her. She had noticed the dress in a shop window and thought it was the most glorious creation she had ever seen. The gown was white brocade with a wide red velvet sash. Jessica smiled as she recalled how she had vowed to save enough money to one day buy the impractical dress.

Her dreams were different now, of course. She never thought about suitors or dances or parties any longer. She had been a foolish, empty-headed young girl back then. Now she was an adult with responsibilities. Her only dream was to be the best mother Caleb could ever have.

Tilly pulled her back to the present with the announcement that the marshals would like to talk to her.

"They're waiting on the porch for you," she said.

"I'll go right out," Jessica promised.

Five minutes later, she was still standing at the kitchen counter. She knew she was being rude by keeping the marshals waiting, but she was so nervous and frightened, she couldn't seem to make herself go outside. She delayed the inevitable for as long as possible by insisting on helping her new friend, Grace Winthrop, finish the dishes and put the food away.

Grace was completely out of place in a kitchen. Jessica didn't think she had ever been inside one until she moved into Tilly's boardinghouse, but what she lacked in experience she made up for with her enthusiasm. She was determined to learn how to cook a decent meal, and there wasn't any chore beneath her. Yesterday she had taken off her gloves and hat, put on one of Tilly's old aprons, and got down on her hands and knees to scrub the floor. It had taken her twice as long as it would have taken Jessica, but when she was finished, the wood had a nice shine.

The two women had become good friends. Each was lost in her own thoughts as they worked side by side.

"I'm scared," Jessica whispered. "I don't want to talk to them."

"I'm scared too," Grace admitted. "After they finish questioning you, they'll probably want to talk to me. Maybe Tilly could convince them to come back tomorrow."

Jessica shook her head. "Then I'd worry all night. I want to get it over and done with now. Otherwise I won't sleep."

"Have you thought about my proposition? Mr. Nelson needs to know if I'm going to purchase his wagon or not. I promised to let him know in the morning. He let me drive it over here," she added.

"I know," Jessica whispered back. "I can see it in the field behind the yard from my window. Yes, I have made up my mind. If you're sure we won't be a burden, Caleb and I would love to go with you."

Grace let out a sigh. "I'm so thankful," she said. "Of course you won't be a burden. I'll admit now I don't think I could manage the horses without help."

"We'll manage together," Jessica promised.

Tilly came back to the kitchen to find out why Jessica was taking so long and decided it was up to her to give her a little nudge.

"They aren't going to go away, girl," she began. "You might as well get on out there and talk to them, and while you're answering their questions, you might want to take the time to notice what fine-looking men the marshals are. It's been a long while since I've seen such big, masculine men. They might give you a scare at first sight, seeing as how they're both so rugged looking, but if you'll look in their eyes, you'll see the kindness there and you'll get over your shivers then. Both of those boys have real pretty blue eyes."

Jessica forced a smile in an attempt to hide her nervousness. "Why would I want to notice how fine looking they are?"

Exasperated, Tilly put her hands on her hips and made a *tisk*ing sound. "Because now you have that little bit of a boy to see raised and it wouldn't hurt you to have a strong man helping."

Jessica folded the damp cloth and put it down on the countertop. "I know you mean well, but I don't need a man to help me raise Caleb. We're doing just fine the way we are."

"Hogwash," Tilly said. "I know you've got the spirit and the heart to do right by that baby, but a man could ease the burden. That's all I'm saying. If I were forty years younger, I'd go after one of them myself. I'd have a devil of a time deciding which one I wanted to put his shoes under my bed, though. All I'm suggesting is that you notice, Jessica, and I want you to notice too, Grace, because a good man would be the answer to your family's prayers. Jessica, take that ribbon out of your hair. It's lopsided."

"Yes, ma'am," Jessica replied. She pulled the ribbon out and quickly threaded her fingers through her curly brown tresses. She wasn't trying to make herself attractive. She was simply placating Tilly.

"You've got such pretty hair, Jessica. You should show it off, and it wouldn't kill you to do a little flirting while you're talking to them. I bet you don't even know how. You ought to try, though. Oh, I know it's a serious matter they're here to discuss, but they're men first and always, and they'll notice both of you. Grace, while you're waiting your turn, you can take all those pins out of your hair and give it a good brushing. Men like women to wear their hair down, not pinned up like an old schoolmarm."

Jessica and Grace had learned that it was pointless to argue. Tilly was in one of her stubborn, I-know-what's-best moods. Grace was smiling at Tilly, but Jessica noticed her cheeks were flushed with embarrassment.

"I guess I should go on out," Jessica said.

"I guess you'd better," Tilly agreed. "I'll take the baby upstairs as soon as I find him."

"You don't feel well tonight, Tilly. Go on up and get in bed. I'll take care of Caleb."

"I'll brew your tea for you and bring it right up," Grace added. "Jessica, Caleb can stay in the kitchen with me. I'll keep an eye on him."

Jessica took a deep breath and slowly let it out. "Lord, I wish I weren't so nervous."

Grace nodded. "I feel like I've done something wrong, but I haven't. Oh, I wish I'd never come to this town. I had such grand hopes . . ."

"I know you did," Jessica said. "But it was wrong of Mr. Wells's son not to honor his father's promise. He should have sold you the grazing land as his father had agreed. A man's word is supposed to be sacred."

"The younger Mr. Wells doesn't know that," Grace said.

"You're going to find your ranch," Jessica promised. "We'll look at the property near Denver first, and if it isn't exactly what you want, I've heard there's lush grazing land to be found in California."

"There's so much to be done, and time's running out. I only have seven months left to purchase the land and buy the cattle, or I must admit defeat and go back home. If I hadn't wasted so much time here, I could be in Denver by now."

"I'm glad you came to Rockford Falls. If you hadn't, I wouldn't have met you, and I believe we've become good friends."

Grace grabbed hold of Jessica's hand. "Oh, we have become good friends."

"And now Caleb and I will be going with you to Colorado. Some good did come out of this, didn't it?"

"Will you two girls stop acting like ninnies. Jessica, get on out to the porch."

Tilly's impatience discouraged further dallying. Straightening her shoulders, Jessica hurried to the front door. She felt as though she were going to her own trial, which was ridiculous, of course. She only had to convince the marshals she hadn't witnessed anything.

Her hand shook when she reached for the doorknob.

"Good evening, Marshals. I'm sorry I've kept you waiting."

She stood poised just inside the door and looked serene, yet her hand gripped the handle tightly, and she appeared ready to bolt. Experience had taught Daniel Ryan that lawmen made people jittery. He quickly stepped forward and tried to put her at ease.

"This should only take a couple of minutes," he explained.

She glanced from one marshal to the other. Neither one of them was smiling. Marshal Ryan looked earnest, but Marshal Clayborne looked bored leaning against the railing. Lord, Tilly had been right. Both men oozed masculinity.

"It's routine," Cole remarked.

She nodded. "Yes, I understand."

He smiled. "It would probably be easier if you came out on the porch."

She took a quick breath and told herself to stop trembling as she walked over to one of the wicker chairs and sat down. She folded her hands in her lap and pressed her knees and ankles together so they wouldn't shake. Then she waited for one or both of the marshals to begin.

"I guess we should introduce ourselves," Ryan began. He dragged a chair across the porch to face her.

"That isn't necessary. I know who you are. You're Marshal Daniel Ryan, and he's Marshal Cole Clayborne. We met at the jail, remember?"

Ryan straddled his chair, and Cole stood a few feet behind.

She stared up at him. "You don't look like a lawman," she blurted out. Her eyes turned back to Ryan. "And neither do you."

"What do we look like?" Cole asked.

"Outlaws."

"We look like outlaws?" Cole asked, laughing.

Their smiles helped, and she began to relax. She wanted Cole to sit down. The man towered over her, and a day's growth of whiskers made him seem menacing. Daniel looked just as ragged. She had to remind herself that both of them were marshals and it was, therefore, their duty to protect innocent citizens. She just needed to let them know she belonged in that group.

"I haven't done anything wrong."

Daniel nodded. "We know you haven't. Lawmen make people jumpy. I'm not sure why."

"I know why," she replied. "You have the power to lock me in jail," she explained.

"Not without a good legal reason," he countered.

She raised an eyebrow. "Is that so? I was locked in jail this afternoon, and there certainly wasn't a good legal reason then."

"We didn't know Sheriff Sloan would go to such lengths," Cole interjected.

"He was convinced one of us was lying, but that still isn't a good reason to lock someone in jail, is it?" She noticed Daniel remove a notepad and pencil from his pocket and gave him her full attention.

"We know you were in the bank the day it was robbed," he began.

"Yes, I was. Caleb was with me."

"Do you happen to remember what time it was?"

She smoothed the wrinkles out of her skirt as she answered, her gaze directed on her lap. "As a matter of fact, I do remember. I was there at two o'clock, give or take ten minutes. I went inside and got into line, but I didn't happen to notice any of the other people there. I wasn't . . ."

"Paying attention?" Cole asked.

"Yes, that's it," she said. "I wasn't paying attention to anyone else."

"You didn't notice anyone in line with you?" Ryan asked with a hint of skepticism.

"I was very busy looking after Caleb. He can be quite mischievous. The gate fascinated him, and he kept trying to swing on it. Mr. MacCorkle became very upset and yelled at the baby. He made quite a scene. I had my hands full, Marshal, and I simply didn't have time to notice anyone else."

While she'd been explaining, she kept glancing up at Cole to get his reaction. He had to know she was nervous because of the way she had rushed through her answer. *Slow down,* she told herself, as she gripped her hands together. *Slow down and calm down, or they'll both think I'm hiding something.*

Cole didn't look as if he thought she was guilty of anything. If she had had to venture a guess, she would have said that the routine questions were putting him to sleep.

She turned back to her inquisitor. "I'm sorry I can't be more helpful."

"Don't babies take naps in the afternoon?" Cole asked. "My little sister always did."

"Yes, Caleb usually takes his nap right after his noon meal, but his schedule has gotten all turned around lately. I was sick with influenza, and because he sleeps in my bedroom, I kept waking him up all night. He slept late today and then had a late nap. That's why he's still running around now." She was rambling like an idiot, she realized, and giving them far too much useless and boring information.

"Did Sheriff Sloan show you the bag we found?"

"Yes, he did," she answered. "He told us he found it under one of the desks. It doesn't belong to me," she added emphatically. "I never carry a bag."

Ryan flipped his notepad shut and put it back in his pocket with his pencil. She noticed he hadn't written a single word.

"Are you positive about the time?" Cole asked.

"You're sure you were in the bank at two?" Ryan asked.

"Give or take ten minutes," she answered.

The marshals exchanged a look. Ryan rubbed the back of his neck.

"Do you have any plans to leave Rockford Falls?" he asked.

"Yes, I'm planning to leave as soon as possible. Caleb and I leave tomorrow as a matter of fact. I'll miss Tilly, but I'll be glad to get away from this town. Ever since the rumors started, I've been very concerned that the men who killed those poor innocent people will come back here. They might believe that one of us saw them, and I'm sure you know what has happened to the witnesses of the other robberies."

"Yeah, we know," Cole said.

"Where are you headed?" Cole asked.

"Colorado," she answered.

Any further information she might have wanted to add was forgotten when Caleb came running out on the porch. The baby spotted his rag doll by the steps and snatched it up by one of its feet. Strutting over to Cole, he leaned against his leg and grinned up at him.

Jessica wasn't surprised. Caleb was always initially shy around strangers, but it never took him long to get over it. He liked men. She thought their size and voices fascinated him.

"It's time for you to go to bed, Caleb," she said, her voice a soothing whisper.

Shaking his head, Caleb pulled his thumb from his mouth long enough to put his arms up to Cole and let out a loud grunt to be picked up. When he spied his mother advancing, he dropped his doll to the floor, threw his arms around Cole's neck, and held on for dear life.

"I don't think this boy wants to go to bed just yet," Cole remarked.

She stood close to Cole and tried to peel her son's hands away from his neck, but she wasn't paying much attention to what she was doing. Tilly was right. The marshal did have beautiful eyes. She wished the dear woman hadn't made such a fuss over the lawmen's appearance because now all Jessica could think about was how fit the two of them were. If Tilly hadn't pointed it out, she surely wouldn't have noticed.

She wasn't in the market for a husband. The reminder helped her concentrate on the task at hand.

"Caleb always goes right to sleep as soon as I tuck him in with his baby doll," she explained. "He's going through a difficult phase and seems to think he has to throw a tantrum at bedtime. He's a very good boy, though. Aren't you, Caleb?"

The baby nodded against Cole's neck. Cole stared at Jessica with a look of amusement in his eyes. She wondered if he knew he was making her uncomfortable. She thought that maybe he did, and, oh, how could she have ever thought him menacing? His hands were big, yet so very gentle as he patted Caleb's back in a circular, rhythmic motion. Caleb rubbed his tiny fist against his nose as he nestled his head under Cole's chin. The child looked blissful.

"You're very good with babies," she remarked.

"Mrs. Summers? Would you mind asking Grace Winthrop to come out on the porch?"

The intrusion of Marshal Ryan's voice startled her. "Yes, of course," she stammered.

"Is it Mrs. Summers?" Cole asked her. "Or Miss?"

"It's Jessica," she answered as she turned away. "Grace is in the kitchen. If you like, you could go on in and sit at the table while you question her."

"That would be fine," Daniel answered. He moved ahead to open the door for her, and Cole followed behind with Caleb. He transferred the sleepy baby to Jessica's arms when they reached the stairs.

"The kitchen's at the end of the hallway," she said.

While Daniel went on ahead, Cole stood in the entry and watched Jessica go up the steps. He liked the way she moved. It was sexy and feminine, and very alluring. He liked her voice too. It was a rich, husky bedroom voice.

He told himself it was all right to notice how good she looked and sounded. There wasn't any harm in appreciating such an attractive woman. It certainly didn't mean he was going to get involved with her. He was a lawman now, and that probably meant that he couldn't and shouldn't dally with a potential witness. It just wouldn't be right. Besides, Jessica Summers came with strings attached. She was carrying one of them up to bed. Any man who became involved with her would have to make a lifetime commitment. Forever. The notion didn't sit well with him. He liked to move around, and no one was going to tie him down. She was also innocent, and he had adopted a hands-off policy with inexperienced women. Their expectations were different. Jessica was definitely the marrying kind. He wasn't.

It was as simple as that.

"Cole, you coming?"

With a nod, he caught up with Daniel at the end of the hallway. "What was that all about?" Daniel whispered with a nod toward the entry.

Cole knew what he was asking. He shrugged in response. "Just noticing. That's all."

Fifteen

❧

Grace Winthrop was standing at the stove. She turned when they entered the kitchen. Daniel stopped cold, then took an involuntary step back, bumping Cole.

He quickly recovered. "Jessica didn't think you would mind if we . . ."

"Oh, please come in," she said. "I'm brewing tea. Would you and Marshal Clayborne like a cup?"

"That sounds fine," Daniel said, pulling out a chair at the table. Cole took the seat across from him, facing the door.

"Have you gentlemen had your supper yet?" she asked.

"No, ma'am, we haven't," Cole answered.

"We aren't hungry," Daniel said at the same time.

"Yes, we are," Cole argued.

Grace went to the counter and returned with a plate of leftover ham. She placed it on the table next to a basket of freshly baked bread and a crock of butter. A minute later she'd added plates and utensils.

114

Cole helped himself. Daniel didn't touch the food. He kept his attention focused on Grace, who was nervously brushing her hands down her apron. She wouldn't, or couldn't, look him in the eyes. The teacups rattled in the saucers as she placed them on the table. She poured a thick, black liquid into each cup that looked more like shoe polish than tea.

"Would you like sugar and cream?" she asked.

Cole was looking suspiciously at his cup, but Daniel was still looking at Grace.

"Is this tea?" Cole asked.

"Yes," she rushed out. "Is something wrong with it?"

"No, no, I'm sure it's fine."

He took a drink and couldn't hide his reaction. It tasted like bitter hair tonic.

"It just needs a little sugar," he lied.

"I boiled it too long, didn't I?" she asked. "That's what I did. I should have timed it. I'll make another pot right away."

"I'd rather have water," Cole said.

Daniel was trying not to smile. He didn't want to embarrass her any more than she already was, for she had seen the grimace Cole made when he tasted her tea, and if Daniel laughed, her discomfort would only intensify.

"I don't think you're supposed to boil the tea leaves," he told her.

With a gesture he found utterly feminine, she brushed her dark curls back over her shoulder. "Cooking is far more difficult than one would ever imagine," she remarked.

"Who did all the cooking in your home?" Cole asked.

She seemed surprised by the question. "The cook did the cooking," she answered. "And her assistants, of course. Sometimes the downstairs maids helped. At least I believe they did. Would you like some sliced pickles, Marshal Clayborne? They're quite good."

"That would be nice," he answered. "Please call me Cole and call him Daniel," he added with a nod toward Ryan.

"Then you must call me Grace. I insist."

She proceeded to slice the pickle with a sharp butcher knife, pulling the sharp blade toward her wrist. The action drove Daniel crazy. He reached out and grabbed hold of both of her hands.

"Always cut with the blade angled away from you," he instructed. "Like this." He slowly glided the knife through the pickle toward the plate. "It's safer that way."

When he didn't let go of her right away, she stared down at his big hands and simply waited. "Thank you, Daniel. I'll try to remember next time."

He noticed the number of cuts on her fingers. "You aren't used to kitchen work, are you?" he asked as he let go and leaned back in his chair.

"No, but I'm learning."

She once again bent over the pickle with her knife. Wrinkling her nose and biting her lower lip in concentration, she cautiously sawed at it until there were half a dozen thin slices neatly arranged on the plate. Then, with a triumphant smile, she washed her hands and set her achievement before them.

Ryan couldn't take his eyes off her, so completely fascinated was he by this delicate woman. Even though she was unskilled and totally out of place, she was not deterred, nor even discouraged.

He had to force himself to get on with the business at hand. Pulling his notepad out of his pocket, he put it on the table and reached for his pencil. "Why don't we get started," he began.

"Yes, of course," she agreed.

"About what time were you in the bank on the day of the robbery?"

She stared at the tabletop when she answered. "I was there at two o'clock, give or take ten minutes."

Cole was about to take a bite of his sandwich when she gave her answer. He put the food back on the plate and shot a glance at Daniel to judge his reaction.

"You're sure it was two o'clock?" Daniel asked, sounding only mildly curious.

"Yes, I'm sure. I noticed the time while I was waiting my turn in line. There's a large clock on the wall behind the tellers' windows."

"Did you notice any of the other people in line?" Cole asked.

She pondered the question for a long moment, and then shook her head. "Actually, no, I didn't notice anyone else. I wasn't paying much attention."

What in God's name was going on? Cole was about to ask Grace that question when Daniel shook his head at him. He obviously didn't want Cole to point out the fact that her answer was identical to Jessica's and Rebecca's—almost word for word. Had the three of them rehearsed what they would say while they were in that cell together, and if so, why?

Daniel closed his notepad and put it back in his pocket. "Did you notice anything unusual?"

"No, I didn't," Grace answered.

"You took your place in line . . ."

"Yes, I did," she said. "And I waited my turn, but I didn't look around. I was thinking about all the things I needed to get done."

Daniel's frustration was mounting, but he was careful not to let it show. "The bag that Sheriff Sloan showed you," he began, "it doesn't belong to you, does it?"

"No, it doesn't. I never carry a bag. All of my dresses have pockets."

"The one you're wearing now doesn't," Cole said.

"Excuse me?"

She was obviously startled by his observation and

was trying to come up with a suitable explanation. "The dress you're wearing doesn't have pockets," Cole repeated.

"No, it doesn't," she agreed. "But the one I wore to the bank does have pockets . . . two of them. Would you like some more tea?"

Cole glanced down at his full cup and wondered where she thought she would put more. He shook his head, but she didn't seem to notice. She turned and rushed back to the stove, then carried the teapot back to the table and placed it next to Cole's cup. A look of acute relief crossed her face when Jessica walked into the kitchen.

Surprised to find the marshals still there, Jessica stopped short.

"I'm sorry. I didn't mean to intrude. I thought you would be finished by now, and I was going to help Grace clean the dishes. I'll do them later." She tried to leave, but Daniel called her back.

"Come and join us," he suggested.

Grace frantically nodded. Jessica's gaze was directed on Cole. He looked irritated and out of sorts, and she thought it was because she had interrupted them.

"No, thank you. I'll just go back upstairs for a little while."

"We insist you join us." He wasn't going to take no for an answer. He stood up and pulled out the chair adjacent to him. Daniel also stood and asked Grace to sit down.

The two women exchanged a look before complying with the request.

Cole then took over the questioning. "Grace, you're planning to leave Rockford Falls tomorrow, aren't you?"

"Yes, I am," she answered. She folded her hands on the tabletop and tried to look composed. "How did you know I was leaving?"

"Just a hunch," he answered dryly. "Where are you headed?"

"Colorado."

"Jessica told us she was also headed to Colorado," Daniel interjected.

"Yes, that's right," Grace said. "We're going to be traveling together."

"Did you come to Rockford Falls together?" Cole asked.

Grace smiled. "Good heavens, no. I came from London, England, several months ago. I stopped in Kentucky, Missouri, and Kansas before I came here. I was looking for property," she thought to add.

"Property?" Cole asked.

"I'm hoping to start a ranching business," she explained. "I'm looking for good grazing land . . ."

"For the cattle she's going to purchase," Jessica interjected.

"Yes, for the cattle," Grace agreed.

"But then Mr. Wells's family decided not to sell the property," Jessica said.

"Who is Mr. Wells?" Cole asked.

"The gentleman I corresponded with from London," Grace said. "I had heard through friends who knew him that he wanted to sell his land and that it was just what I was looking for."

"But it wasn't?" Cole asked.

"Oh, it was," Grace answered. "Acres and acres of lush green land. It was as perfect as my friends had claimed. I had already made an offer sight unseen from London, but when I arrived in Kentucky to sign the official papers, I found out that poor Mr. Wells had passed on. His son refused to honor his father's promise."

"Grace saw an advertisement in the *Rockford Falls Gazette* for available land near Denver, and we're going there together to look at it."

"Do you know anything about raising cattle?" Daniel asked.

"No, but I plan to hire men who do know how," Grace answered. "And I will learn how. I know it's going to be hard work, but I'm not afraid of it."

Cole was trying not to let Grace see how appalled he was. "Ma'am, running cattle is a backbreaking business." He was diplomatic in his caution.

Daniel was blunt. "Are you nuts? You can't run a cattle ranch."

Grace's spine stiffened. "No, I'm not crazy, and I assure you I will achieve my goal. I may not have the experience, but I'm determined."

Daniel was too incredulous to argue. Cole shook his head. "How can you leave tomorrow?" he asked. "The coach doesn't come through here until the day after."

"We aren't taking the coach," Jessica explained.

"We're going by wagon," Grace said. "It's in the field behind the house. Surely you noticed it on your way here."

"We should put our suitcases in it tonight," Jessica said.

Grace agreed. "And get an early start in the morning. That's a good idea."

"Who's driving the team?" Cole wanted to know.

"We are," Grace answered. The look on her face indicated she couldn't imagine why he would ask such a question.

Cole was staring at Jessica's hands. He reached over and took hold of one and turned the palm up. "Your hands are soft."

It sounded like an accusation, and she pulled her hand back. "I'll wear gloves."

"Have you ever driven a team before?" Daniel asked.

"Not exactly," she admitted.

Astonished by their impossible plans, Daniel

looked at Cole, hoping he would be able to talk some sense into them.

Cole was just as astounded, but he tried to be diplomatic. "The two of you . . . and the baby are going to set off on your own across some of the most rugged and dangerous terrain in the country. Have I got that straight?"

Both Grace and Jessica nodded.

Cole lost his patience. "Are you ladies out of your minds?"

Since he was looking at Jessica, she assumed he expected her to answer his rude question. "No, we aren't out of our minds. We've thought it all out, and I assure you we know what we're doing."

Grace nodded. "Yes, we do," she agreed. She turned to Daniel and added, "We won't be traveling alone. We're going to join a wagon train."

"We must be in Gramby by Monday at the latest," Jessica said.

Daniel was staring intently at Grace. More than anything she longed to tell him to stop it. It was rude, and it was also driving her to distraction. She had the feeling he was trying to see into her mind, which was absurd, she told herself. He couldn't possibly read her thoughts.

"Why are you asking us so many personal questions?" she demanded.

"We haven't done anything wrong," Jessica insisted.

"Are you finished questioning us about the bank?" Grace asked. "We both have work to do."

Daniel's anger was evident in his expression and voice when he said, "If one of you has information about the robbery and isn't telling, that's called *obstruction*. It's a punishable crime, ladies."

"Are you trying to intimidate us?" Jessica asked.

Both marshals ignored the question. Daniel turned to Grace. "I've only got one more question for you.

Did you happen to run into Jessica when you were at the bank?"

She looked at Jessica before she answered. "Yes, I passed her on my way out of the bank. She was going inside."

"What about Rebecca?" Cole asked. "Did you bump into her too?"

The men's anger sizzled in the air between them. It had been simmering, Grace realized, all the while they were questioning her. Something she had said must have set them off. She bowed her head when she answered. "Rebecca was just leaving the bank when I went inside."

Jessica also could feel the hostility and was convinced that she had said something that triggered the marshals' anger. She was exhausted from the strain of guarding every word and knew that if she said anything more, she would only make it worse. She decided to show the marshals out as quickly as possible. Pushing her chair back, she stood up and headed for the door.

Daniel stopped her with his command. "Both of you are going to be staying in town tomorrow."

She whirled around and bumped into Cole. She neither apologized nor stepped back.

"Why must we stay?" she asked.

"You can't make us stay here, can you?" Grace asked. "I'm not familiar with the laws in this country, but making someone do something she doesn't wish to do is wrong . . . isn't it?"

"Yes, it is," Jessica said. "Cole, you can't . . ."

He interrupted her. "Yes, I can make you stay. We're using the office in the front of the jail. You ladies know where it is. Why don't you both plan on being there at eight o'clock. Rebecca will be joining you."

Jessica and Grace seemed to wilt. They meekly followed the lawmen to the front of the house.

"This isn't right," Grace whispered.

Daniel heard her and turned back in the doorway. "No, it sure as hell isn't right, but we're going to figure it all out tomorrow, aren't we, Grace?"

Cole turned to address Jessica. "I don't know what kind of a game you ladies are playing, but it ends now. Do I make myself clear?"

He didn't wait for an answer. Jessica was shaking from head to toe as she shut the door and bolted the lock. She turned around and fell back against it.

Tears sprang into Grace's eyes. "Oh, God . . . they know."

Sixteen

The twisted turn of events left Cole and Daniel feeling bewildered and irritated.

"All three of them rehearsed what they were going to say to us when they were in the cell together," Cole remarked on the way back to the hotel.

"Hell, yes, they rehearsed. Now tell me why."

"They're scared, I guess. That's all I can come up with."

"They were all real edgy. Rebecca did the best job of concealing it from us, but I could see it in her eyes."

"And her hands," Cole said. "She was gripping them."

"Yeah, she was," Daniel remembered. He reached up and rubbed the back of his neck, trying to work the knots of tension out.

"I sure was wrong," Cole said. "I thought it was going to be a waste of time talking to Jessica and Grace. What the hell kind of a game are they playing?"

"I don't know," Daniel replied. "I was pretty sure it

was going to be a waste, too. I was just following procedure, hoping one of them might have noticed something unusual. It sure as hell got complicated, didn't it?"

"Yeah, it did," Cole agreed. "And it doesn't make any sense. They've got to know they were seen in the bank earlier that afternoon. They all stood in line with men who would remember them. Why did they go to all the trouble of rehearsing what they were going to say?"

"No, it doesn't make any sense. Which one of them is lying?"

"Maybe all three of them are. They're obviously hell-bent on protecting one another."

"Or . . ."

"Or what?"

"They're protecting someone else, someone we don't know about yet."

"How do we find out the truth?"

"They're going to tell us," Daniel said. "Tomorrow, one way or another, Jessica and Grace and Rebecca are going to tell us what they know."

"And if they don't?"

"No one's going to get in my way, man or woman." Daniel's voice shook with emotion. "If I have to lock them up, by God, I will."

"Don't do anything crazy."

Cole saw the irony in his remark and let out a harsh laugh. "I think this badge is changing me. I'm usually the one doing crazy things, and now I'm cautioning you. I know how bad you want those men. Hell, I'd feel the same way, but you've got to keep it legal."

Daniel disagreed. "I'm going to get them any way that I can. I don't care if it's legal or not. Are you going to help me?"

"I already told you I'd help."

The conversation ended when they reached the hotel and went up to their rooms. Cole threw open his window to get rid of the musty smell, then stripped out of his clothes, washed, and fell into bed. Stacking his hands behind his head, he thought about the women's answers to their questions. One thought led to another, and he was suddenly thinking about Jessica. Damn but she was a tempting woman.

He fell asleep hoping to God she hadn't been hiding under that desk.

Daniel didn't go to sleep right away. He spent a good hour pacing around his shoe box of a room, feeling like a caged animal. He tried to concentrate on the investigation, but Grace Winthrop kept getting in his way.

He'd been stunned by the impact she'd made on him, and honest to God, he didn't know how to handle it. Until tonight, he hadn't so much as glanced at another woman, and he sure as certain hadn't physically wanted any of them. Grace had gotten to him, though, and it seemed so damned disloyal of him to have such unbridled thoughts about her.

He couldn't figure out why he was attracted to her. Granted, she was pretty and her face was about the loveliest he'd seen in a long, long time. She had a nice shape too. No doubt about it, she was well put together, but she still wasn't anything like his sweet Kathleen. No other woman could ever measure up to her. The unspoiled daughter of a farmer, his wife had simple tastes and a passionate zest for life. He'd been drawn to her robust laugh and her generous nature, and he had immediately and completely fallen head over heels in love with her. How he had marveled at the great gift God had given him, and he often would quietly observe her as she went about her daily chores. Her strong, sturdy hands worked tirelessly through the day, but at night they were gentle and soft as they stroked his brow.

Grace was a dainty, petite woman. The top of her head barely reached his shoulders. She came from wealth and status and had obviously moved about in a world that was totally foreign to him. Yet there was a naiveté and gentleness in her that made him want to move close.

But she wasn't Kathleen. Oh, God, how he missed his wife. He ached to take her into his arms and make love to her once again. He longed to listen to her sing a lullaby to their little girl, to hear their laughter, to touch . . .

He forced himself to stop thinking about the past. His life had ended when his wife and baby were taken from him, gunned down like animals, but he had to keep going . . . had to keep pushing and searching until he had gotten every one of the demons responsible. Only then could he stop.

With a weary sigh, he got ready for bed and methodically went through his notes again. He wanted to find something he'd missed before, but that didn't happen. In frustration, he hurled the notepad across the room and fell back against the pillows.

Oh, Kathleen, if one of us had to die, why couldn't it have been me?

He fell asleep thinking about his wife, but he dreamed about Grace.

Seventeen

Cole didn't know what had awakened him. One second he was sound asleep, roping cattle, and the next he was wide awake and as tense as a bow. He was a light sleeper even when he was home at Rosehill in his own bed, and he always heard every little sound. He didn't hear anything unusual, but he still reached for his gun and went to the door.

As he expected, there wasn't anyone lurking in the hallway. He shut the door and crossed to the window to look down at the street, thinking that someone who had had too much to drink had made a racket. The street was deserted.

A faint breeze brushed his face. He let out a loud yawn and thought about going back to sleep, but then he saw the faint orange glow in the distance and realized it was already dawn. The sun was slowly making its way up into the black sky. Damn, but morning had come quick. He was still sleepy, and it seemed to him that he had only just closed his eyes.

He was getting old, he supposed. He stretched his

arms and went to get a drink of water before he got dressed. Because it was still dark in the room, he lit the kerosene lamp. His pocket watch was on the dresser next to his compass, and it wasn't until he happened to glance at the time that he realized it was still the middle of the night.

"What the hell?" he muttered.

He turned toward the streaks of amber light once again . . . and then he started running.

He was pulling his shirt on and trying to button his pants as he ran into the hallway.

"Wake up, Daniel. We've got trouble."

The door opened a second later. Daniel rushed into the hallway brandishing his gun. He was half dressed and half asleep. "What is it?"

"Fire."

"Where?" Daniel demanded as he turned and ran back into his room to get dressed.

"Could be as far away as the mountains, but I don't think so . . . the light's too close. Could be down the street . . . Ah, God, the boardinghouse . . . You don't think . . ." Cole shouted as he raced down the stairs.

Daniel was right behind him. The night manager was sound asleep in his chair behind the front desk, with his head and arms resting on the countertop, when Daniel leapt over the railing and shouted to him to ring the fire bell. Startled by the abrupt noise, the manager struck his head on a lamp and overturned his chair when he jumped to his feet.

"What . . . What did you say?" he cried out.

"The fire bell," Daniel roared as he crossed the lobby and burst through the door in Cole's wake. "Ring the fire bell."

He caught up with Cole at the corner. Side-by-side the two men ran, the only sounds the pounding of their boots against the ground and their harsh breathing as each pushed himself to his limit. They were halfway down the block when they smelled smoke.

Running as though the fire were licking at their heels, they sprinted around the curve in the road and saw the flames. The first floor of the house was a blazing inferno. Glowing red embers, like demon eyes, spewed out the open windows and floated up into the night sky. Tattered remnants of lace curtains, blackened with soot, billowed outward with each burst of dense smoke, and the freshly painted white wood blistered and boiled from the intensity of the heat.

No one was outside.

Cole and Daniel leapt over the fence at the same time and raced across the lawn. Daniel headed for the back of the house, hoping he could find a way inside through the flames, while Cole circled around the opposite side.

The front door crashed open, and they saw Jessica slowly backing out. She was bent at the waist, dragging Grace to safety.

Her friend wasn't moving. Daniel reached the porch before Cole did and lifted the unconscious woman into his arms. In the firelight, he could see the blood trickling down her left temple. Something had struck her hard, and considering the amount of swelling, he thought she was damned lucky to be alive. He held her close against his chest and ran down the steps and out into the yard, where he gently laid her in the grass.

Jessica followed him down the steps, then stopped. Screaming Caleb's name, she was turning in a circle, frantically searching for the baby and for Tilly, when Cole dove from the porch railing and tackled her to the ground.

He landed hard and knocked the breath out of her. She was thrown backward in the grass. She couldn't catch her breath and didn't understand what was happening, or why. All she could think about was Caleb and getting to him in time. Where was he?

Jessica tried to roll to her side so she could get up

and search for her baby, but Cole was suddenly pinning her down. Then he started pounding at her legs with the palms of his hands, shouting to Daniel to help him. She cried out and renewed her struggles to push him off her.

Flames were greedily eating the hem of her robe. Cole was trying to put the fire out and get the robe off her before she was burned. By the time he had rolled her onto her stomach, Daniel was at his side, helping.

The two men were tearing at her clothes. Screaming Caleb's name over and over again she struggled to get up, but they wouldn't let her move until Cole had ripped her robe off her shoulders and Daniel had pulled it free.

Cole lifted her up. She grabbed hold of his shirt and screamed, "I can't find Caleb. You have to help me find him. He's with Tilly . . . She was taking him outside while I searched for Grace. They were beside me upstairs. Where are they? I have to find them."

She jerked away from him and tried to run back to the house, but Cole grabbed her from behind. She fought like a wildcat to get free, clawing at his arms and kicking at his legs.

"I'll find him," he promised. "Do you hear me, Jessie? I'll find him. You stay with Grace. Can you do that?"

His calm voice cut through her hysteria. "Yes, yes, I'll stay with Grace. Please hurry."

"The old lady and the baby are still inside," Cole shouted to Daniel. He jerked Jessica around to face him. "Where are their rooms?"

She pointed to the center window above the porch. "Tilly's room is in the middle. Caleb and I are next to her . . . on the left side . . . by the tree."

Daniel was already on the roof. He'd swung himself up from the overhang above the porch. He used the heel of his boot to break the glass in the center window and jumped back to avoid the flames and smoke that billowed out. Then he dove, headfirst, inside.

The roof above the porch collapsed a second later. Cole had run to the other side of the house to try to get in through one of the windows on the first floor, but he couldn't get close enough, for the heat pouring out was too intense. His eyes burned and watered as he backtracked to the gnarled tree closest to the house. Thick branches hung down over the eaves, and he hoped he could get close enough to jump onto the roof.

He began to climb. Seconds later he swung out, hand over hand, and then dropped down to the roof. Daniel appeared at the window with Tilly wrapped in a blanket and draped over his shoulder. Before Cole could help him, Daniel jumped through the opening and sprinted toward the opposite side of the roof. The branches on that side of the house were lower and easy to grasp hold of.

"Caleb wasn't with Tilly. Get out of here," Daniel shouted. "The roof's going to go."

Ignoring the warning, Cole headed for the window Jessica had pointed out. Tongues of fire were hissing and spitting at him from the opening, but fear lent him strength. He was so damned scared he wouldn't find the baby alive, he recklessly followed Daniel's example and plunged headfirst inside.

He was surprised to find the floor was still there. He landed with a thud on his left shoulder, rolled, and stood up. A thick wall of black smoke knocked him backward to his knees. Ashes poured over his face and matted his eyelashes. His eyes burned so badly he couldn't see where he was, he couldn't breathe, and the heat inside the bedroom made his skin feel as though it were melting. He dropped down to the floor and took a deep breath of cool air. Then he began to crawl forward on his belly. There was almost a foot of clean air trapped between the floorboards and the dense, deadly smoke. Taking another deep breath, he shouted Caleb's name.

The sound of his voice was lost in the crackling inferno. He slowly inched forward. He couldn't see anything, but he hoped he would bump into a clothes closet. Every bedroom had one, and he knew that whenever his little sister had become afraid, she'd hidden there. He hoped to God, Caleb had done the same thing.

The bed was his second choice, but he found it first. He hit the side of the headboard, squeezed himself along the length, and reached underneath, sweeping his arm back and forth in a wide arc.

There wasn't anything there.

Every second that passed was another second closer to the baby's death. Cole was silently praying and begging for God's help as he made one final sweep under the bed. He was just pulling back when Caleb grabbed hold of his hand.

The baby let go just as quickly. Cole rolled his shoulder under the frame, lifted up, and reached for him. Caleb had squeezed himself up against the headboard. Cole found a leg and gently pulled.

He could hear him whimpering and making loud, sucking sounds with his thumb in his mouth, and Cole thought those were the most beautiful noises he'd ever heard, for it meant that Caleb was unharmed.

He lifted the baby into his arms and rolled to his knees. Caleb threw himself backward and grabbed his baby doll off the floor. A forked flame of fire leapt up from between the floorboards as Cole pulled Caleb back.

"Let's get out of here," he whispered to the baby, his voice hoarse and raw from smoke.

He wanted to wrap Caleb in a blanket from the bed, but when he reached for it, he saw the embers raining down from the ceiling on top of it. The blanket ignited and rapidly burned. In desperation, Cole tucked Caleb's head under his chin, wrapped his arms around him, and doubled over, his hope that his own body would shield the baby's.

He figured he had only a couple of seconds left to get out. The bedroom was closing in on him. Flames where shooting up from the cracks in the floor and dropping down from the ceiling above.

And then the walls began to move as though they had suddenly come alive. They bulged forward, hovered; then, with an eerie swooshing sound, they slowly receded before throbbing forward once again. It was the spookiest damned thing he had ever seen. He could hear the heart of the fire beating behind those walls. It pulsated and throbbed as it sucked every breath of air it could find.

Cole knelt near the floor, took a deep breath, rose to his feet, and raced for the window. The monster chased him. He heard a snapping sound behind him, felt the floor shift under his feet, and leapt through the opening as the floor collapsed. The room's walls exploded a heartbeat later. Shards of glass and fragments of burning embers blew out the window. The force of the explosion slammed Cole forward, but he turned in midair so he would land on his back and not crush the baby in his arms. The heat pouring out from the hot roof burned his skin, and he knew he had only seconds left before the whole house collapsed. Staggering to his feet, he turned in one direction and then the other, looking for a way down. Flames, like serpent heads, were creeping toward him from below and closing in on him from the eaves above. Fire cut off the route Daniel had taken with Tilly, and Cole knew he wouldn't be able to go down the way he had come up on the opposite side, for the tree branches were too high for him to reach with a baby in his arms.

He was trapped.

He could hear the faint clanging of a fire bell in the distance. Then he heard a shrill whistle. He turned toward the sound just as Daniel whistled again. Squinting against the black smoke, Cole spotted him straddling the heavy branch.

It was too damned far away. Impossible to reach.

There wasn't any other alternative. "Hang on, Caleb," he whispered. Taking a deep breath, he let out a roar and leapt over the ring of fire directly in front of him. He could feel the wood cracking under his feet and hear the beams crashing behind him, but on he ran until he felt as though his lungs were going to explode.

Daniel watched Cole coming toward him. When Cole was halfway across the roof, Daniel flattened himself on one branch and braced his legs in a wedge of a lower branch. He wrapped his left arm around the limb holding him, then reached down as far as he could extend and put out his right hand.

It was a leap of faith. The distance from the edge of the roof to Daniel's hand was considerable. Cole felt as though he were flying, and for a brief second, he did exactly that. He vaulted out into the night, reaching for Daniel.

Their hands connected. And held.

Cole closed his eyes and let out a sigh of relief.

Daniel grunted from the weight but held tight. When Cole had stopped swaying and Daniel was sure he wasn't going to drop him, he reached down with his other hand to get Caleb, and let go of Cole who dropped down to a lower branch. The baby was screaming as Daniel gently pulled him up in his arms. A few seconds later, they were all on the ground and running for safety.

Jessica ran to Daniel to take Caleb from him, but Cole intercepted her. Looping his arm around her waist, he lifted her up and carried her with him as he continued to run.

Just as they reached Grace and Tilly, the walls of the house and the roof caved in. The horde of townspeople who were running to and fro with buckets of water suddenly stopped to watch the dazzling display of fireworks. Sparks shot up as high as fifty feet and spiraled downward in a popping, cracking arc that was so impressive some of the townsmen actually oohed and aahed.

It was a night none of them would ever forget.

The reporter was rushing around trying to find someone he could interview, while John Cletchem, the photographer, set up his equipment so that he could capture the destruction before the flames stopped feeding.

Tilly was sitting on the grass, quietly weeping. Grace was still unconscious, but Tilly had lifted her up so that her head rested in the older woman's lap. She was gently stroking Grace's forehead while she cried. Daniel knelt down beside the two women. He awkwardly patted Tilly's back in an attempt to comfort her, but his attention was centered on Grace. He was watching her breathe and thanking God every time she drew a breath.

She looked so young and innocent and vulnerable. Daniel shouted for someone to go and get the doctor. The sound of his voice jarred Grace, and she flinched in reaction. He'd almost had himself convinced that his heart was safe, then she opened her eyes and looked at him. His heart started pounding, and his own eyes stung with tears of relief.

What in God's name was the matter with him? He couldn't stop himself from reaching for her. He gently took her into his arms and stood up.

"Daniel? Your face is covered with dirt."

"Yeah, I know. How are you feeling?"

"My head hurts," she said. "I'm not sure why," she added, a puzzled look on her face. She reached up and trailed her fingers down the side of his cheek. "How did you get so dirty?"

He turned around so she could see what was left of the house. She wasn't looking anywhere but at him however, and so he explained. "There was a fire."

She turned her head, grimacing from the pain the movement caused. Her eyes widened in disbelief, and she was suddenly clearheaded again. "Where's Jessica and Caleb and Tilly?"

"They're fine," he assured her. "Everyone got out of the house in time. No one was hurt . . . except you. Do you remember what happened?"

She put her head down on his shoulder. "No, I don't remember. Please put me down. I need to . . ."

"You need to see a doctor." He looked over the crowd and was about to shout for the physician once again when the man suddenly appeared at the head of the townspeople watching the fire. Rebecca was dragging him toward Tilly and Grace.

"Daniel?" Grace whispered, drawing his attention once again. "How did I get out of the house?"

"Jessica pulled you out. If she hadn't . . . Cole and I would never have found you in time."

"She saved my life."

"Yes."

As Grace began to cry, Daniel tightened his hold and tried to comfort her.

Jessica was also crying. She had Caleb cuddled in her arms and was so relieved and thankful her baby was unharmed she kept kissing him and hugging him. Fully recovered from his adventure, Caleb squirmed and wanted to get down and play.

Rebecca found the two of them in the crowd. "My God, Jessica, you could have been killed," she cried out as she lifted the baby. "Are you all right?"

Jessica forced herself to stop crying long enough to answer her friend. "Yes, I'm fine, but Grace is hurt. A beam must have fallen on her head," she explained.

"The doctor's looking at her now," Rebecca said. "She doesn't remember anything?"

"I don't know," Jessica answered. "Will you watch Caleb? Don't let him out of your sight. I have to find someone."

"Jessica, we need to cover you first. Where's your robe?"

"It caught on fire," Jessica said as she turned to search the crowd for Cole.

"I'll find something for you to put on," Rebecca promised.

Jessica didn't hear her. She had finally spotted Cole and hurried toward him. He stood well away from the crowd and was watching the house being devoured by the fire. He looked exhausted and was covered from head to toe in soot.

She thought he was the most beautiful man she had ever seen. "Cole?"

She stopped and simply stared at him. Suddenly he seemed bigger than life to her. The fire blazing in the background enhanced the fantasy, for Cole was silhouetted in a hazy, burnished gold glow. It was as though God had blessed him because of the courage he had shown in the face of such danger.

"Did you want something?" he asked, puzzled by the look of joy and wonder on her face.

She hurried toward him once again with the intention of thanking him for saving Caleb's life, but when she finally reached him, a simple thank-you didn't seem sufficient. She threw herself into his arms.

He buckled under the impact and instinctively put his arms around her.

Leaning up on tiptoe, she embraced his neck, whispered, "Thank you," and kissed him passionately.

It wasn't a chaste kiss by any means, and Cole wasn't about to let the opportunity slip past without taking full advantage. He would have kept right on kissing her if he hadn't felt her tremble in his arms. He pulled back then and tried to move away, but she tightened her grip, and that was all the provocation he needed. He kissed her once again and held her close.

Her head dropped down to the crook of his neck, and she began to sob. All the pent-up emotion inside of her seemed to erupt then. His chin rested on top of her head as she whispered her thank-you again and again.

He gently kissed her forehead. "You're welcome."

The moment would never be forgotten, for the photographer captured the couple embracing so passionately—he, covered in soot, and she, wearing only a thin nightgown.

The photograph was on the front page of the *Rockford Falls Gazette* the following morning.

Eighteen

✿

Rebecca was sickened by the sight of Grace. The left side of her temple was severely swollen from the blow to her head. It was a miracle her friend had survived.

Daniel had placed her on a blanket one of the neighbors provided and knelt by her side while the doctor examined her. Rebecca wasn't usually timid, but the seriousness of the injury took her breath away. Daniel thought she was going to faint and told her to sit down, but she was determined to speak to Grace first.

"How are you feeling, Grace?" she whispered, her voice shivering with fear.

Grace stared up at the woman towering over her. She couldn't help but notice there wasn't a hair out of place. Rebecca hadn't come running to see the fire as everyone else had, dressed in robes and slippers. No, she was fully attired. The unadorned black dress fit the occasion, but her face was stark white in comparison.

"I'm feeling much better now," Grace answered. "I'll be all right, Rebecca. You mustn't worry about me."

Rebecca lifted the hem of her gown and knelt down next to Dr. Lawrence.

The physician patted Grace's hand. "You're going to be all right," he promised. "You're very lucky. I'm still not clear about how you got hit, but I'm guessing the ceiling caved in on you."

The doctor awkwardly got to his feet. He addressed his next remark to Daniel. "She should have been killed, Marshal."

Rebecca leaned over Grace. "Do you remember what happened?"

"No, I can't seem to remember anything at all."

Rebecca nodded sympathetically. "It's just as well you don't remember. You would have horrible nightmares otherwise. Poor Jessica was right in the thick of the fire, but blessedly you slept through it."

Grace became teary-eyed again. "She saved my life. If it weren't for her, I would have died."

Rebecca grasped Grace's hand. "Please don't cry," she whispered. "It's over now and everyone's safe."

"Where is Jessica?" Grace asked.

"She went to the wagon with Marshal Clayborne to fetch some clean clothes," Dr. Lawrence said. "I should probably have a look at her."

Grace struggled to sit up. Daniel put his arm behind her back and helped her. Her head was still throbbing so much she could barely concentrate. "Thank heavens we packed our clothes tonight. Everything we own is in the wagon except what we were going to wear tomorrow. The wagon didn't catch fire, did it?"

"No, no, it didn't," Rebecca assured her.

The fire was still raging, but the street beyond was dark. Someone in the crowd lit a torch. Caleb was sitting on Tilly's lap when the stranger started toward the yard with the fiery light. Terrified, Caleb began to scream for his mama. Rebecca immediately ran to him and lifted him into her arms, holding him tight as she tried to soothe him.

Daniel collared the man with the torch and told him to move back.

Grace tried to stand. She held on to the doctor's arm so she wouldn't fall, but, Lord, she was so dizzy the world was spinning around her.

"What do you think you're doing?" Daniel muttered. "Sit down before you pass out again."

"You're as white as a sheet," the doctor told her. "Do as the marshal says and sit back down. You need to rest."

"I want to find Jessica. I must talk to her."

"I'll find her," Daniel promised.

He headed for the field behind the house and saw Jessica coming toward him. She obviously had heard her son crying, for she'd dropped the clean clothes she'd only just gathered from the wagon and was running toward him. Cole was following behind. He noticed the ground was littered with trash and shouted to Jessica to watch where she was walking, as there were pieces of glass in the grass that could easily cut through her soft slippers.

Daniel shouted to Cole and then stopped near the edge of the lot. He stared down at two empty milk bottles. It had rained hard the past week, yet the bottles were clean. Curious, he picked one up. The smell of kerosene was still strong, and when he looked, he could see the residue in the bottom of the glass.

He showed both to Cole. He took a whiff of one and nodded. "When we first got here, I noticed there didn't seem to be a starting point. The back of the house was burning as fiercely as the front. It was like the whole house was primed."

"Whoever did it must have circled the house with the kerosene."

"You thinking the Blackwater gang's responsible? They might have seen the article in the paper, and a fire in the dead of night would be a sure way to get rid of a couple of possible witnesses. Rebecca's lucky she didn't move in here."

"She could be next on their list," Daniel said, his voice grim. "We're going to have to keep close to all three of them, and as soon as they have had some sleep, they're going to tell us the truth."

"Are you going to tell them the fire was set?"

Daniel took the bottle from Cole and put both of them on the ground next to a tree. "Not yet," he said. "I don't want to scare them any more than they already are."

Cole looked at the house. "What a hell of a night," he muttered.

"Let's get everyone settled," Daniel said. "There's too many people here. I don't like crowds."

The marshals could hear Rebecca issuing orders as they headed back to the front lawn. She had stepped forward and had taken charge with a vengeance. She sounded like a military commander who wasn't going to take no for an answer, and the crowd she was ordering about responded like new recruits. They did whatever she told them to do.

Jessica and Grace didn't know what they would have done if it hadn't been for their friend organizing the townspeople. Neighbors were sent home to fetch blankets for the women and the baby, Dr. Lawrence was encouraged to open his home for Tilly until she could make other arrangements, men were told to bring the wagon to the hotel, and a brigade was established to haul water and put out the fire before it spread to the field beyond.

No one was allowed to stand idle. There was work

to be done, and Rebecca was determined to see that it was completed as quickly as possible.

Less than thirty minutes later, the bone-weary group headed to the hotel. Although Grace protested vehemently, Daniel insisted on carrying her. Cole carried Caleb, who was fast asleep before they reached the street. Rebecca came up with the suggestion that Jessica and Caleb take one of the marshal's rooms for the night and Grace take the other one. Since the hotel was full, the lawmen could sleep outside.

Cole and Daniel had other intentions. They weren't about to let the women out of their sight. Daniel was going to stand guard in the lobby, and Cole would stay upstairs to watch the hallways, but their plans changed when they ran into Sheriff Sloan as he was tiptoeing out of the hotel.

Daniel told him what had happened and ordered him to sit outside Rebecca's door. Sloan readily agreed, for he was extremely embarrassed that he hadn't even known about the fire. He had been otherwise occupied, and from the smug, sated look on his face, Cole and Daniel knew exactly what he'd been doing.

The night manager was appalled at the sight of the soot-covered men and women, but he was also extremely solicitous. He immediately awakened two maids to help prepare the rooms. Everyone took baths. Caleb not only awakened during his bath, but was also full of energy. The nap on the way to the hotel had obviously rejuvenated him.

Jessica and Grace were dead on their feet and fell asleep as soon as they got into their beds. Daniel propped his chair against Grace's door and was asleep seconds later with his hand resting on the hilt of his gun.

Cole was across the hall. He too had stretched out in his chair and had his back up against the door to

Jessica's room. He could hear Caleb chattering away in nonsensical gibberish. After several minutes, the door opened and the baby came running out.

Cole carried him back to his mother, but stopped short just inside the door when he saw Jessica. She was sleeping on her stomach with her arms splayed wide. Apparently she had been too exhausted to pull the covers up, and her pink nightgown had worked its way around her knees. Lord, but she had a shapely backside and legs. Cole noticed she had nice feet too, and he wondered if she was ticklish.

Her face was turned toward the moonlight streaming in through the open window. He stared at her mouth, remembering how soft her lips had been when she'd kissed him. He could still feel her pressed against him, and all he wanted to do now was get into that bed with her and . . .

He blocked the thoughts racing through his mind. The poor woman had been through hell tonight, and he didn't have any business conjuring up such lustful notions. Besides, he was a U.S. marshal and the job carried responsibilities with it. He couldn't act on his impulses, no matter how irresistible they were.

Caleb began to fidget in his arms then, pulling Cole back from his fantasies. The baby was wet. Cole quickly found his nappies and lay him on the side of the bed close to Jessica.

"No," Caleb chanted over and over. He swung his leg up, kicking Cole in the arm, and tried to flip over so that he could slide down on the floor.

"Oh, no you don't," Cole whispered. "You're going to get changed, and then you're going to sleep."

He tied the straps securing the nappy, picked up Caleb, then grabbed his baby doll and shoved it into his arms. The baby was grinning and chattering away as Cole carried him over to the narrow cot the manager had sent up, tucked him in, and quietly left the room.

Caleb was right behind him. Jessica heard Cole mumble something under his breath and covered her mouth with her hands so he wouldn't hear her laugh. She had been horrified to find him in her room, but then she'd heard him whispering to her son and realized his intentions were quite honorable. Cole was a good man, and she and her son were perfectly safe with him.

She fell asleep with good intentions of rescuing Cole.

Caleb ended up sleeping on Cole's lap for a couple of hours, woke up chattering, and then fell asleep on Daniel's shoulder. Needless to say, the marshals didn't get much rest.

Nineteen

❧

Daniel was summoned to the telegraph office at seven the following morning.

Cole met Sloan in the lobby and ordered him to hire two deputies to help guard the women. He waited at the hotel until the sheriff strolled in a few minutes later with Robert York and John Carver. The two men were heavily armed and looked dangerous. They convinced Cole they knew what they were doing, and he quickly filled them in on what was expected of them. Jessica and Rebecca were to stay in their rooms until the marshals returned to meet with them. Grace had been ordered to stay in bed until the doctor looked in on her that afternoon.

"Don't let anyone but Dr. Lawrence go upstairs," he ordered. "York, you stand outside Jessica's door. Carver, you take Rebecca's, and Sloan, you watch Grace's."

"But I haven't had my morning coffee yet. Couldn't I go into the dining room and get something to eat?" Sloan moaned.

"No," Cole answered. "You're going to stay outside Grace's door."

Lack of sleep made Cole more surly than usual, and Sloan was smart enough not to provoke him.

Cole took the key to the jail from the sheriff and headed across town. The office was stuffy, and so he left the door open to get some fresh air. Everything smelled like smoke to him, which was probably why he didn't have an appetite.

It was almost eight when Daniel arrived. He carried a pot of coffee in one hand and a wad of telegrams in the other.

He didn't waste any time telling Cole what he had learned. "One of the Blackwater gang was captured."

"Where did they get him?"

"He was hiding in one of the caverns just inside the Texas border. They've taken him over to Blackwater."

Cole went to get a clean cup from the shelf across the room. He poured himself some coffee, took a drink, and then asked, "Is he alive?"

"Barely," Daniel answered. "The sheriff in Maple Hills put a couple of bullets in him. It was a piece of luck that the sheriff stumbled on him. The man was sick as a dog with influenza, but he still put up a fight. I hope to God he lives long enough to stand trial. Damn, I wish I were there now. I can't wait to talk to him."

"You can't believe he'll tell you anything."

"Oh, yes, I do believe that. He's going to tell me everything I want to know."

"Is talking all you plan to do, or did you have something else in mind?" he asked quietly.

"That depends on how the trial goes. He isn't going to walk away," Daniel said. He shook his head and added, "Judge Rafferty won't let that happen. If the man's one of the Blackwater boys, he'll hang."

"You sound like you know this judge personally."

"I do," Daniel answered. "Everyone in Texas

knows him, or at least has heard of him. Rafferty has quite a reputation for being hard-nosed. Folks think he makes Hangin' Judge Cyrus Burns look like a saint. You don't cross Rafferty and keep on breathing. He's also got a real personal stake in all of this," he added. "Rafferty lost a good friend in a robbery up in Kansas. The two of them went way back, and he took the man's death hard. He wants revenge."

"Then he's personally involved. A fancy lawyer could argue for a new judge."

"Maybe, but he'd lose," Daniel said. "Rafferty's the law in west Texas. Fortunately, he's also an honest man. Hell, if he weren't, he would have handed the man over to a lynching mob by now."

"You think they've had trouble?"

"Yes, I do."

Cole thought about that for a moment, and then asked, "What's in the other telegrams?"

"They're all from Rafferty. He must have been standing inside the telegraph office and was in a talkative mood. He wanted to know if we had any leads, and I wired him back that there was a remote possibility of a witness. He jumped right on that. I told him there might have been a woman hiding in the bank, that we think it's one of three, but none of them will admit it . . ."

"What did he say about that?"

"He wants us to bring all three of them to Blackwater. He says he can get the truth out of them."

"Does he have the authority to make us bring them?"

Daniel leaned back against the wall. "Yes and no," he answered. "We're on special assignment, so we don't have to follow his instructions."

"But?"

"Rafferty's got some powerful friends in Washington. He might be able to exert enough pressure to force us to do what he wants. I don't want to get him riled up, so I'm letting him think we'll cooperate. I promised him that we would know for certain today if we had a witness or not."

"And will we know today?"

"Hell, yes, we'll know."

"Grace might not be up to talking today. We might have to wait."

"We'll talk to her this afternoon, then. By the end of the day, we'll know whether or not we have a witness."

Cole muttered an expletive. He'd just spotted Rebecca on the boardwalk across the street. She was wearing a pink dress and carrying a pink-and-white-striped parasol. She was so lovely, she was literally stopping traffic as men paused to gawk at her. Her guard, Carver, trailed close behind, glancing in all directions.

"Here comes Rebecca," Cole said. "Ah, hell, she just stopped to talk to the reporter."

Ryan looked outside. "He was hanging around the telegraph office while I was inside, and when I came out, he went running in. He probably knows everything now, and from the look on Rebecca's face, I'm guessing he just told her they caught one of the gang."

"How do they know?"

Daniel turned back to Cole. "Know what?"

"That the man they caught is one of the gang."

"He was carrying a large sum of money."

"So? Lots of people carry large sums of money when they travel."

"That's true," Daniel conceded. "But they also found a copy of the *Rockford Falls Gazette* in his saddlebags. The date's the same as the day of the robbery."

"It's still circumstantial evidence, isn't it?"

"Did I mention he tried to kill the sheriff before he was captured?"

Cole shook his head. "No, you didn't mention that.

He won't be walking away free and clear, then. They'll hold him for attempted murder."

"But I want to get him for the robberies. If he's one of the gang, then he's going to talk to me and tell me everything. I want all the other names."

"How do you think you're going to convince him to talk?"

"I'll figure out something," Daniel replied. "It would make it easier if there was a witness to point him out . . ."

"I wouldn't get my hopes up, Daniel. Those women could have told the same story for an altogether different reason. You think two of them are hell-bent to protect the third woman. I'm not sure. It occurs to me that we don't know anything relevant about these women, and I think it's time we looked into their backgrounds."

"I'm not taking anything they tell us as true until I've checked it out."

"Good," Cole replied. He glanced out the window again, just in time to see Rebecca strike the reporter's arm with her parasol. Even from the distance separating them, he could see how pale and upset she was. Not paying any attention to what she was doing, she picked up her skirts and rushed into the street, almost running headfirst into a horse and buggy. Carver pulled her back in the nick of time.

A minute later, she came running into the office, ordering her guard to remain outside to watch the door. Cole and Daniel waited for her to regain her breath.

Daniel offered her a chair, but she declined the invitation to sit and began to pace around the office. It was very apparent that she was highly agitated.

"Why have you assigned a guard to follow me?" she asked.

"For protection," Cole answered.

"But why do you think I need to be protected?"

"After the mob here last night, we thought it was best to hire guards for all three of you just to make sure no one tries to bother you."

"Does the guard upset you?" Cole asked.

"No," she answered. "I am upset, but not because of Mr. Carver. He's only doing his job."

"Then what's bothering you?" Cole asked.

"I've just heard the most startling news from that despicable reporter this morning. He told me that one of the Blackwater gang has been captured. Was the reporter lying or was he telling the truth?"

Because she was looking at Daniel, he stepped forward to answer. "Yes, it's true. One of them was caught."

"Is he dead or alive?" she cried out.

"Alive," Daniel answered. "But just barely."

"I hope he dies," she whispered, and then bowed her head. "No, I shouldn't say that. It's just that there's been so much killing, and if he's responsible, he should pay for his crimes. Do they know the man's name?"

"I don't know if the authorities know his name or not," Daniel said. "I didn't ask."

"Are they bringing him back to Rockford Falls to stand trial?"

"No, they've taken him to Blackwater, Texas."

"Is that a long way from here?"

"Yes," Cole answered.

She looked relieved.

"Good," she whispered. "I won't have to worry about him getting loose and coming after Jessica and Grace and me."

She collapsed into a chair and began to fan herself with her handkerchief. "The murderer has confessed to his crimes, hasn't he?"

"No, he hasn't."

"But they're sure he's one of them? They won't let him out, will they?"

She sounded terrified of the possibility. Daniel quickly put her mind to rest. "They won't let him out," he assured her.

She glanced down at her lap. "Oh, Lord, my hands are shaking. I'm not used to this kind of excitement, and this past week has been hellacious. First, there were the murders at the bank, and then I was named a witness in the paper, and the fire last night . . . It's too much. It's simply too much." Her voice broke.

Daniel sat down on the edge of the desk to face her. "I know how distressing this is, but . . ."

"No, you don't know," she cried out. "I'm . . . so . . . scared."

After whispering the admission, she burst into tears and buried her face in her hands. "I've been such a coward, but I'm going to do the right thing now. You don't need to bother Jessica or Grace any longer because . . ."

She didn't go on. Daniel leaned toward her and tried to look sympathetic, while Cole shoved a glass of water into her hand.

"Here, drink this," he suggested.

She wiped her face with her handkerchief and looked up at him. "Try to understand. I didn't want anyone to know . . . I'm engaged to the most wonderful man. He's a respected businessman and very careful about appearances. A scandal would ruin him. It's taken him five long years to get up the courage to propose to me. I thought I could go back home and pretend none of this happened. You would catch the men eventually. My fiancé runs with a very sophisticated, wealthy crowd. Can you see why I would keep silent?"

"Rebecca, what are you telling us?" Cole asked.

"I'm your witness. I was hiding under the desk when the Blackwater gang came inside. The purse you found belongs to me."

Both marshals tried to contain their reaction to the

news. Relief flooded through Cole, and he felt guilty about that. He was just so damned happy it wasn't Jessica.

Daniel felt a burst of excitement rush through his veins. She was there, and, God willing, she saw all of them.

"They'll try to kill me, won't they?" she whispered.

"We'll protect you," Cole fervently promised.

"You'll try, but they'll find a way to silence me."

"We aren't going to let anyone hurt you," Daniel vowed.

She wiped the tears away from her face before speaking again. "I know I should have come forward sooner, but I was very frightened. I just wanted to pretend it didn't happen, and I kept hoping that you would catch them . . . eventually. I'm so sorry I lied. It isn't like me to act so cowardly."

"You were scared," Cole said.

"Yes," she whispered. "And now poor Jessica and Grace have both been dragged into this nightmare. Neither one of them was in the bank at closing time. I know because I was there, and if I had had the courage to speak up sooner, they wouldn't be living in fear now."

"You were seen inside the bank earlier that afternoon," Cole said.

"Yes, I was there, but I went back. I needed to finish some business. I thought I could just run into the bank and . . ."

A defeated look crossed her face. "I'll go to Blackwater with you and look at the man they've captured," she whispered. "If he's one of the Blackwater gang, I'll point him out and testify in court."

She wiped another tear from her cheek before continuing. "I'm begging you. Let Jessica and Grace get on with their lives. They want to leave town this afternoon, as soon as they can, and I think they should be allowed to," she added. "They shouldn't be hounded or punished any longer because of my cowardice. You don't have to worry that the gang will come after them. I've thought about this long and hard, and I think I've come up with the perfect solution to ensure they'll be left alone."

"And what's that?" Daniel asked.

"I'm going to tell the reporter for the newspaper that I'm the witness. I'm certain he'll put the announcement on the front page of tomorrow's edition. I'll go over to his office as soon as I leave here."

Daniel was shaking his head. Cole put his coffee cup down and took a step toward her. "We can't let you do that."

"You can't stop me," she cried out. "I will protect Jessica and Grace as best I can. It's my fault they're caught in the middle of this nightmare. Hopefully, one of the Blackwater gang will see the interview and leave those poor innocent women alone."

"I can stop you," Daniel countered. "You are *not* going to talk to any reporters. Do I make myself clear?"

"But I must let everyone know Jessica and Grace weren't there. Don't you understand? They're being treated like lepers in this town, and they haven't done anything wrong."

She sounded on the verge of hysteria. Cole quickly tried to calm her down. "You didn't do anything wrong either, Rebecca. You were simply in the wrong place at the wrong time."

"Do Jessica and Grace know that you've come forward?" Daniel asked. "When Sloan locked the three of you in the cell together, did you tell them then that you were the witness? Is that why all of you told us the same story?"

She seemed surprised. "They were both very frightened. I remember telling them exactly what I was going to say to you. Why? Did they say the very same thing?"

Neither marshal answered her question. "Did you tell them you saw the robbery and the murders?" Cole pressed.

"No, I didn't, but I think they knew. They were protecting me by not telling you what they suspected. They're both very kindhearted ladies, and they wanted to help me. I could pack and be ready to leave in an hour. I'd like to get going as soon as possible."

With a tilt of his head, Daniel motioned Cole to step outside with him. They left the door open but spoke in low whispers so Rebecca wouldn't overhear.

"She isn't going to get near the reporter," Daniel muttered.

"I agree," Cole said. "She's right, though, about leaving. We better get her out of town as quickly as possible."

"I wanted to wait . . ."

"For what?" Cole demanded.

"Marhsal Cooper and a couple of deputies are coming up from Salt Lake City to help. They should be here any time, and I'll let them take charge of Jessica and Grace, while you and I escort Rebecca to Blackwater."

"And if Jessica and Grace want to leave Rockford Falls in the meantime? Are they going to be safe?"

"Yes," Daniel answered. "Cooper and his deputies will go with them to make certain no one bothers them."

"Do you trust this Cooper?"

"Yeah," Daniel answered. "He's a good man. I've worked with him on other cases. Trust me. He knows what he's doing."

Rebecca drew both marshals back to her side when she burst into tears again.

"They're going to come after me, aren't they?"

Cole wanted to lie to her, but Daniel was quicker and was bluntly truthful. "Yes, they'll probably come after you, but we aren't going to let them touch you."

"We have to leave. Now," she demanded. "I won't stay here another minute. It's too dangerous," she added in a panic.

"Before any decisions are made, you need to tell us exactly what happened from the minute you walked into the bank."

"No, we must leave now. I'll tell you everything you want to know on the train when I feel safe."

"Rebecca, we need to hear the details now," Daniel insisted.

She was sobbing in earnest now and trembling. Gripping her hands together, she whispered, "It was horrible. I remember I was in a hurry, and I didn't like having to stand in line again. I didn't talk to any of the other customers while I waited. The bank was going to close and the tellers were very slow. I worried I wouldn't get all of my errands done. Oh, God, Franklin helped me, and now he's dead. I met him at church and he was such a kind man."

Before she could continue, a messenger from the hotel came rushing inside. He was a tall, lanky boy with pockmarks on his face. "Marshal Ryan? I'm sorry to intrude, but this message I'm supposed to give you is urgent."

He stared at Rebecca while he handed the sealed envelope to Daniel. "Why's she crying?" he asked.

No one answered him. "Ma'am, is there anything I can do to make you feel better?" he asked.

She shook her head. He shrugged in response, then asked Daniel if he wanted him to take back a reply.

Daniel read the contents before answering. "Tell Miss Winthrop I'll be along in a little while."

"She said it was urgent, Marshal," the messenger repeated. "She wants to leave town. She told me so herself just before the doctor went into her room to check on her."

"Go back to the hotel and tell her I'll be there as soon as I finish up a couple of things."

"It ain't *Miss* Winthrop," the messenger said as he started out the doorway. "It's *Lady* Winthrop. She's titled," he added importantly. "The night manager told me so."

Daniel wasn't paying any attention to the boy. Rebecca was using Cole's handkerchief to wipe her tears away. As soon as the door closed behind the messenger, Daniel began to grill Rebecca with questions.

"How many were there?"

"Seven," she answered. "There were seven men. I didn't see all of their faces."

"Start at the beginning and tell us everything," Cole demanded.

She bowed her head, closed her eyes, and then gave a concise account of what had happened inside the bank. By the time she was finished, she was openly sobbing again and clinging to Cole's hand.

"Reliving the nightmare is almost as awful as being there . . ."

Cole patted her. "We know how hard this was for you," he sympathized.

"You've been a tremendous help," Daniel said.

Cole agreed with a nod. "Do you have any more questions for her?" he asked Daniel.

"No, she's told us everything we need to know."

Rebecca stood up, took a calming breath, and said, "You will get all of them, won't you? Promise me you will."

"We promise," Cole answered.

Daniel walked her to the door. "Why don't you take a few minutes to relax before you pack."

"Like it or not, I'm leaving this town today," she threatened. "If you have any decency at all, you won't tell Jessica and Grace that I'm the witness because it would only upset them, and I don't want them to hate me for not coming forward sooner."

"I'm sure they would both understand why you

kept silent, but don't worry. Cole and I don't plan to tell them. And we will leave today," he promised.

"Thank you, Marshal. I shall be ready in one hour."

The guard was waiting to escort Rebecca back to the hotel. He suggested that they alter their route and take one of the streets parallel to the hotel. He was armed to the teeth with a pair of six-shooters and a shotgun. Daniel noticed the way he watched the street as he walked along and decided that Rebecca was in good hands.

"What does Grace want that's so urgent?" Cole asked him.

"Her note just says she wants to talk to me at the hotel before she leaves town. She thinks she's going to get out of her sickbed and drive a wagon. The woman doesn't have the sense God gave her."

"She's got the determination, though," Cole said. "I've got the feeling she could pull it off if we let her."

"We aren't going to let her go anywhere alone," Daniel countered. "Cooper's going to stick to both women until every member of the Blackwater gang has been captured."

"That could take a hell of a long time."

"I don't think so," Daniel said. "If the gang finds out about Rebecca, they'll be coming after her, and, God willing, we'll get every last one of them."

"You're going to use her as bait, aren't you?"

"I'm going to get her to Blackwater alive."

Cole nodded agreement. "I thought Rebecca was the witness, but it was just a guess. No—that isn't true. I hoped it wasn't Jessica."

"I can understand why. She's got enough on her plate now, raising that baby on her own."

Cole was staring out the front window. "Didn't you tell me Grace wanted you to see her at the hotel?"

"That's what her note said," Daniel answered.

"She's crossing the street with Sloan hot on her trail."

"Son of a . . ."

Daniel ran out the doorway just as Grace came hurrying down the boardwalk. He grabbed hold of her hand and pulled her inside the office.

"What in God's name are you doing out of bed?"

His concern for her well-being was evident in his expression. He thought she looked like the walking dead, and he fully expected her to faint at any moment. The left side of her face was still slightly swollen. Daniel wanted to pick her up and carry her back to the hotel. He pulled her to his side and looked out at the street beyond. Sloan was lounging against the hitching post.

"I had to see you," she explained. "The sheriff was eating his breakfast in the dining room, so I slipped out the side door."

"I saw her going down the steps out of the corner of my eye," Sloan interjected. "I had to leave a full plate of food to chase after her."

Grace was trying to hold on to her patience. "Daniel, I must speak to you. I'm sorry if it isn't convenient, but it's terribly important. She looked around the office and then asked, "Isn't Jessica here yet? You did tell us to be here this morning."

"York walked her over to Dr. Lawrence's house to look in on Tilly," Sloan said. "She took the boy with her."

"What in thunder are you women thinking?" Cole snapped. "Three potential witnesses strolling around town without a care in the world. It's enough to make the saints scream. I'm going over to Lawrence's house and take Jessica back to the hotel." He glared at Sloan when he added, "And if I have to drag her, by God I will."

The sheriff backed out of Cole's way and watched him cross the street. Daniel slammed the door in Sloan's face then, giving Grace privacy for their talk.

"Why is Cole so upset?"

"He's upset because you and Rebecca and Jessica are making it impossible for us to protect you."

"You don't think in broad daylight that someone might try . . ."

He interrupted her. "I'm taking you back to the hotel."

"No," she insisted. "I need to tell you something. It's important, Daniel."

She tried to make herself let go of his hand, since she felt it was a sign of weakness for her to cling to the lawman, but she couldn't pull away. She was so scared, she could barely gather her thoughts. What she was about to do was going to change her future irrevocably, and all of her dreams were going to be crushed. There wasn't any other choice, though. She had to do the right thing.

He gave in. "All right, Grace. What did you want to tell me?"

"I'm your witness," she blurted out. "I was the one hiding in the kneehole."

Aside from the muscle in his clenched jaw twitching, Daniel didn't show any reaction to her announcement.

"You're the witness?" he demanded.

"Yes. I'm so sorry I didn't have the courage to come forward sooner, but I was frightened. Jessica and Rebecca had already left the bank. They were telling you the truth. I wasn't, and now I've caused them all sorts of trouble. You'll let them leave now, won't you?"

Daniel didn't answer her. His gut was telling him she was lying. The longer he stood there the angrier he became.

"How many were there?"

Without a pause, she answered, "Seven."

Tears brimmed in her eyes, and Daniel suddenly had the urge to comfort her and shake her at the same time. He didn't give in to either inclination. "All right, I'm taking you back to the hotel, and you can tell me everything."

"But I'm worried about Jessica and Rebecca," she cried. "I believe I've found a way to make certain that they'll be left alone."

Daniel guessed what was coming and let out a loud groan. "Ah, hell, you didn't talk to the reporter, did you?"

The question surprised her, for she had only just come up with the idea. "No, but I want to," she said. "I thought I would go to the newspaper office and ask the gentleman there to print the truth in tomorrow's paper. I'm sure the reporter will be happy to listen to what I have to say."

"You are not going to talk to the reporter." He snapped the command and squeezed her hand to let her know he meant what he said.

She was stunned by his burst of anger. He was furious, she realized, for his blue eyes had turned as cold as winter. She bowed her head. "I thought you would be pleased with my confession. I don't understand your anger, Daniel."

He took a deep breath. "Grace," he began. "Are you telling the truth?"

She jerked her hand away from his and tried to get around him. "There's something else you should know."

"Yes?" Daniel asked.

"The fire . . . it wasn't an accident," she blurted out. "I remember what happened, and I remember . . . apples."

"Apples?" he repeated, clearly not understanding.

She nodded. "I was having trouble sleeping. That isn't unusual," she thought to add. "I never sleep through the night. I thought I heard a peculiar noise coming from downstairs. It sounded like glasses tinkling."

"I don't understand."

"You know . . . when you toast someone and your glass clinks against another glass . . . It was that sound that I thought I heard."

"So what did you do?"

"Tilly wasn't feeling very well, and I didn't want to disturb her, so I put on my robe and my slippers and went downstairs to investigate. If someone was knocking on the front door, I wasn't going to open it, of course. I was going to tell whoever it was to come back in the morning. When I reached the foyer, I noticed the dining room window was wide open. The wind was making the curtains billow into the room. I became alarmed because I remembered closing it before I went up to bed, and I was the last one to go up the stairs."

"What did you do then?" Daniel asked.

"I went into the dining room to shut the window, and that's when I smelled coal oil."

"You mean kerosene?"

"Yes, kerosene," she answered. "I put my hand on the windowsill and it was covered with oil. It was as though someone had only just poured it there."

"And then what happened?"

"Tilly had placed a basket of apples on the kitchen table after supper. One of her daughters had given them to her."

"What do apples have to do with the fire?"

"I could smell apples. I know it sounds crazy, but I think someone was eating one. I wanted to run upstairs and wake Jessica and Tilly, but I was suddenly afraid to move. I could feel the breeze on my arms from the swinging door that connects the kitchen with the dining room, and I heard the squeak the hinges make. I knew someone was rushing toward me. I could feel him coming. I turned and started to scream, but I don't know if I made a sound or not."

"That's when you were struck, wasn't it?"

"I don't remember being hit. I just remember turning, and then you were leaning over me, Daniel, and I was outside . . . in the grass. If Jessica hadn't found me and dragged me out, I would have died in the fire.

"I'm your witness," she whispered once again. "I don't want them to hurt Jessica or Rebecca. They're innocent."

Daniel couldn't resist touching her. He reached out to wipe away a tear from her cheek. "You're also innocent, Grace."

They stared into one another's eyes for a long minute. Daniel was overwhelmed with the desire to keep her safe. He had failed with his wife and his daughter because he hadn't been there to protect them. He decided then and there that he wouldn't let Grace out of his sight. Anyone who tried to harm her would have to go through him first.

"Daniel, are you all right?"

"Yeah, I am."

"You look terribly . . . angry."

"I don't want anything to happen to you, Grace."

He was gripping her shoulders, his hold fierce, protective. He was hurting her, but she knew if she told him so, he'd feel terrible. She gently pulled his hands away and held on to them. "Nothing's going to happen to me."

"I'm going to protect you."

"Yes, you are," she agreed. "And I must protect Jessica and Caleb."

He raised an eyebrow. "Why?" he asked.

"She risked her life for me," she answered.

"What about Rebecca? Do you feel responsible for her too?"

"In a sense I do. She's been so kind and thoughtful."

He put his arm around her shoulders. "Come on. I'm taking you home, Miss Winthrop. No, that isn't right," he teased. "It's Lady Winthrop, isn't it?"

"No, Daniel, it's Grace. Just plain old Grace."

"Ah, Grace. There's nothing plain about you. Nothing at all."

Twenty

$\mathcal{T}$he baby was in his line of fire. He wanted to kill the boy first, but he wouldn't give in to the inclination because the mother would have time to run for cover, and she was his primary target. It was imperative that she die. There was a deputy walking by her side who was fully armed, watchful, and who just might get off a lucky shot of his own if he was given the chance.

Mr. Johnson shifted his position on his belly, determined to wait until all three of them were crossing the street. From his perch on the roof above the general store, he had a nice clear view of the road below, and with his Winchester, he wouldn't miss. *Patience,* he told himself as he felt the surge of excitement rush through him. The guard first, then the woman, then the boy. One, two, three, as easy as can be.

Anticipation made him giddy. The thrill he felt before a kill was as good as being with a woman. No, it was better than that, he thought. Much better.

They were taking their time, strolling along the

boardwalk, stupidly ignorant and blissfully unaware that they had only seconds left to live. Their executioner giggled like a young boy while he waited to seize the opportunity.

Jessica argued with the guard about their destination. She wanted to walk over to the jail, but York was determined to take her back to the hotel. The dourfaced deputy Sloan had hired was a rather plain man with only one vanity, his handlebar mustache. The long black hairs on his upper lip curled out and up over the sides of his nose. The pomade he'd used stiffened and starched each hair, so that when he talked, his mustache didn't move at all.

Jessica took hold of Caleb's hand as she stepped off the boardwalk. York had hold of her elbow and was trying to guide her across. There wasn't any traffic on the road behind the physician's house, for it deadended at the stable around the curve. When Caleb wanted to run ahead, she made certain it was safe for him to do so and then let go of him.

Cole had just turned the corner and was striding down the center of the street toward them when Caleb spotted him. The baby started running. He stumbled twice as he tripped along but quickly regained his feet and continued on. Jessica and York increased their pace to catch up with him. Caleb was chattering away, and Jessica was smiling like a proud mother while she watched her baby's antics. When Caleb was about thirty feet away from Cole, he raised his arms and demanded, "Up," in a roar that echoed down the street.

Mr. Johnson edged up to his knees, swung his Winchester into position, and fired. The guard dropped. Like a pigeon in a shooting gallery, York was moving forward one second and dead on the ground the next.

Jessica screamed. York was facedown in the dirt.

The bullet had sliced through his heart, just as Mr. Johnson intended. He never ever missed.

Jessica fell to her knees and struggled to turn the guard over so that she could help him. There was blood everywhere. "Mr. York," she whimpered. "No . . . no . . . Mr. York . . ."

She reached for the gun in his holster and had just pulled it out when a shot spit the dirt up next to her side. She screamed again, dropped the weapon, and then grabbed hold once again.

"Get down," Cole roared to her as he raced forward. The shots were coming from the roof above the general store, but he couldn't see the gunman's exact position. He kept shouting at Jessica to get the hell out of the street, to duck, but she wasn't listening to him.

She squinted up at the roof as she lifted the gun with both hands and tried to fire. She was shaking so much she almost dropped the gun again, and when she finally fired, the bullet shattered the glass of the second-story window.

The sound of gunfire had frightened Caleb, and he was running back to his mother. "No," Jessica cried out.

Mr. Johnson watched as she ran to intercept her baby. He was toying with her. He was having such a fine time, he couldn't resist playing cat with his little mouse. Because he so enjoyed the look of stark terror on the woman's face, he wanted to prolong the thrill. The boy had quickly come back into range. That was nice. Mr. Johnson smiled as he once again considered killing the boy before the mother so that he could watch her expression. It was bound to be priceless.

She was moving too quickly to suit him. *We can't have that,* he thought with a chuckle as he fired at the ground in front of her. She came to a dead stop. "That's better," he whispered, but then she was moving again, and he had to fire at the ground to get her to stop. Dust sprayed up into her face.

Damned if she didn't start running yet again. God love her—and He would soon have that opportunity, Mr. Johnson thought, if she went right to heaven. Was she as pure as she looked? Mr. Johnson sincerely doubted that. There was no such thing as a pure woman, and he wasn't going to dispatch this woman to heaven or hell quite yet. She had to suffer first. His rules, not God's, but in his mind he was just as omniscient because he too had the power to determine who lived and who died.

"Time's up," he whispered as he aimed the barrel of the rifle at her heart.

Only a few precious seconds had passed since the first shot was fired, but it seemed a lifetime before Cole could reach Jessica. He dove, knocking her to the ground. He rolled onto his back on top of her, his guns drawn and ready as he squinted against the sunlight to find the target.

There . . . in the corner of the roof . . . a flash of metal. "Got you," he muttered a scant second before he opened fire.

His second shot struck his target. The gunman lurched up and back, stumbled forward on his knees, and then plummeted to the ground. Cole shot him three more times as he was falling to his death.

His attention stayed on the outlaw as he slowly rolled to his feet and moved forward. His anger was beyond control. Caleb's screams echoed in his ears. The baby was sitting in the dirt, crying for his mama.

Staggering to her feet, Jessica ran to him. She was too weak to pick Caleb up and fell to her knees beside him. He clawed at her skirt and threw himself against her. She wrapped him in her arms and began to rock back and forth, her sobs overpowering her.

Daniel had heard the shots from the jail and ran the three blocks to Lawrence's house. He saw Jessica and

Caleb in the street, slowed down to make sure they were all right, and then continued on to Cole, who was standing over the dead gunman. Panting, Daniel watched as Cole kicked the man over onto his back. Every bone in the man's face had been crushed by the fall. The damage was so severe his own mother wouldn't have recognized him now.

"Do you know who he is?" Daniel asked.

Cole shook his head. "Maybe Rebecca can tell us . . . if she can recognize him. He was probably one of the gang."

"Yeah, well, Grace just told me she was in the bank. She swears she's the witness."

Cole was taken aback by the announcement. "Which one's telling the truth?"

"Damned if I know," Daniel muttered. He squatted down next to the body and began to search the pockets, looking for identification.

Cole waited for another minute or two until he was certain he'd gotten his anger under control. Then he slowly crossed the street to Jessica, who was doubled over, hugging her son. Cole put his arms around her and lifted her up. She tried to jerk away from him. He noticed the six-shooter in her hand and quickly grabbed it, tossing it on the ground behind him.

Caleb reached for him, but Jessica wouldn't let the boy go. She was still trembling and taking deep, gasping breaths.

"Why the hell didn't you drop when I told you to?" Cole asked in a voice as smooth as molasses.

What he said and how he said it confused her. She couldn't tell if he was angry or not. "What did you say?"

"I asked you to explain why you didn't dive for cover when I ordered you to," he repeated.

"You're angry."

"Yes, I am."

"You want to shout at me, don't you?"

"Yes, I do," he admitted. "But I won't. It would upset Caleb, and yelling is pointless. Next time, Jessica, do as I say. I can't protect you unless you do."

"Next time?" she shouted.

Caleb burst into tears again.

"Ah, hell, now look what you've done," Cole muttered.

Daniel joined them. Without a thought as to what he was doing, he took the baby away from Jessica, turning so that Caleb wouldn't see the body behind them.

"Poor baby," he whispered as he gently patted Caleb's back.

Properly soothed, the baby put his head down on Daniel's shoulder and stuck his thumb in his mouth.

"Did you find any identification?" Cole asked him.

"No," Daniel answered. "His pockets were empty."

Jessica grabbed hold of Cole's hand. It had finally dawned on her what he had said. "I didn't do as you ordered because I wasn't thinking. I only wanted to get to my son to protect him from that madman."

"I understand," he said. "But, Jessica, I can't . . ."

She squeezed his hand as she interrupted. "I'm sorry if my conduct upsets you or offends you, but I swear to you, I'd do it again. No one's going to hurt my son. Dear God, I can't . . . stop . . . thinking what almost happened. Caleb could have been killed."

He didn't have to reach for her. She came into his arms willingly, desperately needing to be comforted.

He hugged her tight. "You aren't going to cry, are you?" he asked gruffly. "You're going to upset Caleb if you do."

"No, I won't cry, but you don't understand," she whispered. "It's my fault Mr. York is dead. He was such a nice man. He'd be alive if it weren't for me."

"Hush now," he ordered. "None of this was your doing. Poor baby. It's all over now. I know it was frightening."

"You don't understand."

"What don't I understand, sweetheart?"

He was more stunned than she appeared to be that he had used the endearment. What was even more amazing to him was the fact that it had come so easily.

"I didn't know how to shoot that gun."

"You did just fine."

"No, I didn't," she argued. "And I have to know how."

"Jessie, I know it was a close call, but I did get the bastard. I can protect you. Have a little faith in me and let me do my job."

"I do have faith in you, but I still have to know how to protect my son."

Daniel carried Caleb back to his mother. "Is she all right?" he asked Cole.

"Yeah, she's just shaken."

"It was me," she blurted out. "I was there."

"What?" Daniel said.

It suddenly dawned on Cole what she was trying to tell him. "Let me guess," he muttered.

She stared up at Daniel over Cole's shoulder. "I'm your witness."

"Ah, hell." Daniel whispered the expletive with a sigh.

Caleb promptly repeated it.

"Now what?" Cole asked as he tightened his hold on Jessica. She had willingly gone to him, and he wasn't going to let go.

"What's going on here?" Daniel asked, his anger mounting as he spoke.

"Know what I think?" Cole said. He squeezed Jessica before adding, "It was damned crowded under that desk."

Twenty-One

The office in the front of the jail was crowded with lawmen. Marshal Jack Cooper, head of operations in Salt Lake City, and two young deputies named Spencer and Cobb, had just arrived in Rockford Falls. The three men had ridden hard and were parched and covered with a layer of dust.

Cooper was a good friend of Daniel's. The two men had worked on several investigations in the past, though admittedly none of them had involved women, and all of the cases had been far less convoluted. Like Daniel, Cooper was no stranger to danger or the bizarre behavior of criminals. He once escorted a smooth-tongued self-proclaimed reverend who had brutally killed and mutilated sixteen redheaded men because he believed the color of their hair indicated that they were spawns of the devil. The crazy loon constantly misquoted scripture, insisted that he heard God's voice every day at noon on the dot, and refused counsel. The Lord, he declared, would step forward and testify on his behalf. Ironically, the judge who heard the case just happened to have carrot orange hair, and it didn't take him any time at all to recommend to the jury that the guilty man be hanged.

Cooper had done and seen it all. Deeply tanned with creases at the corners of his brown eyes and prematurely silver-tipped hair, he looked more like a senator than a lawman. Nothing ever fazed him. After reading Daniel's notes, he tossed the pad on the desk and sat down. The two deputies leaned against the wall behind him.

"It seems to me that you're letting these three women run your investigation," he remarked as he stretched his long legs out and crossed one ankle over the other.

Cole heard the comment as he came in the door. He had just returned from the hotel.

Daniel introduced him to Cooper and his deputies. "This is Marshal Clayborne," he said. "He's new to the job."

The deputies rushed forward to shake his hand. Spencer looked awestruck and asked, "Is your first name Cole? Are you *that* Clayborne brother?"

"Yes," Cole answered.

"I've heard all about you, sir."

"Is that right?" Cole asked, wondering what he had heard.

"Yes, sir," Spencer said. He looked at the other deputy and whispered, "Clayborne's a legend in Montana."

Cobb was dutifully impressed. Cooper saw Cole roll his eyes in exasperation, and grinned in reaction.

"Why don't you boys go on over to the hotel now and get cleaned up. After you eat, take the watch from the sheriff and his men for a while."

"Yes, sir," Spencer said. He nudged Cobb out the doorway but paused to look at Cole. "Marshal Clayborne, sir? Is it true what happened down in Spring-field?"

"Don't believe everything you hear," Cole replied.

"But it's true, isn't it? You shot all four of the Murphy gang before any of them could get their guns out, didn't you, sir?"

"Get going, Spencer," Cooper ordered. "You're embarrassing Marshal Clayborne."

Cole laughed. As soon as the door closed behind the deputies, he said, "They look awfully young."

"They are young," Cooper agreed. "But they're fast with a gun and they want to be lawmen. They're both tougher than they look."

Daniel spoke to Cole then. "I've decided to change the plans. Cooper's going to take Rebecca to Blackwater, and you and I will take Grace and Jessica. We'll split up and all meet in Red Arrow on Thursday, barring any unforeseen problems."

"That's fine with me," Cole said.

"I thought we should all travel together," Cooper interjected. "But Daniel thinks it's safer if we take separate trains."

"Three beautiful women are bound to draw a lot of attention," Cole said.

"Cooper just told me there's a signed order from Judge Abbott," Daniel said.

"Who's Abbott?"

"A judge in Salt Lake," Daniel answered. "The judge in Blackwater wired Abbott asking for his help in getting our cooperation. Since we're on special assignment, we don't have to do as they ask, but I think we should go along. One of these women saw the murders, and by God, she will testify."

"The judge in Blackwater is hopping mad," Cooper interjected. "I can't blame him. First, Daniel wires him and tells him he might have a witness. Then the women say they weren't there, and then they all say that they were. Have you figured out which one was really inside the bank at the time of the robbery?"

"Not yet," Daniel said. "I thought I'd know after each one gave me the details of what happened."

"But?" Cooper prodded.

"They each have their own version. It's maddening."

"If you had to guess, which one do you think was really there?" Cooper asked.

Daniel and Cole said the name at the same time. "Rebecca."

"Interesting," Cooper replied.

"The details she gave us are convincing. She was able to describe some of the men, and she even knew a couple of their names."

"Jessica hasn't been able to tell us much yet. She's still pretty shaken over the shooting."

Cooper said, "I've gotta tell you one thing. These women sure do intrigue me. I can understand why they would all deny being there. They'd be scared and they have all surely heard about the witnesses the Blackwater boys butchered. What I can't understand is why they'd all change their tune and say they were there."

"Daniel thinks they all joined forces," Cole said. "Sheriff Sloan put the three of them together in one of the cells, and Daniel thinks that's when they hatched their plan."

"What do you know about these women? Have you looked into their backgrounds?"

"We don't know much . . . yet," Daniel said. "I'm having each one of them investigated. It's a slow process, though, and we'll probably be in Blackwater before the information comes back. I do know bits and pieces, but even that hasn't been verified."

"Such as?" Cooper asked.

"According to people she's met in Rockford Falls, Rebecca was born in New York City and lived with her parents and her cousins in a tenement. There were nine of them in a two-bedroom apartment. Both the parents drank themselves into early graves. Rebecca is self-educated, and about three years ago, she moved to St. Louis and severed ties with her relatives. She met a businessman and she's planning to marry him in the fall. She goes to church every Sunday and works in the library."

"If she's in love, she's probably trying to protect him. She's got to know this gang could use him to get to her," Cooper said. "What about Grace and Jessica? What do you know about them?"

"I don't know anything about Grace yet, other than the fact that she came here from England and that she wants to buy a ranch. I wired some contacts in London, but I haven't heard back from them yet."

"And Jessica?" Cooper asked.

"Her mother died about two years ago. Her father deserted the family when she was a little girl. Jessica came to Rockford Falls from Chicago to help with the delivery of her aunt's baby. The aunt was her mother's sister, and she was the only family she had left."

"You're talking as though she's dead. Is she?" Cooper asked.

"Yes," Daniel answered. "She died a couple of hours after childbirth from hemorrhage. She and her husband had been married for over fifteen years when she finally got pregnant. Her husband didn't want the baby, though. After his wife died, he didn't stay around long enough to name the baby. He left town the very next day and hasn't been heard of since."

"What happened to the baby?" Cooper asked.

"Jessica happened," Daniel answered. "She's very young, but she's doing a hell of a job raising the boy on her own."

"That's a hard burden for a single woman to take on," Cooper said.

"She's up to the task," Cole said. "Jessica's strong."

"Sounds like she is," Cooper agreed. "Her baby would be a good reason for her to keep silent if she were your witness. She'd probably go to great lengths to protect him."

"Grace probably had someone she was trying to protect too," Cole said.

"She does," Daniel replied. "Her parents."

"Where did you get all this information?"

"Tilly MacGuire," Daniel answered. "Like I said before, it hasn't been verified. The woman's a wealth of information. She seems to know everything about everyone in this town and all the folks passing through. She's been very helpful."

Cooper stood up and stretched his arms. "When are you going to leave for Blackwater?" he asked.

"I can't go until tomorrow. The doctor wants Grace to stay in bed another day. It's too bad you can't get some sleep before you head out. You look like hell."

"You don't look so good yourself, Daniel."

"I'm fine," he replied. "Cole, when are you going to take Jessica?"

"Wait a minute," Cole said. "I can't take Caleb with us. That's out of the question."

Daniel agreed. "What are we going to do with him?"

Cole had already considered the problem. "I don't want to leave him here. Everyone knows who he belongs to," he explained. "I want to hide him, and I think I've thought of the perfect place."

"Are you thinking about Rosehill?"

"What's Rosehill?" Cooper asked.

"My ranch," Cole answered. "My mother lives there, and my brothers and my sister come and go. Mama Rose is in Scotland now with my sister and her husband, and they won't be back for another month."

"Then where are you going to put Caleb?"

"Tom and Josey Norton."

Daniel smiled. "That's good, Cole. Tom won't let

anything happen to the boy, but Josey just might kill him with her cooking."

"That's a risk we have to take," Cole replied. "I'm going to tell Tom to disappear with Caleb for a little while. If Jessica is the witness, I don't want the Blackwater gang going after her son."

He motioned to the map spread out on Daniel's desk. "Where's Red Arrow?" he asked. "I've never heard of it before."

"Blink and you'll miss it," Cooper said. "It's a tiny hole in the ground and the turning-around point for the train. The town boasts a saloon, a whorehouse, and a stable. In Red Arrow you sleep outside 'cause they don't have any hotels. It's a godforsaken place."

"It's surrounded by deep caverns," Daniel remarked. "It's barren, but beautiful."

"I think I should leave Jessica with Spencer and Cobb while I take Caleb to the Nortons. I'll swing back here for her."

"That won't work," Daniel said.

"It's safer for Jessica."

"It still won't work."

"Why not?" Cole asked.

"Because Jessica will be going with you."

Cole didn't like the idea one bit. "She'll slow me down," he said. "And like I said, it's safer. Once I get Caleb to the Nortons, I plan to cut down through some rough terrain. It's hard riding."

"You aren't married, are you, son?" Cooper said.

"No, I'm not married, and I'm sure as certain not your son. You're old, Cooper, but you aren't that old."

Cooper laughed. "I've never been married," he admitted. "Daniel wouldn't let me in on this investigation if I were a family man. He only wants bachelors in case one of us gets shot. My brother's married, though."

"Is that right?" Cole said, wondering why Cooper was telling him about his family.

"Yes, he is," Cooper said. "He's got five girls and two boys, and I swear to you that if you tried to take one of those seven children away from his mama, there would be hell to pay. Just how do you suppose you're going to get Caleb away from his mama?"

Cole didn't anticipate any problems. "I'll simply explain the situation to her."

He paused when he saw the look of disbelief on Cooper's face, then went on to defend his position. "I know Jessica won't like being separated from her son, and I expect she'll argue, but in the end, she'll go along. I've gotten to know her pretty well in the last two days, and after I've explained the situation, I'm positive she'll be reasonable."

Twenty-Two

She threatened to kill him. Jessica was anything but reasonable. Cole had believed that, because he was a U.S. marshal, she would do whatever he told her to do. That was his first mistake. Letting her get close to his gun was his second. He hadn't realized how arrogant he'd been with his assumptions until she grabbed his gun and threatened to put a hole through his black heart if he touched her son.

After packing his satchels, he had gone to her hotel room, knocked on the door, and when she'd let him inside—keeping the door open so that the deputy assigned to protect her could see that nothing inappropriate was going on—he had quickly explained that he was going to take Caleb north and that she was going to wait in Rockford Falls until he returned—then she was going to Texas.

Fortunately, Caleb slept through the whispered argument that followed. The baby was curled up in a ball on the cot, his chin wet with drool. He looked like an angel—but the fire in his mother's eyes was anything but angelic. She was acting like a bear determined to protect her young.

"You're out of your mind if you think I'm going to let you take my son."

"Jessica, stop waving my gun around. It might go off. Give it back to me."

Deputy Spencer stepped into the room. "Marshal, do you need some help?"

Cole shook his head. "No, it's all right."

Jessica stood at the foot of the double bed, the gun pointing to the floor now. She was tense and out of sorts, and there were dark circles under her eyes. The strain was beginning to show on her.

"You're going to be reasonable about this," he said.

She shook her head. "I'm not going to Blackwater, and you're not going to touch Caleb."

"I know it's difficult for you to give me your son, but I promise you he'll be safe and well taken care of."

"Get out."

He ignored the command as he crossed to the chair adjacent to the bed and sat down. His arm deliberately brushed hers when he walked past her, and he could have easily snatched the gun out of her hand then, but didn't.

"I told you to leave."

"I'm not going anywhere until you listen to reason."

She glanced from the deputy to Cole and then back again. Cole had a gun in his other holster, which made him armed and dangerous, and Spencer had his hand on the hilt of his gun.

"I can't make up my mind which one of you I'm going to shoot first."

Spencer glanced at Cole to see what he was going to do about her threat.

Cole ignored the deputy and kept his gaze on Jessica.

"Please leave before I do something you'll regret."

"Spencer," Cole said, "close the door. Jessica and I are going to have a private talk."

"We are not," she whispered.

"Are you sure you don't want me to stay, Marshal Clayborne?" Spencer asked as he reached for the doorknob.

"I'm sure."

Spencer looked disappointed. Cole waited until the door was shut and then told Jessica to sit down. She shook her head and continued to stand there glaring at him.

He smiled at her. In fact, he couldn't take his eyes off her. She'd changed her dress and looked even prettier than she had an hour before. She wore an old, faded honey-colored dress that had probably been the color of gold at one time. The dress, noticeably threadbare at the elbows and frayed at the cuffs, was probably a hand-me-down, but on her it was still beautiful. Her hair was tied back behind her neck with a thin white ribbon. Strands had worked free of the confinement and curled around her ears. She defined sensuality and femininity, and when she took a step toward him, the light scent of lilacs came with her.

Damn, but she was something else.

"What are you staring at?" she demanded.

"You," he answered. "You're a very beautiful woman, Jessica."

The compliment took the wind out of her. He didn't order her to sit down this time. He asked.

"I want you to listen to what I have to say, and when I'm finished, if you still want to shoot me, I'll let you."

"You know I won't shoot you," she muttered as she handed the gun back to him. "I'd like to," she hastily qualified. "But I won't. The noise would wake the baby."

He laughed. "You're all talk, Jessie."

"You can't make me go to Texas."

"Yes, I can," he countered, his voice firm now, unyielding.

She buried her face in her hands. "I didn't do anything wrong. Why don't you leave Caleb and me alone?"

"You know I can't do that."

She put her head down on his shoulder and quietly wept. He dug his handkerchief out of his pocket and handed it to her. He didn't tell her to stop crying, figuring she needed to get rid of the tension inside her, but he hated knowing that he was part of the reason she was so distressed.

Long minutes passed before she was able to gain control. Cole held her close, noticing how soft she felt against him.

"I know you didn't do anything wrong," he whispered. "The judge down in Texas wants you to come to Blackwater."

"But what about Rebecca and Grace," she cried out. "Are they—"

"Hush, you'll wake the baby," he reminded her. "I don't want you to worry about your friends. Daniel will watch out for them."

"How can I not worry?"

"Trust me," he replied.

"I'll try. But, I can't stop thinking about Rebecca and Grace. They're in danger because of me, aren't they?"

"Yes, they are. Your names were published in the paper as potential witnesses, and I don't think the men who murdered those innocent people will stop until they've gotten every one of you. I can understand why none of you would want to admit you were there, but . . ."

She started crying. The sight of her tears made Cole feel like a heel. He started to reach for her, then stopped himself.

"I don't like women who cry," he said.

"Then you must hate me. I cry all the time. I don't cry in front of Caleb, though. It would upset him. Sometimes . . . late at night, I pull the covers over my head so no one can hear me and I have a good cry."

He put his arm around her and pulled her to his side. "I don't like hearing that. What makes you cry at night?"

"I get scared."

"Of what?"

"Failing."

"You have a hard life, Jessie."

"Oh, no, I have a wonderful life with Caleb," she whispered. "I'm very content. I just get . . . tired sometimes. Everything was going so well until the day I walked into the bank. I'm ready to tell you what happened if you want me to," she added. "Then you'll believe me. I know I've lied to you. I shouldn't have told you I wasn't there, but I was trying to protect Caleb."

"I'm going to help you protect your son. I've found a safe place for him, Jessica. You can't take him with you to Blackwater, and you know you have to go."

She finally accepted the inevitable. "Yes, I know. Couldn't I leave him with Tilly? She loves him and would take care of him. Caleb knows her. He wouldn't be afraid or feel abandoned."

Cole wouldn't hear of it. "Jessie, everyone here knows who Caleb belongs to, and it would be easy to get him away from Tilly. She's an old woman. I don't want to leave him in Rockford Falls."

"Why would anyone want to take him?" she asked.

"Holding your son hostage is a good way to make you keep silent during the trial."

"Oh, God."

"Jessica, the couple I've thought of will take good care of him. Let me tell you about them. They're older . . . like grandparents . . ."

He spent a good fifteen minutes telling her everything he knew about Tom and Josey Norton. He went into great detail about Tom's background, stressing the fact that he had quite a reputation with a gun and that he was now a lawman, but he didn't mention Josey's lack of skills in the kitchen. When he had run out of things to tell her, Jessica didn't seem to be quite as resistant to the idea.

"You said they always wanted children?" she asked.

"Yes," he answered.

"If you had a son, would you leave him with the Nortons?"

"Yes," he said again.

"I'll have to meet them before I decide. If I don't like them and I don't feel that they'll take good care of Caleb, I'm not leaving him with them."

She was determined to go with him, and nothing he could say would make her budge on that issue.

"When do we leave?" she asked. "To go north with Caleb?"

"Ah, Jessie, don't start crying again. It's going to be all right. You want to know that he's safe, don't you?"

"Yes, yes, of course I do. It's just that I don't know the Nortons, and I . . ."

He started for the door. "Pack light, Jessica. One bag for you and one for Caleb."

"I have to talk to Grace before I go anywhere."

"It's out of the question."

"Will we be coming back to Rockford Falls after we take Caleb?"

"No, we're going directly to Texas."

"What about my things? Everything I own is packed in Grace's wagon."

"I'll have it taken over to the livery stable. The owner can keep an eye on it. You can ride a horse, can't you?"

"Yes," she said, though she didn't add the fact that she couldn't ride well. "I'd like to purchase a gun before we leave, and I'd like you to teach me how to use it. I want to be accurate."

He didn't like hearing that she wanted a weapon. "Just aim and shoot," he said. "That's all there is to it. You don't need to carry a gun anyway."

"Yes, I do," she argued. "Will you teach me how to use it?"

"You already shot York's gun."

"I want to be accurate," she insisted.

He didn't waste time debating the point. "We'll leave as soon as Caleb wakes up. Now what?" he asked when she shook her head at him.

"He has to eat first."

"Fine," he said. "After he eats, we'll leave. You might want to pack some food he likes," he thought to add.

"How long will it take us to get to the Nortons' home?"

"Not long," he promised. "And, Jessie, I don't want you to tell anyone where we're taking Caleb. Don't even say Norton's name again, because someone might overhear. All right?"

"Yes."

He was walking out the doorway when she called out to him. "Cole?"

"Yes?"

"Promise me you won't let anything happen to my son."

"I promise."

Part Three

And time remembered is grief forgotten,
And frosts are slain and flowers begotten,

Twenty-Three

Rebecca sat on the stone bench in the small garden in the back of the hotel. Her packed valises were on the ground beside her. It was safe and quiet, and very secluded this time of day, for none of the other guests wanted to venture out into the hot afternoon sun. The garden was surrounded on all sides by a high brick wall and thick pruned evergreens. Spencer and Cobb stood guard by the door leading out from the atrium, while their superior, Marshal Cooper, paced in agitation. Impatient to get going, he was waiting for the private coach they'd ordered to arrive.

She was concerned that Grace and Jessica would see her leave.

After checking the time, she glanced at the doorway. "I feel terrible not saying good-bye to Jessica and Grace, but I don't want them to know I'm going to Texas to look at the man they're holding. They'll worry about me," she added. "I hope we don't run into them when we leave the hotel."

"You don't have to worry about that," Cooper said. "Neither lady will see you leave."

"How can you be so certain?"

"Grace has been ordered to stay in bed until tomorrow, and Marshal Ryan has a guard posted at her door. He isn't going to let her out, and he isn't going to let her have visitors."

"What about Jessica?"

"She left with Marshal Clayborne a couple of hours ago."

"What do you mean, she left? Where did she go?" Rebecca cried out. "Did she have an errand to do? Will she be back today?"

"No."

"Where is she?"

"She's in good hands," Cooper said. "You shouldn't worry about her."

"How long ago did she leave? Did you say a couple of hours?"

"Yes," he answered. "We should have left then too, but finding a decent coach has taken time. You're certain you won't ride a horse to the train station?"

"I'm certain. I was raised in the city, Marshal, and as I explained before, I have absolutely no experience riding. I'd break my neck."

"All right then," he said. "It shouldn't be much longer before the coach gets here. We'll just wait."

"You still haven't told me where Jessica has gone."

Cooper braced himself before looking directly at Rebecca. He didn't want her to know the effect she was having on him, but, Lord, it was difficult to keep himself from staring. She was an incredibly beautiful woman, and with the sun beating down on her golden hair, she looked as though she were wearing a halo. The first sight of her angelic face had all but knocked the legs out from under him. Daniel really should have warned him, he decided, so that he could have prepared himself.

Spencer and Cobb were openly besotted with all three women. Since meeting them, they had behaved like boys who had just discovered the opposite sex. It was damned disgusting.

Slowly lowering his gaze, he asked Rebecca to repeat her question.

"I want to know where Jessica and Cole have gone."

"I don't know their destination."

"North," Spencer blurted out.

Cooper gave the deputy a look that suggested he not say another word. "Cole and Jessica took the baby to a friend's house."

"Was it one of Cole's friends?" she asked. "It must be," she added. "Jessica's friends are in Chicago . . . except for Grace and me. We're her dear friends. Why did she need to take Caleb away? And why won't you tell me where she's gone? You're a marshal, for heaven's sake. You should know."

"Sorry, but I don't know," he said.

"I just worry about her."

"The three of you have become close, haven't you?"

"Tragic circumstances forced us together, and we found we had quite a lot in common."

Cooper felt sorry for Rebecca. She sounded so forlorn and looked so damned vulnerable.

"You're going to see both of your friends real soon," he promised.

"I will?" she asked eagerly. "When?"

"Jessica and Cole and Grace and Daniel will all catch up with us."

She frowned in confusion. "I don't understand. Are you telling me that Grace and Jessica are going to Texas too?"

"Yes."

"But why? I'm the witness."

"I realize that," he replied. "However, we have to keep the other women safe until after the trial. Once you've testified, the ordeal will be over. Until then, all of you need guards. Besides, Judge Rafferty wants all three of you."

"How soon will I see them?"

"They're meeting us in Red Arrow," he answered. "We'll probably get there before Cole and Jessica, but they might surprise us and meet our train."

"Red Arrow's the last stop then? Does that mean I have to ride a horse to Blackwater?"

Her worry made him smile. "You can ride with me, or I'll find a buggy somewhere."

She stared down at her hands and whispered, "This is all wrong. If I had come forward sooner, Grace and Jessica wouldn't be living in fear."

"Why didn't you tell the truth in the beginning? Was it fear?"

"Yes," she said.

"Ma'am, you can get into serious trouble lying to an officer of the law," Deputy Cobb called out. His friend Spencer nodded his agreement.

"You could go to jail for that offense," Spencer added.

"What does it matter?" Rebecca asked. "I'm already in trouble. I'm going to be hunted by those criminals, and it will be a miracle if I survive. I don't understand why they haven't tried yet. What are they waiting for? Why haven't they tried to silence me?"

"They've been busy, that's why." Daniel answered her question from the doorway.

He came down the stairs and handed Cooper a telegram. "Another bank's been robbed," he said. "Sixty miles southeast of here."

Cooper swore. "Was it clean?"

Daniel looked grim. "No."

"What did you mean when you asked Daniel if it was clean?" Rebecca asked.

Daniel turned to answer her. "He was asking me if there were any casualties."

Rebecca paled. "How many were killed?"

"Three men," Daniel answered. "All of them were employees of the bank."

"Those poor men," she whispered.

Daniel had motioned to Cooper to follow him to the corner of the garden. In a low voice he said, "There was something different about this one."

"What?" Cooper asked.

"Every desk inside the bank was overturned, and a copy of the *Rockford Gazette* was nailed to the wall. There was blood all over it."

"They're telling us they know we have a witness."

Daniel nodded. "Let's get the hell out of here."

Twenty-Four

Traveling with a toddler wasn't difficult; it was a nightmare. The baby didn't know how to be quiet. Most of what he said didn't make any sense, but he still expected and demanded an answer anyway, and Cole was pretty certain he chattered nonstop just to hear the sound of his voice echoing through the forest. His favorite word was still *no*. He whispered it, shouted it, whined it, and sang it, and by the time they stopped for the night, Cole was sure he'd said the word at least two hundred times.

It was almost sunset when they finally made camp in a secluded area by a small horseshoe-shaped lake. Jagged rock ledges, some as high as fifty feet, jutted out over the water in spots and offered protection from the rain and wind. More important, no one could sneak up on them during the night. There was only one way into camp, and that was on the path that bordered one side of the lake.

While Cole saw to the horses, Jessica fed Caleb his dinner. The baby was far more interested in exploring his surroundings than eating, and it took considerable coaxing by his mother to get him to cooperate.

Cole wasn't worried about all the noise Caleb was making, because he knew they weren't being followed. He'd backtracked twice just to make certain. The baby needed to run and play. He had been forced to sit still on his mother's lap for most of the day, but he seemed to be making up for lost time now. Full of vitality, he raced in circles from one end of the clearing to the other, chattering away a mile a minute. Every once in a while he would burst into laughter over what Cole decided must have been a private joke only a toddler could appreciate. His shoulders would shake with merriment.

The kid was a charmer, even when he was having a full-blown tantrum because Jessica wouldn't let him go into the water. All her energies were spent trying to turn his attention, but for some reason, when Cole told Caleb to do something, he did it. He told him to sit, and the baby promptly did just that. Caleb had already taken off his shoes and socks and sat perched on top of one of the saddles under the overhang, watching Cole brush the horses. His undershirt had ridden up to the top of his belly, his nappy had slid to the tilt of his hips, and he looked about as happy as a baby could be.

His mother, on the other hand, looked like hell. She was clearly exhausted. She reminded him of his little sister's rag doll after it had been left out in the rain and the sun too long. Her hair hung in clumps, her white blouse was covered with dust and the strawberry jam Caleb had smeared on it while eating his biscuit, and there were smudges all over her cheeks. He still thought she looked too damned sexy for her own good . . . and his peace of mind.

Jessica was too tired to eat, until he convinced her she needed the nourishment. He coaxed her in much the same way she'd coaxed her son, but he was smart enough not to mention that fact to her. In her present state of mind, she wouldn't be amused.

He was starving and ate two helpings of the ham, beans, biscuits, and sugar cookies. He kept his eye on her while he ate. She was definitely in a mood tonight if her frowns were any indication. After suffering her stony silence for several minutes, he gave up and asked her to tell him what was wrong.

"Why didn't you tell me we would be camping out tonight? You should have warned me."

"Would you have done anything different if I had told you?"

She started to nod, then stopped. "I don't know, but I would have insisted that you select a safer spot," she said.

"This is about as safe as I could find," he replied. "No one can get to us from behind, and I can hear anyone coming down the path."

"That isn't what I mean," she said. "And now you've started a fire. I can't be in three places at once."

He wasn't sure what she was riled up about. He leaned back against the rock and stared at her. "We'll need the fire later," he said. "It's going to get cold in the middle of the night. It always does up here in the mountains."

She threaded her fingers through her hair and closed her eyes. "Did you have to set up camp next to a lake?"

"The horses need water, Jessie, and so do we," he reasoned.

She didn't care if his explanation was logical or not. "Don't you realize the enticement the water is for Caleb? I won't sleep a wink tonight, worrying about him. What if he wakes up and wanders away? He could get lost in the forest, or drown, or step on a snake . . ."

"Jessica, calm down. I'm not going to let anything happen to him."

She acted as though he hadn't said a word. "He could fall in the fire or step on a hot ember," she continued. "What were you thinking?"

Although he did understand her concerns, he was a little insulted that she didn't trust him to look after her and her son. "I'm not going to let him get burned, drowned, bitten, or lost."

"I'm still going to worry," she whispered. She glanced over at Caleb to make sure he was all right, saw that he was digging in the dirt with a stick he'd found, and turned back to the lake. In the fading light, the water appeared to be on fire. The burnished orange sheen was a lovely sight.

"You know what I think?" Cole said, drawing her back to the conversation.

"No, what?" she asked on a weary sigh.

"You need a bath."

She turned back to him. "Excuse me?"

"I said you need a bath. Take your clothes off and go swimming. It'll be good for you. You're hot and tired, and the water will make you feel better. Go ahead. I'll take Caleb in with me. I'll keep my back turned if you're worried about your modesty, but out here folks have to be practical."

She glanced back over her shoulder at the lake. "I'm not worried about modesty. I know you wouldn't take advantage of our circumstances. You can't."

If she hadn't added the last comment, he would have taken what she had said as a compliment, for in his mind, she had just admitted that she trusted him.

"I can't?" he repeated, his curiosity piqued. "Why can't I?"

"Why can't you take advantage of our situation?"

"Yes."

Her smile was heart-stopping. The woman was something else all right, and he realized then how difficult it was becoming for him to keep his hands off her.

"Because you're a United States marshal," she patiently reminded him.

"And that means?" he prodded.

"It means you've taken an oath. You're here to protect me, not . . ." She was going to say the word "dally," then changed her mind. ". . . you know."

He couldn't make up his mind if he wanted to laugh or groan. He gritted his teeth in frustration, for he finally understood what she was telling him. He decided to set her straight.

"Jessica, contrary to what you might imagine, marshals aren't neutered when they're sworn in. Giving up sex isn't part of the job description."

Her eyes widened. "Are you saying . . ."

"Damned right I am."

He expected her to blush or at the very least try to change the subject. She shrugged instead. "I'm not going to worry," she announced. She stared at the lake a long minute before nervously adding, "Should I?"

The longer he thought about the conversation and her bizarre opinions, the more exasperated he became. "I'll tell you when you should worry. All right?"

She laughed. "Yes, all right."

"Do you want to go swimming or not?" he asked. "Caleb, quit throwing dirt and come here."

The baby dropped his stick and came running. Cole sat him on his lap and took his undershirt off.

"Is the water deep?" Jessica asked.

"I don't know," Cole answered as he unfastened the ties holding Caleb's nappy secure. "It probably is in the middle. Why? Can't you swim?"

"Not very well," she admitted. "I haven't had much practice."

"Didn't you go swimming when you were a little girl?"

She shook her head. "There wasn't time for such frivolity."

Cole looked at her. "Why wasn't there time?"

"I was busy."

He could tell from her tone of voice she didn't want to talk about growing up. If he'd been a sensitive man, he might have heeded the unspoken suggestion and changed the subject. Sensitivity wasn't one of his attributes, however. "Doing what?" he asked.

She sighed. "I helped my mother in the shop where she worked . . . a lady's dress shop," she qualified. "When I was younger, I stayed with neighbors or helped at school. There wasn't much time to play."

"It was just the two of you, wasn't it? Your father left."

"Yes, he left."

"Do you know where he is?"

"I heard that he died, but I don't know if that's true or not. Are you taking Caleb in the water now?"

"Yes."

"You'll hold him tight?" she asked. "He's slippery when he's wet."

Cole pulled his shirt over his head and tossed it aside. Then he removed his gunbelt and stood up. She hastily turned her attention to the lake, but not before she noticed how muscled his chest and upper arms were. His skin was deeply tanned, indicating he had spent long hours in the sun bare-chested. There was a mat of dark blond hair trailing down to his belly button, and, God, she really shouldn't have been looking. Cole was a handsome man. She would have had to be blind not to notice his steely blue eyes, but what made him most attractive to her was his behavior toward her son. He had the patience of Job. He was gentle and soft-spoken with Caleb, and nothing the little one did seemed to bother him.

He'd make a wonderful father. She pushed the thought aside the second it popped into her mind. She didn't need him or any other man, she reminded herself. She and Caleb were doing just fine the way they were.

"I wish I had been able to talk to Grace before we left. I promised to help her find a ranch. She offered me a job, and it would have been an ideal setting to raise my son. He'd have room to run."

"What could you do on a ranch?"

Her spine stiffened. "I could do lots of things. I've never been afraid of hard work," she added.

"You don't need to get mad. I wasn't insulting you or challenging you. I was simply curious."

"Grace should know what's going on. I would have told her to go ahead and leave without Caleb and me and that we'd catch up with her in Denver. She's under tremendous pressure, and time's running out for her."

Cole didn't understand, but Jessica refused to explain. "If Grace wants you to know her personal business, she'll tell you. I should have taken my belongings out of the wagon. I hope Grace doesn't feel she has to look after them."

"Quit worrying," he ordered. "She'll be fine, and you'll be seeing her real soon."

Her attention was turned when Caleb threw himself into her arms. He wasn't wearing a stitch of clothing, and he was rank.

"I'll get the soap," she said.

"Jessie?"

"Yes?" she answered as she eased the baby off her lap.

"You might want to close your eyes for a minute."

She didn't ask why. She simply squeezed her eyes shut. Curiosity got the better of her, though, and she finally had to know. "You didn't take all of your clothes off, did you?"

"Sure did," he answered cheerfully. "Caleb and I are buck naked."

She wanted to look. She convinced herself that she was merely curious because she'd never seen a naked man before. She really ought to, shouldn't she, since she was a mother? She peeked, but with only one eye. She was disappointed because she'd waited too long. All she saw was Cole's backside and thighs as he moved into the water. She found it quite odd that every inch of his back was also tanned. What did the man do? Work outside naked? The possibility was so ludicrous, she smiled.

Caleb had his arms wrapped around Cole's neck and was happily chattering into his ear. He didn't look at all scared, and Jessica suddenly yearned to be in the water with both of them.

She went to fetch the soap instead. As she was searching through the valise, she heard a loud splash, promptly followed by the baby's squeal of delight. Nothing seemed to frighten Caleb, which meant that he was feeling secure, she hoped.

"So far so good," she whispered. Caleb hadn't been harmed by her lack of skills as a mother. Each day she learned a little bit more, and hopefully, by the time he was five or six, she'd be comfortable in the role she'd taken on. She would always worry, she supposed, but then didn't all mothers? She wanted to do the right thing for her son so that he would grow up with fond memories and a strong sense of self-worth. Unlike the other men in her life, Caleb would have values.

"Jessie, bring the soap."

She jumped at the sound of Cole's voice. Grabbing the misshapen clump of rose-scented soap she'd made, she hurried to the edge of the bank.

"Should I throw it?"

"Sure," he called back.

She aimed but missed by a good ten feet. Cole was able to retrieve the soap before it sank to the bottom. "You throw like a girl," he shouted.

"I am a girl," she called back as she kicked off her shoes and sat down on the grassy slope.

She also took her stockings off, but that was as far as she would go while Cole was in the lake. It wouldn't have been proper for her to do what she wanted to do. Mothers couldn't be wanton. And so she watched him scrub her son from top to bottom and then play with him, wishing all the while she were part of the antics.

Her heart fell to the bottom of her stomach when Cole casually tossed Caleb into the air and let him go under the water. Before she could shout a warning, Cole had scooped him up, waited until he'd stopped sputtering, and then tossed him in the air again.

Caleb was having the time of his life and hopefully getting all worn out. Jessica sat on the bank with her toes in the cool water until it was almost completely dark. The temperature was rapidly dropping. She fetched a towel for Caleb and waited until Cole swam over to give her son to her.

The baby's lower lip was trembling from the cold, but he still put up a fight when she lifted him out of the water. He wanted to go back in. Jessica carried him back to the fire and quickly got him ready for bed. She'd already spread a blanket out and placed his baby doll in the center, and as soon as she put him down, he grabbed the toy, put his thumb in his mouth, and closed his eyes.

"I'll watch him if you want to get in the water, Jessie," Cole said from behind.

"Thank you," she whispered.

There was laughter in his voice when he told her she could look at him. "I'm dressed."

Barely, she thought to herself. He was wearing only a pair of snug-fitting buckskin pants. His hair was slicked back from his brow, and droplets of water glistened on his arms and chest.

A bath did sound wonderful. She waited until Caleb had drifted off to sleep, then gathered clean clothes, soap, and a towel. She walked a good distance away from the campsite so that Cole wouldn't see her, draped her garments on a fat, leafy bush, and slowly removed her clothes. Every muscle in her neck and shoulders ached, and she was suddenly so tired, she could barely concentrate on what she was doing. The water felt luxurious against her bare skin. She sighed deeply as she cautiously moved further into the lake, feeling her way with her toes to make certain the rocky bottom wasn't going to disappear.

It was sheer heaven. She didn't even mind the cold, but by the time she had scrubbed herself and washed her hair, her fingertips were as wrinkled as prunes.

It would have been nice to slip into her nightgown, but that would have been inappropriate with Cole there, of course, and so she put on a clean chemise and a dark gray dress that was at least two sizes too big for her. Like most of her other clothes, the gown was a hand-me-down. Jessica hadn't had time to take it in because she was always too tired in the evening after spending her days chasing after Caleb. As she slipped the dress over her head, she vowed once again to become more organized and headed back to camp.

Caleb was sound asleep with his back squeezed up against Cole's side. She thought Cole was also asleep. He was resting on his back and using one of the saddles for his pillow.

She sat across the campfire from him. Kicking her shoes off and tucking her feet under her, she proceeded to brush the tangles out of her hair. She loved this time of night, when everything was so peaceful and she had a few minutes to herself. She knew she should go to sleep, for tomorrow promised to be as exhausting as today, but she was enjoying the solitude too much to do the practical thing. The heat from the fire warmed her face. She tilted her head to the side so that her hair was draped down past her shoulder and leaned close to the flames.

"You're going to catch on fire," Cole said.

She jerked back. "I thought you were asleep," she whispered so that Caleb wouldn't be disturbed.

"You don't have to whisper. Your son's out cold. Nothing's going to disturb him."

"He's put in a long day," she said, a smile in her voice.

A few minutes passed in silence, and then he spoke again. "You're a good mother, Jessica."

She put her brush down. "No, I'm not, but I'm trying," she said. "I had never been around babies when I was growing up, and I know I've made mistakes with Caleb. I'm more relaxed with him now, and hopefully I haven't done anything that's going to permanently damage him. I've spoiled him, though, but I don't care. Babies should be spoiled."

"The boy needs a father," he said. "Are you going to find him one?"

Her answer was quick and forceful. "No, I'm not. Caleb had a father. He deserted him, remember?"

"Like your father deserted you?"

She didn't answer the question. "I'm never going to get married. It would be too much of a complication."

"Do you have any idea how difficult it's going to be raising Caleb on your own?"

"We'll get along."

Cole stared into the fire for a long while, thinking about Jessica's circumstances. She was too young to hold such opinions about men and marriage. "Not all men leave."

"Most do."

"No, most do not," he argued. "You've got guts, I'll give you that, but you have to be practical. You're a fine-looking woman, and men are going to want you."

You were made for loving, he thought, but didn't add. He didn't want to give her the false impression that he was interested. Granted, he was interested in making love to her and knew it would be a night he would never forget, but he wasn't interested in marriage.

"What makes you think I need help raising Caleb?" she asked.

He ignored her question. "I like the color of your hair."

The compliment startled her. "You do? Most men don't like brown hair."

"Where did you get that crazy notion? When a man first notices a woman, he isn't looking at her hair anyway."

"Then what's he looking at?"

Cole smiled. "The whole package. We take in every curve from the neck down."

She blushed and had to keep herself from laughing. "You shouldn't be talking like this."

"Like what? I simply answered your question. Your hair isn't brown, by the way. It's cinnamon."

She didn't like being the focus of his attention. It was wrong of him to try to fill her head with sugared remarks that weren't true. She wasn't a fine-looking woman, as he'd declared. She was a plain, sensible one.

"Why haven't you married?" she asked.

"I never wanted to," he replied. "Besides, in my line of work, marriage is out of the question."

"But why haven't you wanted to?" she prodded.

"I don't like the idea of being tied down. I don't want any strings."

She nodded agreement. "I understand. I don't want any either."

"You're too young to be set in your ways."

"Are you trying to tell me I'm cynical? I am, you know."

"The right man will change your mind."

"The right woman might change yours," she countered.

He stared at her for several seconds, then turned his gaze to the fire. There was a brooding expression on his face that puzzled her, and she wondered what he was thinking about now.

She got up and put her brush away, dug through her valise for one of her ribbons, and then went to sit on the blanket next to Caleb.

"I've decided I'm going to tie my son's wrist to mine. If he tries to get up, he'll wake me."

"Jessie, that isn't necessary. I'll hear him."

She wasn't willing to take the chance. She looped the yellow ribbon around Caleb's left wrist and secured it to hers. Then she lay down and closed her eyes.

"I won't sleep a wink worrying about him."

She was sound asleep less than a minute later. Cole added some twigs to the fire, then reached over and untied the ribbon from Caleb's wrist. Jessica had left a long strip of ribbon between them so that Caleb could move, but Cole was concerned that in his sleep the baby would get the ribbon around his neck. He wasn't about to take the chance. Besides, he would hear the baby if he stirred. When Cole was away from home, he never slept straight through the night, and he always heard every little sound.

Jessica sighed in her sleep and rolled on her side, facing him. He stared at her lovely face, knowing in his heart that if ever there was a right woman for him, Jessie was the one, and that realization made him angry.

It could get complicated, and he hated complications.

He stretched out on his back again, closed his eyes, and let the cool night air soothe the fire inside him while he reminded himself of his basic philosophy of life.

No strings.

Twenty-Five

Sheriff Tom Norton and his wife, Josey, lived in a two-story gray clapboard house on Grant Lane, just two blocks east of Middleton's town square, where Tom's jail was located. Three stone steps led up to the front door, and there were recently painted black wicker chairs on the porch. Two large black flower pots filled with pink and red summer flowers flanked the top step. Tendrils of ivy trailed down the sides. The house, though small, was charming.

It was dark out, but Cole still insisted on going around to the back door. He carried Caleb in one arm and half dragged Jessica with his free hand.

"I'm sure they've gone up to bed. It's late."

"It isn't that late," he argued. "And they wouldn't have left all the lights on if they'd gone to bed. Come on, Jessie. We have to do this."

She pulled on his arm as he tried to lead her forward on the cobblestone path.

"If I don't like these people, I'm not leaving Caleb with them. Agreed?"

He held on to his patience. "We've been over this. I agreed two hours ago, remember?"

"I just didn't want you to forget."

He put his arm around her shoulders and squeezed. "It's going to be all right, just like I promised."

He was just about to knock on the back door when she asked him to wait a moment. Then she reached up and threaded her fingers like a comb through Caleb's hair. The baby promptly dodged her hand.

"You ready?"

She took a deep breath. "Yes," she answered. "I hope we aren't disturbing them. It's late," she stubbornly added once again.

The Nortons were thrilled to have company and weren't at all put out. Josey had just finished the supper dishes when Cole knocked on her back door, and Tom Norton was still sitting at the table, having his second cup of coffee.

Cole had to gently nudge Jessica to go inside as he followed with Caleb into the brightly painted kitchen.

Josey was already making over the baby, who was overcome with a sudden bout of shyness and tucked his face into the crook of Cole's neck.

"My, he's a handsome boy, and just look at those curls, Tom. I didn't know you had a family, Cole, and this pretty lady must be your wife. It's right nice to make your acquaintance," she added.

"I'm not his wife," Jessica explained. "But this is my son. His name is Caleb."

Tom Norton stepped forward to shake Cole's hand, then pulled out a chair for him and one for Jessica.

"Sit down and tell us what in thunderation you're doing back in Middleton. You don't think there's going to be another robbery, do you?"

"No," Cole answered as he sat down and perched Caleb on his lap. "We came here to talk to you."

"Is that right?" Tom asked. "I was just thinking about you the other day. Yes, sir, I was. I see you're still wearing the star. Have you taken to the notion of being a marshal then?"

"For the time being," Cole answered. He thanked Josey for the cup of coffee she placed on the table in front of him, and then turned back to Tom.

"I haven't been a marshal long enough to know if I like the job or not." After making the comment, he glanced at Jessica. She was watching Josey closely and seemed to be weighing every move the older woman made.

Caleb reached for the hot coffee. Before either Jessica or Cole could react, Josey moved the cup out of his reach.

"Can the little imp have a cookie? I just made some fresh. They've got nuts in them, though, and some babies don't like nuts. What about some milk? I've got plenty."

"I'm sure he'd like some milk and a cookie," Jessica answered. "But he'll make a mess. Will you mind?"

"No, of course not. He's too young not to be messy," she added. "Have you folks had your supper yet? I could fry up—"

"No, we've eaten," Cole hastily interjected. "But thanks for offering."

"I'm not at all hungry, thank you," Jessica answered.

"Tom, could I have a word alone with you for a minute?" Cole asked.

The sheriff led the way into the living room. Caleb was still a little suspicious of his strange surroundings and wouldn't let go of Cole. He handed him to Jessica, winked at her, and then left the room.

Jessica wrapped her arms around her baby and held him protectively against her. The kitchen was clean. She noticed there wasn't a speck of dirt anywhere. Josey was obviously a good housekeeper, but if she and Tom agreed to look after Caleb, would she be able to keep up with him? And would she be patient?

She wished there were more time for her to find out everything she needed to know. She was relying on Cole's judgment, but he was a man and he wouldn't have the concerns a mother had. He trusted the Nortons. She didn't, at least not yet, and she wasn't going to leave an innocent baby in the hands of fiends.

They weren't monsters, though. The kindness in Josey's eyes told her she loved babies. She'd already taken to Caleb, and he was quickly warming up to her. Granted, his thumb was still in his mouth, but he was smiling at her.

What did he know? He was just a toddler. It was up to her to make certain he was well cared for, and, oh, God, how could she leave him with anyone? No one could love him the way she did.

Josey put a plate of cookies on the table. She poured two glasses of milk, the taller one for Jessica and the smaller one for Caleb, then sat down across from her and let out a loud sigh.

"It sure was hot today, wasn't it?"

"Yes, it was," Jessica agreed. She smiled at Josey and tightened her hold on Caleb when he tried to scoot off her lap. "You have a lovely home."

"You've only seen the kitchen," Josey said with a chuckle.

"Do you have children?"

"No, we don't. We always wanted a large family, but we just weren't blessed. I've taken care of a bushel of nieces and nephews, and I sure do know my way around babies, but I've got a longing in my heart to raise some of my own."

"You could still have children. How old are you?"

It was a bold question, but Josey didn't seem to mind. "I'm too old to start having babies. Why, I'm going to be forty-seven next month. It seems kind of odd for you to be asking me such a question."

"It was rude," Jessica said. "And I apologize if I seem a bit abrupt. It's just that there's so little time to decide, and I . . ."

She couldn't go on. She'd start crying if she tried to explain. She took several deep breaths in an effort to control her emotions before she started questioning Josey once again.

Josey was watching her closely. She noticed how pale Jessica was and how sad her eyes looked. She wanted to ask her if she was in trouble and if so, if there was anything that she and Tom could do to help, but Jessica spoke before she could get the words out.

"Do you consider yourself patient?"

"I beg your pardon?"

"Are you patient?"

"Tom seems to think I am," she answered.

"What do you do when you get angry?"

Josey leaned back in her chair. She was thoroughly perplexed by her guest's peculiar questions.

"I clean."

"I'm sorry?" Jessica asked, not understanding.

"I clean," Josey repeated. "When I get into a lather about something or other, I scrub my floors and wash my walls and do whatever else I need to do until I've gotten rid of my anger. Then I talk it out with Tom. Are you going to tell me why you're asking me these questions?"

Tears sprang into Jessica's eyes. "Yes, I'll explain just as soon as Cole finishes talking to your husband. Do you keep lye under your counter?"

"Do I what?"

"Keep lye under your counter."

"Good heavens, no," Josey answered. "Like I told you before, I'm used to watching my nieces and nephews. A couple of them are about your baby's age. They can walk and get into mischief, but they don't have a lick of sense yet. Lye could kill them, so I keep it up where they can't get to it. You're in trouble, aren't you, Jessica?"

"Yes," she whispered. "I'm sorry I've been so . . . suspicious, but I needed to know."

"Know what?" Josey asked.

"Cole will explain," she replied. "But I promise I won't hound you with any more questions."

Josey reached over to pat Jessica's hand. "You're with a good, strong man to help you through this trouble."

"Cole's a marshal and he's part of my problem. If it weren't for him, I wouldn't be on my way to Texas."

Josey's frown deepened. "I guess I'm just gonna have to wait until Tom tells me what's going on, then. That baby's been trying to get to his cookie for a good five minutes now," she added, deliberately changing the subject because Jessica looked on the verge of tears again. "Why don't you lessen your grip on him and let him have one. Can he drink out of a glass yet?"

Jessica turned her attention to her son. She moved the glass toward him and told him to show Josey how he could manage a glass. She was bragging about his ability when he spilled the milk.

Josey chuckled. "It's usually my Tom who does that," she commented. She mopped up the milk with a dishcloth and then held Jessica's glass while Caleb took a drink.

Caleb was finally ready to get down and explore the kitchen. Jessica followed him and held the drawers closed so he couldn't empty them.

"Sit back down and let him play," Josey suggested.

"He'll destroy your kitchen," she warned. "Caleb's a very curious child."

Josey opened the doors under the counters. "My nieces and nephews like to play with my pots and pans. That's the way," she said when Caleb squatted down and reached for one of the wooden spoons.

Jessica sat down next to Josey once again, and while

they got to know one another, Caleb made a fine mess banging on the pots and pans. Within ten minutes he had warmed up to Josey enough to let her pick him up and kiss him.

Cole and Tom came back into the kitchen then, and Cole gave Jessica a quick nod.

"Josey, you and I are going to be keeping this little boy a spell," Tom announced.

Josey patted the baby and looked at Jessica. "No wonder you were asking those questions. I'll be proud to watch him for you," she added. "And Tom and I won't let anything happen to him."

"Jessica's a witness, and she's got to go to Texas to testify," Tom said. "Cole doesn't think it's a good idea to take the baby with them."

"When do you think you'll be back?" Josey asked Cole.

"I don't know," he answered. "Maybe two weeks . . . or longer."

"He won't remember me."

Everyone turned to Jessica.

"Of course he'll remember you," Josey said. "We won't let him forget."

Tom suggested Jessica and Cole spend the night with them so that the adjustment for Caleb would be easier on him. Jessica let Josey bathe Caleb but hovered over her like a mother hen. Josey did know her way around babies. She filled a basin in the sink and let Caleb splash water everywhere while she lathered him up.

"You're very good with him," Jessica told her.

She followed Josey up the stairs to the guest room. Caleb, wrapped in a thick towel, was peeking at his mother over Josey's shoulder.

"He always sleeps with a rag doll. It's in his valise," Jessica said. "Oh, and he hates carrots. He'll spit them out if you try to force them on him."

"I wouldn't do that," Josey said. "I hate carrots too.

I know you're gonna worry, no matter what assurances I give you, but I promise you I'm gonna love this boy like he was my own. Why don't you go on downstairs for a bit and let Caleb get used to me. I'll call out if I need help."

"Yes, that's a good idea," Jessica said. It was also a test. Putting Caleb to bed required stamina and patience. Every once in a while, if he was overly tired, Caleb would throw a tantrum. The baby was all wound up now, and that was a sure indication that trouble was coming. Jessica left the valise on the bed and closed the door behind her.

When she came downstairs, she found Cole in the living room standing by the window, looking out. She glared at him before turning her back on him.

"What was that all about?"

She began to pace. "This is all your fault," she whispered. "Can't you see that this is breaking my heart?"

He started toward her, but she put her hand out to keep him at bay. "I can't leave him. I'm sorry, but that's the way it is. He'll be lost without me, and he'll be afraid and he'll be miserable and . . ."

As if to mock her, Caleb's peal of laughter echoed down the stairs. Cole shook his head. "He sure doesn't sound miserable."

"I'm not going to go through with this. My mind's made up," she whispered.

She turned to go back up the stairs, but Cole grabbed hold of her hand and pulled her up against him.

"Tom?" he called out. "Jessica and I are going for a walk."

The way he was squeezing her hand told her not to argue. She let him drag her out the back door and into the yard. He didn't stop pulling her along until he reached a cluster of trees that shielded them from the street and gave them privacy.

"Now you listen to me——" he began.

She cut him off. "Don't you dare take that tone of voice with me. I will not leave my baby with strangers. I'm sorry, Cole, but that's the way it's going to be."

She tried to jerk her hand away, but he tightened his hold and pulled her close until she was pressed against his chest. His face was inches away from hers. He was going to give her a hard lecture because she was being so stubborn, but then he saw her tears and relented. Now wasn't the time to lecture.

"I know how hard this is . . ."

"No, you don't know. You aren't a mother."

"No, I'm not," he agreed. "You're going to have to be sensible. I know Tom Norton, and I'm telling you he's trustworthy. When Luke MacFarland and his wife were killed, Tom and Josey wanted to raise their children."

"Why didn't they?"

"Luke's relatives wouldn't let them. They farmed the children out among them."

"They separated brothers?" she whispered.

"Yes, but Tom tried to keep them all together. I'm telling you he's a good man. So is his wife. Josey took care of me when I got sick. I was a stranger to her, but she still nursed me back to health. The Nortons aren't going to let anything bad happen to your baby. They'll love him, Jessie, and we can't take Caleb with us. You know that, don't you?"

"I'm not going to go to Texas."

"Must you be so stubborn about this? It's out of your hands. You have to go, and Caleb has to stay."

"I hate this," she cried out.

He wrapped his arms around her and held her tight. "I know you do."

"I'm beginning to hate you too, Cole Clayborne. This is all your fault."

"All right. It's all my fault," he whispered. His chin dropped down on top of her head, and he continued to hold her and stroke her back for several minutes until she had calmed down. He couldn't help but notice how good she felt in his arms.

She couldn't stop thinking about the danger Caleb had been in when that monster had killed her guard. Her son could have been killed too.

The Nortons would keep him safe. In her heart she knew that to be true. She suddenly pulled away from Cole. "None of this is your fault. You're only doing your job. You're right too. Caleb should stay out of harm's way."

She straightened her shoulders, turned around, and walked back inside.

Josey was waiting at the kitchen table. She wanted to tell Jessica that Caleb had gone right to sleep, but when she saw the heartache on the poor mother's face, she got up and went to her. "I'm going to take good care of your boy. I promise you, Jessica. Tom and I will treat him like he was our own son."

"I want to thank you for agreeing to watch him, and I know I don't have the right to ask . . ."

"You can ask anything you want to ask. If I can do it, I will."

"If I don't come back . . ."

"Don't talk like that," Josey interrupted.

"You're coming back," Cole said from behind.

Jessica ignored both protests. "If I don't come back, Josey, will you raise my son?"

Josey looked over Jessica's head at Cole. He gave a quick nod. "Yes, Tom and I will raise him. You've got my word."

"Thank you," Jessica said, her voice flat. "I would also like you to change his name legally so that he won't feel like an outsider. I want him to belong to a family."

"Jessica, for God's sake, stop talking like that. Nothing's going to happen to you."

"I have to make arrangements just in case. I owe it to Caleb."

Josey understood. "We'll make it legal," she promised. "I give you my word."

Jessica grabbed hold of her hand. "One last promise, Josey, and I'll be able to go. Please, don't ever leave him."

Twenty-Six

$\mathcal{D}$aniel was torn between responsibilities. His primary obligation was to escort Grace to Texas, and he was doing exactly that, but he also wanted to head over to the small town of Clarkston, where the latest robbery had occurred, to look for evidence that might help him in his investigation.

He couldn't send Cooper to the bank in his place, as he was with Rebecca, making certain she got to Texas alive and unharmed. The two of them had left for the depot an hour ago, but not before Cooper had dispatched his two young and inexperienced deputies to Clarkston to help the sheriff there. Rebecca had insisted on sending a telegram to the hotel in Salt Lake City to cancel the reservation she'd made the day before and to alert her friends that her plans had been changed, and as soon as she came out of the telegraph office, she was put in a coach with Cooper and sent on her way.

Cooper had suggested that he and Rebecca wait until Grace could travel so that he could take both women with him and Daniel could go to Clarkston, but Daniel refused. Each of the women believed herself to be the only one claiming to have witnessed the robbery, and he was determined to keep all three of them separated on the trip to Red Arrow because he didn't want them making any more joint plans. Although he personally believed that Rebecca was the real witness—she had given descriptions and details to prove she had been there—he would let the judge in Blackwater decide for himself which one of the three was telling the truth.

He hadn't seen Cole before he left town with Jessica and Caleb. They had taken off an hour or so after the gunman had tried to kill her. Daniel still didn't know the name of the dead man, but he was certain he was one of the Blackwater gang. Past reports told him that there were seven men in the gang. One was in jail in Blackwater, another was dead now, thanks to Cole's expertise, and five were still out there somewhere . . . waiting for an opportunity, Daniel believed, to silence all three women.

There was also another reason he didn't want Cooper to take Grace with him, but one Daniel would never admit. While he trusted Cooper to do his job, he didn't want to let Grace out of his sight. In his mind, no one could protect her as diligently as he could. There was also the fact that he was drawn to her, and it was his hope that by the time they reached the stopping point in Red Arrow, he would have gotten over his bizarre and unexplainable infatuation.

Daniel stayed in Rockford Falls that night and slept in a chair outside of Grace's door. He went downstairs early the next morning, but didn't plan to leave the town until late that afternoon when the coach arrived.

Grace had other ideas. Daniel had just returned from the bathhouse, where he'd washed and changed into clean clothes, and was standing on the veranda talking to Dr. Lawrence when Grace came down the stairs. Dressed in a pale pink skirt and matching blouse, she carried her white gloves and hat in her hands, and went directly to the manager's desk to inform him that she was leaving. Sloan trailed behind her, carrying her valise.

Daniel didn't like the crowd in the lobby. Folks were checking out of the hotel, and it was chaotic. He quickly went to Grace's side and ordered her back upstairs.

"You can rest until this afternoon when the coach arrives."

"I don't wish to rest any longer. I feel fine," she insisted. "Have you changed your mind about taking me to Texas?"

"No."

"I didn't think so, but I was compelled to ask. We need to talk, Daniel."

"Upstairs."

"No, not upstairs. Now, right this minute, then I expect you'll take me off to jail."

"I'm taking you to Texas," he whispered as he half dragged her into a corner.

"Sheriff Sloan just told me they're holding a man in Blackwater and they think he's one of the gang. Is that true?"

"Yes."

"Then why didn't you tell me?" she demanded. "I never would have . . ."

"You never would have what?"

"I lied to you," she cried out. "I'm not your witness. I only said that I was to protect Rebecca and Jessica. It was wrong and I'm sorry. Please don't be angry with me. Will I have to stay in jail long?"

"You aren't going to jail," he muttered.

"But I lied to an officer of the law."

"The three of you have done nothing but lie," he said. "I honestly don't know who to believe."

"I'm telling you the truth now. I wasn't there."

"At this point I don't care if you were there or not. The judge has ordered all three of you to Blackwater, and that's where we're going as soon as the coach arrives."

"Why are the others going?"

"I just explained that Judge Rafferty wants all of you there."

"Will he put me in jail for lying?"

The thought of her behind bars was so outrageous, he lost some of his anger.

"You've got bigger things to worry about than jail. Come on. You're going back upstairs to wait in your room until the coach gets here."

She shook her head. "If I must go . . ."

"You must."

"I don't want to wait for a coach. Can't we go by horseback? The sheriff told me it would be quicker because we could take some cut throughs."

He smiled. "Shortcuts," he corrected.

A stout, elderly woman was pushing her way through the crowd toward Grace. Daniel noticed her out of the corner of his eye and moved to put himself in front of Grace.

"I beg your pardon," the woman said. "Please get out of my way. I wish to speak to Lady Winthrop."

Grace gave Daniel a little nudge and stepped forward. "Good morning," she said.

The woman made an attempt at a curtsy. "It's an honor to meet you," she said. "My name is Winifred Larson," she added with a blush. "And I couldn't help but notice your lovely hat. Could you tell me where you purchased it? I would like to get one just like it. Would you mind if I looked at it more closely?"

Grace smiled and handed the hat to Winifred. The straw brim was covered in lace and flowers, and there were two purple plumes feathering up and out on one side.

"It's exquisite," Winifred declared. "I must have one just like it. I have a purple dress, you see, and it would be lovely with it."

A tall, thin man with a receding hairline came over to join them. She quickly introduced him. "This is my husband, Lionel," she said. In a loud whisper she told her husband to bow to Lady Winthrop.

"That isn't necessary," Grace said.

"Do you mind telling me where you purchased this divine creation?" Winifred asked again.

Grace explained. "I purchased the basic straw hat, but I decorated it."

"Then there's not another one in all the world like it?"

"I know where this is headed," her husband interjected with a chuckle.

Grace didn't understand. "Excuse me?"

"When Winifred gets a notion she wants something . . ."

"May I buy it from you?" Winifred blurted out. "To own a Lady Winthrop creation would be so thrilling for me. I simply must have it. How much will you take for it? Will five dollars do?"

Grace was incredulous. She glanced at Daniel to see how he was reacting and smiled because he looked genuinely puzzled.

"Actually, Mrs. Larson, I hadn't considered selling . . ."

"If it's an original, Mother," Lionel whispered loudly, "you've got to offer more."

"Yes, yes, you're right. Ten dollars then. Will that do?"

Daniel decided it was time for him to interfere. Grace's face was turning pink, and he figured she was embarrassed.

"I don't think the lady wants—"

"Sold," Grace blurted out. "For ten dollars."

Lionel quickly paid her. She tucked the money into

her pocket, told Winifred she hoped she enjoyed the hat, and then bid them good-bye.

"Shouldn't we go to the stables now?" she asked Daniel.

From the glint in her eyes, Daniel knew she was determined to get her way. "You're in no condition to ride a horse. You should sit inside a coach and try to rest."

"I don't need to rest."

He still felt compelled to argue with her for several more minutes before giving in. In the back of his mind, he kept thinking that if they took the shortcuts and didn't follow the winding roads, they could possibly reach the train station in time to board the late afternoon train. If they didn't make it in time, the next train wouldn't come through until the following morning.

He stood there, hesitating, as he studied her. Her hair was down around the sides of her face, and he gently lifted a silky strand away to look at the bruise near her temple. It didn't look as bad as it had last night.

His fingers trailed down the side of her face. "Are you sure, Grace?"

She gently removed his hand. "I'm sure."

He was staring intently at her, and she thought he might be looking for a sign of weakness from her. She straightened her shoulders, smiled, and suggested once again that they get going.

"Is there time for me to stop by the wagon? I must get another hat," she explained. "A lady should never appear in public without her head covered. It just isn't done."

"Then why did you sell the one you had?"

"Daniel, it was ten whole dollars."

He grinned. "It took you by surprise, didn't it?"

"Not really," she admitted. "It's the third hat I've sold since I arrived, and I didn't even try," she added.

"The poor ladies here don't have the shops we have in London. They must order through the catalog, but quite often what they think they're buying and what they get are two different things. It can be very disappointing."

"I'm sure it can be," he said dryly.

She laughed. "Hats are important to ladies, but not to men. Isn't that right?"

"Come on then," he said. "The wagon was moved to the stable. You can get another hat out of your boxes there."

He took hold of her arm and tried to go out the front door. She pulled away.

"It would be rude to leave without saying good-bye to Jessica and Rebecca."

"They've already left. Jessica went with Cole yesterday to take Caleb to a friend's house, and Rebecca left with Marshal Cooper. You'll see them again in Red Arrow," he explained as he picked up her valise, grabbed hold of her arm, and headed out the doorway again.

"Are we going to run to the stables?"

He immediately slowed down. Once they were outside, his full attention was directed on the street.

"Do you think we'll be able to catch up with Jessica or Rebecca?"

"No."

"It would have been nice to sit with them on the train."

"Even if we took the same train, I wouldn't let you sit with them."

"Why not?"

"I'll explain later," he hedged.

She pulled her arm away from him. "Daniel, it's rude to look away when you're speaking to someone."

He smiled over the censure in her voice. She sounded like a teacher explaining simple manners to a little boy. "Grace, I'm trying to make sure no one takes a shot at you, but if you would rather I looked at you . . ."

"No, no, I would rather you watch the street. Do you think there's someone waiting to shoot me?"

"Besides me?"

"That isn't funny."

They arrived at the stable a moment later. The wagon was in the back, and Grace went through the crates until she had found three more hats to take with her. She stuffed two inside her valise and kept the third one with her. Daniel made her stand away from the door while he went to ready his horse.

The owner, a short, squat man with a thick neck and a round belly, came forward to introduce himself. He had a sincere smile and smelled of horses. "My name's Harry, and I'd shake your hand, Miss, but it's real dirty. Can I be of assistance?"

She smiled at the eager young man. "Yes, you may be of assistance," she replied.

"The lady needs a sound horse," Daniel called out. He was saddling his own horse, a beautiful gray stallion with a surprisingly calm disposition, but he was also keeping a watchful eye on Grace.

She looked completely out of place. "Pink fluff," he whispered. The woman belonged in a fancy parlor, dressed the way she was in that ridiculously feminine hat and those impractical leather slippers. Harry sure did like her though. The man had a rapturous look on his face and kept trying to edge closer to her. Probably because she smelled so good, Daniel thought, but he didn't care what Harry's reason was. He wanted him to back away.

"How about getting the lady a horse, Harry?" Daniel called out, his tone just as sharp as he intended.

"Your husband sounds a might possessive," Harry whispered before turning to Daniel. "I'll fix your woman up with the best I got."

A few minutes later, Harry came strutting forward leading a swaybacked gelding that Grace suspected had lost all of his teeth. The poor thing was obviously on his last legs.

She took one look at the sorry beast and politely declined. "No, thank you."

Harry rubbed his jowls while he considered which of the other horses to show her. "I only just inherited this stable from my brother, and I'm not familiar with his stock," he said. "But I recall one pretty little mare. You're gonna like her just fine," he promised as he turned and hurried away. "I guess you could say I was saving the best for last."

Grace politely but firmly declined the pretty little mare too.

"What's the matter with this one?" Harry wanted to know.

"She simply won't do," Grace replied. "She should be put out to pasture. With such spindly legs she wouldn't have enough stamina for a trip down the street. May I have a look at the other horses?"

Harry got his back up. "No, you may not. You stay right here, and I'll fetch the best I got and bring him out to you."

Grace didn't think it was a good idea to remind Harry that he had already brought out the "best" of the lot. She patiently waited, and when he showed her yet another swaybacked horse, she shook her head.

Harry threw his hands up in defeat. "Go ahead and look, ma'am. I'll let you have whatever you think you want."

It only took her a couple of minutes to find a sound horse. She was a fiesty mare Harry had hidden in one of the rear stalls.

Harry immediately tried to talk her out of her choice. "I'll grant you, she's sound, but she's mean," he explained. "You don't want the lady riding her," he told Daniel.

"Grace?"

"Yes, Daniel?"

"Can you handle her?"

"Yes, I can."

"Well, now, she will get you where you want to go," Harry agreed. "But . . ."

Grace reached up with her gloved hand and patted the animal. "Oh, she's lovely. She'll do just fine. What's her name?"

"Damnation."

Grace's eyes widened. "Harry, if you don't wish to sell her to me, simply say so. Cursing isn't necessary."

"I wasn't cursing. That's her name," he insisted. "The owner that sold her to me told me her name after the bargain was struck. I'm telling you plain and simple. Her name's Damnation."

"That won't do," Grace announced. "I'll call her Daisy."

Harry rolled his eyes. "I don't think you understand, ma'am. You can call her anything you want, but she'll only answer to Damnation. Do you still want to take her?"

"Yes, please. Daniel, isn't she lovely?"

Daniel was trying not to laugh. When Harry had told them the name of the horse, Grace's cheeks had turned as pink as her blouse. She thought Damnation was lovely, and he agreed just to get going.

After accepting the money from Daniel for the horse and saddle, Harry began to have second thoughts.

"Are you certain your wife can handle such a mean-spirited animal?"

"He's sure," Grace answered before Daniel could speak.

Harry gave up. "I'll fetch you a riding crop then. You're going to need it with this hell-raiser."

"No, thank you," Grace said.

"I'm telling you, she won't do what you want unless you lash her. You're going to need the riding crop."

The argument would have escalated if Daniel hadn't stepped in. Harry, he decided, was in the wrong line of work. The man was afraid to get near the horse. Daniel quickly saddled the mare and led her out to Grace.

Harry was pleading with Grace now. She wouldn't accept the crop, even when he told her he'd give it to her for free.

"It's time to get going," Daniel announced. He tied her valise behind the saddle and then lifted her up so that he could adjust the stirrups.

She felt as light as a handful of feathers. He couldn't hide his smile when she put her straw hat back on her head. White ribbons trailed down her back. He thought she looked as though she was about to go for a Sunday ride through the park.

Looks could be deceiving, he knew. She'd surprised him when she'd proven to be so knowledgeable about horses, and the way she sat in the saddle told him she hadn't exaggerated about her riding experience.

"Why are you smiling?" she asked.

"We just might make it to the train," he replied. "That's what I was thinking."

There was a speck of dirt on his chin. Before she could think better of it, she reached over and gently brushed it away.

He reacted as though she'd just struck him a hard blow. He jerked back and turned away from her.

"Let's go," he ordered. "Harry, open the back doors for us. We'll go out that way."

"How long will we be in Texas?" Grace asked.

Daniel was about to swing up into his saddle when she asked the question. He turned to her. His arm was casually draped over his saddle, his head was tilted ever so slightly to the side, and she thought he looked exactly like one of the wild and rugged gunmen of the West she'd read stories about. The wilderness men, as they were called, were bigger than life and couldn't be tied down. They roamed the land seeking adventure and danger, and left broken hearts behind them. Was Daniel like that? she wondered. She thought perhaps that he was. He just looked the type who would never, ever settle down.

"There's no way of knowing," Daniel answered, wondering why she was frowning so intently. "Why do you need to know?"

"I have other commitments," she said. "They're personal. Could you please make a calculated guess, Daniel? I really do need to know."

"It's going to take us a week or two to get to Blackwater, depending on the amount of trouble we run into," he said. "Then you'll have to stay until the trial's over and the other men have been caught—"

"Why?" she interrupted. "That could take months."

"I can't let you go on your way until I'm certain none of the other gang members will come after you."

She closed her eyes. "All right then," she agreed. "You're telling me I could be in Texas for as little as a few weeks or as long as two months."

"Could be longer," he told her.

Her reaction surprised him. Tears came into her eyes. "Then it's settled."

"What's settled?" he asked, confused by the sadness he heard in her voice.

She was so disheartened she could barely think what to do. "It's over," she whispered. "And I've lost."

"Grace, what are you talking about?"

"I don't blame you, Daniel. Really I don't."

"Will you make sense?" he demanded. "Explain why you're so upset."

"My future," she cried out. "It's ruined. Even one

month's too long. Don't you understand? No, of course you don't, but it doesn't matter. It's all my own fault for having such silly dreams. I've wasted too much time already, and I'd never be able to become established in the amount of time I have left." Her sigh was long and weary. "I have to make a stop at the telegraph office before we leave town."

"No," Daniel said.

"I'm sorry, but I must insist."

"Tell me why," he argued.

"When a person dreads something, isn't it best to hurry and get it over with as soon as possible so he'll stop dreading it?"

Daniel didn't have any idea what she was talking about. Harry obviously did though, for he stepped forward to offer his opinion.

"Do you mean like getting a tooth pulled?" he asked.

"Yes, it's exactly like that," she agreed.

"She's telling you she's got to send a wire now so she'll stop dreading it," he told Daniel.

"I don't need an interpreter," Daniel snapped. "You can send the wire from Blackwater. Now let's get going."

She shook her head. "Waiting would only put off the inevitable."

After making that statement of fact, she turned the mare and tried to ride out the front doors. Daniel muttered a blasphemy before chasing after her.

Harry grabbed hold of the mare's reins and held tight. "Your husband's getting irritated, ma'am. What have you got to do that's so almighty important it can't wait?"

She burst into tears. "I have to get married."

Twenty-Seven

❧

"**I** don't wish to talk about it."

"I don't care if you wish to or not," Daniel said. "You're going to tell me why you have to get married."

She decided to ignore him. She leaned back against the padded seat inside their private compartment and looked out the window at the passing scenery. The train was traveling at a neck-breaking speed, and because they were in the last car, the compartment violently swayed every time the train slowed to go around a curve. The motion was making her nauseous, and judging from the tightness around Daniel's mouth and his gray countenance, she thought the motion was making him sick too.

"Are you feeling all right?"

"I'm fine," he snapped.

"You needn't be surly with me, Daniel."

They sat across from one another in the tiny room. There was supposed to be seating for four adults, but he swallowed up all the space on his side. His long legs were sprawled out in front of him, making it impossible for her to leave without making him move first. She wasn't going anywhere, however. The door was bolted from the inside so that no one could intrude.

"This probably isn't at all proper," she remarked.

"What isn't proper?"

"Traveling together. It would be frowned on in England for an unattached man and woman to share a compartment together without a chaperone."

"I'm a lawman," he reminded her. "That changes things."

"You're still a man."

"Last time I looked I was," he told her with a grin.

She looked out the window again, but not before he saw her smile. "Are you ready to tell me why you have to get married?"

"No, I'm not ready to tell you."

"Are you in trouble, Grace?"

She didn't look at him when she answered. "Yes, I suppose I am."

His mind leapt from one possibility to another, but she wasn't the type of woman who would let a man touch her before marriage. She was innocent and sweet and definitely untouched.

"You aren't pregnant."

"Good heavens, no," she stammered out. "How could you think that I . . ."

"You said you had to get married, and you said you were in trouble. I simply put the two together, but then I changed my mind. It's a long trip to Texas, Grace, and eventually you will tell me what I want to know. You might as well do it now."

"Daniel, I had no idea that men could be such nags. Very well, you win. I made a promise to my parents that I would marry Lord Nigel Edmonds if things didn't work out here. They haven't," she added.

"I still don't understand. What didn't work out?"

She frowned in vexation. "My parents are titled

and therefore highly positioned in society. They're also quite poor, and it's been very difficult for them to keep up appearances. They've borrowed against their land, and they haven't been able to make the interest payments to their banker. They've been terribly humiliated."

"Has anyone suggested to your father that maybe he ought to think about getting a job?"

"Oh, no, that wouldn't do. He's titled," she repeated.

"Being titled won't put food on the table."

"No, it won't," she agreed.

"If he can't or won't work, then he's going to have to sell his land and whatever else he has of value."

"That's why I'm getting married."

"I still don't understand."

"I'm all my father has left, Daniel . . ."

He leaned forward. "Are you telling me he's selling you?"

"No, no, of course not. He simply arranged a suitable marriage for me."

"And will this marriage solve his financial problems?"

"Yes, it will."

"Then he's selling you."

"No, he isn't," she snapped. "Arranged marriages that benefit both families have been going on for centuries. My father isn't doing anything wrong. In fact, he's been extremely patient with me. I asked him for a year's grace, and it was my hope . . . my dream really, foolish though it was . . : that I could make a go of it here. I wanted to purchase land with my inheritance from an uncle—"

"And make enough to support your parents in the style they're accustomed to?"

"No, you've jumped to the wrong conclusion. My parents are quite elderly. They were in their forties when I was born," she explained. "But they aren't set in their ways. If the ranch could support them, they could leave England and come to me. Isn't that adventurous of them? You'd like my parents, Daniel. They're very practical, and you'd have that in common."

"You're not old enough to be shouldering such responsibilities."

"Age doesn't have anything to do with it. The day I was born my future was determined."

"Why?"

"Because I was born a lady."

"I know you're a lady," he replied, smiling.

"No, you don't understand. I was born Lady Grace Winthrop. The title carries certain responsibilities, and I would shame my parents if I didn't honor their wishes."

Daniel was intrigued by the vast cultural differences between the two of them. What was important in England didn't matter at all in the United States.

"Titles don't mean anything here."

"I know," she said. "What is important here? Money?"

"To some," he allowed.

"What's important to you?"

"Honor."

"But that's exactly what I was trying to say. My honor is at stake. I must do the right thing."

"A man's word is more important in the United States than his position in society."

"Being responsible is extremely important to me," she countered. "I have specific duties."

"Like getting yourself hitched to a man with money and power?"

"If it will help my family, then yes."

"You don't like it much, do you, Grace?"

She refused to answer him.

"No, you don't like it much at all," he said. "You wouldn't have asked for a stay of execution if you agreed with your parents. Do you love the man they've chosen for you?"

"I'm sure I'll learn to love him. He seems a decent sort."

"Seems decent?"

She blushed. "I don't know him well. In fact, I've only met him once. I was introduced to him at a charity ball, and I'll admit he didn't make much of an impression on me. I shouldn't be talking like this, should I?"

"There's nothing wrong with being honest," he told her. "You must have made quite an impression on him."

"It seems I did," she said. "He sent a note to my father the very next day requesting an audience. Mother told me Nigel fell in love with me immediately, but I don't believe that nonsense."

"I'll wager it was lust at first sight."

"I don't think we should talk about this anymore. It seems to upset you."

"I'm not upset," he snapped. "It just seems so barbaric of your father."

"Daniel, arranged marriages are customary in some societies."

"And you're a dutiful daughter."

Her spine stiffened. "As a matter of fact, I am. It was quite wonderful of my parents to give me a year's . . ."

"Reprieve?"

"Sabbatical," she corrected. "They wanted me to have the chance of fulfilling my dream. They have tremendous faith in me."

His blue eyes bored into her. "But you don't have much faith in yourself, do you, Grace?"

"Of course I do."

"Then why are you giving up so easily?"

"Because I'm going to Texas," she answered. "I

cannot be in two places at once. I've already used up four months, and going to Texas might take as much as two more. I won't have much of a life until you've caught all of the members of that horrible gang, because you're going to insist on protecting me and that might take you months and months."

"You're giving up," he repeated.

He was hitting too close to the mark, and she didn't like that one bit. He was making her acknowledge what she had been trying to ignore. As soon as the road became bumpy, she was ready to quit.

"I'm not a quitter."

"It seems to me that you are."

"Oh, what do you know? Things are different for you."

"Because I live in the United States."

"Because you're a man," she said. "You don't ever have to get married unless you want to, and I sincerely doubt that will ever happen. You aren't the type to settle down and raise a family."

He shifted his position on the bench so his legs could have more room to stretch out.

"I was married."

She was astonished. "You were?"

He nodded. "For almost seven years. We had a daughter named Bridget."

She didn't ask him any more questions, but the silence didn't make him uncomfortable. He didn't know why he felt compelled to tell her about his past, but the words wouldn't stay locked inside of him any longer.

"They're both dead . . . two years now."

"I'm so sorry."

"Yeah. So am I."

He sounded as though he had been talking about strangers, for all the emotion in his voice, but the pain was there in his eyes, and it was devastating. She wanted to go to him and take him into her arms and give him what small comfort she could, and the only reason she didn't was because she knew he wouldn't accept it.

She didn't want him to see how shaken she was, and so she turned to look out the window again.

She didn't speak again for several minutes, and then she asked, "What was your wife's name?"

"Kathleen."

"It's a beautiful name. You loved her very much, didn't you, Daniel?"

"Yes," he answered without hesitation. "I loved her. I still do."

"Do you think you'll ever marry again?"

"No," he answered.

"In time . . ."

He shook his head. "Don't tell me that time heals."

She didn't understand why he had suddenly become so antagonistic. "I wasn't going to say that."

"Then what were you going to say?"

"That in time you'll be able to smile when you think of Kathleen and Bridget because you'll remember the joyous times you had with them. The pain won't ever go away, but it will lessen."

"How the hell would you know?"

She tried to ignore his hostility. "I don't know firsthand. It's only a hope I have for you."

"It's hot in here, isn't it?"

She agreed with a nod as she reached over to unlatch the lock on the window. She pushed and prodded but couldn't get the window up. "I think it's been sealed shut."

Daniel reached over, gave the frame one good push, and the window opened. A hot breeze rushed into the compartment.

"Tell me, what was Kathleen like?" Grace asked.

"Why?"

"I'm curious, that's all."

Daniel propped his feet up on the bench next to Grace, leaned back, and closed his eyes. His arms were folded across his chest, and he looked as though he was going to sleep.

"She was the complete opposite of you," he answered. "In appearance and in disposition."

"What did she look like?"

"She was tall and had brown hair and brown eyes, and lots of freckles," he added. "She worried about her weight all the time, but she didn't need to because she was perfect just the way she was. Kathleen was a beautiful woman, inside and out. So was our daughter. She looked just like her mother."

Several minutes went by in silence before Grace asked another question. "How did you meet her?"

"I stopped by her father's farm on my way into Dillon, and she was working in the garden. She was down on her knees pulling weeds with the sun beating down on her, and all she had to do was look up at me and smile. I think I fell in love with her then and there."

"I love to garden," Grace said, believing that she and Kathleen shared a common interest after all. "I had the most beautiful cutting flowers, all the colors of the rainbow."

Daniel shook his head. "Kathleen's garden was filled with vegetables. She was raised on a farm, and she didn't have time to grow flowers. They raised crops so they could put food on the table. You were raised in the city, weren't you?"

"We had a house in the country too," she said. "We would go there when the heat in the city became unbearable."

He scoffed at the notion. "Kathleen wasn't privileged, and she sure didn't have time to worry about the heat or society. She worked from dawn to dusk, no matter what the weather. She didn't have a closet full of fancy ball gowns, but what she did have was honor and courage and loyalty."

"And I don't? Is that what you're telling me, Daniel? You said that Kathleen and I are complete opposites. She had honor, and I don't?"

"I'm just saying you're different."

She stared into his eyes and asked, "Did you mean to hurt me on purpose?"

He didn't answer her. She looked out the window so he wouldn't see how he had wounded her with his backhanded insults. What had she done to make him think so little of her, she wondered, and why did his opinion of her matter so much?

She squeezed her eyes shut to keep from crying. If he saw a single tear, she was sure he'd think she was a weakling, and she wasn't weak, she was strong. Granted, she had never plowed a field before or planted a vegetable garden, but that didn't mean she couldn't.

Getting angry lessened the hurt. How dare he make such sweeping judgments about her.

"I'm sorry, Grace. I didn't mean to insult you."

She didn't look at him when she replied. "Yes, you did."

"Damn it, you aren't going to cry, are you?"

She glared at him. "No, I'm not," she snapped. "Just don't lie to me. You meant to hurt me, and the very least you could do is admit it."

"Fine. I meant to hurt you. Close the window, will you? It's getting cold in here."

"It's as hot as the inside of an oven," she argued.

"Just close it."

She stood up to do as he asked, then turned to him once again. "Are you getting sick?"

"No, I'm not," he muttered. "I'm just tired."

"You were hot a few minutes ago, and now you're cold."

She sat down on the bench beside him, squeezing herself in between the wall and his side. Before he could stop her, she reached up and touched his brow with the back of her hand. "You have a fever. Daniel, I think you're getting influenza."

"Grace, go sit on your own bench and leave me alone. Please."

She moved back to her seat and sat there fretting about him. "Now I understand why you're so surly. You aren't feeling well."

The train flew around another curve in the tracks, the compartment swayed back and forth, and Daniel's stomach felt as though it had just lurched out the window.

"I'm not surly," he growled. "I said those things so you'd stay away from me. It was stupid and cruel, and I shouldn't have done it, but you need to keep your distance, Grace. That's just the way it is. Why in God's name does this train have to go so fast?"

"It isn't going fast. It's slowing down, and how in heaven's name can I keep away from you? We're locked in this compartment together, and you won't let me out of your sight. What did I do to offend you so?"

"Ah, hell, Grace, you haven't done anything wrong. You're just so damned pretty and sweet."

She didn't know what to think. The words were flattering, but the way he'd said them made them seem like accusations of some sort. Why did the fact that he thought she was pretty and sweet anger him?

"Daniel, you aren't making any sense at all."

He could feel the bile rising in his throat. He took a deep breath to try to keep his stomach from overturning. "Look, it's real simple."

"It is?" she asked quietly.

"Yes," he growled. "I haven't wanted any woman since my wife, but lately . . . since I met you anyway, I've . . ."

She waited for him to continue, then gave in and prodded him. "You what?"

He figured he had about fifteen seconds, at the most, to make it to the washroom at the end of the car. He bolted for the door.

"I want you, Grace. Now do you get it? Lock the door behind me, and don't let anyone in."

She was so stunned she couldn't move. He roared her name to get her to do what he wanted, then stood outside the door until he heard the bolt clicking into place.

He made it to the washroom the first time he threw up. He didn't make it all of the other times. He threw up on the floor and in the bucket the porter brought in to him. He thought he might have thrown up on Grace too, but he hoped to God he had imagined that. He did know he'd never felt this awful in his whole life. The illness drained every ounce of strength from his body. He could barely lift his head, and no matter how many blankets Grace covered him with, he couldn't seem to get warm.

Grace fixed a bed for him. She sat with him all through the night, cradling his head in her lap, stroking his brow with cool, wet compresses, and he was sure he would have rolled over and died if she hadn't been there.

By midnight, he stopped throwing up and actually slept. She shook him awake around dawn to tell him they had reached the station and needed to change trains. He honestly didn't know how he managed to get from one compartment to the other, and he was surprised when he saw that the valises had also been transferred. Had she carried them? No, she couldn't have. She had her hands full trying to hold him up. He had been completely useless, and when he realized what an easy target she had been while they were moving from one train to the other, he got chills again.

As soon as the door was bolted behind him, he went back to sleep. He woke up with his head in Grace's lap again. She was leaning against the window, her eyes were closed, and she looked very peaceful and serene.

He tried to be quiet so he wouldn't disturb her. After he washed and changed his shirt, he sat down on the bench across from her.

He noticed then that she had changed her clothes. She was wearing a white blouse with a pretty brooch at her neck and a dark blue skirt. She'd changed her shoes too. The ones she had on now matched her skirt.

When had she had the time? he wondered, and why had she bothered?

"Good morning, Daniel. Are you feeling better today?"

"Yes, I'm feeling better. Did I wake you?"

"No, I wasn't asleep. I was just resting. You don't look like you feel better. Lean forward and let me touch your brow."

"Don't fuss over me, Grace. I'm fine."

She was totally unaffected by his gruff manner. "Where have I heard that before?"

"Heard what?"

"You kept telling me you were fine all through the night, but you weren't fine, of course. Now lean forward."

There was a thread of iron in her command, and Daniel ended up obeying just to placate her. "You're a stubborn woman," he muttered.

She put the back of her hand against his forehead and frowned. "I just can't tell," she admitted. "If you have a fever, it isn't much. You mustn't eat or drink anything yet, or you'll get sick again. You're very fortunate."

He leaned back against the cushions and crossed his arms over his chest. "How's that?"

"You have a mild case of influenza. It could have

245

been much worse. Jessica was throwing up, off and on, for three days. I thought she was going to die."

"I wanted to die last night," he admitted. "By the way, thanks for . . . you know."

"You're welcome."

Curious, he asked, "Why did you change your clothes? Did I get them all wrinkled? I must have," he added before she could answer him. "Seems like a waste, though. No one's going to see you but me."

"It was necessary."

"Why?"

She let out a little sigh. "You threw up all over me."

"Ah, Grace, I'm sorry."

She laughed. "Daniel, you didn't do it on purpose."

"Did the porter help you . . ."

He didn't finish the question because she was shaking her head.

"I didn't let the porter come inside the compartment because you made me promise not to let anyone in, remember?"

"No," he admitted. "I don't remember. If he didn't come in, who cleaned up the floor?"

"I did."

He looked miserable, and she was suddenly sorry she'd told him the truth. "Why don't we talk about something else?"

"Like what?"

"The weather," she suggested.

"You're joking."

"It was all I could think of on the spur of the moment. Would you mind if I opened the window and let some fresh air inside?"

He got up and opened the window for her. The breeze felt soothing against his skin. He sat down again and looked at her. "Do you want something to drink or eat?"

"Would you be able to stomach it if I ate in front of you?"

"Maybe you should wait a little while."

Grace hadn't eaten anything since yesterday morning, and even though she was starving, she nodded her agreement. "I'll be happy to wait."

"Do you want a glass of water? I do."

"You're not going to have it," she said in that commanding voice he was beginning to dislike intensely.

"Why not?"

"You know why not. You'll get sick again. I'm not in the mood to clean up another mess."

"Now who's being surly?"

He sounded like a bear. He resembled one too with the day's growth of whiskers on his jaw. His hair was in disarray, his shirttail was hanging out, and there was a definite menacing quality about him now. Yet, she still thought he was handsome.

He wanted her. She still couldn't seem to get past that remarkable fact, and she really wished she could talk to him about it. She didn't dare say a word, at least not while he was in his present irritable mood. She supposed she would have to wait until later to bring up the topic, and perhaps by then she would have figured out why his admission had stunned her and left her breathless.

No, she wouldn't mention it now because it would be indelicate.

Daniel didn't have any such reservations. "About what I said yesterday . . ."

"And what was that?"

"You know . . . that I wanted you."

She folded her hands together. "You didn't mean it. Is that what you want to tell me now? It was the fever talking."

"No, I meant it all right."

"You did?" she whispered, astounded that he was being so forthright. She had just given him an out, but he hadn't taken it.

"Yes," he said. "I'm not going to do anything about it, though; so don't let it go to your head."

Her mouth dropped open. "Excuse me?" she said.

Daniel realized he'd made a bit of a blunder when he saw the fire in her eyes. "I just meant that I guess you could take what I said as a compliment, but don't make too much out of it because I don't plan to do anything about it."

"Oh, yes, it was a compliment all right. You told me you wanted me, and then you promptly threw up all over me."

He burst into laughter. "I'm real sorry, Grace."

"Oh, go stick your head in a bucket."

He laughed again. "I got you all riled up, didn't I? I didn't think you were capable of ever getting angry, but you are, aren't you? You've got a temper underneath that thick layer of sugar, Lady Winthrop. I wonder what good old Nigel would think about that."

"Must you be so exasperating?"

"Do you still want to send the telegram agreeing to marry Nigel?"

"Could we please change the subject?"

"Sure," he agreed. "Do you want to talk about the weather again?"

"We didn't talk about it, but no, I don't want to now. I was thinking about Jessica and Rebecca. I had hoped to run into them when we were changing trains, but I didn't see either one of them."

"Cole and Jessica wouldn't have had time to catch up with us. They're a full day behind us, and Cooper and Rebecca left yesterday."

"But we made up time going by horseback, and they could have missed their train yesterday."

"Maybe, but it's unlikely," he said. "I looked for them too, but I didn't see them."

"Of course you didn't. You were draped all over me. You could barely keep your eyes open."

"I'm sure your friend is doing just fine. Don't worry. Cooper will keep her safe."

"You really think so?"

"Yes," he insisted. "Now stop worrying. Knowing Cooper, he's probably already taught her how to play poker. I'll bet she's having the time of her life."

Twenty-Eight

Rebecca was going stir-crazy. She thought she would go out of her mind if she had to stay locked inside the tiny compartment with Marshal Cooper much longer. As attractive and attentive as he was, he was still driving her to distraction. He did try to make the time pass quickly. They played cards for several hours, chatted, and ate a boxed lunch the porter fetched for them. Boredom set in then, and all she wanted was to be left alone for a few minutes. In desperation, she finally came up with a plausible reason to send him away. She asked him to please fetch her brown suitcase the porter had put in the luggage compartment so that she could get her medicine. Pleading a headache, she insisted that if she didn't drink her tonic before the pain intensified, she would have to leave the train at the next town and take to her bed.

She felt guilty lying to him because he was being so sympathetic and understanding.

"I know I should have packed the medicine in my little valise, but I forgot."

"Is the pain bad?" Cooper asked, his concern apparent.

"It's becoming unbearable," she replied. "If I don't nip it now, I'll be sick for a week. The pain becomes blinding."

Cooper couldn't have been any more solicitous. After promising to hurry, he told her to bolt the door after him, and she did exactly that. Then she stood in the center of the claustrophobic cubicle and let out a blissful sigh because she finally had the room to herself and it was so wonderfully quiet. She needed time alone to think about the future and formulate her plans. Lord only knew, there was so much to be done in such a short time.

She expected Cooper to be gone at least fifteen minutes and probably more. The luggage compartment was three cars away, and once he'd made his way there, he would have to search through the baggage to find hers. Yet, less than a minute after he had left, a knock sounded at the door.

"Now what?" she muttered, assuming that the marshal had thought of yet another order to give her before he went on the errand. She forced a smile back on her face, flipped the bolt, and opened the door a crack.

The door seemed to explode against the interior wall, then bounced back. She couldn't even scream. All she saw as she staggered backward was the barrel of a gleaming black pistol. It was pointed at her.

She fell on the bench, clutching her bosom. Panting with fear, she cried out, "What are you doing here?"

In answer, the gunman rushed inside and kicked the door shut behind him. He was dressed in a dark business suit and wore shiny black shoes. He didn't look like a murderer.

"Get up, bitch," he hissed.

She didn't move fast enough. He grabbed her arm and jerked her toward him, his gun pressed into her belly. When he let go of her arm, she tried to step back, shaking her head at him in a silent plea not to hurt her, but he was indifferent to her fear.

"Please," she whimpered.

Her plea fueled his excitement. "That's it, bitch. Beg me," he crooned. "I want you to beg."

He reached between them and tore the front of her dress open to the waist, smiling when she cried out again. Before she could cover herself, his hand was painfully squeezing one of her breasts.

"No, don't do this," she whispered.

He tossed the gun on the bench, laughing now, and pulled her up against him. His fingers tore through her hair as his mouth slammed against hers. The kiss was wet, hot, crude. He bit her lower lip until he'd drawn blood and hungrily licked the red drops with his tongue.

He kissed her again and again, holding her prisoner in his arms as she fought him, and when he finally pulled back, he stared into her eyes as he slowly took hold of her hand and forced her to caress him intimately through his trousers.

"I want you."

Her eyes closed in blissful surrender, and she sagged against him. Her laugh was that of an enchantress. "You always want me."

His grip tightened, and he panted against her ear. The sound aroused her. She wrapped her arms around his neck and boldly rubbed against him. "You ruined my blouse. You're too rough."

"You like it rough."

A shudder passed through her. "Yes, I like it that way," she whispered.

He began to kiss the side of her neck. She purred like a contented cat. "We shouldn't . . . The marshal will be back soon. Oh, God, that feels good."

She leaned back so she could see his eyes. "I see you received my telegram. Are the boys with you?"

He kissed her mouth once again before he answered her. "Johnson's in Rockford Falls waiting for the opportunity to kill both those women. The others have gone on ahead to Red Arrow. If Johnson fails, they'll kill them when they get off the train. You are sure that's where the women are headed, aren't you?"

"Yes, I'm sure," she answered smugly.

"Have you figured out which one was in that bank?"

"No," she said. "Both of them are as scared as mice and neither one confided in me. It's a pity the fire didn't kill them," she added as she slid her fingers through the hair at the back of his neck. "I went to a considerable amount of trouble."

"Don't you pout," he crooned. "If Johnson can't get them, the rest of my boys will take care of them in Red Arrow."

"And then I'm the witness."

Her throaty laugh inflamed him. "Yes, yes," he whispered. "Oh, that's fine. Just fine."

Her hand slowly moved down his chest and then lower still until she was once again stroking his arousal. She knew the effect she was having on him and thrilled with the feeling of such power.

He reached for her skirts. She shook her head. "No, we mustn't," she whispered as he began to tear at the buttons. "There isn't time. It's too dangerous."

"We'll make time. I want you, Rebecca. Now."

She gave in to his seduction and stepped back to strip for him. Her blouse was in tatters, and she quickly discarded it, then unbuttoned her skirt and let it fall to the floor. "We're fools to take such a chance, Donald," she said as she unfastened her petticoats.

He was panting while he watched her disrobe. He waited until only a silk-and-lace chemise covered her golden body, and then impatience got the better of him. He rushed forward, thrust his hand between her thighs and roughly shoved her back on the bench. She peeled the undergarment down her body, kicked it aside, then stretched out along the length of the cushioned seat and spread her legs wide, beckoning him to take her. He wet his lips in anticipation as he greedily stared at her breasts. He knelt on one knee between her thighs. He couldn't wait another second, for he knew he would burst with his need if he didn't mate with her quickly.

"You know you drive me crazy, don't you, bitch?"

She laughed. "Oh, yes, I know," she whispered. "Who would have thought such a stuffy and prim gentleman could have such a violent appetite."

"How much time do we have?"

"At least fifteen minutes," she answered.

Donald was fumbling with the buttons on his trousers when he heard a knock on the door. Had he locked it? He couldn't remember. He jumped up and turned just as Cooper opened the door.

"Rebecca, I told you to lock . . ." he began as he pushed the door wide. He was so startled to see her naked, he stopped. He couldn't seem to take in the scene.

Donald stood behind the door, waiting for the marshal to come inside. He frantically searched for his pistol in his pockets.

"What the hell?" Cooper muttered as he stepped forward.

She leaned up on one elbow, her heart slamming inside her chest, and stared at Donald, silently willing him to take action. Cooper saw where she was looking and turned just as Donald moved forward.

"Son of a bitch," Cooper shouted.

Rebecca panicked. She spotted Donald's pistol on the bench an arm's length away from her and rolled to her side, grabbed hold of the weapon, and fired.

Cooper was going for his gun when the bullet struck him. The force was so powerful, he was thrown backward into the corridor against the windowpane. The glass shuddered from the impact.

Rebecca scrambled to her feet. To keep from screaming, she covered her mouth with her hand and fired once again. She'd aimed too high the second time. Cooper was already crumbling to the floor. The bullet missed him but shattered the glass. It rained down on top of his prone body.

"Oh, God . . . Oh, God," she whimpered. "Did I kill him? Make sure I killed him. Hurry, Donald."

Growling low in his throat like a cornered animal, Donald rushed into the hallway. His eyes darted from side to side to make sure no one else was coming down the aisle.

"If he isn't dead, he will be," Donald muttered. "Stop crying and get dressed. We have to get off the train."

"Yes, yes," she whimpered before turning to do as he ordered.

Donald quickly dragged the unconscious lawman to the door connecting the cars, leaving a smeared trail of blood in his wake. The train was slowing to take the curved trestle above a yawning black lake when Donald opened the door. He could see a small town looming up in the distance on the other side of the lake. He bent down, half lifted Cooper, grunting from his weight, and then shoved and kicked him out. He stood there watching as the train clattered on around the bend, smiling when the marshal hit the water.

No one had seen him. He was sure of it, and he doubted that anyone had heard the gunshots either, for the sound the train made as it thundered along the tracks muffled any other noises.

Once again he had gotten away with murder. Excitement surged through his blood, and he began to pant with euphoria. He thought he saw a movement out of the corner of his eye, but he couldn't be certain. He turned away as a precaution so that his face wouldn't be seen, and then took his time strolling back to Rebecca's compartment. The carpet had already absorbed the blood, and it looked as though the stains had been there for some time. No one would know how fresh they were unless he got down on his knees and felt the wetness.

Donald remembered to bolt the door this time. Rebecca hadn't gotten dressed yet. Her clothes were laid out on the bench, and she was frantically shoving her torn garments into her valise. He grabbed hold of her from behind, slammed her up against the wall, and violently took her.

No one heard her screams.

Twenty-Nine

❧

$\mathcal{P}$arting wasn't sweet sorrow; it was agony. Jessica looked as though her heart were being torn apart when she said good-bye to Caleb. She didn't shed a single tear, however, and neither did her son. Her departure didn't faze him, for he'd taken quite a liking to Josey and Tom Norton. He squirmed in Jessica's arms when she kissed him good-bye, couldn't be bothered with waving farewell, and didn't give his mama a backward glance when she walked out the doorway. He was busy wreaking havoc in Josey's kitchen.

Jessica surprised Cole. He knew she wouldn't make a scene in front of the baby, but he expected her to cry and carry on as soon as they were outside. He even had an "it's for the best" lecture all ready. But Jessie didn't carry on. She remained solemn, but dry-eyed, throughout the journey.

She deserved a reward for holding up so well. They'd pressed hard all day, only stopping twice to rest their horses for a short spell, and by sunset, she was clearly physically and emotionally spent.

At dusk, he stopped his horse alongside hers and silently berated himself for pushing her so hard. She wasn't a skilled horsewoman, and the long ride must have been extremely difficult for her, yet she never once voiced a complaint.

"We'll catch the train in Edwardsville tomorrow morning," he said. "The town's about five miles south from here. I doubt we'll find fancy accommodations there, but you would be able to sleep in a bed," he explained. "Or we could make a little detour and sleep outside by the waterfalls."

"You aren't thinking about going back to Rockford Falls?" she asked, already shaking her head.

"We're a long way from Rockford Falls," he assured her. "The spot I'm thinking about has a little waterfall that spills into a clear, blue water basin. It's real secluded."

"How much of a detour is it?" she asked tiredly. She pushed a strand of hair out of her eyes and noticed the dust on her hands. A bath sounded luxurious to her.

"About a mile from here," he said. "If we do sleep out, it means getting up a little earlier."

"What would you like to do?"

He always preferred sleeping out under the stars, away from the noise and crowds and congestion of a big town, but he wasn't going to sway Jessica. It was her choice, not his.

"Whatever you decide is fine with me."

"I'd love to have a bath."

"I'm sure we can find a bath for you in Edwardsville."

"But I'd rather sleep outside. Is it really secluded by the waterfall?"

"Yeah, it is."

"Then I'll be able to practice."

258

"Practice what?" he asked.

"You'll see," she said. "I can't do it alone. You're going to have to help."

He raised an eyebrow. "Does practice involve touching?"

He was teasing her and fully expected to make her blush. She didn't, though. She agreed instead.

"Oh, yes, you'll have to put your arms around me. At least I think you will. I'm not sure. I don't have any experience."

He nudged his horse into a trot and led the way down a narrow slope. She was right behind him.

His mind jumped from one licentious thought to another. What in thunder did she want to practice?

He glanced back. "This practice . . . it requires seclusion?"

She hid her smile. "Oh, yes, it does."

"Why?"

"Because I'm going to make a lot of noise. If there were other people around, I would be inhibited."

He pulled back on the reins and waited for her to catch up to him. He could see the sparkle in her eyes and knew she was up to mischief.

"You aren't talking about what I think you're talking about, are you?"

She batted her eyelashes at him. He burst into laughter.

"What do you think I'm talking about?" she asked innocently.

"Sex."

"No," she blurted out before she too burst into laughter.

"Men don't like to be teased, Jessie. Remember that."

He took the lead once again. She trailed behind him just as she had for the last eight hours. She didn't say another word for a long while, until curiosity got the better of her.

"Cole?"

"Yes?"

"Were you disappointed?"

"About what?"

"That I wasn't talking about sex."

"No," he snapped. "I wasn't."

Her shoulders slumped, and she felt an acute wave of disappointment. "Then you never once thought about it . . . with me?"

He couldn't believe they were having this conversation. Didn't she realize the effect she was having on him? Probably not, he decided. It was apparent she was innocent, but she wouldn't be for long if she kept asking him such personal questions.

"Yeah, I thought about it."

"And?"

"And what? It isn't gonna happen, Jessica."

"No, of course not," she hastily agreed. "But I've thought about it too, several times, as a matter of fact."

He almost fell off his horse. "Will you stop talking about it?!"

"You don't have to yell at me. I was just being honest with you. You're very easy to talk to, at least you were until you got upset, and admitting that I've thought about making love to you isn't a crime. I'm not going to act on it. I wouldn't even know what to do."

"Then I don't have to worry you'll do anything stupid."

"Like what?"

He didn't answer her. He swore he wasn't going to say another word, and he definitely wasn't going to look back at her, at least not until he had gotten rid of the notion of dragging her off her horse, pulling her clothes off, and making love to her.

"I hope the water's warm," she remarked.

He hoped it was cold . . . icy cold.

The last mile seemed like twenty to her, and by the time they finally arrived, she was bone weary.

Cole helped her dismount. His hands stayed around her waist much longer than necessary, and she leaned into him, thankful for his assistance. Her legs were so shaky she was sure she would have fallen flat on her backside if he hadn't held on to her.

She glanced up to thank him, noticed his clenched jaw, and quickly moved away from him. He was obviously still irritated by her inappropriate remarks.

She decided to ignore him until he was in a better mood. Her surroundings enthralled her, for everything was so lush and green. She worked the stiffness out of her legs by walking along the bank of the basin. The waterfall wasn't anything like Rockford Falls. It was much smaller and not nearly as grand, yet just as enchanting. A steady stream of water poured across a jagged ledge above, and as it spilled into the pool below, the drops of water, like prisms, caught the sunlight and refracted it into a sparkling rainbow of colors.

While Cole took care of their horses, she prepared their camp. After gathering sticks for the fire, she laid out their bedrolls and the picnic Josey had prepared for them.

"Food's ready," she called out.

"I'll eat later," he called back.

He finished brushing the horses and let them graze on the sweet grass. The sound of the water rushing down the rocks was soothing and too enticing to resist, and while she ate, he went to the edge of the waterfall, stripped out of his clothes, and dove into the crystalline waters.

The cold water did help him take his mind off of Jessica, and he was able to remember why he didn't want to touch her. Strings, he thought to himself. The woman was definitely desirable, but she came with strings. Besides, she wasn't the kind of woman a man could bed and leave. She deserved better than that— someone better than he was, he qualified. Why, then, did he get so hot and bothered when he pictured her with another man? He had no right to be possessive, and yet that was exactly what he was.

"Are you going to stay in the water all night?"

The question pulled him out of his dark thoughts. He got out of the water, haphazardly dried himself off, and put on his pants. When he returned to camp, he moved their bedrolls closer to the rock ledge as a precaution in case of rain, restacked the kindling she'd collected, struck a match to light the fire, and then sat down on his bedroll to eat.

Since he knew that Josey had prepared the food, he wasn't surprised it tasted terrible. Jessica hadn't complained about the taste, but from the amount of food left over, he knew she hadn't eaten much.

She did eat most of the peppermints Josey had packed. She was chewing on one while she gathered clean clothes, a towel, and soap. She removed her clothes, got into the water, and used the gently cascading waterfall as a screen to shield her from Cole. It was cold but not unbearable. She lifted her hair away from the nape of her neck and backed into the running water with her legs braced apart, her head back, and her eyes closed. The gentle massage soothed the tension out of her, and in no time at all she was completely relaxed. It was sheer heaven.

He felt as if he were in purgatory, and he had no one to blame but himself. He shouldn't have been watching her bathe. It was wrong and intrusive. He couldn't make himself turn away, though, and if that made him a voyeur or a lecher, so be it. She was incredibly lovely. She stood waist high in the water, and her every movement was so sensual and graceful. He watched her lather her neck and arms; then he had to close his eyes while he battled the urge to dive into the water and join her. Maybe strings weren't so bad after all. He pushed the thought aside and opened his eyes again. The erotic scene was so compelling he could barely breathe. His entire body reacted, and every muscle felt hard and coiled with the need to touch her.

His mind was flooded with one lustful intention after another, and he realized he was going to be in real trouble if he didn't control his thoughts soon. With a loud groan, he stretched out on his bedroll and stacked his hands behind his head. He was a light sleeper, and if she got into trouble or needed him, all she had to do was call out.

He counted cattle; he counted sheep. Then he started counting the number of ways he wanted to make love to her.

"Cole, are you asleep?"

He didn't open his eyes when he answered her. "No."

"Is something wrong? You sound hoarse."

"I'm fine. What do you want?"

"I wanted to know if it would bother you if I made noise."

"Doing what?"

"Target practice."

He sat up and spotted the gun in her lap. "Where did you get that?"

"Tom Norton gave it to me."

"Put it away."

"I want to learn to shoot with some degree of accuracy."

"No, you don't."

"I'm going to learn how to protect myself. I don't particularly like guns, and I had hoped never to own one, but the Blackwater gang changed everything. I'm responsible for taking care of myself and my son, and I'm not going to let anyone hurt us."

"Dry your hair and go to sleep."

She pushed a wet strand of hair over her shoulder, then opened the box of bullets Tom had purchased for her, and began to load the gun.

He tried not to get mad as he watched her shoot at an impossible target. She was driving him nuts because she kept making the same mistakes over and over again, and when he simply couldn't stand it a second longer, he got up.

He came up behind her, wrapped his arm around her waist, and pulled her up against him, then took hold of her hand that held the gun.

"Exactly what are you shooting at?" he demanded.

"The tree straight ahead. What did you think I was shooting at?" she asked.

"The stars. You're too high, sugar."

He spent the next twenty minutes teaching her, and, honest to Pete, he hated every second of it. She shouldn't have to be learning such a skill. She should be in a parlor somewhere sipping tea while Caleb played at her feet. She was a lady, and ladies didn't carry guns.

He made the mistake of giving her his opinions. She vehemently disagreed. "I've admitted I don't like the idea of carrying a gun, but I'm going to until every one of the Blackwater gang has been captured, and if that means I'm no longer a lady, so be it."

"You sure are pretty when you're angry. Your eyes sparkle."

"A lot of women carry weapons for . . . What did you say?"

She turned her head to look at him and bumped into his chin. "I said you're pretty," he repeated.

He rattled her with the compliment. "Thank you," she stammered before looking away so that she could concentrate.

"Women who live in the Wild West must carry guns

because there are all sorts of . . . What are you do-ing?"

He had bent down and was nuzzling her neck. "I'm kissing you, but don't let me interrupt your tirade. You were saying?"

"There are wild animals . . . like bears and other predators . . . and . . ." She paused to sigh, then tilted her head to one side so he would have more room to explore the side of her neck. The sweet warmth of his breath against her felt wonderful and made her shiver. She knew she should stop him from taking such liberties, and she would do just that, she promised herself, in just a little while.

"Predators?" he asked when she didn't continue.

"Yes, there are lots of predators."

"Where?"

She had lost her train of thought. "I don't know . . . somewhere."

He laughed softly. "I'm getting to you, aren't I?"

He asked the question as he slowly turned her in his arms and lowered his head so that he could give her a proper kiss. His body had other ideas. The second she put her arms around his neck, he roughly pulled her up against him until her breasts were pressed against his chest, and hungrily kissed her. His mouth took complete possession of hers, his tongue penetrated, and for long breathless minutes he made love to her with his mouth. Her body fit his perfectly, as though she had been made just for him. She was so sweet and sensual and loving.

And innocent. The reminder helped him regain his senses. He couldn't quite make himself let go of her, but he did let her catch her breath. Gently tugging on her lower lip with his teeth so she would open her mouth again, he kissed hard and thoroughly, and then released her.

She wouldn't let go of him. Trembling with desire,

she kissed him with all the pent-up passion and longing inside her. She became the aggressor, imitating the erotic way that he had kissed her, timidly at first and then boldly when he wrapped her in his arms again. He growled low in his throat when her tongue touched his.

God, she was sweet. She tasted like candy. Her abandon shook him, and he knew that if he persisted, he could overwhelm her senses and make love to her. She was too innocent to think about consequences.

One of them had to think about tomorrow, and he knew it was up to him to stop now.

He pulled her arms away from his neck and took a step away from her.

"I shouldn't have done that," he said gruffly.

Dazed, she watched him walk away. "I'm glad you did," she whispered. "I wanted to know what it would feel like . . ."

He turned back to her. "I'm not an experiment, Jessica."

She could see the anger in his eyes and in his stance. She took a step toward him, then stopped. "No, you're not. It's just that I've wanted to kiss you for a long time."

"Yeah, well, it isn't going to happen again."

"Why not?"

He couldn't believe she had to ask. "You do know what kissing leads to, don't you?"

She slowly nodded. "I'm pretty sure I do, but since I've never . . ."

He cut her off, for the topic was making him ache with his need to touch her again, and if he did that, he knew he wouldn't stop.

"We're just going to have to stay away from each other. You got that?"

She nodded, then shook her head. "How in heaven's name are we going to be able to do that? We're traveling together."

"Just keep your hands to yourself." After giving her the command, he laughed harshly. Never before had he said those words to a woman, and he couldn't believe he'd said them to Jessica.

It's the damned badge, he thought to himself. It had made him noble.

She folded her hands. "If that's what you want, I shall of course be happy to accommodate you."

He was suddenly furious with her. "No, that's not what I want. I want to take your clothes off, toss you down on the ground, and do all the things I've been dreaming about."

Her eyes widened. "You dreamed about me?"

"Let it go, Jessie."

"I dreamed about you too. Cole, do you want to make love to me?"

"No, not make love," he corrected. "Have sex. Do you understand the difference? If we had sex, tomorrow morning you would realize the mistake you'd made and you'd live with that regret for the rest of your life."

She could feel the anger building inside her. "And you? Would you realize it was a mistake?"

"Yeah, I would."

"Would you also live with regret the rest of your life?"

"I'd regret all right, but not for long. Now do you get it? It wouldn't mean all that much to me."

She spotted the empty gun on the ground, picked it up, and marched past Cole.

"Of all the arrogant . . ."

"I'm being honest, Jessie. Most men would lie to get a woman like you in bed."

"A woman like me?"

He followed her to the campfire. "Yeah," he said. "Like you . . . innocent and pure and sexy as hell. With your fine body, you can't afford to be naive. It's dangerous and stupid."

"So now I'm stupid? Being inexperienced doesn't mean I'm stupid."

She dropped the gun in the bedroll and stood there glaring at him. "Answer one question for me, and then we'll never discuss this topic again."

"What?"

"What makes you so certain that I would live with the regret the rest of my life? Is it because I'm a woman, or is it because I'm stupid?"

"Are you telling me you wouldn't regret it?"

She didn't answer him. "Sure you would," he decided. "Women want strings."

"Strings?"

"Commitment," he explained. "Men don't."

"Then all those married men were hog-tied and dragged to the altar?"

He thought the image fit perfectly. "Yeah, they probably were."

"Was your brother-in-law forced into marrying your sister?"

He'd forgotten he'd told her about his family. "Mary Rose and Harrison?"

Before she could say another word, he shook his head. "Harrison wanted to marry her."

She sat down and began to untie her shoelaces. He stood there watching her while he tried to figure out how they had gotten into such an intense discussion.

"Look, Jessie, all I'm saying is that . . ."

"You don't want strings."

"Exactly." He almost shouted the word.

"Brace yourself, Cole. I don't want strings either," she whispered. "I don't want to get married, and I'm never going to," she added with a nod.

"You'll get married one of these days," he predicted, and immediately frowned over the possibility.

"Because life would be easier?"

He stretched out on the bedroll and stared at the stars while he considered his answer.

"Yeah, it would be easier, and it would also be good for Caleb to have a father around."

"My son and I don't need a man to make our family complete. Oh, you make me so angry, Cole. You're like the majority of people I've encountered who want to push their expectations and beliefs on me."

"It's difficult to be a single mother."

"I know how difficult it is, but I'm happy . . . genuinely happy, and if I married someone just to gain respectability, I'd be miserable and would have no one to blame but myself."

"Respectability? What does that have to do with anything?"

"Never mind."

"You brought it up. Tell me what you meant."

"As soon as strangers find out I'm not married and never have been, they assume I had Caleb out of wedlock, and then . . ."

He prodded her to continue. "Then what?"

"They're compelled to make sure I know exactly how they feel about it."

He was watching her closely. "How do they do that? Give me an example."

She shrugged and tried to pretend that all the hurt she'd suffered had barely mattered to her. "When Grace and I went shopping for supplies, a woman slapped me across the face when she found out I'd never been married. I had Caleb with me, and when she asked who he belonged to, Grace told her he was my son."

Cole was outraged by the incident. "What did you do?"

"I took Caleb outside."

"I'm sorry you didn't punch her."

She smiled. "I wanted to, but I didn't give in to my urge because it wouldn't have been ladylike, and I had Caleb with me. I didn't want him to see his mother behave in such a manner. Grace took care of her, though," she added. She put her hand over her mouth and giggled. "It was a sight to see. I watched her through the window."

He smiled in anticipation of what she was going to tell him. "What did she do?"

"She snatched up a ruler from the counter and backed the woman against the wall. She didn't hit her, but she blistered her all the same with her lecture, and by the time she was done, the woman was crying. It was ridiculous really. Grace was half the other woman's size. Later, we laughed about it."

"But it still hurt, didn't it?"

She didn't answer him. "Grace is the first real friend I've ever had," she whispered. "I would do anything for her."

"And she would do anything for you, wouldn't she?"

"Yes, she would," she agreed. "Do you have any close friends?"

"My family," he answered. "I'm close to my brothers. They drive me crazy sometimes, but I'd kill anyone who tried to hurt them."

She couldn't imagine having siblings and pleaded with him to tell her what his life had been like growing up in such a large family. She was clearly astounded to find out that his brothers and sister and mother weren't blood relatives.

He spent over an hour talking about his growing up years, sharing both humorous and poignant stories with her. The warmth in his eyes and his voice indicated the love he felt for his family, and by the time he finished, she ached with her own loneliness. She yearned to belong . . . and to be loved.

"We joined together to become a family," Cole said. "And never once did I think any of them would run out on me. That's what you think always happens, though, don't you?"

"Experience has taught me not to trust anyone else."

"What about your friend Grace?"

"Oh, I trust her implicitly."

"And Rebecca?"

"I don't know her well, but I could probably trust her, I suppose. She's been very kind to Caleb and me."

"The three of you have been loyal to one another."

"Neither one of them jumped to the conclusion that Caleb was illegitimate," she pointed out. She sat up and stretched her arms over her head to work out the tension.

"I've decided that when Grace and I get to Denver, if anyone asks, I'm going to tell them I'm widowed."

"One lie will only lead to another and another," he told her. "Look at the mess the three of you have gotten into by lying about being a witness. If all of you had simply stepped forward and told the truth before the reporter made you front-page news, your life would have been far less complicated. The judge wouldn't have insisted that Daniel and I haul you and Grace and Rebecca to Blackwater. I imagine you and Grace would already be in Denver."

"I told you I was the witness," she reminded him. "Grace and Rebecca are going to Blackwater?"

"They're on their way now."

She was flabbergasted. "Why didn't you tell me earlier?"

"You were about to leave your son. You had enough to worry about," he said.

"Why does this judge want all three of us? I told you I was the witness."

"Yeah, well, so did Grace and Rebecca."

"But that can't be," she nearly shouted.

"All three of you have come forward to tell us that you were there hiding under the desk."

"No."

"Yes," he countered.

"No wonder you didn't believe me. You wouldn't let me tell you what happened. I did try."

"I didn't want to hear any more lies."

She took a calming breath and tried not to get angry, for he had every right to doubt her. She had lied to him in the past.

"Why would Grace and Rebecca say they were there?"

"You tell me."

She thought about it a long while before venturing a guess. "Grace must feel she has to protect me . . . She knows I'd do the same for her, but I still don't understand why Rebecca would lie."

"She didn't lie, Jessie. She is our witness. Now go to sleep. I'm tired, and I'm not in the mood to argue."

She lay down and rolled to her side so she could stare at the fire. Her mind was filled with questions. Cole had sounded so certain Rebecca was the witness, and she couldn't figure out why.

"Cole?"

"Now what?"

"I saw the man on the roof of the building in Rockford Falls. . . . He killed Mr. York, and I tried to shoot him, but I dropped the gun."

"I remember. What about him?"

"I've seen him before, and I recognized him."

He let out a weary sigh. "Where'd you see him?"

"In the bank. His name is Johnson. Mr. Johnson. I watched him kill those innocent people."

Thirty

She told him everything. She remembered every word that was spoken, every laugh, every scream. As she related the sequence of events to him, beginning with her untied shoelace, she remained dry-eyed and calm. Too calm, Cole thought, for her voice was completely devoid of emotion. He didn't ask her any questions, and when she was finished, she got up and walked to the lake.

He didn't know if she wanted to be alone or not, but it didn't matter to him because he was compelled to go to her. She stood with her arms folded at her waist, her stance was rigid, and when he tried to put his arm around her, she jerked away.

"Don't."

Ignoring her protest, he moved in front of her, blocking her view of the lake, and forcefully pulled her into his arms.

"I don't need you to comfort me," she said angrily, and it was the first show of emotion he'd heard since she'd told him the truth. He was glad of it and continued to hug her tightly.

"But I need to," he said softly.

She struggled to get away, and Cole finally let go.

"You don't understand. I was such a coward. I should have done something, but I didn't do anything. I let it happen. I watched."

She took a deep breath in an attempt to control herself and put her hand out to ward him off when he took a step toward her.

"Okay, I'll agree with you if you want me to," he said. "You should have done something to prevent it. Now, tell me, what should you have done?"

She shook her head. "I don't know. I was so scared I couldn't think. My God, when they first rushed into the bank, I was worried about my stupid money. I should have . . ."

"What?" he persisted. "What could you have done? You could have died with Franklin and the others. Is that what you feel guilty about? That you survived and they didn't? Do you think you should have crawled out from your hiding place and knelt down with the others and let them kill you too?"

"No, but maybe . . . if I had screamed, someone outside might have heard . . ."

"Enough." He roughly pulled her into his arms again and was pleased because she didn't fight him this time. "You couldn't have done anything."

"You would have," she whispered against his chest.

"Yeah, maybe I would have," he allowed. "If I had had a gun, but I would have died. I couldn't have gotten all of them."

"But you would have tried. I didn't."

"Did you have a weapon to use against all of them?"

"No, but—"

"There wasn't a damned thing you could do, and

somewhere in that head of yours you know that's true."

Trembling, she wrapped her arms around him and held tight. "I want . . ."

"What, sweetheart?" he asked as he leaned down and kissed the top of her head.

She tucked her head under his chin and closed her eyes. She needed his strength tonight, and she desperately needed his comfort . . . and his love.

"You should get some sleep," he told her as he gently lifted her into his arms and carried her back to the campfire. He laid her down and knelt beside her, frowning at her with worry.

"You're going to be all right." He said the words, not so much to convince her, but to convince himself.

He started to turn away then, but she grabbed hold of his hand. "Sleep with me," she whispered.

Outwardly he didn't show any reaction to her plea. Inwardly his heart felt as though it had just fallen to the pit of his stomach.

"No," he answered, his voice harsh, his need to touch her almost overwhelming.

In the firelight, her hair had turned a vibrant red, and all he could think about was threading his fingers through the silky mass and coming down on top of her sweet, soft body. . . .

"It's out of the question."

"Just for a little while," she begged. "I don't want to be alone."

"You're not alone. I'm two feet away. I'm telling you it's not a good idea."

"Why not?"

"You want me to spell it out for you? Fine. I want to stay with you, but I sure don't want to sleep."

"You want to make love to me."

"Hell, yes."

His eyes had turned a deep intense blue, and the

hand she held had turned into a fist. "I don't want you to do anything you don't want to do." She let go of him and rolled to her side, away from him. "Good night."

He didn't move. He knelt there, fighting a silent war for what seemed an eternity before he finally gave in.

He stretched out beside her, closed his eyes, and tried to pretend she wasn't there.

No matter what, he vowed, he wouldn't touch her. Granted, a man had only so much discipline and she was definitely pushing him to his limit, but she didn't realize what she was doing to him. She needed him, though not in the physical way he wanted or needed her, he reminded himself. She was feeling all alone and craved human contact.

She was killing him. Her hair tickled his nose. Just as he was brushing the silky strands away, she lifted up and pulled his arm under her so that her head was pillowed against him. She smelled like roses tonight, and he was suddenly reminded of home. That was it, he decided. He'd think about all the things he wanted to get done when he got back to Rosehill.

He couldn't come up with a single chore.

"Five minutes, Jessie. I'm only staying with you for five minutes." He grimaced over the sound of his voice.

She obviously wasn't upset by his gruff manner. She scooted against him, until her back was pressed against his chest and her bottom cuddled his groin.

A cold sweat broke out on his brow. This was hell, he decided, to be so near the woman he craved and not be able to touch her. His only saving grace was the thought that it couldn't possibly get any worse.

He was wrong about that. She wiggled against him and a bolt of white hot longing shot through him.

"Don't move," he ordered. "Just go to sleep."

Evidently unaffected by his harshness, she reached

up to grab hold of his hand and pull his arm around her waist. He couldn't stop himself from tightening his hold and snuggling closer. His hand rested beneath the swell of her breasts, and all he had to do was spread his fingers and touch her soft . . .

The erotic picture was interrupted when she tried to turn in his arms.

He had promised her five minutes. He must have been out of his mind, but he had given his word, and so he began to count off the seconds. Heaven help him, if he lasted one full minute without kissing her, he figured he could last a lifetime.

He wanted a lifetime with her.

The admission stunned him. He realized he'd been ignoring the truth for a long time, but somewhere in the back of his mind, he'd known, and accepted. He could even name the moment he knew he loved her. It was when that bastard, Johnson, was on the roof with his rifle trying to kill her. Cole had never felt such rage before. As he raced toward her, thinking he wouldn't be able to get to her in time, the possibility of losing her had scared the hell out of him. In the aftermath, he'd been so shaken with fear, he'd reacted with anger, not love.

If this was true love, he wanted no part of it. Yet he didn't want to ever let go of her.

It seemed the most natural thing in the world for him to kiss her shoulder, the side of her neck, her ear. He kept telling himself to stop this torment, but his senses were already responding. She smelled so good and felt so soft.

Had five minutes gone by? Maybe she'd gone to sleep, he thought desperately, and he clung to that hope like a man hanging from a rope on the side of a cliff.

She tried to turn in his arms again. "Don't move," he whispered.

"I want to kiss you good night."

His heart soared at her shyly whispered request. "No," he snapped.

"Please?"

He sighed into her hair. "If you kiss me, I swear I won't stop. Now leave me alone and go to sleep."

He made a mockery of his own ultimatum by nuzzling her neck again. He loved the feel of her skin against his mouth. He loved the little sound she made in the back of her throat, like a gasp but not quite.

Jessica stayed perfectly still for several heartbeats, and when she slowly turned in his arms, she knew exactly what she was doing and what it would lead to. Heedless of the consequences, she stroked the side of his face, stared into his beautiful eyes, and then slipped her hand behind his neck.

"I want this one night with you . . . just one night."

"Jessica," he whispered, his voice filled with anguish, "you don't know what you're saying. . . . Tomorrow, you'll regret . . ."

"I need you, Cole. Love me tonight."

He couldn't be noble any longer. He sought her mouth hungrily, desperate with his desire to make her completely his.

For long minutes he made love to her with his mouth as his hand cupped her breast through her clothing. She was tugging at the buttons on his shirt.

He buried his face in her hair. "Slow down, sweetheart," he whispered. "Or I'll . . ."

He wanted the first time to be perfect for her, but her eagerness so excited him he was finding it impossible to follow his own instructions. His hands shook as he roughly removed her clothes, and when he pulled the straps of her chemise down over her shoulders and saw her beautiful breasts, he let out a groan. The pain of wanting her for so long blended with the sheer ecstasy he felt as he slowly came down on top of her, her smooth skin against his.

Her gasp of pleasure drove him wild. Her caresses became as bold as his, and when her nails scored the back of his thighs, the feeling was so exquisite, he thought he would die from it.

He wanted to kiss every inch of her body, and he did exactly that, spurred on by her cries of pleasure. When his hand slipped between her thighs, she tried to push him away, but he wouldn't be denied and within seconds was richly rewarded when she begged him not to stop.

Her passionate response equaled his own. He kissed her navel, smiling when she inhaled sharply, then moved lower to taste all of her.

"Now, Cole," she cried out.

She was more than ready to receive him, but he wanted to prolong the blissful agony until he had so overwhelmed her she wouldn't notice the pain of his invasion.

She was writhing in his arms as he knelt between her thighs. "Look at me," he demanded, his voice shaky with raw passion.

"This is forever."

"Please . . ."

"Say it," he demanded, his eyes piercing hers as he waited.

"Forever," she cried out.

His mouth claimed hers for another searing kiss as he moved to make her his completely. His invasion was gentle but swift; as he thrust forward, he buried his head in her fragrant hair and closed his eyes in surrender.

She was exactly as he had fantasized she would be . . . perfect. He heard her cry, knew he'd hurt her, and stilled inside her, giving her time to adjust to him. He whispered loving words, but he was so out of his mind with his own raging need he didn't know if he was making any sense at all.

How could anything hurt like this and feel so

wonderful at the same time? Beyond control, she wanted to tell him to stop, but she didn't want him to leave her.

"It'll be all right in a minute," he promised her.

He sounded out of breath. Then she realized she was panting. She wrapped her arms around his neck, and the slight movement caused a burst of pleasure to rush through her. She moved again, heard his groan, and realized then he liked it as much as she did.

He slowly withdrew and then just as slowly moved forward again.

"Will you stop teasing me?" she cried out.

His laugh was throaty. "I'm trying to be gentle."

"Stop it," she begged. "I want . . . ."

He silenced her with another kiss and then began to move again inside of her. Her passion shook him. He had never been with a woman who was so honest and open with her desire, and the fact that she gave herself to him willingly and with love in her heart was surely the reason he completely let go of his control.

Determined to make their loving last as long as possible, he tried to slow the pace. She made it impossible, and when she arched up against him, the fire surged between them.

Their lovemaking was wild, free, beyond anything he had ever experienced before. He felt her tighten around him, heard her call his name, and as she found her own fulfillment, he thrust deep and gave in to his own.

His surrender was complete, body, heart, and soul. He collapsed on top of her but couldn't find enough strength to move.

She was quietly crying. He felt her hot tears on his shoulder and finally lifted his head to look at her.

"I hurt you, didn't I, sweetheart?"

He was filled with self-loathing, condemned himself for being too rough, too savage in his own desire. It was her first experience, and he should have been more careful, much more tender . . .

"Jessie, say something."

His anxiety pulled her out of her daze. She opened her eyes and looked into his, and the warmth she saw there made her tremble with a burst of love.

"Oh, no, you didn't . . . Well, you did, but it didn't . . . It was . . . amazing."

He grinned with arrogant satisfaction. God, he loved her face. Her eyes were still glazed with passion, her mouth was red and swollen from his kisses. She looked thoroughly sated and pleased with herself, and how could he not love such a woman?

"Yeah, it was pretty amazing." He reluctantly moved away from her. "But . . ."

She put her hand over his mouth. "Don't," she whispered. "No regrets."

"No regrets," he agreed.

She rolled into his arms then and laid her head on his shoulder.

Nothing lasted forever.

She squeezed her eyes shut so she wouldn't cry. How she wanted to believe him. No, he did love her, she knew, until tomorrow or the day after or the year after, but eventually, inevitably, he would leave.

"I love you too," she whispered. Until forever.

Thirty-One

She had seduced him. Jessica stood by the water's edge and let the truth sink in. The acknowledgment was promptly followed by another truth just as shocking. She wasn't sorry. For the rest of her life she would have the memory of his touch and his loving words to cherish and hold dear. It would have to be enough.

He came up behind her and wrapped his arms around her waist and kissed her shoulder.

He knew something was wrong the minute he touched her, for he felt her stiffen against him.

"Tell me what's wrong."

"It's morning. That's what's wrong."

"No, you're supposed to say, *good* morning, not, *it's* morning," he explained as he turned her in his arms.

She avoided his mouth when he tried to kiss her.

"All right, Jessie. What's this all about?"

"Last night . . ."

When she didn't continue, he tilted her face up

toward him so he could gauge her mood. She was clearly upset, and he thought he knew why.

"You're regretting what happened, aren't you?"

She vehemently shook her head. "No, I meant what I said last night. I'll never have regrets."

He jerked her up against him and tried to kiss her again, but she turned her head away, and he ended up kissing her ear.

"Please don't make this any more difficult than it already is," she pleaded. "We had last night."

"We have forever."

She stared at his collarbone and tried to stay determined in her decision. "We should leave now. We'll miss the train if we don't hurry."

He didn't move. He simply stood there, holding her, while he patiently waited for her to look up at him again. "We aren't going anywhere until you tell me what's going on inside that head of yours."

"We had last night, Cole, but now we have to . . . move on."

It finally dawned on him what was happening. "You don't believe I meant any of the things I said to you last night, do you? That's what this is all about. You think I told you I loved you so you'd let me touch you."

"I wanted you, and you wanted me. It was a mutual decision."

"Yes, it was."

"And I have no regrets. I don't expect a commitment from you, and I'm not giving you one."

He couldn't believe what he was hearing. "Are you telling me you don't want any strings?"

"Yes."

"Son of a—"

She turned away and ran to the horses. Cole followed her, grabbed her from behind, and lifted her into the saddle.

He noticed her grimace and asked, "Are you going to be all right riding today?"

"Yes, of course."

"Jessie, I know I hurt you last night."

"But I'm fine now."

Her blush took some of his anger away. She was so sweet and loving and exasperating. His hand rested on her thigh. "Will you please look at me?"

She slowly lifted her gaze. The tenderness in his eyes tested her determination. She wanted to throw herself into his arms and never let go.

"Yes?" she asked quietly.

"Do you love me?"

He squeezed her thigh until she finally answered him. "I won't lie to you, Cole. Yes, I do love you, but—"

He cut her off. "How many other men have you told you loved them?"

"I haven't told any other man that I love him."

He grinned. "Good. That's all I wanted to know."

There was a definite swagger in his gait as he walked away. She watched him swing up into his saddle. He took the reins, rode to her side, and then, before she could ward him off, his hand was behind her neck and he was pulling her toward him. His mouth took absolute possession, his tongue thrust inside, and he kissed her passionately.

When he finally lifted his head and saw the bemused look in her eyes, he nodded with satisfaction. "Listen to me, woman. That's how I want to be kissed every morning. I want a whole lot more than that, but we'll start with a kiss."

"For how long, Cole?"

She didn't realize she'd spoken the thought aloud until he answered her.

"For the rest of our lives, and yours is going to be real short if you keep having such crazy thoughts."

"You can't possibly know what I'm thinking."

"Sure I can," he boasted. "It's like looking in a mirror." He shook his head in self-deprecation. "My brother Adam used to tell me I'd get it all back."

"Get what back?"

"My attitude," he answered. "I'm the one who never wanted any strings, and it's galling to know you feel the same way."

"I do feel that way," she cried out.

"All you're doing is striking first."

"And what does that mean?"

"You're so certain I'll leave you, you're taking action first and leaving me. Isn't that right?"

He wouldn't give her time to answer, but plunged ahead. "Well, I've got news for you, baby. That isn't going to happen. I'm not going anywhere, and neither are you. I meant what I said. It's forever, Jessie, and I seem to recall you gave me the same promise."

She didn't believe she could be any more miserable than she was at this very moment. Memory served her well, and she knew that even the most fervent promises were empty. He loved her now, yes, but in time he would change his mind.

"I don't want you to stay with me because of what happened. I asked you for one single night, and you gave me that."

"Are you going to thank me now?"

His tone suggested she not comply. "It's time to go."

"You're trying my patience," he whispered.

He didn't say another word to her for almost an hour. He kept looking back over his shoulder to make sure she was all right, and she noticed that his expression grew more hostile with each glance.

She knew she had hurt him, but it was for the best to end it now. She told herself she was simply protecting herself and her son, because if she opened her heart to him, she would be giving him the power to destroy her. She couldn't take that chance. Yet, thinking about life without him made her miserable, and she didn't know what to do to stop the ache. She hated being afraid, and loving Cole terrified her because it meant she would have to trust him.

Why, oh, why, hadn't she considered all the ramifications before she attacked the man? Because, she wanted to know what it felt like to be loved. Dear God, what had she done?

"Jessie, we did it all wrong."

She stared at his back, her heart already shattering, while she waited for him to tell her he had finally come to his senses.

He didn't turn around as he explained, but took the lead down the last slope that led into the town where they would catch the train.

"We had our wedding night before our wedding. We just did it backwards, that's all. If there's time, we'll fix that when we get to town."

"How do you plan to do that?"

"Find a preacher."

Her mouth dropped open. "I'm not marrying you."

"I'm not asking."

"Good, because I . . ."

"I'm telling you we're getting married. You made that decision when you gave yourself to me last night."

He let her hear the anger in his voice, but he was careful not to let her know how worried he was. If he hadn't known better, he would have thought he was scared. Loving her shook him to the core, and he didn't know how to make her understand that his love was real . . . and forever.

"Caleb . . ."

"I'll be a good father."

"I won't subject him to heartache. He'll become attached to you, and then . . ." She didn't go on because of the scathing look he shot her over his shoulder.

"There's something I think you'd better know about me."

"What's that?" she asked.

"I always win."

Thirty-Two

❧

Of the one hundred twenty-three passengers on the train headed south, only one person happened to be looking out the window at the precise second that Marshal Cooper was thrown over the trestle into the water, but one passenger was quite enough. Mildred Sparrow, a spry woman of advanced years and a sedentary disposition, was seated on a hard wooden bench in the rear car with her husband, George, at her side. He was slumped against her, sound asleep, and was using her shoulder as a pillow. Mildred was quietly admiring the lovely view one second and screaming like a madwoman the next. She was so distraught she could barely tell her husband what she had just witnessed. George didn't believe her. Insisting she'd dozed off and imagined that a man was hurled to his death, he opened the window and stuck his head out to have a look himself.

He didn't see anything. Mildred wouldn't be hushed, though. She caused quite a scene, and the only way the porter could get her to stop screaming was to promise to stop the train and investigate. He too believed that Mildred had let her imagination run away with her.

The train came to a screeching halt about a quarter of a mile from the nearest town. The conductor led the curious across the dry, barren land to a hill overlooking the lake. More than twenty men and women were in his entourage, and all of them doubting Thomases. More would have ventured out if they hadn't been afraid of the possibility of stepping on a rattlesnake.

The conductor was out of breath by the time he reached the top of the hill. He looked down, let out a startled gasp, and whispered, "Dear God, it's true."

The group stood with their heads bowed in silent prayer as they watched a fisherman drag a body out of the lake.

Black Creek Junction was a quiet little town in the middle of an isolated and desolate stretch of land. There wasn't a tree or a bush or a flower for as far as the eye could see. The sunsets were the town's only vanity. Each day as the sun descended, orange shards of light struck the red clay soil and the western sky exploded in color, giving the appreciative audience the illusion that the horizon was on fire. Those who stood in the town square swore that they could see flames dancing across the land. It was a spectacular sight, made even more magical when old man Towers felt up to playing his fiddle. The townspeople told newcomers that they had actually seen flickering flames keeping time to the fiddler's tunes.

Grace was transfixed by the magnificent sunset and was watching the phenomenon from the train.

Though reluctant to pull her away from the window, Daniel had to be practical. "We only have an hour to eat and stretch our legs," he reminded her.

The mention of food reminded her how hungry she

was. She put on her gloves and her hat and followed him down the corridor.

"Do you wear your gloves everywhere you go?" he asked.

"A lady must always wear her gloves in public."

He smiled as he shook his head. She was so very proper all the time, ridiculously so, and sweet . . . Lord, but she was sweet. He wondered how proper she'd be in bed. The second the thought popped into his head, he pushed it aside.

"Do you think you'll be able to eat a little something?" she asked. "Has your stomach settled down?"

"Quit fussing over me. I'm fine."

Dinner was being served inside a two-story way station on the outskirts of town, about half a block from the depot. Daniel hadn't even stepped off the train when he was summoned.

"Marshal Ryan?"

He turned and saw a heavyset, bowlegged man running toward him. "Yes?" he said as he put his arm across the opening so Grace would have to stay inside the train.

"I thought that was you, being so tall and all. The porter gave me a good description of you. My name's Owen Wheeler, and I'm the sheriff in this here town. Folks who know me good call me by my nickname, Bobcat. You can too if you want," he added as he shook Daniel's hand. "It's a right pleasure to make your acquaintance."

"What can I do for you, Sheriff?"

Bobcat spotted Grace behind Daniel, tipped the brim of his hat, and said, "Howdy, ma'am."

"Hello, Mr. Bobcat."

"Just plain old Bobcat will do," he explained. "Don't need a 'mister' in front of it."

"How did you ever get such a nickname?" she asked, her curiosity piqued.

He grinned at her. "A while back, I ran into a bobcat and had to wrestle with him. I got the scars all over my belly to prove it. If you'd like to see . . ."

"No, no, that's quite all right. I believe you," Grace rushed out.

The sheriff couldn't seem to take his eyes off Grace, and the rudeness irritated Daniel. "Was there something I could help you with?" he asked impatiently.

Bobcat vigorously nodded. "We've got some trouble here. I was telling the porter about it, and he mentioned he'd seen you wearing a badge and thought maybe you could help."

"What exactly is the problem?" Daniel asked, wishing the sheriff would get to the point.

"Yesterday, Gladys Anderson's boy, Billy, pulled a man out of the lake. Billy was doing some fishing instead of going to work at the stables like he was supposed to, but it was fortunate he's such a slacker. The man would have drowned if Billy hadn't been there, and that's the truth. Billy saw it happen too."

"Saw what happen?"

"Billy was sitting on his boat watching the train go over the trestle when all of a sudden he sees a man come flying out and plunging down into the water. The poor fella hit hard and went right under, but Billy fished him out, and that's when he noticed the man had been shot. I'm thinking he was thrown off that train."

Grace was horrified. "How awful," she said. "Is the gentleman going to recover?"

Bobcat mournfully shook his head. "Doc says he's in a real bad way, ma'am. Real bad. The bullet went through, so Doc didn't have to dig it out, but infection already set in. I figured you'd want to know, Marshal, being as the dying man is one of yours."

Daniel was already reaching for Grace to pull her off the train.

"He was wearing a badge," Bobcat explained. "And the porter told me his name is Cooper. Do you know him?"

"Where is he?" Daniel asked, his voice sharp with fear and anger.

"Inside the way station. Doc wouldn't let us take him any further. He's in one of the sleeping rooms upstairs. The marshal's fighting for his life, but Doc doesn't think he's gonna make it."

Shaken by what he had just heard, Daniel grabbed Grace and quickened his pace toward the building. The sheriff ran by his side.

"Did you question everyone on the train?" Daniel demanded.

"I did," the sheriff answered. "One woman saw him going over the trestle, but she didn't see anything else. No one heard the gunshot either," he added in a pant. "A window was shattered by one bullet, and I figure two were fired. The second went through the marshal."

Daniel reached the door to the way station, threw it open, and rushed inside. His gaze was on the crowd sitting at the long tables waiting for their food to be served. He kept Grace tucked into his side, spotted the stairs in the corner, and headed across the room.

As they raced up the narrow steps, he glanced back at the sheriff. "What about the woman Marshal Cooper was traveling with? Where is she?"

"There weren't no woman."

"Yes, there was," Daniel muttered.

"The porter told me the marshal had a woman with him, and other folks remember seeing her getting on the train. She might have been there when they started, but she weren't there when the train was stopped. That's the God's truth."

"What about her things?" Grace asked. "Did you find a valise or a bag?"

"No, ma'am. We didn't find anything. That compartment was empty, and there weren't nothing left behind to prove a woman had ever been there."

They reached the end of the hallway, where the physician was standing. He nodded to Daniel and then opened the door and went back inside.

"Grace, wait with the sheriff out here," Daniel said. "Sheriff, don't let anyone up those stairs. You understand me?"

"What do you want me to do if someone wants to come up?"

"Shoot him."

The sheriff's eyes widened. Grace waited until Daniel had gone inside Cooper's room before bowing her head and saying a silent prayer that his friend would survive.

"Was the missing woman Marshal Cooper's wife?" Bobcat asked.

"No," she answered. "They weren't related. Marshal Cooper was escorting Rebecca to Texas."

"Well, where in tarnation is she?"

Grace shook her head. "I don't know," she whispered.

A shiver passed down her arms. Rebecca had vanished.

God help her.

Thirty-Three

Daniel kept vigil by his friend's side all through the night. Cooper, locked in a fitful sleep, was having nightmares and mumbling words about monsters and traitors that didn't make any sense.

Grace took care of practical matters. She asked the porter to remove their bags from the train, ordered a tray of food be sent up for Daniel to eat later if and when his appetite returned, and kept Sheriff Bobcat company at the small round table in the corridor adjacent to Cooper's room.

The sheriff kept up a constant flow of chatter while he and Grace ate supper together. The food was bland but filling, and an hour later she couldn't remember what had been served. Her mind was filled with fear for Marshal Cooper and Rebecca.

The physician came out of Cooper's room around nine that evening. He shook his head sorrowfully and told the sheriff there was little improvement.

"I opened the wound near the rib cage to drain the infection. I don't know what good it will do now, though. The man's burning up with fever. I mixed up a batch of my herb brew, and if I could only get him to wake up long enough to swallow some, I know it would do him some good."

"You can't get Marshal Cooper to wake up?" Grace asked, her worry apparent in her trembling voice.

"No, ma'am, I can't," the doctor answered. He scratched his whiskered jaw and added, "That poor man is delirious and ranting and raving about monsters."

"Sounds like he's plumb out of his head," Bobcat interjected.

The physician agreed with his friend's diagnosis. "It looks that way. I don't believe there's anything more to be done tonight. I'm going to go on home and get a couple of hours sleep. Then I'll venture back here and have another look at him. Miss, if you don't mind me saying so, you look awful weary. Why don't you find a bed with clean sheets and get some rest."

"We got her all fixed up in the room next to your patient. It's the only door with a lock on it up here."

After the doctor went down the stairs, Bobcat turned to Grace. "I'm right proud to be of help to Marshal Ryan, and now that I know you need protecting, I'll just set myself outside your door with my loaded rifle."

"Do you think that's necessary? The train left hours ago, and the only other people here are the owners."

"Of course it's necessary. The Blackwater gang ain't going to knock on the door and ask if they can come inside and shoot you. They'll try to sneak in. Now, don't argue with me. You go on ahead into your room and get some sleep. I'll keep my eyes open."

Grace didn't argue. The room she'd been assigned was sparsely furnished. There was a bed with a wooden headboard, a chest of drawers, and three hooks on the wall to hang her clothes on. She put her gloves and hat on top of the dresser, and then went right back out into the hallway.

"I'm just going to look in on Daniel for a moment," she explained as she hurried past the sheriff before he could try to stop her. "I won't be long."

She didn't knock on Cooper's door, for she knew that Daniel would send her back to her room. She simply went inside and quietly shut the door behind her.

Daniel was standing at the window but turned when she entered the room. His surprise at seeing her was quickly replaced with a frown.

"What are you doing here? You should be getting ready for bed. You're going to have to get up early tomorrow."

"I would like to help you take care of your friend."

"There isn't anything you can do."

He looked haggard and sounded defeated. It was as though he had already accepted Cooper's death and was mourning him. She wanted to tell him to have hope, but she didn't think anything that she said would change his attitude.

"You're exhausted," she said. "Why don't you get some sleep? I'll sit with Marshal Cooper. You still haven't recovered from the influenza."

"Don't fuss over me," he growled.

She gave up trying to talk sense to the obstinate man and turned her attention to Cooper. He was sleeping on his back in the double bed with just a sheet covering him to his waist. He was as still as death. A thick bandage was wrapped around his middle, and there were spots of bright red blood seeping through the white packing. His complexion was a chalky gray, and in the dim light from the two lanterns on the bedside tables, Cooper looked as though his next breath would be his last.

"The doctor couldn't get him to wake up and drink the medicine?"

"No. He kept choking."

She got down to business, unbuttoned the cuffs of her sleeves and rolled them up to her elbows. Then she went to the basin and washed her hands.

"What do you think you're going to do?"

"Daniel, try not to take your anger out on me. All right? I know how upset you are about your friend, but being hostile isn't going to help. To answer your question," she continued. "I'm going to try to bring his fever down."

"What makes you think you can do what the doctor couldn't?"

"I'm going to try. That's all. I have had some experience nursing the sick. My grandmother was ill for a very long time."

"What happened to her?"

"She died."

"So much for your nursing expertise."

She lost her temper. "Will you stop being so sarcastic? I simply don't have the time or inclination to deal with it. Come over here and help me. One way or another, Marshal Cooper is going to swallow the medicine."

"I don't think—"

She wouldn't let him finish. "Either help me or stay out of my way. Understood?"

Daniel was astonished by her burst of anger. This was the second time he'd seen her lose her composure. Lady Winthrop, he decided, definitely had a dark side. The discovery made him smile.

Between the two of them, they were able to get most of the medicine down him. She then pulled a chair up next to Cooper's side and began to apply cold compresses to his forehead.

"Your fever was just as high as his," she remarked.

"Maybe, but I didn't have a bullet hole in my side, and I wasn't riddled with infection. The doctor says that's what's going to kill him."

"When did you become such a pessimist?" she asked.

"When my wife and daughter were gunned down in a bank."

The horrifying admission stunned her. She dropped the compress she was holding and watched Daniel restlessly pace in front of the window. She didn't know what to say to him, and all she could think about was not crying in front of him because she knew her reaction would make him angry.

Neither one of them spoke again for almost an hour. Then Grace finally broke the silence. "Do you blame yourself?"

"Yes."

"Why?"

"I wasn't there to protect them," he whispered. "That's why."

"I see."

"Aren't you going to argue?"

She picked up the soaked cloth from the basin, wrung the excess water out, and gently placed it on Cooper's forehead.

"What would you like me to say, Daniel? You've already made up your mind and condemned yourself because you couldn't stop it from happening. Isn't that right?"

"I wasn't even in town when they died."

"Were you working?"

"Yes."

"But if you had been in town, then you would have gone to the bank for your wife? Would you have done that?"

"I don't know. I don't want to talk about it."

He sprawled out in the chair on the opposite side of the bed. "I should have been there, and I wasn't. It's as simple as that."

"Did you always do the banking business for your wife?"

He shook his head. "No."

"Did you do other errands?"

"Like what?"

She shrugged. "Like going into the general store to shop or—"

He interrupted impatiently. "No, Kathleen did all the shopping."

"I see."

"What do you see, Grace? Enlighten me."

She ignored his hostility. "If your wife and daughter had been killed while they were shopping or while they were walking down the street, you would still blame yourself. I think I understand why. It's because you're a lawman, and it's your duty to protect the innocent."

"Yes. I should have prevented it from ever happening."

"By staying with your family day and night and never letting them out of your sight?"

"I didn't say that."

"Yes, you did."

He bowed his head. His eyes burned, and he rubbed them with one hand. Then he reached over and turned down the lamp on the table next to him. The orange glow from the flame was irritating him. "You don't need all this light, do you?"

"No."

She was stroking Cooper's brow while she thought about their conversation. She still hadn't recovered from the stunning news that his family had been murdered.

"I'm surprised you didn't hand your badge back to your superiors," she remarked. "Or turn to drink after your wife died. Some men do."

"I didn't. I wanted to die all right, but I figured it would take too long if I tried to drink myself to death. One night, I got my gun and I put the barrel up against my temple . . ."

"Stop it. I don't want to hear this."

He didn't realize he was breaking her heart by telling her what he had attempted to do. He didn't know how much he meant to her. How could he? She had been cold and so appallingly proper from the moment she'd met him. Ladies never revealed their true emotions. It wasn't acceptable to let others see a burst of anger or passion or joy. Grace had been well trained by experts, and there were times when she honestly didn't know what she was feeling.

"I obviously didn't have the courage to kill myself," he said dryly. "I'm still here, aren't I?"

"Courage has nothing to do with it," she snapped. "Killing yourself is a coward's way out. It takes courage to go on."

"Maybe," he allowed. "I even thought about trying to get Cole riled up enough to shoot me, but that was before I heard all the stories about him. He's far more honorable than I am," he added.

"Sheriff Sloan told me he shot a woman in Abilene. Is that true?"

"Ah, he just winged her," Daniel replied.

She gasped.

"It was the only way he could get the man who was going to kill her," he said.

"Then it was necessary?"

"Yes."

"Daniel . . . do you still think about . . . it?"

He knew what she was asking. "No, I don't think about it anymore. Thoughts about doing myself in happened right after I buried my family. I was pretty much out of my mind then."

"Yes, I think maybe you were."

"I figure there has to be a reason I'm still around."

"I think so too," she whispered.

He was warmed by the fact that she was worried about him. It had been a long time since anyone had been concerned about his welfare. The world had been such a cold place for the past two years . . . until Grace.

"When this is over . . ."

"Yes?"

He shook his head. "Never mind."

She'd been sitting by Cooper's side for so long her back was aching. She moved the basin of water out of the way and stood up to stretch. What she needed, she decided, was fresh air.

The window was on Daniel's side of the bed. As she tried to walk past him, he reached out and took hold of her hand.

"I thought I'd open the window."

He gently pulled her down onto his lap. She was caught off guard and put her hands around his neck before she realized what she was doing. Then she pulled back.

"You don't want me to open the window?"

"I want you to sit here with me."

"It probably isn't very proper."

"And you're always proper, aren't you?"

The yearning in his eyes was her undoing. She gently stroked his cheek with her fingertips. "I try to be," she whispered. "May I ask you something?"

"Anything at all."

He wanted to wrap her in his arms and hold her for the rest of the night. He didn't know what had come over him, but maybe it was all the talk about Kathleen that made him melancholy and lonely. No, that wasn't true, he admitted. Grace made him feel this way. He had been wanting to hold her from the moment he'd walked into Tilly MacGuire's kitchen and seen her standing at the counter.

He was tired of fighting the attraction.

"Grace, what I said to you on the train . . . about wanting you. Does that offend you?"

She didn't answer him. He cupped her chin with his

hand and leisurely ran his thumb back and forth across her lower lip. "Does it?" he asked again.

She studied him. His eyes were captivating, and she wondered if he had any idea how amazingly handsome and virile he was.

"I'm sorry . . . What did you ask me?"

He laughed softly. "What were you thinking about?"

"How handsome you are," she admitted. "I'm glad you want me," she blurted out. "But I'm not Kathleen."

"No, you're not."

"I can't replace her."

"I don't want you to replace her. I just want . . ."

"Yes?"

"You, Grace. Just you."

His hand moved to the back of her neck, and he pulled her toward him. "I want to kiss you. Is that all right?"

She loved the fact that he'd asked permission. "Yes, Daniel. I want you to kiss me. I've waited for such a long time."

He was stunned by her honesty and felt a tightness in his chest when she shyly put her arms back around his neck.

His mouth captured hers in a kiss that was anything but proper. His touch was possessive, almost violently so, and yet there was a tenderness in the way he coaxed her into responding. His tongue swept inside to taste the sweetness within.

The kiss was long and thorough, but when it ended, he wanted another.

She pulled away and walked to the window, staring vacantly for a full minute before she remembered what she'd wanted to do. Her hands were trembling, and it took considerable effort to get the lock unlatched and the window up.

When she passed Daniel again, she hoped he'd grab

her once more, but he didn't. His eyes were closed, and his head rested against the back of the chair.

She resumed her vigil by Cooper's side. Daniel slept until the middle of the night and came awake with a start when Cooper began to thrash about. Grace was sitting on the bed, trying to calm him. Her soft voice did the trick, for within seconds Cooper was quiet once again.

"How's he doing?" he whispered.

"I can't tell," she answered. "He's fitful, but the fever doesn't seem to be as high."

"I'll sit with him, Grace. You should try to get some sleep. You look worn out."

"I'll rest in a little while," she promised. "My mind is racing now. I've been worrying about Rebecca. Do you think she's still alive? I pray she is."

"I doubt it," he said. "My mind's also racing with questions. I can't figure out why the compartment was empty. It doesn't make any sense."

"I don't understand."

He leaned forward and braced his hands on his knees. "The porter said the compartment Cooper and Rebecca shared looked as though it hadn't been occupied."

"Yes, I remember."

"So where are her clothes?"

"Cooper's things were also missing, weren't they?"

"No," he answered. "His saddlebags were in the luggage compartment."

"Maybe Rebecca's satchels were thrown out the window."

"The sheriff assured me that he and his men searched the area. They were looking for Rebecca, and they would have found her bags. They didn't."

"Maybe the men who shot Marshal Cooper let her take her things with her," she said. "That would be a good sign, wouldn't it, that they plan to keep her alive?"

"But they wouldn't want to do that," he argued. "They'd want to silence her as quickly as possible."

"Because they think she's the witness?"

"Yes."

"How awful," she whispered. "Poor Rebecca. She wasn't even there."

The matter-of-fact comment caught his attention. "She told Cole and me she was."

"She what?" Grace asked, clearly flabbergasted.

"Rebecca said she witnessed the robbery. She gave us a detailed accounting of what happened and descriptions of the men she saw."

"She couldn't have," she argued, shaking her head.

"She could have and she did."

"If you'll remember, I told you I was in the bank too. Rebecca was probably just trying to protect Jessica and me and she lied to you."

"Why are you assuming she lied?"

Before Grace could answer the question, he said, "Jessica also told us she was the witness. She didn't give us any real details, though, but Rebecca did. She told us everything."

She shook her head again. "No, that isn't possible."

"I'm telling you she gave us specific details," he insisted. "What's wrong?"

"It doesn't make any sense. That's what's wrong . . ."

She was exasperating. He held on to his patience and asked, "Why doesn't it?"

"Because she couldn't have given you details. I promised I would keep silent. . . . I gave my word . . . but that was before . . . and now . . ."

"Grace, what are you trying to tell me?"

"Rebecca isn't the witness. Jessica is."

Thirty-Four

Daniel was white with anger. "Do you realize what you're saying? I swear to God, if you're lying now . . ."

"I'm telling you the truth," she insisted. "Jessica was in the bank during the robbery, not Rebecca."

He was pacing about the room like a caged animal. He kept telling himself that shouting at Grace wouldn't accomplish anything, but the urge was nearly overwhelming. He took a deep breath and then asked in a chillingly soft voice, "Why didn't you tell me the truth before? Why in God's name did you wait so long?"

"I promised Jessica I wouldn't tell anyone. I gave her my word."

"Dear God," he muttered. He threaded his fingers through his hair and sat down.

"Try to understand," she pleaded. "Jessica was terrified."

"Does Rebecca know that Jessica is the witness?"

"No, she doesn't."

"Are you sure?"

"Yes." She turned away then so that she wouldn't have to look at the fury etched on his face. She had never seen him this angry before, and it frightened her.

"Now do you understand why I was so bewildered when you told me Rebecca gave you specific details?"

"Ah, Grace," he whispered as he tried to control his anger.

"Daniel—"

He cut her off. "Tell me how you know Jessica was in the bank," he demanded.

"I watched Caleb for her," she explained. "She had taken him with her to the bank earlier that afternoon, and he was cranky and out of sorts. She put him down for his nap and then went back."

"Why?"

"She had tried to close her aunt's account, but she'd left one of the signed documents on Tilly's kitchen table. That's why she went back."

"Then what happened?"

"It was awful," she whispered. "She'd run all the way, and when she got to the back door, she started throwing up. She was barely coherent," she added. "I tried to get her to calm down, but she was out of her mind with terror. I put her to bed and stayed with her until Caleb woke up."

"Was Tilly there?"

"No. She had gone out to do some errands. I told her that Jessica had come down with influenza and that she needed to stay in bed and rest."

A tear slipped down her cheek, and she impatiently wiped it away. "I took care of Caleb the rest of that day, and when it was his bedtime, I took him upstairs and found Jessica frantically packing. She wanted to leave Rockford Falls that night, but I was finally able to convince her to stay."

"Did she tell you exactly what happened while she was in the bank?"

"Yes, she did. After Caleb fell asleep, we went out on the porch and she told me everything but their names."

He erupted in rage. "Are you telling me she knows their names?"

Grace gripped her hands together. She knew how wrong it had been of her to keep silent and how she had magnified her culpability by adding the lie that she was the witness. Daniel would never forgive her. He should arrest her and put her in jail, but she didn't think that would be half as horrible as the guilt she now felt.

"She heard the man in charge call the others by their names. She didn't see all of them . . . or hear all their names . . . just some."

"Why in God's name didn't she tell Cole or me?"

Desperate to make him understand, she stood up to plead with him. "She couldn't trust anyone."

"She trusted you."

"Yes, she did. I don't know if she would have told me what happened, though, if I hadn't been there in the kitchen when she came back. I saw the condition she was in. She couldn't control her panic, and all she could think about was keeping her son safe. Can you blame her? I would have done the same thing."

Daniel nodded, for he did understand. "What happened then?"

"Jessica was sure that the authorities . . . you . . . would apprehend the men and wouldn't need an eyewitness. She desperately wanted to believe that would happen."

"When she wanted to run . . . is that when you suggested she go with you?"

"Yes."

"When did she remember she'd left her bag behind?"

"Not until we heard that one was found under the desk."

"Why was it empty?"

"When the men came in, she stuffed the money in her dress. She was afraid they'd take it. She didn't realize they were going to . . ."

"Massacre them?"

"Yes."

Daniel closed his eyes for a moment. "If Jessica hadn't left her bag behind, Cole and I would never have known she saw it happen."

"I don't know if she would have eventually come forward or not," Grace said. "It wasn't her bag, though. It was mine. She borrowed it so she would have something to put the money in to carry it home."

"It was your bag?" He didn't know why that information infuriated him so, but it did.

"Honest to God, you and Jessica have obstructed this investigation from the very beginning. I ought to lock the two of you in a cell and let you grow old together."

"Will you please lower your voice? You're going to wake up Marshal Cooper."

"We want him to wake up," he roared.

She had had enough of his temper and started for the door. "I won't let you shout at me, Daniel. I know what I did was wrong, and if you want to arrest me, then do so."

"Grace . . ."

"I realize I should have tried harder to convince my friend to tell the truth, but I can't change the past."

"Come back here."

She was too tired to argue and did as he ordered. "I'd like to go to bed."

"You're too upset to sleep."

"How do you know how I feel?"

"I can see it in your face. I know I shouldn't have raised my voice to you, and I'm sorry about that, but I'm damned well not going to apologize for my anger. I lost the only two women I'm ever going to love, and I don't care how scared Jessica was. She and you should have come forward."

The impact of what he had just said was devastating, and she realized for the very first time just how much his opinion had come to matter to her. He had just told her he could never love again, and, dear God, she was already falling in love with him. She wouldn't let that happen. Only a fool would love a man who couldn't open his heart to her.

"Why did you kiss me?"

The question caught him off guard. "I wanted to."

She folded her arms across her waist. "Don't ever do it again. Promise me you won't."

He wouldn't make a promise he had no intention of keeping, and so he said nothing at all, until she pushed him.

"I want your word, Daniel."

"No."

"No? Do you mean . . . after what just happened . . . you would want to kiss me again?"

"Yeah, I would and I will."

"Have you figured it all out yet, Daniel?" Cooper's raspy voice intruded.

Daniel jumped to his feet. "You're awake."

Grace rushed to his side. "How do you feel, Marshal?"

"Like I'm in the middle of a war. What's the matter with you two, fighting with a dying man between you?"

Daniel was so relieved to see his friend awake a huge grin crossed his face.

Grace was teary-eyed. "I'm sorry we disturbed you."

"You shouldn't shout at a lady," Cooper told Daniel before turning to Grace. "And you should have told us what you knew. Now, don't cry, darlin'."

"You're not dying, are you, Cooper?" Daniel asked.

Cooper would have laughed, but he didn't have the stamina. He felt as weak and used up as a hundred-year-old plow horse. "I don't suppose I am," he said. "I asked you a question," he reminded him. "Help me sit up, fetch me a glass of water, and then tell me if you've figured it out yet."

Grace hurried to place two pillows behind the marshal's back while Daniel lifted him up. A moment later, Daniel handed him a glass of water, then pulled his chair closer to the bed.

Grace felt Cooper's brow, smiled because it didn't feel overly warm to her, and then politely excused herself and tried to leave the room so that they would have privacy for their talk.

"Grace, come back here," Daniel ordered.

When she went back to the chair across from him, Daniel shook his head at her and motioned for her to come to him.

"Are you going to introduce me to the lady?" Cooper asked.

"My name is Grace Winthrop," she said, and instinctively started to curtsy.

"She's Lady Grace Winthrop," Daniel told his friend. "She already knows who you are, Cooper."

He patted the side of the bed next to Daniel. "Sit with me, darlin'."

"She isn't your darlin'."

"She isn't?" he asked before taking a long swallow of the cool water.

"No, she isn't," Daniel replied. "She's mine."

Grace stumbled and fell on the foot of the bed. She was too astounded by his comment to argue. Did all men make so little sense? Daniel had kissed her, then shouted at her, and then he said the most ridiculously romantic thing she'd ever heard.

She simply had to get away from him as quickly as possible before he turned her mind into mush.

"Cooper fancies himself a lady's man," Daniel remarked.

"I am a lady's man," Cooper corrected.

Daniel settled back in his chair and relaxed. His friend was going to make it. Now it was time to talk about what had happened. He was pretty sure he had it all figured out, but he wanted confirmation.

"So tell me, Cooper, did Rebecca shoot you or was it someone else?"

Grace was so taken aback by the question, she jumped to her feet to protest. "You cannot be serious, Daniel. You can't possibly believe that sweet Rebecca had anything to do with this." Images of Rebecca cuddling little Caleb flashed in her mind. She remembered how worried and frightened Rebecca had been when she first arrived at Tilly's house after the fire. What would they have done if she hadn't stepped forward to take charge in their time of need? No, Grace thought, Daniel was wrong.

"Rebecca did the shooting," Cooper said quietly. "I never saw it coming, never once suspected. There was a man there, but I only got a fleeting glance at him before I was blown into the hallway. I was going down when she shot at me again. The last thing I remember is the sound of glass breaking."

Grace was too stunned to speak.

Cooper told Daniel every detail he could recall, including the fact that Rebecca had been naked. "I opened the door and was so surprised by the sight of her, I think I hesitated before I went for my gun. Those seconds almost cost me my life. I should have been prepared for any eventuality."

Grace fell back on the bed. "She's one of them?"

she gasped, trying to come to terms with the truth. "The fire," she cried out. "Did she start the fire? Did she hit me?" By the time she finished her questions, she was shaking.

Daniel nodded. "Most likely," he said. "Unless one of the other men stayed behind, but I don't think that happened. All Rebecca had to do was sprinkle some kerosene around the house and light a match. She was real sure of herself," he told Cooper. "She went inside the house—"

Grace jumped to her feet again. "And helped herself to an apple," she blurted out. "She tried to kill all of us . . . Tilly and Caleb and Jessica . . . and she wore black, Daniel. Didn't she? She was dressed all in black."

Daniel noticed that Cooper grimaced in pain when Grace sat on the bed again. She didn't realize that every time she moved, she was causing him discomfort. Knowing Cooper the way he did, he also knew he wouldn't say anything to her. Daniel gently pulled Grace toward him and deposited her on the arm of his chair.

She barely noticed she'd moved, so caught up was she in the horror of Rebecca's treachery.

"She's a good actress," Cooper remarked.

Grace tried to stand again, but Daniel put his arm around her waist and held her down. "Yes, she is a good actress," she agreed. "She was complacent and smug, and I thought she was my friend. Can you believe that, Marshal Cooper? I believed she was my friend."

Cooper nodded. "I felt sorry for her."

"Everything was a lie, wasn't it? She pretended to be so worried about Jessica and me, and she kept telling us we had to stick together."

"When you were locked in the jail together?" Daniel asked.

"Yes," she answered. "She told us what she was

going to say to you. She went over it again and again until we had all but memorized it."

"Did she try to find out which one of you was the witness?"

"No, she didn't."

"She had probably already made up her mind to kill both of you."

Grace visibly shivered. "She almost succeeded. If you and Cole hadn't come when you did, we all would have died. Jessica would never have left the house without Caleb and Tilly and me, and the smoke would have gotten her."

"The very first robbery . . . wasn't the building burned to the ground?"

"Yes," Daniel answered. "The first thought all of us had was that someone was trying to cover embezzlement. The bank manager swore that the receipts balanced every night. Every penny was accounted for," he added. "And we ran a thorough check on all the officers and employees. Everyone came up squeaky clean."

"Marshal, can you ever forgive me?" Grace asked. "If Jessica and I had told Daniel the truth, you wouldn't have been shot. All of this could have been avoided."

"That's one way to think about it," Cooper told her. "But there's also another. If you two had told the truth at the beginning, Rebecca wouldn't have said she was the witness. She could have happily gone on her way and let her friends go after Jessica. We might never have known that Rebecca was involved."

"Then it wasn't terribly wrong of Jessica and me to withhold the truth?"

"Grace, if you're expecting me to thank you, it isn't gonna happen," Daniel said. "You should have told me the truth."

His mind was consumed with Rebecca. "I let her slip right through my fingers."

"I bent over backwards to accommodate the woman," Cooper admitted. "I even let her . . . Ah, Daniel, I told her Grace and Jessica were going to meet her in Red Arrow, and I also let her send a telegram. She told me she wanted to let her friends know she wouldn't be joining them, but we now know that was a lie. If you go into Red Arrow, they're going to be waiting for you."

"What about Cole and Jessica?" Grace whispered. "They'll be walking into a trap."

Daniel didn't seem very upset by the possibility. A gleam had come into his eyes, and he rubbed his hands together in anticipation.

"What are you thinking?" she asked. "Aren't you worried about Cole and Jessica?"

"No, they have to come through here to get to Red Arrow," he explained. "And they're at least a day behind us. Maybe two."

"Then you won't go into Red Arrow at all. You'll take a cut through to Blackwater?"

She was nodding over her own conclusion when he contradicted her. "Oh, no, we're going into Red Arrow all right."

"But they'll be waiting. . . ."

"God, I hope so."

Cooper had been listening to the conversation with his eyes closed. He didn't bother to open them when he asked, "You do have a plan in mind, don't you?"

"Yes," Daniel answered. "But it involves you, Cooper."

"Daniel, he's been seriously wounded, and his fever only just broke."

"He won't have to do much," he promised.

"So what do you want me to do?" Cooper asked.

Daniel smiled. "I want you to die."

Part Four

And in green underwood and cover
Blossom by blossom the spring begins.

Thirty-Five

For two long days and nights, four members of the Blackwater gang impatiently waited to ambush the women when they got off the train in Red Arrow. Three of them kept vigil at the depot, while the fourth kept to the shadows as a backup in the event his friends didn't succeed.

Two trains arrived daily, one at ten in the morning and the other at six at night. The men were thorough in their search. After the passengers departed, a clean sweep was made of every car just to make certain the women weren't hiding.

The hours in between the trains' arrivals were spent in the town saloon. The four of them drank hard whiskey together, but none of them got drunk. Mr. Robertson did get a little careless, though, and the others had to help him cover up his spot of trouble. Robertson blamed his lack of control on boredom, for surely that was why he had taken the homely little whore named Flo out to one of the caverns and cut her. He hadn't meant to kill her, just scare her a little;

317

at least that's what he believed when he started out with her perched on his saddle, but once he took his knife out and started carving, he got such a kick out of hearing her scream he didn't want to stop.

His friends helped him bury the body, and aside from having to listen to Robertson boast about how she had squealed like a pig, they all put the inconvenience behind them. Flo was just a whore, after all, and no one was going to miss her.

Because they still hadn't heard from Johnson, they assumed he'd failed to kill the women himself. Robertson told the others he wished their boss were there because he was much smarter than they were and would surely be able to figure out where the women were hiding. He wasn't there though, for he and his mistress had gone south to get Bell out of jail.

On the third morning of their watch, they heard through the grapevine that a U.S. marshal named Cooper had been killed. Someone had shot him and thrown him off a train. A wire had been sent to the sheriff in Red Arrow telling him to be on the lookout for any suspicious characters. He relayed the information to the owner of the saloon, who told it to everyone who came into his bar for a drink.

The four men felt they had cause for celebration. They sat together in the corner and shared a bottle of Rabbit Rye among them.

Robertson, bleary-eyed from lack of sleep, wasn't in a festive mood. "What's taking those women so long to get here? According to the boss's calculations, they should have gotten off the train yesterday or the day before."

He had only just made the remarks when an old coot, with long straggly hair and a smell about him as rank as a skunk's spray, came walking into the saloon.

He strutted up to the bar and draped himself across the counter. "Give me a drink, Harley. I just seen something real special, and I'll tell you about it after I wet my whistle."

The bartender, a big man with beefy arms and missing front teeth no one ever noticed because he never smiled, sauntered over to his customer and squinted at him.

"You got money today, Gus?"

In answer, the misshapen, scrawny man slammed a coin down on the countertop. "I sure do," he boasted. "I got a lot of money today, almost three whole dollars."

"Where'd you get it?" Harley asked as he poured Gus a watered-down drink of whiskey.

"Never you mind," Gus answered. "Do you want to hear what I seen or not?"

"I'm listening."

"I think maybe we're getting us some new whores, and the two I saw were real perty and fresh looking. I seen them both, and I can't make up my mind which one I want to diddle with first. Maybe I'll do them both."

"Are you drunk?" Harley asked.

"No, I ain't drunk yet, but I plan to get that way as soon as you'll pour me another drink. I seen what I seen," he insisted. "Two men were with them," he added before taking a long gulp. In his greed to quench his insatiable thirst, he spilled liquor down the sides of his face and quickly tried to catch the drops with the back of his hands and then licked them dry.

"They hid them all right, but I seen where. I went looking for Flo. Didn't find her," he said. "But I seen the women all right."

"What are you talking about, you old goat? There aren't any fresh whores coming here. I would have known about it. Don't I run this town?"

"Yes, Harley, you surely do."

"That's right," he growled. "And I'm telling you, I didn't hire any new women."

"I'm telling you what I seen. Two men hid those perty girls in the cavern just south of town. Maybe these men are gonna give you some competition and start up a whoring business of their own."

Harley slammed his hand on the bar. "We'll just see about that," he hissed. "Now that Flo took off, I could use a couple more good women. Did you say there were only two men with them? Just two?"

"That's what I said," Gus agreed. "Not too smart neither. Those two fellers left those women on their own, tucked inside the cavern, but one of them must have gotten curious, because she poked her head out the entrance to have herself a look around. Then the other one had to look too, and I seen them both. They're mighty fine looking," he added with a snicker. "Nice and young, and sure to be feisty."

Harley was fuming. He was considering riding out to the cavern to steal the women when Robertson strolled over to the bar.

Gus's stench ensured that Robertson wouldn't get too close. "Tell me what you saw, old man," he demanded, his hand caressing the handle on his knife. "I want to hear all about those women."

It had been a long while since Gus had been the center of attention, and he gloated while he repeated the story, but before he got the chance to describe the two ladies in detail, Robertson had motioned to his friends and left the saloon. The three others followed him out the door.

They were gone a long time, almost three hours, and when they returned to the saloon, Gus was nowhere in sight. Robertson wanted to go looking for him, but the others talked him out of it. They reclaimed their table in the corner to discuss the situation.

Cole strode through the swinging barroom doors a

moment later. Harley took one look at the badge on his vest and reached for the shotgun he kept tucked under the counter.

"Put your hands on the counter, where I can see them," Cole ordered. He was being inordinately polite. Inwardly, he wanted to wait until the bartender had gone for his weapon and then shoot the insolent look off his face, but now that he was a marshal, he knew he couldn't give in to all of his urges.

"The sheriff told me all about you, Harley," Cole said. "He said you think you run this one-block town."

"It's true," Harley boasted. "I do run it."

"He also told me you shot a man in the back."

"The sheriff couldn't prove it was me," the bartender said, his face turning red with anger. "I don't want any trouble."

The four men at the table were watching Cole closely. Cole's attention was riveted on them, but he still noticed that Harley's hands were down at his sides.

"I told you to put your hands up where I can see them. Do it now."

The force of his voice, added to the dangerous look in his eyes, should have convinced Harley to do as he ordered. The bartender was obviously weighing the possible consequences as his glance darted back and forth between the men in the corner and the lawman.

He tested Cole sorely when he put one hand on the counter and waited.

"I wasn't thinking about shooting you," Harley lied. "You being a lawman and all. I just don't want any trouble. I got me a brand-new mirror, and I . . ."

Before Harley could blink, Cole drew his gun and shot the mirror. Glass shattered down on Harley's shoulders. The bartender roared an obscenity and put both hands on the counter.

Besides the four men at the back table, there were

only three other customers inside the saloon, and those three went running for safety. Cole made certain none of them were armed as they filed past him, as the notion of getting a bullet in his back didn't sit well.

"What did you want here?" Harley demanded.

Cole nodded toward the four men. "It's a personal matter."

The tallest of the gang stood up first. "We don't know you, mister."

"You will by the time I'm finished with you," he promised. "Now, all of you get up, and take it slow and easy. I'm taking you boys to jail."

"You've got no right to arrest us," a man with a puckered scar across his cheek protested. "We haven't done anything wrong."

Cole's attention stayed on the man with the knife. "Is your name Robertson?"

The question got a swift reaction. Robertson's eyes bulged. "What of it?"

Cole didn't explain. "Which one of you is Bell?"

"None of us go by that name," Robertson said.

"Never heard of him," one of the others said.

"What's this all about, Marshal?" Robertson asked, his voice reeking congeniality. "Like my friend told you, we haven't done anything wrong."

"I'm not arresting you," Cole said. "At least not yet. We're going to go on over to the jail. There's a lady waiting there to have a look at you."

The men's demeanor rapidly changed, and they suddenly turned into a pack of cornered jackals.

"I don't know what you're talking about," one of the others protested.

Robertson glanced at the man on his left. "We can take him."

"You're welcome to try," Cole said, and finally let some of his fury explode. "Damn, but I want you to try."

Scar Face snickered. "Four against one? You must think you're fast, Marshal."

Cole shrugged. "Why don't you find out? I'll get every one of you, and I won't make you kneel down first."

Scar Face twitched, and Robertson paled.

"We can take you," Robertson said, his eyes narrowing as he studied his adversary. "You think you're as fast as lightning?"

Cole smiled. "Nah," he drawled out, deliberately baiting them. "Folks say I'm all thunder." With a tilt of his head, he added, "He's lightning."

Daniel was standing inside the back door. The men whirled around and then turned back to Cole. They were trapped, and they knew it.

"You've got five seconds to put your guns on the table," Daniel said.

Robertson was the first to go for his gun. Shouting, "Now," he swung left and dropped. Cole shot him in the chest just as his hand reached his holster. The other three had also gone for their guns. Daniel shot two dead and left the last man for Cole, who put a bullet through his throat.

Cole was putting his gun away when he and Daniel saw the bartender raise his shotgun. They fired simultaneously and watched without expression as Harley fell across the counter. His shotgun crashed to the floor.

Cole hadn't killed Robertson. He was sprawled on the floor, his back against the wall, whimpering in pain. Blood trickled down from the wound in his chest.

Daniel squatted beside him. "Tell me the name of the man in charge."

He put the barrel of his gun to Robertson's temple. "If you want to die quick, give me the name. Otherwise you're going to die real slow." He started counting.

Cole rushed across the room. "Don't do it, Daniel. He isn't worth it."

Daniel didn't hear him. "Give me the name."

Robertson started crying. "I'm hurt. I'm hurt bad," he sobbed. "You've got to get the doc to fix me up."

Cole ignored his whining. The hate in Daniel's eyes scared the hell out of him, and he knew he had to figure out some way to make him let go of his rage before it was too late.

"Put the gun away," Cole said softly. "Jessica saw him. She can point him out to us."

Daniel's eyes were glazed with anguish as he glanced up at Cole. Then he shook his head and pressed the gun against Robertson's temple.

"No, she only saw his eyes and heard his voice. Without a name . . ."

Cole put his hand on Daniel's shoulder. "We'll get him," he promised. "Don't do it this way. You have to keep him alive."

"No."

"Yes," Cole argued. "Don't do it this way. I can't let you kill him."

"Then walk away," Daniel demanded.

Cole reached down and pushed the gun away from Robertson. "We're in this together," he said. "We will get him . . . We'll get all of them."

Daniel suddenly came to his senses. With a shudder, he jerked back and stood. "Bring Jessica in here."

Cole shook his head. "I don't want her to see this mess. There's blood everywhere."

"She has to look at them, just to make certain."

Gus came charging into the saloon but staggered to a quick stop when he saw the marshals' guns pointed at him.

"It's just me," he stammered.

Cole and Daniel holstered their guns. "You gave me a start, drawing on me like that," Gus said.

He strutted across the room, looking as pleased as

could be. "I did all right, didn't I?" he asked, craving a compliment.

"Yeah, you did just fine," Cole said.

"I was worried Harley wouldn't believe me, but he fell right into my hands, and then those four went running out of here. Did you follow them to the cavern?"

"Yes," Cole answered.

"I'm real good at lying," Gus said. "But I got to ask you just one question before I leave you to your jobs. I was wondering . . . are there really two women here?"

"Yes, there are."

"Are they fresh whores?"

Neither marshal liked the question. Gus hurriedly put his hand up in conciliation. "I don't mean no disrespect if they ain't."

"You're the one who came up with that lie, not us," Cole reminded him.

"It was a good lie, wasn't it? Where do you have them hidden?"

"The safest place in town," Cole answered.

"Gus, go get help for me," Robertson cried out. "I'm hurting bad."

"I ain't gonna help you. I know you did something bad to Flo, 'cause I seen you riding out of town with her. She was a sweet old gal and I know you hurt her."

Gus realized a golden opportunity was slipping by and ran to the bar to grab two bottles of whiskey. Three sounded better to him, and he snatched up another one. He rounded the corner of the bar with his booty clutched to his chest, stopped to spit on Harley's head, then hurried to the door, his fervent hope to get away before the marshals noticed his thievery.

Daniel and Cole searched through the dead men's pockets, looking for identification, while Robertson continued to blubber like a baby. The noise was distracting. Frustrated at not being able to find anything, Cole grabbed Robertson and demanded that he tell his friends' names.

"I'm not telling you anything," Robertson answered in a near shout. "The boss will kill me."

"I'll kill you if you don't," Daniel threatened.

Cole spied Gus still hovering in the doorway. "Is there something you wanted?"

"Did you find any money in their pockets? I could sure use some extra, I know you already gave me three dollars, but I hate to see good money buried with them."

"You can take the whiskey, Gus," Daniel called out. "But that's all."

"Marshal?"

"What now?" Cole asked.

"I sure would like to get a look at them women. Could you maybe tell me what cavern they're in?"

"They aren't in a cavern," Daniel said. "They're in jail."

Gus grimaced. "Never mind, then. I ain't going over there."

Daniel left Cole to watch over Robertson while he went to get Jessica. The sheriff was waiting outside the front door, and Daniel asked him to find a doctor for Robertson.

"Are you sure you want to save him?" the sheriff asked.

"No, but get the doctor anyway."

Jessica and Grace were sitting at the desk, but both jumped up as soon as they saw Daniel. Grace was so overwhelmed at the sight of him alive and well she threw herself into his arms.

Shocked by how much he needed to hold her, he hugged her tight.

"We heard the shots, but we didn't know . . . Oh, Daniel, I'm so happy you weren't hurt."

"Is Cole . . . ?" Jessica began.

"He's fine."

She was so relieved she had to sit again. Daniel continued to hold Grace until she calmed down and stopped shaking. Then he realized she wasn't shaking; he was. It had been a close call, and he wanted—no, he needed to tell her what had happened and how he had almost crossed the line between the law and a personal vendetta. Grace would understand the torment he was going through.

"Did you get all of them, Daniel?" Jessica asked.

"No. There's still one unaccounted for. You're going to have to look at the men. Three are dead." He added the warning so she could prepare herself for what she was going to see. "I hate to ask, but I have to know if they were hired thugs or part of the gang."

"I understand."

"I'm going with you," Grace told Jessica, ignoring the fact that Daniel was shaking his head at her.

"I would rather you waited here."

She patted his chest. "I know you would, but I'm going with her," she insisted, and before he could argue, she went to the door and pulled it open. "Come on, Jessica. Let's get this over and done with."

Jessica led the way. She was worried about how she would react to the sight of the dead men and didn't want to disgrace herself in front of Cole. She was a strong woman, she reminded herself. She could and would get through this.

Grace's hand kept brushing against Daniel's as they walked along, but she couldn't make herself move away from him. She couldn't stop looking at him either and kept glancing up just to make certain he wasn't going to vanish. When she had heard the gunshots, her heart had felt as though it had stopped, and it wasn't until that very moment that she realized how much she loved him. No, that wasn't true, she thought. She'd known for a long time; she just hadn't been willing to acknowledge it because of the complications and the pain he would cause her. He had been honest from the very beginning. He loved his Kathleen and no other.

"Daniel, I know now isn't the time . . . in fact, it's a terrible time to tell you . . ."

He was barely paying attention to her as his gaze scanned the buildings on either side of the street. There was at least one member of the Blackwater gang still out there, and Daniel wasn't taking any chances.

"Tell me what?" he asked.

"I've become attached to you."

She didn't think he'd heard her whispered admission, for he showed absolutely no reaction, and she was glad of it. She shouldn't have said a word, because the timing was all wrong. She should have waited until they had a quiet moment together and then admitted how she felt, but she was compelled to tell him this very moment, fully expecting a rebuke.

"Yeah, I know."

It was such an arrogant response she smiled. "Should I try to stop?"

He looked straight ahead when he answered. "No, I don't want you to stop."

"Well then," she whispered on a sigh.

Jessica had increased her pace until she was running to the saloon. She certainly wasn't in a hurry to view the gruesome scene, but Cole was inside and she desperately needed to see for herself that he hadn't been hurt.

When she reached the swinging doors, she straightened her shoulders and then pushed the doors aside. She found Cole right away. He was leaning against the far wall, watching her. A wave of relief made her weak, and it took all she had not to run to him. She had expected to be frightened and was prepared to hide her reaction, but what she didn't expect was the surge of rage that rushed through her. Three of the men were already dead, but she had the insane urge to shoot them again.

She pointed to the first body. "He was there," she said. "I didn't hear his name, but I saw him."

She moved to the second and third man, shook her head, and said, "I don't know if these two were in the bank or not. I didn't see all their faces."

She turned to the wounded man. Hate radiated from his eyes as he stared up at her. She neither flinched nor trembled, her gaze dispassionate as she stared back.

"Yes, he was there. His name is Robertson."

She was more shaken than she realized, for she hadn't noticed that Cole had moved to her side and that she was holding his hand. She held tight and let him pull her out the door while Grace and Daniel waited for the sheriff to return with the doctor.

As soon as Jessica stepped outside, she turned to Cole. "There's another one," she told him. "You shot Johnson, they're holding a man in jail in Blackwater, and if all four of the men inside were in the gang, that leaves one missing."

"And Rebecca," he said.

"And Rebecca," she agreed. "I really want you to get her."

"We will," he promised.

Thirty-Six

𝒲

It was a race against the clock to get to Blackwater, and Daniel pressed hard. He was obsessed now with getting to the jail so Jessica could tell him if the man they were holding was Bell. He hadn't thought the rest of it through, and didn't know what he would do if she confirmed that this was the man who had killed his little girl.

The women didn't complain about the grueling pace, but the group stopped when the sun was going down and made camp by a clear stream. Daniel had wanted to push on, but Cole refused.

While Grace and Jessica unpacked the food Cole had gotten in town, Daniel paced.

"We should keep going," he said. "The moonlight's good tonight."

Cole shook his head again. "Look at Jessie and Grace," he suggested. "They're both half dead. The horses aren't in much better shape."

"But we could—"

Cole cut him off. "The idea is to get a live witness there, not a dead one."

Daniel came to his senses. "Yeah, you're right."

While he helped Cole with the horses, he kept glancing at Grace and Jessica. The two of them were covered with dust and looked too tired to move.

"Maybe I did push a little hard today," he conceded.

Cole was already thinking about tomorrow. "Did you send a wire to the sheriff in Blackwater?"

"Yes, but I didn't get an answer. That worries me."

"We'll be there tomorrow afternoon, and then maybe we can finish this."

"It still won't be over," Daniel said. "We have to get Rebecca and the man in charge."

"Do you think the man they're holding is Bell?"

"Jessica saw him and said he turned when the leader called his name, and he wasn't one of the four in the saloon. It has to be Bell."

"Rebecca could be with Bell."

"No, she'd align herself with the one running the show. She wouldn't take up with one of the hirelings."

"Maybe, but don't get your hopes up."

Several minutes passed in silence while Daniel carried the saddles over to the camp and Cole brushed the horses.

"Daniel?" Cole said. "I've been thinking."

"Yes?"

"If Jessica tells you it is Bell, you aren't thinking about doing anything you'd regret, are you?"

"What would you do if you knew he killed your wife and your baby?"

Cole thought it over a long while before answering. "I honestly don't know."

"Neither do I. I won't know until I look at him."

"If you kill him, they'll lock you away or hang you."

"I realize that."

"You know what's worse than hanging?"

"There's lots of things worse than hanging."

"Sitting in a cell somewhere knowing that because of you, two of the gang got away."

"You'd get them."

Cole didn't want to argue the point. "What about Grace?"

Daniel shook his head. "I don't know what to do about her. She kind of . . . took me by surprise."

"I know all about that," Cole admitted.

"Meaning Jessica?"

"I'm that transparent?"

"No, but she is," he said. "She's always looking at you like she's thinking about shooting you."

Cole grinned. "It's love all right."

"How can you be so sure? Everyone who meets you wants to shoot you."

"We're getting married."

"Has she agreed?"

"No."

Daniel burst into laughter and was surprised at how good it made him feel to let his guard down and relax for a few minutes.

"Then how do you think you're going to get her to marry you?"

Cole smiled. "Ever hear of a shotgun wedding?"

"No, but I've got a feeling I won't want to miss it."

"Good," Cole said, "because your attendance is going to be required."

"Why?"

"Who do you think is going to hold the shotgun?" They both laughed.

Grace turned to smile at Daniel. She and Jessica were sitting side by side at the edge of the creek, dangling their feet in the water.

"What do you think they're laughing about?" she asked Jessica.

"I don't know. I'm trying to figure out where they found the strength. I'm too tired to eat."

"Me too."

Jessica was walking back to camp when she spotted Cole coming toward her. He wasn't smiling now, but looked terribly serious, and when he reached her, he didn't say a word. He simply caught her hand in his and kept walking. She either had to follow him or fall down.

"What are you doing?"

"You need to work the stiffness out of your muscles."

"I'm too exhausted to walk."

"Walking isn't what I had in mind."

Her heart felt as though it had just skipped a beat. "Oh, no . . . you can't think . . ."

"I can if you'll let me."

She tried to tug her hand away, but it was a halfhearted attempt, and when he tightened his hold, she gave in. He continued on until they were well away from camp, then turned to her.

In the moonlight, his face was golden. She stared into his amazingly beautiful blue eyes, and she thought he was surely the most handsome man in the whole world. How could he possibly love her? She was so ordinary and plain, and he could have any woman he wanted. Why had he chosen her?

"Do you still love me?"

He couldn't believe she had to ask. "Do you think I would change my mind so swiftly? No, don't answer that," he cautioned, " 'cause then I'll get mad. Yes, I do still love you."

"Why?"

She was genuinely perplexed. Cole was astonished and realized then that she had absolutely no idea of her appeal. Hadn't anyone ever told her how perfect she was?

"Jessie, when you were a little girl, didn't your mother or father ever tell you that you were smart and clever and sweet and good-hearted and—"

He would have gone on and on if she hadn't interrupted him. "My father left when I was very young. I don't remember much about him except that I had to stay away from him when he was drinking, and it seemed he was always holding a glass in one hand and a bottle in the other."

"What about your mother?"

"I think his leaving changed her, but I can't be certain. She dried up inside. She used to tell me she had to be hard on me so I wouldn't make the same mistakes she made."

"Did she ever praise you?"

"I don't remember," she said. "I loved my mother, but I don't want to be like her, and I'm afraid that maybe it's too late for me to change."

"You aren't like her," he said. "You don't know how to be hard."

When she tried to turn away, he tilted her chin so she would look at him again.

"You praise Caleb all the time. I've heard you tell him how smart he is and how sweet . . ."

"Children need to know they're loved. They must have constant reassurance."

"You need to be reassured too, don't you?"

She didn't answer him.

"Do you know what attracted me to you?"

She shook her head.

"When I first met you, you were standing behind a screen door at Tilly's house. Remember?"

"I was terrified."

"Yeah, I know you were. Well, I thought you were about the prettiest woman in the territory."

"You did?" she whispered breathlessly. "I was wearing an old, faded dress."

He laughed. "I didn't pay much attention to what you had on. I was trying to picture what was underneath. You have a very shapely body, Jessie, and I couldn't wait to get my hands on you."

He couldn't believe she was blushing, yet she was, and he thought that was one of the hundred or so reasons why he loved her.

"I was already intrigued, because I had heard about this young lady who went to visit her aunt and ended up taking on the responsibility of becoming a mother to a newborn. Do you know how few women would have done what you did? The responsibility of raising a child alone is staggering, and a lot of women couldn't or wouldn't have done it. They would have dropped him off at the nearest foundling home and gone on their way."

"It isn't a hardship. Caleb's the joy of my life."

"Remember I told you how my brothers and I became a family? I was part of a gang back then and awfully young when we found Mary Rose in the alley we called home. I was headed for disaster," he added. "Mary Rose changed my life and so did my brothers. I didn't raise my sister alone, though. I had three brothers to help."

"But I—"

Before she could continue, he interrupted. "I love your strength and your courage, and I love the fact that you bring out the best in me. Those are just a couple of the reasons." He gently cupped the sides of her face. "I didn't want to fall in love with you."

"Then why don't you stop?" she asked gently.

"Sweetheart, that's like asking me to stop breathing. Ah, Jessie, I need you in my life."

He bent down and proceeded to drive her crazy by kissing every inch of her throat.

"How come you always smell like flowers?"

The question was simply too complicated to answer. She should stop him, she thought, even as she tilted her head so he could kiss the spot directly under her earlobe that was so sensitive to his touch.

"You're doing it on purpose . . . You know how much I like . . . but we can't . . ."

"One kiss, Jessie. Just one kiss."

Her hands were gripping his shirt, and she didn't protest at all or turn away.

It felt so wonderful, so right, to be in his arms. The seduction of his loving words was her undoing. She leaned up on tiptoe and willingly let herself be swept away. His mouth moved over hers greedily. Passion was instantaneous, explosive. One kiss wasn't enough for either one of them, and as his mouth slanted over hers again and again, she began to shiver with her need.

She didn't want him to stop. When he lifted his head, she leaned up and kissed him again.

He stopped her from going any further. He pried her hands away from his shirt, wrapped her in his arms, and tried to catch his breath. "You don't know how to hold back, do you, sweetheart?"

He sounded happy about that fact, and so she didn't ask him to explain.

Draping his arm around her shoulder, he led her back to camp. "I'm going to have to teach you all about pacing." He smiled just thinking about it.

She tried to pay attention to what he was saying, but his kisses had robbed her of the ability to think about anything at all but making love to him. "I don't know what's wrong with me. I used to be a lady until you came into my life."

"You still are a lady."

"I knew what I was doing the other night. I practically seduced you, and I promised myself that we would have one night together, but just a couple of minutes ago, I was thinking about having one more night."

He groaned. "Jessie, we need to talk about something else."

"Why?"

He decided to be blunt. "Because I'm already hot and bothered, and if you keep talking about making love again, I won't be able to hold out until after we're married."

"Cole . . ."

He squeezed her. "Don't you dare ask me how long I'll stay with you."

"I wasn't going to ask you that."

"Yes, you were."

"What if I can't ever give you what you want, what you deserve? A wife should be able to trust her husband, but I don't think I could ever . . . What if . . ."

He didn't let her finish. "Then I guess you're going to be real worried every time I leave the house. I'll always come back to you and Caleb, though, and maybe in about twenty years or so, you'll catch on. I'm in this for the long haul. I meant it when I told you it was forever. And by the way, you will tell me you love me before our wedding day. Now please change the subject."

"Do you think Caleb's all right?"

"Yes," he answered. "He's probably going to have an aversion to fried foods for the rest of his life, but he's being loved and spoiled."

"I had a nice long talk with Tom," she remarked.

"What'd you talk about?"

"You."

He shot her a glance. "What'd he tell you?"

"He was full of stories about you."

"Like what?"

"Abilene."

His shoulders sagged. "I had hoped to get married before you found out about that."

"You act like you did something wrong."

"I shot a woman, Jessie."

He waited for her to grill him with questions or tell him he'd been wrong to take that chance with a woman's life hanging in the balance.

"It was very clever of you."

He stopped dead in his tracks. "What?"

"I said it was very clever of you."

"I shot the woman," he reminded her.

"Oh, it was a flesh wound. You're very good with a gun, aren't you?"

"Jessie, you act like we're talking about the weather. You aren't at all shocked, are you?"

"Of course not."

"The end doesn't justify the means."

"You feel guilty."

"Yes."

"It was a practical solution."

"Yes, but . . ."

"You saved her life."

"Then how come I felt so rotten afterwards?" It was the first time since it had happened that he had admitted the truth to anyone, even himself.

He was giving her another glimpse into his heart by letting her see his vulnerability. He showed the world such a hard, unbending exterior, but underneath all the shields was a kind, gentle man who cared deeply about others.

"Because you're honorable." She leaned up and kissed him, then took hold of his hand and started walking again. "Grace sold another hat today."

"What?" he asked, confused by the rapid change in subjects.

"I said Grace sold another hat today. Isn't that nice?"

Jessica was ready to move on, and that practical side of her was yet another reason he had to add to his list when she asked him again why he loved her.

"Who'd she sell it to?"

"A very nice woman . . . Well, she wasn't nice at first, she was actually quite hostile, but Grace has a way of putting people at ease and within minutes they were chatting like old friends. She gave Grace seven dollars. I think she would have paid more, but Grace said this was a working woman and couldn't spare another cent. Grace tried to give the woman her hat until she realized pride was involved. It was a good bargain, don't you think?"

"What kind of job could a woman get in that fleabag town?"

"Her office is in one of the rooms above the saloon."

He grinned. "You do know what she does for a living, don't you?"

"Yes, but I wanted to see you smile again. You worry too much."

He would have argued with her, but they'd reached camp and Grace was sleeping, so he didn't say another word. He did kiss her good night, though, and was pleased to notice that she looked thoroughly dazed when he was finished.

Daniel ignored them. Grace was curled up on her side, facing him.

After Cole moved his bedroll close to Jessica's, Daniel moved his so that he could sleep next to Grace. He fell asleep thinking about her, and sometime during the night he felt her take hold of his hand. For now, it was enough.

Thirty-Seven

The curtain was about to rise on the final act.

Rebecca dressed with care, choosing a virginal white dress with a modest, yet seductive, neckline. There was just enough cleavage to ensure that the recently widowed judge would stare. Donald had told her she would have to convince Rafferty of Bell's innocence before he could be released by the sheriff.

She thought about carrying a Bible with her, then changed her mind. She mustn't overdo the role she was going to play.

She finished brushing her hair and stood up to preen in front of the mirror. Men liked women who wore their hair long and free, and hers was exceptional. The lustrous curls shimmered in the sunlight like strands of gold.

The bedroom door suddenly opened, and her lover strolled inside. She tossed the brush on the table and turned to him. "You took a chance coming here. Did anyone see you?"

"Of course not. I'm always careful. I came up the

back way." Rebecca dressed in white was such a mockery he wanted to laugh. She actually looked pure and untouched.

"Donald, is everything all right? You look perplexed," she said.

"Sorry," he replied. "I was preoccupied. The sight of you in white stunned me."

She smiled. "I thought it was a nice touch."

"It's fine, just fine," he said before finally getting down to the business at hand. "I'm sorry you couldn't be in the courtroom this morning to watch the pathetic sheriff from Maple Hills make a complete fool of himself," he said with a laugh. "He admitted under oath that he surprised Bell when he snuck up on him and drew his gun. He also admitted he wasn't wearing his badge and he didn't identify himself. By the time Bell's attorney finished reminding the jury that his client was deathly ill at the time and blinded with a raging fever, he had all twelve men in the palm of his hands. I swear they were glaring at the sheriff when he shuffled away from the stand. I doubt he'll get re-elected."

The news thrilled her. "Then the attempted murder charge has been thrown out?"

"Not yet, but it will be this afternoon," he assured her. "The judge is dragging the trial out for as long as he can."

"If Bell is going to be released, there's no reason for me to carry on with the charade."

He shook his head. "You're still going to have to go through with it," he told her. "The judge is itching to hang Bell. He knows he's got his man, and if he can't get him on the charge of attempted murder, he'll keep him locked up until you convince him Bell wasn't in the bank."

"All right, then." She sat down at her dressing table and began to brush her hair again. "What are you going to do about Bell? Now that people are suspicious of him, he's become a liability."

"I'm going to kill him, of course," Donald said.

"Have you told the others?"

"Burton, Harris, and Andrews know."

"What about Robertson?"

"The boys are going to take care of Robertson for me. It was their idea, not mine. Burton says Robertson is getting out of control. Andrews calls him knife happy."

She put her brush down and turned to him. "Have you heard from Burton yet?"

"Don't start fretting."

"But he was supposed to wire you after they killed Grace and Jessica. Have you gotten word from him yet?"

"I'm sure they got the job done. They always do," he added with a grin. "Burton couldn't send a wire."

"Why not?"

"The telegraph office here has been shut down for the last two days. The equipment broke down," he explained. "Don't worry. I checked it out to make sure it was true."

"No one in town is getting telegrams?"

"Oh, they're getting them, but they're being rerouted through the next town and that's twenty miles away."

"His wire will probably come tomorrow, then."

"And we'll be long gone," he told her.

"You never told me how Burton and the others feel about disbanding."

"They're ready to stop for a while. By the time they get the urge again or run out of money, we'll be setting up house in Paris."

"If you take care of Bell tonight, we could leave tomorrow."

He headed back to the door. "No, we're leaving

tonight. Pack your things and bring them with you when you meet me outside of town. You know where."

"Yes," she called out. "I wish you could go with me to see the judge. It would amuse you to watch."

"You know I can't be seen with you in this town. Everyone knows me here, and they might start wondering how I got hooked up with you. I'll be in the courtroom."

"Yes, I know. Where should I go now, straight to the courthouse?"

"Go to the sheriff's office. He'll take you to the courthouse."

After giving the order, he pulled the door closed. He was surprised by the twinge of regret he felt. He was going to kill her, and he was surprised that he actually felt sorry for her. Then he started thinking about how he would kill her tonight, and within minutes he was hard and throbbing. All feelings of remorse vanished. He would keep her alive for as long as he could to prolong his own enjoyment, and he must remember to gag her so no one would hear her screams for mercy.

It was a pity really. He had considered taking her with him and then decided against it. Rebecca was such a striking woman she drew attention wherever she went. The flawless beauty made her a risk because everyone, even strangers, remembered her.

He would miss her though, for he doubted he could ever find another woman with such a twisted sexual appetite.

He jerked the door open again, walked inside, and began to unbutton his pants.

"No, Donald," she cried out as she backed away from him. Her face was already flushed with excitement and fear. "There isn't time."

His laugh was harsh. "There's always time."

* * *

Rebecca didn't arrive at the jail until one-thirty that afternoon. It had taken almost two full hours to pull herself together after she and Donald had finished with one another. Fortunately, he'd let her take her dress off before it was ruined. She was still hurting, but she wasn't upset about it because pain would make her look all the more vulnerable and frightened.

The sheriff wasn't there. His deputy, a young man with a horridly pockmarked complexion, fastened his eyes on her breasts the second she walked inside. Amused, she stepped forward to shake his hand. His palms were sweaty, and she had to resist the urge to wipe her hand on her dress. She introduced herself and explained why she was there.

"The sheriff was hoping you'd get here soon," he said. "He's over at the courthouse waiting to either drag the prisoner back here or let him go. I think we ought to head over there, because Judge Rafferty won't end the trial until you eyewitness Bell for him."

"And if he isn't one of the men I saw in the bank?"

She tried to dazzle him with a smile, but it was wasted on him because he wouldn't take his gaze off her chest. She really had to remember to tell Donald about the deputy. He'd get a good laugh out of the story.

"We're all hoping Bell is one of the Blackwater gang," he told her. "Would it be all right if I held your arm while I walked you to the courthouse?"

"I won't mind at all. It's very gentlemanly of you."

The courthouse was only two blocks away. He took her to the back entrance and showed her to the judge's chambers adjacent to the courtroom. She sat down near the desk to wait, while the deputy wrote a note for the clerk to hand to the judge.

"I'll bet Rafferty interrupts Bell's closing speech when he reads this," he said, waving the note he'd just folded. "Is it okay if I leave you alone for a few minutes? I'd like to watch old sour face's expression and hear what he has to say to the fancy attorney."

"I'll be fine," she whispered.

She fought the urge to open the door just a crack and look into the courtroom, but she didn't dare take the chance because Donald was in the audience, and if he saw her peeking out, he'd be furious.

She closed her eyes, cleared her mind, and prepared for her role.

Thirty-Eight

❧

he moment had arrived.

As soon as the deputy returned and opened the door for her, Rebecca stepped into the courtroom and waited until she was summoned. She surveyed her audience, noting with pleasure that the room was packed. A center aisle leading to a pair of front doors divided the courtroom in half. Two deputies with rifles stood guard on either side. She noticed a side door directly across from the door to the judge's chambers. It too was guarded.

She was called forward to the witness-box. Every eye in the room was on her. Her head held high, her expression fearful, she half expected applause. She was, after all, about to give the performance of her life.

Judge Rafferty was so eager to hear her testimony he interrupted the closing arguments so that she could take the stand. As she walked past him to take her seat behind the railing, she looked him over closely and came to the conclusion that it would take very little

346

effort on her part to get him in the palm of her hand. Rafferty was a heavyset, middle-aged man with eyeglasses so thick his owlish eyes appeared to be three times the normal size.

She also noticed he was taken with her. He smiled, he gawked, and she couldn't have been happier.

She was being sworn in by the clerk when the defense attorney leapt to his feet and demanded the judge's attention.

"Your Honor, this is highly irregular," he protested. "Couldn't you wait until the prosecutor and I have finished up and the jury has left the courtroom to deliberate? My client is being tried on the charge of attempted murder. The prosecutor is trying to prove that my client willfully and with malice in mind tried to kill the Maple Hills sheriff. This case shouldn't be muddled up with a witness testifying about an altogether different matter."

The judge peered at the upstart over the top of his glasses. "I'm fully aware of what this case is all about. Do you think I've been sitting up here twiddling my thumbs and daydreaming about fishing, Mr. Proctor? Is that what you think I've been doing?"

"No, Your Honor, I don't—"

The judge wouldn't let him continue. "What you're saying, Proctor, is that you don't think that what the witness has to say is relevant, but I say it is. If your client is who I think he is, then the jury needs to know it because he would have been fleeing and he would have tried to kill the sheriff and he would have tried it with what you call malice in mind."

"But, Your Honor—"

"Mr. Proctor, you need to understand. No one tells me what to do in my own courtroom, and that includes fancy-pants lawyers like you. I know you're young and inexperienced and that you think you know just about everything there is to know, but I make the rules here. Now sit down and be quiet until I finish with my witness. You understand me?"

"Yes, Your Honor."

"Then why aren't you sitting?"

The crowd burst into laughter when Proctor tripped in his hurry to take his seat.

The judge wasn't amused. He slammed his gavel on the desk and demanded silence. "I'll have order in my court. If I hear another sound out of any of you, I'll clear you out.

"Like I said before, I make the rules here, not you. Sit." He bellowed the command, but by the time he swung around to Rebecca, he had mellowed considerably.

"I sure would like to cut to the chase and ask you plain out, but I'm not going to do that. First, I want you to tell the jury who you are and what happened to you."

Her moment had finally arrived. Gripping her hands together on the railing so the jury could see them, she took a shuddering breath and began. She told them why she had been in the bank and what she had seen. Tears came easily, and her voice had a halting quality she was quite proud of, and by the time her story ended, she was sure there wasn't a dry eye in the courtroom.

The judge was as shaken as the jury by her gut-wrenching recollection of the murders. He sat hunched over his desk, leaning toward her as though he thought his nearness would somehow comfort her.

"All right, then," he said. "I know how hard it was for you to go through it again, and I appreciate it. Now, I want you to look at the man shackled to the table over on your right and tell me if he was one of the men in the bank."

Rebecca stared at Bell for several seconds before shaking her head. "No," she cried out. "He wasn't there."

The judge's face betrayed his disappointment. His frustration was palpable, but he wasn't ready to give up. "Take your time and look him over real good before you make up your mind."

She did as he instructed. "I'm so sorry, Your Honor. I wish he were one of the Blackwater gang, but he isn't. I swear to you he wasn't there."

Bell's attorney was grinning from ear to ear, and that offended the judge almost as much as her devastating testimony.

"Don't even think about getting to your feet again, Proctor. You keep your seat glued to your chair until I'm finished. I've got a couple of nagging points I want to clear up before I let this young lady leave the stand."

Rebecca bowed her head and pretended she was desperately trying to compose herself. She knew the judge was watching her closely, and when she looked up at him again, she felt a burst of gloating satisfaction over Rafferty's compassionate gaze.

"I'm going to make this quick," he promised. "I just have a couple of questions. Are you up to answering them now, or would you like a recess?"

"I'd like to finish now, please."

He immediately asked his first question. "I ordered three women brought here, and I'm curious to know where the other two are. Do you have any information about their whereabouts?"

"No, I don't. When Marshal Cooper told me Grace and Jessica were also being brought here I felt terrible, just terrible. Their lives have been uprooted because of me. If I had told the truth from the beginning, none of this would be happening to them. They've become dear friends. I expected them to be here when I arrived, and I was looking forward to seeing them and telling them how sorry I am. I'm sure they were just delayed. Grace wasn't feeling well when I left her. She might have had a relapse."

"Let's move on to the next question. You said you got on the train with Marshal Cooper and that he left your compartment and didn't come back. Why did he leave?"

"I had a pounding headache and my medicine was in my suitcase. Because Marshal Cooper was such a gentleman, he insisted on going to the baggage compartment to fetch it for me. If I hadn't complained . . . if I had suffered in silence . . . he would still be alive. It's my fault he's dead, all . . . my . . . fault."

She buried her face in her hands and began to sob. Rafferty looked at the jury and noticed their united sympathy for the poor woman. He realized he had better hurry up then before a rebellion broke out.

"We're almost done," he announced. "Tell me what happened when you heard the gunshots. Do you recollect how many you heard?"

She wiped her face with the handkerchief as she nodded. "I'm pretty sure I heard two shots fired. I was too frightened to find out what was happening. The train made an unexpected stop, and that's when I heard that poor Marshal Cooper had been killed."

"And then what did you do?"

"I was afraid to get back on the train. I didn't know what to do," she cried out. "I hid in the brush and waited until everyone had gone. I don't know how long I stayed there . . . It could have been hours," she stammered. "When I was finally able to pull myself together, I ran into town."

"But you didn't go to the sheriff there, and that's one of the little nagging points I'm confused about. Why didn't you seek his help?"

"I was terrified," she cried out. "And I didn't know who to trust. I wanted to get away from there. I knew you were waiting for me, Your Honor, and that you would protect me. All I could think about was getting here . . . to you."

His expression was comical to her. Rafferty looked as though his dog had just been put down.

"You did the right thing," he said gruffly. "I'm not going to fault you because you came here, and that's exactly what I ordered you to do. You've been very brave. Very brave indeed."

The prosecutor stood up. "Your Honor, before we go any further, will you please ask Miss James one last time to look at the defendant. Maybe recalling the sequence of events . . ."

"This poor woman has been through a terrible time," the judge said. "You and I both have to accept that we were about to hang an innocent man."

"Please, Your Honor," the prosecutor pleaded.

"I don't mind," Bell's attorney called out.

The judge ordered the sheriff to unshackle the defendant and bring him over so that the witness could get a close look at him. When Bell stood in front of the railing, the judge reluctantly turned back to Rebecca. "This is the last time I'll ask you. Is the man standing in front of you one of the Blackwater gang?"

"No, he isn't," she insisted.

"Yes, he is!"

The shout came from the doorway of the judge's chambers. Everyone turned as Jessica slowly walked forward into the courtroom. She wanted to run to the stand and tear Rebecca from her seat so outraged was she, but Daniel had made her promise not to go any farther than the defense table so that she wouldn't be near the killers she was condemning.

The rage was building momentum inside her. Images kept flashing into her mind. Malcolm down on his knees looking up earnestly as he tried to be helpful . . . Cole carrying her baby across the fiery inferno, the roof collapsing behind him . . . Franklin's head exploding . . .

Daniel grabbed her arm to keep her from going any farther. He stayed by her side, but Cole had already moved to the center aisle and was diligently searching the audience for signs of hidden weapons.

"He was in the bank. I saw him put his gun to the back of a man's head and shoot him. I saw everything," she shouted, "because I was there."

She was pointing at Bell when she made her accusations, but her attention was centered on the woman who'd tried to kill Caleb and who'd shot Marshal Cooper. Rebecca was shaking her head in denial as she started to stand, then fell back against the chair. Her face was so white she looked as though she were rapidly bleeding to death.

The crowd was going wild, the judge was pounding his gavel, and in the fracas a young deputy in the back of the room shouted, "Those men are armed, Judge." He then tried to bring his rifle up.

Before anyone in the crowd could summon a scream or dive for cover, Daniel's gun was out, his arm fully extended, his target the center of the deputy's forehead. The man hadn't even gotten his rifle past his waist when he realized it was too late.

"Put the gun down, boy." The command was given in a deep, yet surprisingly calm, voice.

Out of the corner of his eye, Cole had seen Daniel draw his gun on the deputy and had already whirled around to face the only other men in the courtroom who were armed. The sheriff was one, a deputy standing in front of the side door was the other.

It was an instinctive reaction on the sheriff's part to go for his gun as soon as his deputy shouted, but Cole had his gun trained on him the second his fingers wiggled. Cole simply shook his head at the sheriff. The message was clear.

Rebecca frantically searched the audience for Donald. He had promised her he would sit in the third or fourth row. She slowly slipped her hand into her pocket.

The judge came out of his seat and leaned forward

with both hands planted on his desk as he roared, "What's the matter with you people? Don't you know better than to draw on two U.S. marshals? Even I can see their badges, and I'm as blind as a bat."

Rafferty's voice lashed out over the crowd and was so thunderous he was able to get through to them and avert a panic. A collective sigh rolled through the assembly as everyone calmed down. Several men chuckled with relief.

Rebecca was slowly bringing her derringer out of her pocket, holding it steady in the palm of her hand with her thumb pressed against the barrel. She found Donald quickly; he was sitting at the end of the fourth row next to the aisle on her side of the courtroom. He was close, very close, and as she watched him, he gave her a barely perceptible nod before turning his attention to the deputy guarding the side door on her left. She understood what he was telling her and looked at Bell.

The judge took his seat, adjusted his flowing black robe, and squinted at the assembly. They still appeared to be a little unnerved, and he decided to give them another minute to recover.

"Marshals, you can holster your guns," he ordered. "Which one of you is Daniel Ryan?"

"I am, Your Honor."

The judge motioned him to the bench. "You sure cut it awfully close getting here," he remarked.

Daniel didn't offer any excuses or explanations. "Yes, Your Honor, we did."

"I happen to know a great deal about you, son, because I make it my business to find out everything I can about men like you, and I have only one thing to say. It's an honor and a privilege to finally meet you."

Daniel didn't know what to say in response. The judge had already turned his attention to Cole. "What's your name, Marshal?"

"Cole Clayborne."

Rafferty nodded. "I've heard a tale or two about you as well. Of course, I know the stories can't possibly be true."

"I'm sure they aren't, Your Honor," Cole answered, wondering why the man wasn't getting to the urgent matter at hand. Cole kept glancing at Daniel to make sure he was still in control. He noticed the way Daniel was watching Bell, and knew that wasn't a good sign.

The judge rose to address his assembly. "All right now. I've given you enough time to soothe your ruffled feathers and settle down. From this point on, I don't want to hear one peep out of any of you. If I do, I swear I'll order these fine marshals to escort you out the front doors."

Silence resulted from his firm decree. Rafferty turned to Jessica and sat back. "Young lady, who are you?"

"My name is Jessica Summers."

"State your business with this court."

She took a step closer to the center of the bench and looked up at the judge.

"I witnessed—"

"I'm your witness," Rebecca screamed.

"I'm telling the truth," Jessica insisted.

"She's lying, Judge," Rebecca countered. "I was there."

Heads turned back and forth from one side of the courtroom to the other as accusations were volleyed. Daniel crossed behind Jessica and handed the judge a paper.

Rafferty noted the seal at the bottom of the sheet, read the contents, and nodded. "Well . . . well . . ."

Shaking with rage, Jessica was irrationally determined to make Rebecca tell the truth. First, she knew, she would have to make the woman lose her control.

"Move back, Jessica," Cole ordered when she took a step forward.

Jessica quickly did as he ordered, but didn't take

her attention off the woman she was determined to destroy.

"Cuff that prisoner, Sheriff," Daniel ordered.

"It was you," Jessica shouted. "You set the fire. You tried to kill my son. You hurt Grace. You shot Marshal Cooper. Surprise, Rebecca—Cooper didn't die. Oh, yes, he's alive and well," she taunted. "And quite able to recall who he saw and what happened. The judge is reading all about it right now. Cooper wrote a nice long letter."

The news staggered Rebecca. She collapsed against the back of her chair and stared at Donald, imploring him with her eyes to help her.

Donald was thoroughly enjoying himself. There was a hint of a smile on his face as he sat there with his head tilted ever so slightly to the wall while he watched and listened. How thoughtful of the marshal to insist that the only living person who could possibly identify him stay on the opposite side of the courtroom. She couldn't see him in the crowd, not with the sea of faces gawking at her and Rebecca. Thanks to the overly cautious marshal, Donald didn't have to worry.

He would continue to sit back and patiently bide his time. He knew Rebecca expected him to help her escape, but he had no such intention, of course. He would wait it out and then sneak away. The poor dear was looking quite desperate now. Donald knew exactly what would happen as soon as he gave her a signal. She would jump to her feet and attempt to use that pathetic little gun she had hidden in her pocket. One of the lawmen would shoot her, of course.

Donald also knew what Bell would do. He wouldn't continue to stand there with his head hanging down, his shoulders stooped, and his hands limp at his sides, looking like the sheriff's whipping boy. Why, he hadn't moved a muscle since he'd shuffled across the room to the railing in front of the star witness.

The cold-blooded murderer was as cunning as a fox. He was waiting for his opportunity to spring into action. The sheriff had already relaxed his guard—the old fool was still looking around for his handcuffs—and barely paying his prisoner any notice at all, which Donald knew was just fine with Bell. The sheriff was going to have to get close to Bell in order to shackle him, and when he did, Bell would attack. Donald expected him to go down in a blaze of bullets, and while the deputies and the marshals were firing, Donald would fold into the inevitable stampede as the crowd swarmed out the doors to escape.

A man in the back row jumped to his feet and reached into his hip pocket, drawing both Cole's and Daniel's attention.

"Hands up," Cole shouted as he strode up the center aisle amid the spectators, his gun trained on the stranger.

"I'm unarmed, I'm unarmed," the man stammered. "I just needed my handkerchief." He then sneezed, drawing smiles from those around him.

Jessica was trying to figure out who Rebecca was looking at in the crowd. Who would she know in Blackwater . . .

"Cole," Jessie screamed as she rushed across the room, "he's here. The leader . . . he's here."

Daniel raced toward her and jerked her back just as Donald gave the signal to Rebecca.

Rebecca leapt to her feet and fired one shot through the sheriff's temple, but before his legs could begin to fold, Bell was behind him and had his gun. He fired at the deputy guarding the side door, hitting him in the center of the chest, then whirled and fired at Jessica. Daniel shoved her to the floor in the nick of time, but the bullet caught him in the left shoulder.

Pandemonium broke loose as the crowd jumped to its feet, obstructing Cole's view.

Bell, diving for cover at the side of the witness-box,

fired at Daniel, but the shot went wild, for Daniel was already in motion. He shot the gun out of Rebecca's hand. She screamed and fell backward. Daniel hit the table, slid across on his side, his gun blazing. Bell lunged back and froze. Daniel fired again as he dropped to the floor, rolled, and fired again, this time at point-blank range.

Indifferent to the ear-shattering screams surrounding him as people tried to escape, Daniel dropped his empty gun, grabbed the other one out of his left holster, and slowly got to his feet.

It wasn't over yet. Daniel slowly extended his arm, cocked his gun, and waited. His eyes bored into those of his enemy. Golden brown eyes stared back.

Cole was desperate to get to Jessica. He fought like an animal to get through the crazed people clawing their way to the doors. He hadn't been able to get a clear shot since the first gunshots were fired, for the crowd had swelled to its feet and surged in on him, screaming and shoving and pushing to get away.

Cole was finally able to shove his way through the crowd. His gun was out, but when the last men were shoved aside and he finally had a clear view, his heart dropped.

Donald had Jessica in front of him and was backing toward the side door. One arm held her tightly around the waist. The other held a gun under her chin, the barrel pressed against her throat.

Jessica was fighting like a wildcat, scraping his arm with her nails and kicking his legs with her heels.

He seemed impervious to her struggles. "What we have here, gentlemen, is called a standoff. I'll blow her head off, and I'm sure that by now, with my rather colorful history, you know I'd get a kick out of watching your expressions after I kill her. Oh, I know you'll get me, but not before I see how you react when her head explodes." His voice hardened into concrete. "It'll be messy. I've done it before."

Jessica dug her nails into his skin, drawing blood. "Stop it," he ordered. "What's it going to be, Marshals?" he demanded as he edged back.

Cole was slowly advancing down the center aisle. He was about five feet away from Daniel, coming toward him at an angle now, when Donald shouted to him. "Stop right there. I don't mind dying," he boasted. "I've seen so much of it lately. If you want her to keep on breathing, you'll stop right there and drop your guns."

Neither marshal reacted. Cole's arm was rigid. Daniel shook his head. "You aren't getting out of here. Let her go."

"I can't do that," he said. "She's going with me. Look there. Rebecca's crawling toward the judge's chambers. That's my girl."

Jessica kicked hard and struck bone. She felt as if she were being cut in half, so forcefully did he squeeze her.

"I told you to stop," he shouted in her ear.

"I won't stop until you let me tell Cole I love him. I have to tell him," she whispered. "I'll help you escape, I'll do anything you say . . ."

Donald laughed. "Isn't that sweet," he called out to the marshals. "The little lady wants to say something to you."

"You got a clear shot?" Daniel asked Cole.

"No," Cole answered, his voice harsh.

"Go ahead, angel," Donald urged. "You can tell him."

"Cole," she cried out.

He was dying inside. Dear God, please don't let him hurt her . . . don't let him . . .

"Abilene."

He knew what she was asking him to do. He had her permission, he had his target, his gun was cocked, but God help him, he couldn't do it.

Daniel took the shot for him.

"No." Cole roared the denial. In his mind's eye, everything happened in slow motion. He saw Jessica's eyes flutter closed, saw her body drift downward to the floor. His mind wouldn't accept any more. He emptied his gun into the bastard, spraying him up against the wall. Cole didn't stop. He kept pulling the trigger again and again and again, the only sound now the clicking as the empty chambers rotated, until Daniel grabbed the gun out of his hand.

"I didn't shoot her," Daniel shouted in hopes that his words would cut through Cole's stupor. "She's all right. She just fainted. Get her off the floor."

Cole rushed to her side and fell to his knees. His hand shook as he pressed his finger against the pulse point at the base of her throat. He felt the heartbeat, strong and rapid, and felt the tears sting his eyes. He gently lifted her into his arms and stood, cradling her against his chest.

Jessica heard someone sobbing. She opened her eyes and saw Grace running toward Daniel.

There was a deputy standing in the doorway of the judge's chambers, watching Rebecca. The woman had her bloody hand pressed against her bosom. Her other hand was braced against the wall and she was slowly struggling to her feet when Grace ran past her.

"I'm all right, Grace," Daniel called out as soon as he saw her tears. He fully expected her to throw herself into his arms, but Grace suddenly stopped. A funny look crossed her face before she turned around and ran back to Rebecca.

Daniel didn't have time to stop her. Grace made a fist, swung, and coldcocked her. Rebecca crumpled to the floor.

Grace stepped back and looked at her. "It hurts, doesn't it?"

Daniel was so shocked he laughed. He stopped when Grace was in his arms, kissing him.

"I love you, Daniel. I love you," she fervently whispered as she kissed his brow, his nose, his chin.

He tilted her head up so he could look into her eyes, and then he whispered his declaration of love. "Don't marry Nigel."

"Because you love me, Daniel?"

"I was getting to that, Grace . . . because I love you."

Thirty-Nine

Everyone had gathered in the judge's chambers to watch the doctor work on Daniel's shoulder. He was sprawled out on the leather settee. Grace leaned against his side, holding his hand.

Cole sat nearby in an overstuffed wing chair with Jessica on his lap. She had tried to sit next to him, but Cole wouldn't let her move.

The judge was still in the courtroom giving orders to two deputies before they dragged Rebecca to jail.

Cole was deliberately taunting Daniel as the physician prodded the injury with his instruments in search of the bullet.

"You're being awful brave, Daniel."

"Don't push me, Cole."

"It hurts, doesn't it, Daniel?" Grace asked.

"If I answer yes, are you going to coldcock me?" Daniel asked dryly.

Everyone laughed but Grace, who was clearly mortified. "You're never going to let me live that one down, are you?"

"No," Daniel assured her.

"I'm having the last laugh," Grace boasted.

"How's that?" Daniel asked. His voice sounded calm, but his brow was covered with beads of perspiration. He wanted to yell at the doctor to hurry up and find the damned bullet, but he didn't say a word because Grace was already anxious and upset.

"I never was going to marry Nigel."

"I know. I wouldn't have let you."

Cole tugged on Jessica's blouse to get her to look at him.

"I want to hear you tell me you love me. No more messing around, Jessie. I mean it. This is your last chance or . . ."

"Or what?"

He leaned down and whispered into her ear. She immediately turned scarlet. "You wouldn't . . . not here in front of Grace and Daniel . . ."

"I'm a desperate man. If taking your clothes off is the only way I can get you to cooperate, I'll do it."

"It sure would take my mind off this torture," Daniel drawled out.

Grace covered her face and laughed. Jessica put her arms around Cole's neck.

"I'm waiting," Cole reminded her.

"I love you, Cole Clayborne. I love you."

His expression turned somber. "Forever, Jessica?"

"Forever."

The judge came striding into his chambers with a full bottle of good whiskey. He poured drinks for everyone and then sat down behind his desk.

"I'm still in shock," Rafferty announced. "I can't believe that Donald Curtis, a respected businessman in this town, a pillar of our community, was the leader of the Blackwater gang. Whatever possessed him to turn like that?"

"Greed," Daniel speculated.

"The thrill," Cole suggested.

"Maybe Rebecca will be able to answer your questions about Donald. She knew him well," Jessica said.

"I know I shouldn't feel sorry for her, but I do," Grace said. "She loved him, and some women will do anything for the men they love, even kill."

The judge raised his glass and said, "Why don't one of you marshals make the toast?"

Daniel looked at Cole. "Are you keeping your badge?"

"Maybe. What about you?"

"Maybe."

Cole raised his glass to Daniel. "To justice."

Epilogue

❧

Rosehill Ranch, Montana Territory

Mama Rose was sitting on the front porch enjoying the sunset. It was her daily ritual and one she tried never to miss, for, in her opinion, sunsets were one of God's special gifts to the world, and it was her duty to take a moment to appreciate His wonders.

She wasn't alone, for squeezed up next to her was the newest addition to the family, Caleb. The two of them had taken to one another immediately, and he was happily chattering away now in a language only he understood.

He was the most adorable child, and every now and then, she couldn't resist brushing her hand across his dark, silky curls.

The family had all returned home to celebrate the wedding of Jessica and Cole and to welcome Jessica and her son into the fold. The house was bursting at the seams, and Mama Rose couldn't have been happier.

She glanced up and saw Cole standing in the doorway, watching her.

"I knew I'd find you out here," he said. He came out and pulled up a chair next to her. With a nod toward Caleb, he said, "He's a piece of work, isn't he, Mama?"

"My, yes," she answered. "He's busy every minute. He was just telling me a remarkable story."

Cole laughed. "He keeps Jessie on her toes," he remarked. "By the end of the day, we're both worn out from chasing after him."

"That's the way it's supposed to be," she replied. She grew serious then and said, "You do know how blessed you've been, don't you? Jessica is a treasure and so is this little boy."

"I know," he agreed. "Sometimes . . . at night . . . I watch her sleep and I get this choked-up feeling. . . . I'm a man in love," he ended. "No doubt about it."

"I expect you at services Sunday," she said. "You'll want to thank God."

"We'll be there," he promised. "Are you going to wear your new hat Grace sent you?"

"Oh my, yes," she replied. "It's almost too grand for me."

"Nothing's too grand for you, Mama Rose."

Praise flustered her, and she quickly changed the subject. "Jessica told me that Grace has decided to open a hat shop in Dillon."

Cole nodded. "Her parents are coming over from London to help her get started. Daniel hopes they'll stay."

"When is Daniel going to marry her?"

"The date hasn't been set yet. He has to wait and ask Grace's father for permission first, but he's hoping to tie the knot next year, come the spring. He expects you to be there."

"Oh, I'll be there, and I'll wear my new hat. Daniel's at peace now, isn't he?"

Cole smiled. "He's getting there, Mama."

The screen door opened, and her other sons, Adam

and Douglas and Travis, came outside. A moment later, her daughter, Mary Rose, joined them. Mama Rose's heart swelled with love and pride, and she suddenly became quite teary-eyed.

"I was about to tell this baby a story."

"We'll listen too," Adam said.

"What's it about?" Douglas wanted to know.

"A circle," she answered, "that began in New York City when four young boys and an infant became a family."

Caleb climbed up on her lap and cuddled against her chest. She put her arms around him and began to rock.

"Once upon a time . . ."

Add these

JULIE GARWOOD

books to your collection:

Mercy

✳

Heartbreaker

✳

Guardian Angel

✳

Come the Spring

✳

Ransom

✳

The Bride

✴

Prince Charming

✴

For the Roses

✴

The Gift

✴

Saving Grace

✴

Gentle Warrior

✴

Honor's Splendor

✴

The Claybourne Brides:
One Pink Rose, One White Rose,
One Red Rose

✴

Rebellious Desire

✴

The Lion's Lady

✴

The Wedding

✴

POCKET
Books

2 of 2   2418-02

Visit

JULIE GARWOOD